CW01082205

ICE BET

SJ SYLVIS

Ice Bet
Special Edition
Copyright © 2023 S.J. Sylvis
All rights reserved. No part of this publication may be reproduced or
transmitted in any form including electronic or mechanical, without
written permission from the publisher, except in case of brief quotations
embodied in critical articles or reviews. This work is a piece of fiction.
Names, characters, places, and incidents are the product of the author's
imagination or are used fictitiously. Any resemblance to actual events,
locales, or persons, living or dead, is entirely coincidental.
Published: SJ Sylvis Books LLC
sjsylvisbooks@gmail.com
Cover Design: Ashes and Vellichor
Editing: Jenn Lockwood Editing / My Brother's Editor
Proofing: Emma Cook | Booktastic Blonde / Wordsmith Publicity / All
Encompassing Books

For Booktastic Blonde (Emma)- You're the Taytum to my Claire - never ever change. <3

USA TODAY BESTSELLING AUTHOR

S.J. SYLVIS

PREFACE

AASHER

A long, drawn-out breath drew from the pit of my stomach and quietly drifted between the open space that separated me from Coach's messy desk. Papers were spewed all over the place, and the white board propped behind his back had yesterday's practice notes scribbled all over it. The longer I stared at the chaotic jottings, the more I wondered if that was what the inside of my brain looked like when I was seven beers deep after winning a game.

"Aasher!"

Coach entered through his office door, and my spine straightened. I caught a glimpse of my teammates and grinned at their loud laughter. The stench of perspiration-covered hockey gear traveled through the opening, and I saw Theo—*my best friend and captain*—raise his eyebrow at me. If he was wondering why Coach Lennon wanted to chat, I wouldn't be able to answer him. I had been killing it at practice. Zero flaws.

The door slammed, and the locker room disappeared.

By the growing red on my coach's round cheeks, I knew why I'd been called into his office.

Jesus Christ.

"Coach," I eased into the conversation, trying to hide my agitation. *All I said was hi to his daughter...that was it.* "If this is about your—"

"It is."

It took every ounce of strength to keep my chill, and that was saying something because off the ice, I was pretty easygoing. Put me in a room with overzealous puck bunnies fighting for my attention, and I would stay as cool as a cucumber. Better yet, put me in a room with overzealous puck bunnies *and* their moms...I'd still be sporting my natural, smug smile.

"Coach." Again, I eased into the conversation. I loosened my tight shoulders and evened my tone. I would be lying if I said a flame of anger didn't dance on the inside at his constant nagging. "I swear to you, I wasn't trying to hit on your daughter."

Our gazes snagged, and I watched the visual come to life right behind his glare. *Was he picturing me with his daughter?* I shifted my attention to his ears, and they grew redder by the second. *Oh, shit.* I began writing my own obituary and accepting my fate.

"I know you weren't, damn it!"

I blew out a breath. My forehead was damp from sweat, and it wasn't because we had just finished with practice. I was prepared to go into the logistics of why I wasn't actually hitting on his daughter, but Coach Lennon was hard to read. Would he be happy that his quiet, seemingly uptight daughter wasn't my type, or would he be offended?

You never knew with him, and I didn't want to take my chances.

Coach snapped his arm out and spun the gold frame around on his desk. I sliced my attention to the girl I'd simply said *hello* to a year prior at our game against Shadow Valley.

There was the slightest twitch on my face before I pulled away from the girl staring at me in the photo. The Riley Lennon I met a year ago didn't exactly resemble the brief glimpse of her that I just caught inside the golden frame. Her long, dark hair and icy eyes were the same, but the soft smile below her cheeks was new. When I met her, she was as tight as the laces on my skates. She wouldn't even look at me.

"I know the story, Aasher. You didn't know she was my daughter at the time."

Even so, I wasn't trying to sleep with her.

I sat up straighter in the hard chair. "I also don't sleep with every girl I say hello to, despite what campus says about me. I was standing beside her, so I simply said hello because where I'm from, it would be rude not to."

Coach snickered. I tightened the hold on my smirk because, truth be told, I had a reputation. But so did almost every other athlete at Bexley U. Personally, I didn't slut shame, because what was the issue in two consenting adults having sex with one another? I was always upfront with my partners too—they were aware it was a one-time deal.

"You have your eye on the Hops, don't you?"

That was a sudden shift in the conversation, but instead of noting the abrupt segue, I slowly nodded. "Yes, that's correct. Season just started, though. Their scouts aren't coming out yet, are they?"

The Hops had been a top NHL team for the last several years. They were also notorious for waiting until the very last second to secure their contracts.

Coach leaned back in his squeaky swivel chair and steepled his fingers together. His lips puckered with his rapid eye movement, and my pulse raced. Once he pinned his gaze to me and smirked, he was the smuggest one in the room.

"I need you to know that this is *not* a bribe. Bribes do not fly on my team."

I said nothing. Instead, I tipped my chin to show my understanding. *Not a bribe. Got it.*

"It's a promise."

Uh, what?

"I've been watching you, Aasher."

I grew antsy. "And what do you see?" *Hopefully a skilled hockey player.*

"I've seen you on the ice, looking out for your teammates. I've seen you do it off the ice too."

My antenna was up. I was seconds away from aborting whatever mission Coach was about to put me on. "I'm just being a good teammate and friend. We all look out for each other. It's part of why we're so good this year." I didn't technically *like* every teammate, but you didn't have to like someone on the ice to work well together. We weren't there to be best friends. We were there to win.

Coach nodded, and my spine tingled, urging my brain to send the *abort mission* signal to my legs so I could walk the fuck out of his office.

"Riley is moving into the apartment across from you."

And just like that, we were back on Riley. I skimmed over to the framed photo of his daughter again before I swung my gaze back to him.

"Oh?" I didn't mean for my response to sound like a question, but nonetheless...

"Yes, *oh.*"

I paused. I blinked. Then I thought over his words before trying to recover. "Your off-limits daughter is moving into the apartment complex littered with..." I cleared my throat and skirted past the word *horny* and continued on, "Bexley U athletes?" Everyone on the team knew that when Coach's daughter was anywhere on the ice, we were to keep our eyes elsewhere. The coach's daughter was *always* off-limits. Didn't matter the coach, or the girl...she was *always* off-limits.

"What are you? A parrot? That's what I said, isn't it?"

I couldn't hold back my laughter. "Why would you ever do that?"

"It doesn't matter why." There was a bite to his tone that I'd heard plenty of times in the rink, and thankfully, I could recognize the *shut-up* cue when given. "I need you to watch her."

"What do you mean?" I was fully fucking invested. *What drama lies between Coach and his daughter?*

"I mean, just watch out for her. Treat her like you would your sister if you saw her at a party with a bunch of simple-minded, immature young men who only want one thing."

I didn't have a sister.

"So..." I gripped the arms of the chair. "You want me to *stalk* your daughter?" My question was slightly sarcastic, and I could tell with the rising tension in the office that Coach didn't appreciate it.

The grinding of his teeth caused me to slink backward. "No! Yes! But don't be obvious about it! Don't tell her you're...watching her. I need to let Riley have a little breathing room and given the circumstances..." Coach's stern gaze pulled away, and I one hundred percent noted the change of direction the conversation was going. "I just need someone I can count on that will make sure she's with the right crowd, making the right choices, staying safe."

In other words, not fucking his hockey players? Or if she is, maybe throwing a condom at her?

"And you want that person to be me?" I raised an eyebrow. "You've given me so much harassment over the fact that I said hello to her a year ago, but now you want me to make friends with her?"

"Whatever you have to do to make sure she's making the right choices. You know, make sure she gets home if she shows up to one of your parties...and remind your team-mates that they are to keep their hands to themselves when it comes to her." He paused before leaning back in his chair again. "The same rule applies to you. Do not cross the line, Aasher."

My brows furrowed. There was obviously much more to the dynamic of their father/daughter relationship, but it wasn't exactly my business, and the last time I meddled in the family drama of someone other than myself, it bit me in the ass.

"Can you do that? Because I promise you that I can ruin your dreams of wearing a Hops jersey with a snap of my fingers."

I gripped the arms of the chair harder.

Coach put his hand up. "I'm not going to unless you break my trust. I need someone that has good morals and someone who is so focused on the game that they won't think twice about crossing a line with her. Given the fact that Theo lives in the dorms and is currently dealing with having a new roommate..."

There was a slip in his armor, and the hope lingering behind his words was enough to get me to nod, but there was an edge to my acceptance too. I didn't like to be intimidated or bullied into something. I was at a crossroads, though, and Coach held all the marbles in his hands. Sure, there were other NHL teams that would sign me, but if I wanted to make it big and accept the future that was once taken from me, I didn't really have a choice.

"Yeah, sure. If she happens to show up at one of our parties, I'll make sure she gets home safe." *And I'll keep my teammates' sleazy hands off her.*

"I can count on you?" he asked, placing his elbows on the desk. "And I can count on you to keep your dick in your pants, right?"

I chuckled, purposefully shielding my eyes from the blue-eyed baby doll staring at me from the picture frame. "Coach"—I stood and took a few steps toward his office door —"your daughter isn't my type. Not to mention, you just promised to screw my chances with the Hops. So, yeah, you can count on me." I wondered if Coach knew about my little bump in the road before I started at Bexley U, but I refused to go back down that road. "No one will touch her." *Including me.*

He nodded before flicking his hand. "Keep this between us. Now get. I've got game plans to work on."

"Yes, sir," I said, opening the door to face my teammates who would demand to know what Coach wanted to talk to me about. I already had a plan. I'd tell them he was stroking my ego because I'm the best player he's ever had, which will cause nothing but chaos and verbal jabs, changing the entire direction of the conversation.

[1]

I LIVED in a world that was highly unrealistic and slightly unhealthy—at least according to those who were closest to me. I didn't see an issue in spending my evenings hanging out with fictional characters in fictitious settings, and I was sticking to that angle, even as I balanced twelve books on top of one another as I walked up the third flight of stairs to my new apartment.

Of course the elevator was out of order.

The semester had already started at Bexley U. The changing autumn leaves were no longer crunching beneath my shoes on my walks to class. Instead, they turned to dust as each day grew colder, preparing New England for the dreadful snowy months. Not that I was anti-winter or anything. I grew up on the ice. At one point, it was my entire personality. When I was in middle school, there was a rumor traveling around the local ice rink that my eyes were the color of ice because of how much time I spent skating. My nickname was *Ice Queen,* which was both flattering and disheartening considering I wasn't only described as that because of my dexterity in the rink but also because of my reserved personality. I could be friendly and even sweet at times, but on the ice wasn't one of them.

Unapproachable.

Withdrawn.

Icy.

Controlling.

Those were the traits that truly granted me my nickname.

I sighed as I stood in front of apartment 3B, balancing the books on my leg. I dug my free hand in my back pocket and rested my chin on the top of a paperback book, pulling on the end of my keychain. The jingle of my keys was a whisper compared to the throaty laughter behind me.

"Stop fucking around. We're going to be late."

A fleeting spark raced down my spine at the smooth, commanding voice from across the hall. I quickly shoved my key into the keyhole and turned the knob before hastily putting my shoe back on the floor and gripping my books even tighter.

"Think fast."

If I would have taken a step into my apartment a second sooner, I wouldn't have had the most humiliating three seconds of my life in front of what were likely *multiple* gorgeous guys if their robust voices had anything to say about it.

I'd fallen a lot over the years and have had many bruises and bumps from landing sideways on the ice. Typically, I try to avoid falling, but I would've loved nothing more than to collide with the wooden floor of my new home rather than feel two steady hands on my waist, staring at all twelve of my books splayed out beneath my face.

"Jesus, Berkley. Watch what you're doing!"

I was hauled up so quickly that my dark hair whizzed past my face and stuck to the sticky gloss on my upper lip.

A pair of bright-green eyes shadowed by a strong, furrowed browline peered at me, and just like that, my exciting new venture of being independent for the first time in a year flew right out the window along with the very fragile trust my parents and I shared.

"Hockey players," I mumbled, peeling the stuck strand of hair from my lip. My feet were on flat ground again, but I felt like I was floating as Aasher Matthews—one of my father's best players—tightened his hands on my waist. My fixed spine was unrelenting with his attention glued to me. I swallowed my thick spit and abruptly stepped away from his overbearing presence. *Ugh.*

I wish I could say I wasn't familiar with any of Bexley U's hockey players, but it was hard not to be when my father spent more time with them than he did me. I wasn't complaining, nor was I jealous. I was simply stating facts.

Aasher Matthews and his posse continued to stand in front of me without so much as a peep. Two of them wore devilish smirks, elbowing one another like they had a secret to tell. My cheeks flamed like the torch I was going to throw at my father's head the moment I walked into his office. *First the elevator doesn't work, and now this?*

The longer I stood there, staring at my father's players, who were *apparently* my new neighbors, the more my suspicion grew. Now I knew why my father urged me to move into *this* apartment instead of the other ones we looked at.

I was likely the only girl attending Bexley U that looked at this situation like a punishment. What normal college girl wouldn't be thrilled to live across the hall from some of the best hockey players in the division with their hot smirks and muscular bodies. But, unfortunately for them, I wasn't your average college girl. I was *pissed*.

"We've stunned The Duster, man."

Berkley would have been burned to ash by my scornful gaze if he had more than two brain cells and noticed my glare. *The Duster.* Really?

"Are you okay?" Aasher bounced his eyes between mine. I stayed quiet even though I knew he was waiting for my answer.

Efrain stepped forward and swooped down to pick up a set of keys that separated Aasher and me. "We're gonna be late." The keys jingled in his large hand as he started down the hall. Neither Berkley nor Aasher followed after him, and I started to grow irritated.

"Who cares if we're late? I think Coach would let it slide if we were late because we were making sure his daughter was okay after almost falling to the floor." Berkley smiled at me, but I knew from past experience that when a hockey player tipped his lips the way he was, it was loaded.

"I'm fine," I snapped. Aasher raised an eyebrow at my tone.

The faint sound of a horn caught all of our attention, and it wasn't long before I recognized the melody of "We Will Rock You," which was the traditional warm-up song the hockey team skated to before each game.

"And that's our cue." Berkley winked in my direction before skillfully hopping down the stairs.

Aasher stayed kneeled on the ground below me as he started stacking up my fallen books like some type of gentle-man. I popped my hip out and crossed my arms, unwilling to trust him. We shared a tense silence that didn't lessen, even after he stacked my books on top of one another and walked away.

"Wait." I stepped forward just as quickly as the word flew from my mouth.

Aasher stopped at the top of the steps and peeked over his shoulder. The hood of his BU hoodie pulled back just a little as his messy brown hair fell over his forehead slightly. "Yeah?"

"Why don't you look surprised to see me?" I asked, already knowing the answer.

All I got in response was one long blink.

My heart thumped violently. "You knew I was moving in across the hall from you guys, didn't you?"

The air in the hallway stiffened. A breathy laugh fell from my mouth before I bit down on my tongue with hot cheeks. I turned my back to him like it was a punishment, but Aasher's smooth, arrogant voice broke through the punitive measure. "I had no idea you were moving across the hall."

"And there goes my respect for you," I said.

I already had a vengeance for hockey players. Aasher just sealed his own deal in making it permanent.

"Excuse me?"

We turned at the same time, facing each other despite sharing the same scowl.

I shrugged. "I don't like guys who lie."

The furrowing along his forehead didn't last long. He regrouped quickly. "Do you even like guys in general?" Aasher erased the rest of the space between us with the same confident stride that *every* hockey player had. He bent down beside my stiff legs and grabbed the last book that had fallen from my pile. When he rose to his full six-foot height, I held my breath. "Here you go, *Duster.*"

I opened my mouth to insult him back, but surprise

killed the words on the tip of my tongue when he pushed the book into my chest.

I recovered after a few seconds and scoffed before answering his irritating question. "What kind of question is that? And why does it matter to you?"

Aasher gripped me by the wrist and squeezed it tightly while clamping it over the paperback he had pressed against my chest. He stepped away, leaving me breathless.

"I was hoping you'd say no." His back was to me, but I still heard him.

"Why?"

"Because your dad forbids any of his players to touch you, and that's tempting to the majority of them."

"I do like guys," I said. "Just not hockey players."

[2]

THE DRIVE to Bexley U's rink takes no more than five minutes. That was part of the reason why I loved the proximity of my apartment so much, but now that I knew I was living across the hall from my father's boisterous hockey players—who will *absolutely* run to my dad and tell him my every move—I wasn't so fond of the idea of my new living arrangements.

My dad had already asked me to find a *female* roommate, and I say that lightly because it was more of a demand, but now I was going to be a hop, skip, and a jump away from his players? *Unbelievable.*

I slammed my door and stomped along the pavement, ignoring all the parked cars. Practice was about to start, so I knew my time was limited. I gripped my phone tightly. My mother's texts sat unread as I pushed it into my back pocket. I refused to open them and feel guilty, because that was exactly how I'd feel after reading them. I knew my parents loved me, and I also knew how lucky I was to have such caring parents, but it was a major slap to my *already* brittle self-respect. The little trust I had repaired with my parents was nonexistent again, and that was almost as disappointing as my entire future slipping through my fingers the moment I slipped on the ice last year.

I whizzed past the empty ice rink—unsuccessfully, I might add—and ignored the pang of regret burrowing in my bones. My confidence was unbreakable until I reached the locker room where I knew what lay behind the door. My hackles rose with my hand on the knob, but I hid from the distant memory.

Ignore the looks and get to the point.

Pushing on the door, it was clear that it was before practice and not after. The team was rowdy, loud, and annoying. The majority of them did a double take and smirked, like I was their reward for after practice.

I gave away nothing. My chin was sturdy, and my mouth tugged my lips into a scowl. The thoughts in my head were unsafe, because if you were a six-foot tall guy covered in hockey pads and attempted to flirt, I was going to plow right through you—or try to, at least.

"Hey, *Duster*." I glared across the locker room and caught the eye of Berkley, who was shirtless and clearly proud of his toned stomach.

"Eyes elsewhere," someone barked from the back.

My cheeks flamed.

I didn't need a rescuer.

Theo Brooks, the team captain, and his right-hand man, who just so happened to be my new neighbor, Aasher, were standing side by side like a pair of broody bodyguards. Aasher's brow raised in my direction. *Is he challenging me?*

I quickly realized that it was my defense mechanisms coming to play, because Aasher's eyes squinted before he flicked his chin to his coach's office. *Oh, right.* My teeth clenched, and my stomps were the only sound throughout the entire locker room.

Control of the situation was slowly slipping from my fingers, which did nothing but irritate me. It was intimidating to walk into a locker room full of arrogant jocks, and the more I stood there, the more flustered I became. *Ugh.*

I used a little more force than I meant to when I pushed on my father's office door. He flew up from his squeaky chair at the sound of it hitting the wall. Once he saw it was me, his expression changed from angry to concerned.

I counted the worry lines on his forehead. "Riley? What are you doing here? Is everything okay?"

Not even a breath left my mouth before the question raced past my lips. "You wanted me to move into that apartment because your players are living across the hall from me, didn't you?" My hands went to my waist, slipping underneath my sweater. I pinched the bare skin above the waist of my jeans to stay present. "Did you ask them to babysit me too?" I lowered my voice and peeked up at my father as he came around and leaned against the edge of his desk. "Do you understand how humiliating that is? Did you tell them the whole reason I'm here at Bexley U?" *Kill me now.*

"Of course not, Ry." My dad's tone softened. I glanced at the dry-erase board behind his desk to hide from the remorse. I was furious. Embarrassed, even. But it *was* my fault in the end. "I agreed to that apartment because it's close to campus, in a safe neighborhood, and—"

I dropped my purse on the chair in front of his desk. "And because your players live across the hall." *Don't lie to me.*

The little wrinkles around my father's eyes hinted at the

truth, and I wanted to act like a spoiled child and stomp my way out of his office while shooting every hockey player the middle finger on my way out, but I remained calm.

"Dad." I tried to move toward him, but my feet were heavy bricks, keeping me in my spot. "I really need you to trust me. I'll never get back on the ice if you don't give me space." *To breathe* was the last part of that sentence, but I left that out. It was the truth, though. My parents' breath had permanently coated my neck since leaving Rosewood.

A throat cleared behind me, and I jumped. The blood drained from my face, and I was mistaken to think I was bitten by a vampire. It wasn't Edward Cullen. Instead, it was Aasher Matthews, standing there with his hand enveloping the doorknob. He briefly caught my eye and raced his gaze down my body before pulling the door closed.

Great, they're already starting to get all up in my business.

A frustrated breath slowly floated from my mouth as I tried fighting my way back to the girl who was just mere points away from winning the World Figure Skating Championship before everything fell apart. *Including me.* I was confident and level-headed, and I surely didn't let a little misstep in my day ruin the entire twenty-four hours. Just like I wasn't going to allow a few brawny hockey players to ruin my newfound freedom after having my every move watched for an entire year.

I stared at my father from across his office and smoothed my voice. "It's uncalled for. I don't need a babysitter." *Especially not his crew of pompous jocks.* "You're going to have to trust me eventually."

My father, one of the stoniest college hockey coaches in the United States, took off his steely mask when his eyes glazed over. His fists went to his lap, and the sternness in his voice that his hockey players were used to was replaced with something that ate away at my conscience. "I *do* trust you. I just don't trust anyone else." He chuckled, which was his own attempt at hiding emotions. I wouldn't call him out, nor would I poke the bear and point out how he didn't dismiss my accusation of his hockey players acting like my babysitters. "I just want you to get back to the girl who was on fire instead of the girl who hides from the fire." *Meaning, he wants me back on the ice.*

I tried joking to lighten the mood. "Fire and ice don't mix, Dad."

His lips tugged into a smile. I dropped my hands from my hips and headed for the door. I glanced over my shoulder and pushed my hair away so I could meet his gaze. "I don't want your meaty hockey players watching my every move, so I suggest you take that thought right out of their heads."

He threw his hands up and skirted around to the other side of his desk. "They won't be bothering you. Trust me." He didn't look me in the eye when he said it. "But if you happen to need anything, they're across the hall."

My scoff threatened to fill his office, but I kept it in. I refused to look at any of his *trusting* hockey players as I left the locker room because, to be honest, I didn't trust a single one of them.

[3]

AASHER

RILEY LENNON WASN'T my type, but she seemed to be everyone else's. The moment Coach's daughter walked out of his office and swung her hourglass hips through the locker room with her dainty chin held high, was the exact moment a spell of lustful silence fell over my teammates. It was witchcraft. Their longing gazes followed every one of her feisty steps, and their shared curiosity morphed to desire within seconds.

I'd admit, my eyes clung to her too, but I wasn't under Riley's little spell. I wasn't as tempted as these other fools. It wasn't because she wasn't attractive. If anything, she was more desirable than most of the girls that attended Bexley U, and that was simply because she didn't fall over her own feet to get our attention. She wasn't blown away by our masculinity and ability to conquer the ice. In fact, her loathing for us was more obvious than the boners most of my teammates were currently sporting.

When I'd walked over and closed Coach's office door—because apparently eavesdropping was a form of foreplay for the team—Riley looked even angrier than before. Her creamy cheeks blasted with heat, and her glare was laser-like. I only heard snippets of her conversation, though. Something about how degrading it was to have the hockey players watching her every move. *I agreed, but nonetheless...*

Coach shot through his door a second after Riley disappeared, leaving a bad taste in my mouth. My teammates' heads were on a swivel as they pulled their attention from the lingering essence of Riley and clicked back into reality. Their gazes dropped, and they engaged in meaningless conversations, as if Coach Lennon didn't realize that each of them just played out several different scenarios of fucking his daughter all over this very locker room.

I gave Theo a sideways glance, and he rolled his eyes. He and I were on the same page. We were both more focused on hockey than your typical college player. We were at Bexley U to secure our careers. We weren't at Bexley U to chase girls. That wasn't to say we didn't let them chase us, but we weren't bewildered by something as futile as simple attraction.

"Listen up." Coach left little time for any of us to fully give him our attention. He whizzed right into a lecture. "My daughter is now attending Bexley U on campus instead of online, which I'm sure some of you already were aware of." No one spoke up and admitted to knowing, probably because they didn't have a death wish. "She is *off-limits.* You got that?"

"Coach, I could fall on the ice during practice, get a critical concussion, forget my name and my family members, and *still* remember that your daughter is off-limits." Efrain was only half-joking, but truth be told, the gravity of his joke was heavier than the humor.

I swore I saw a quick dash of amusement on Coach's face. "I will personally go out of my way to destroy your future at this school if you try anything. Do not tempt me."

"So we can't even be her friend?" I didn't care to see who asked the question, and if Coach hadn't tasked me with being his daughter's glorified babysitter, I might not have cared to hear the answer.

"You? Absolutely not. You don't know how to have friends who are females!"

The team snickered under their breath, but I didn't. Instead, I continued digging through my locker for the rest of my practice gear.

"With that said..." He paused for dramatic effect. "I don't think I need to remind you all to watch out for her. Or any other female at Bexley U. I do *not* tolerate foul play on this team."

That was Coach Lennon's recycled unwritten law that he repeated often.

There was a huge scandal a few years ago that completely destroyed the hockey team's chances of having their own hockey house. Most of the athletes at Bexley U had their own sanctuary where their teammates lived, but not the hockey team. Coach put an end to that when a girl was roofied at one of the parties. He shut it down *real* quick —thus the hockey players either getting their own apartment off campus or living in the dorms, like our captain, Theo. Poor guy.

Coach didn't wait for us to confirm we had heard his threat—I mean, *team discussion.* Instead, he stormed out of the locker room and barked, *"Ten minutes,"* on his way out.

The locker room talk started up almost immediately.

Ford tried to lighten the mood. "We've gotta get some blinders, fellas. Coach's daughter is..." He took his finger and ran it across his neck very slowly, pretending to cut his head off. "Off-limits."

I chuckled before pulling my practice jersey over my head. Some of my teammates had already gone onto the ice to begin warming up, but I slowed my movements, too caught up in my thoughts, wondering why Coach needed me to keep an eye on his daughter. The choices were endless, but my first guess was that she flunked out of her previous school and got in some trouble with ol' daddy. Even as uptight as she seemed, she very well could have been a party girl. Maybe that was why he was so adamant that I make sure she's 'making the right choices.' *Fuck, why do I care? Move on.*

"Off-limits." Berkley stood up after putting his skates on. "Doesn't he understand that we are feral when it comes to things we aren't supposed to do? Like her?"

"Coach would strangle you with the laces of your skates if you touched her." I briefly looked at Emory, our goalie, before he knocked Berkley on the back of the head and continued through the locker room. "Just like I'd strangle anyone if they touched my sister."

Someone from the next line of lockers mumbled under their breath, but I caught every last word. "It would be worth it. I'll gladly be strangled if it means touching her." Emory stopped walking and spun around. The poor freshman was quick to add, "I mean the coach's daughter! Not your sister."

Locker room talk. That was all it was.

I glanced at Theo. His jaw worked back and forth, and I

knew him well enough to know he was trying to hold back his reprimanding. Theo was a good team captain, meaning he knew when to put his foot down. There was a very thin line between admired captain and controlling asshole, but Theo did it well. The one thing you didn't want to disrupt on a team like this was the dynamic. It wasn't that we were all best friends, but we had a strong team bond. No one wanted to fuck that up.

Winning the Frozen Four was something we all wanted.

Berkley waited until Emory left the locker room before saying, "He is going to kill you on the ice now. You know that, right?"

The freshman was shaking in his skates.

"Don't worry." Efrain slapped him on the shoulder. "You wouldn't have a chance with either girl. Em's sister isn't swayed by hockey players, and Riley looked like she wanted to kill us earlier. That was well before you idiots drooled over her."

"Earlier?" Theo asked.

"Yep." Efrain nodded. "Riley lives across the hall from us."

"Whose idea was that?" Theo glanced at me.

I turned my head and lowered my voice. "Believe it or not, Coach's."

"Shit, can I move in with you guys?" Ford wiggled his eyebrows before pulling his jersey over his head.

"You practically have." Efrain threw his shirt at Ford's face. "And stop using my fucking body wash."

"Oh, will you relax? I'll buy you some more."

"No, you won't. And you'll probably use my cologne now too, hoping that the scent makes its way across the hall and sways Riley off her feet and into your arms."

"Will you two fucking stop?" I snapped. "No one is touching Riley." I didn't plan to sound so gruff, but the longer I listened to everyone lusting over Riley, whether they were kidding or not, the more irritated I became. Probably because *I* was the one who was supposed to keep them in check.

"Why?" Berkley loved pressing everyone's buttons, including mine. "Do you want her for yourself?"

As if on fucking cue, Graham Sullivan slithered out from behind the second row of lockers with his arrogance intact and the ability to piss me off in full effect. Sully was a transfer, but I knew him well before he relocated to Bexley U and found a spot on the team. He was my own personal antagonist. *A foe.* I have considered him an enemy on more than one occasion, and he thought the same of me.

We had always been neck and neck. Every accredited sports news outlet had compared us at one point over the years, and I was certain there was a meme floating around the internet about us.

Rosewood University was my first choice.

Bexley U was my second.

It was no surprise that it was the same for Sully.

His ego exploded when the scouts chose him over me. I was the first to admit that the reason they didn't choose me was because of the shitstorm I'd found myself in my senior year of high school, but Sully believed otherwise. The chip on his shoulder formed shortly after Bexley U started to climb to the top, and he was still stuck at Rosewood, thinking he was the better player.

But now, here he was, attending Bexley U, where we both had to shelve our hidden rival.

"I'd like to know the same. You got your eye on the coach's daughter, Aash?"

I instantly zeroed in on Sully's cheeky smirk as he pulled his shirt over his head and began getting dressed for practice. *Fucker.* I couldn't help but swell in victory when I noticed that my stomach was more defined than his. I wanted to puff my chest out like a twelve-year-old boy for winning an *ab competition* that he was unaware of. My competitiveness ramped up near him. It was simply out of my control.

Theo's sigh hit the back of my neck on his way over to Sully. He grabbed on to his bicep. I waited eagerly for Sully to recoil at his touch, but to my surprise, he didn't even blink. Theo's voice carried throughout the locker room and caught the ear of every player who was still in the vicinity. "Don't fuck around, Sully. This year is about the Frozen Four, and even *thinking* about Riley is going to be a distraction." Theo swung his firm stare around the locker room. "Get her out of your heads and focus on the game." He let go of Sully and started to walk past our silent teammates. "I can assure all of you that Coach didn't say those things to bait you. He meant what he said. Riley is off-limits. Don't fuck up our chances at being the best or ruin your futures over your need to be defiant."

Silence ensued when Theo disappeared out of the locker room, and the majority of us followed him out onto the ice. Our pucks had a little more fire to them, and Sully was a little more antagonizing than usual when we were pinned against one another for a practice scrimmage. The puck sliced past my head, clipping my padded shoulder. It took everything in me to keep my stick hovering over the ice instead of thrusting it outward to cross-check him.

"Were you going to take a bite out of that biscuit, Aash?"

I hated when he shortened my name. We were not on a nickname basis with one another.

"Jealous of my hat-trick, *Sul?*"

Theo skated in between us, and his disapproving frown did nothing to sway me from continuing my banter with Sully. It was rare when we shared words, but considering the fact that we had been enemies for years up until now, I think we both deserved a little leeway.

Coach blew his whistle, signaling that practice was over. I glanced at him, wondering if he was going to give me shit for my spar with Sully, and that was when I saw Riley quickly climbing the stands. I was already annoyed with her for reasons she was unaware of, but distracting her father so I could talk shit back to Sully wasn't one of them. *Thank you, Riley Lennon.*

Once back in the locker room, I began stripping out of my practice gear. Theo was the first to leave, and I wasn't really sure why, because he had been avoiding his dorm room since finding out that his new roommate was a chick, but I was glad he'd dipped out quickly. If he had stuck around, then he'd hear the team talking about Riley again and likely pop a blood vessel.

"Sounds like some of you are trying to score with Riley. Who will be the first to make her fall?" Ford was joking. I knew him well enough to know he didn't take many things seriously, but I also knew the mind of a twenty-something-year-old college guy because, well, I was one, and the wheels were fucking spinning in my teammates' heads.

"Maybe *you?*" Ford wiggled his eyebrows in my direction, and I laughed him off.

Sully peeked around the edge of the lockers and waited for my answer. I ignored him and answered truthfully. "Nope. Uptight and cold aren't my type, even without the thought of Coach coming at me with a shotgun." *Or worse, a quick call to my future NHL team, sending me packing.*

I'd already been disappointed once when it came to my future—ironically, over a girl. I wouldn't make that mistake twice.

"I can loosen her up," Nate said, pulling off his skates.

"Doubtful," someone quipped.

"Watch me."

I denied myself the energy to engage in their fruitless arguing. They were all likely to go home and ponder Coach's threat along with the look of disapproval on their captain's face and snuggle up with a puck bunny instead.

Riley Lennon was too much work, and our effort went onto the ice. There was no room for anything else.

Ford began heading toward the door with all his gear. "She's been surrounded by hockey players all her life. Let's face it, fellas. We just don't do it for her. Why do you think we call her duster? That girl never plays the game. The few times I've seen her around, she sticks her nose in the air and ignores every single guy who approaches her."

"That's not true."

My fingers stopped undoing the laces of my skates. I didn't have to look up to see that it was Sully who argued. His voice was nails on a chalkboard.

"What isn't true?" someone asked in between shutting a locker.

"Ry not liking hockey players. She used to date a hockey player."

He calls her Ry? What are they, fucking besties?

I suppressed a growl. "And how exactly do you know that?"

Sully's chuckle rubbed me the wrong way. I cursed Coach for propositioning me and leaving me no choice but to agree to being Riley's handler. If it weren't for our covert conversation, I wouldn't have cared. "Do any of you know where Riley used to go to school? Before transferring here?"

The answer was obvious by the haughty sound of his voice. "Rosewood."

Of fucking course.

My teammates broke out into hushed conversations, but there was one question that snagged my ear. "So what? Have you tapped that or something?"

Suddenly, it felt like I was the prey and Sully was the predator. "No. But I know her type."

The collective, "*Ooh,*" provoked an eye roll from me. *A bunch of idiots who weren't focused on hockey even in the slightest.*

"So, it's settled, then. She's into hockey players."

No, she isn't. She better not be.

"Let's see who can tap that first. Winner gets to fuck Leon's mom."

"What the fuck?" Leon came barreling out of the steamy showers like a wild animal. He took the towel off his hips and zeroed in on Nate. The sound of a wet towel on skin sliced through the stuffy locker room. My teammates laughed, and I walked away before I got too riled up by their talk. I was headed toward the door, rounding the last set of lockers when I paused. Their conversation was hushed, but I had excellent hearing.

"Winner gets *her.* There's no need for anything else."

For fuck's sake.

"Let's make an ice bet."

I stayed hidden and cursed under my breath. An *ice bet* was the oldest trick in the book. It was an unwritten tradition that I had thought died down but *apparently* not. It was considered hazing, and not only did Coach have a no-hazing rule, but Bexley U itself had a zero-tolerance policy for it. My heart picked up speed the longer I listened.

"So it's settled. Whoever gets to her first, wins."

"But you have to do so without Coach finding out."

"Obviously. We will all keep it on the down low."

"Are we talkin' sex or what?"

"We should do a point system."

"The hotter the act, the more points you get."

They laughed while I silently teetered between my choices. I listed them off quickly in my head and grew more irritated with each stupid remark from my teammates. Coach had no idea that putting a no-touch rule on his daughter would be like dangling a piece of steak in front of hound dogs. He also had no idea that I would quickly grow to resent her for taking up space in my head that wasn't reserved for her.

The obvious choice would be to tell Coach about the little hazing activity, *but* there was a problem with doing something like that: *the team*.

Bexley U was number one in our division. We were elite, and although there were lead players on every team, we all worked together on the ice to secure a win. We had a good relationship and an even better team dynamic. Tattling on my teammates—Sully in particular because he was the one who started it—would ruin that in a heartbeat, because if Coach didn't kill him with his bare hands, he'd definitely kick him off the team for poor morals and hazing. Then I'd be the team pariah for fucking up our chances at the Frozen Four, thus ruining my future and everyone else's. It was a snowball effect that I wanted no part in.

The other choice—and the one I was happily replaying in my head—was to knock Sully's teeth out.

"Oh, it's fucking on."

"Ice bet secured, baby."

I pushed off the lockers and stormed out of the locker room.

Riley told me that she didn't like hockey players, and unfortunately, my future was balancing on whether or not that would hold true.

[4]

RILEY

I WAS SO CLOSE.

I had one foot in the locker room and one in my father's office when the clanking of hockey skates against the floor filled the locker room.

After sitting in the stands and watching the hockey team skate along the ice with ease for ten minutes, I was more than ready to grab my purse that I had *regrettably* left on the chair perched in front of my dad's desk and head to my apartment.

It was dire that he gave me his office keys so I could rush to his office, snag my purse, and head to my car all before he dismissed his players. But here I was. *Stuck.*

Never mind the few seconds I had to take to gather my breath after almost stepping foot onto the ice. It was pathetic, yes, but my shaky hands and clammy palms reminded me that I had *a lot* to accomplish before tryouts.

Now I was trapped, waiting for the hockey team to stop messing around and leave so I could slip out. I was meeting

Sutton at our apartment with all her stuff so I could help her move in.

I popped open my texts to message her. Sutton and I met last semester when I had to come take a final in person instead of online, and we hit it off immediately. She was the first friend I made at Bexley U, but since we both had an intense hatred for hockey players, we were instant besties— at least according to her.

It was girl math. We didn't make the rules.

Plus, most of my previous friendships ended when I abruptly took my sabbatical from skating and transferred from Rosewood. It proved that the majority of them weren't true friendships anyway.

> Me: I'm going to be a little late. I'm stuck in my dad's office because there is no way I'm walking through the locker room while the guys undress from practice.

My legs dangled off the edge of the desk as I waited for Sutton to text back. I ignored the photos of me in various figure skating poses from past routines hanging along the wall, because they only reminded me of what I'd lost.

Instead, my gaze traveled to the office door. I caught the loud "oohs" and "ahhs" floating in from the locker room, and I rolled my eyes. *Why were they so loud?* The men's locker room was vastly different from the women's. Or maybe it was just the difference in hockey players and figure skaters. We were poised and composed. There wasn't much conversation that occurred between us, and there was certainly no yelling.

. . .

> Sutton: Why refuse? Sneak a glimpse of those muscles. You and I both know those boys are ripped. That's how they get away with being complete assholes.

I suppressed a laugh. *It was true.* I went to text her back but stopped mid-sentence when I heard my name.

"*Sounds like some of you are trying to score with Riley. Who will be the first to make her fall?*"

I popped up from the edge of my father's desk and shoved my phone in my back pocket. *Excuse me, what?*

"*Maybe you?*"

I had no idea who was talking or who the person was directing their conversation to, but I suppressed the need to get closer to the door and find out. The mortification of them knowing I was in here while they walked around butt-ass naked would be enough to make me self-combust. I didn't necessarily care what they thought about me, but the rumors would start immediately, and they'd think I was either a stalker or a puck bunny.

Not that there was much of a difference.

"*Uptight and cold aren't my type, even without the thought of Coach coming at me with a shotgun.*"

My mouth fell open at the jab. I could fool anyone with my blasé front of hating hockey players, but I couldn't pretend I didn't feel the sting of that insult. I was too focused on ignoring the irrational hurt to continue listening to their conversation, only catching snippets here and there.

"*So it's settled. Whoever gets to her first, wins.*"

They were assholes. Every one of them.

"Are we talkin' sex or what?"

"We should do a point system."

A point system?! As if I were a game? My palms stung with the clenching of my fists.

"Ice bet secured."

My face was hot. I wanted to stomp my way into their locker room and stare each of them in the eye to give them a little scare. It would be *so* easy for me to run to my dad and get their asses handed to them, or *worse*. I could probably get them kicked off their precious little hockey team that they were all so passionate about, but some games were better played with slow manipulation.

I wouldn't appear like an opponent to them. They were too blind to see me for what I really was: *an enemy*.

They could try all they wanted, despite my father's threats, but none of them would ever get close enough to win their little *ice bet*. In fact, the entire Bexley U hockey team was going to have the biggest case of blue balls there ever was.

I sure hope it didn't affect their skill on the ice.

⸺

Eventually, I made my way back to my apartment. It didn't take long for the locker room to clear, but it was enough time for my irritation to lessen. That was, until I stepped out of the elevator and was reminded who my neighbors were.

"Finally!" Sutton flung herself off our door and rushed over to me, leaving my enemies to linger in the open space. Sutton leaned in close. "What took you so long? I've been standing here having a pointless conversation with the new guy for entirely too long."

New guy?

I peeked around the curtain of Sutton's summery blonde hair and shuffled backward in surprise. "What is he doing here at Bexley U?"

"You know him?" she asked.

The unease in my stomach didn't stop me from walking toward Graham Sullivan. He was likely the only person on this campus that knew me beyond my label of being Coach Lennon's daughter.

His cheek pulled, revealing his white smile. "I was wondering when I'd run into you. You were on a mission earlier in the locker room, or I would have said hi."

"The locker room?" *You mean the same dreaded locker room where my name was being thrown around like fucking confetti.* "Are you a student at Bexley U now? What happened to Rosewood?"

"I could ask you the same."

My eyes immediately fell to the speckled tile that lined the hallway. I knew no one heard my pulse strumming like a guitar, but I felt it everywhere.

"The last time I saw you was at the Delta house with Gray." he said.

Ah, yes. The memories.

Delta Kappa was the fraternity that my ex was in, and their house was the most popular party spot on campus.

Sutton made an obnoxious noise that sounded like a buzzer, pulling my attention away. Her hand fell into mine, and she tsked her tongue. "We don't talk about exes here. Now scoot along, boys. I'm moving in this evening, and we have plans that don't involve hockey players."

"You're living here too?" Efrain asked over his shoulder while putting his key in the door. "What happened to the house on Fourth with Crew?"

Ford smacked Efrain against the chest. "She just said we don't talk about exes. Keep up, bro."

"Wait, you and Crew broke up?"

Sutton pulled me toward our door, and I almost tripped because I was too busy trying to match Ford's, Efrain's, and Graham's—or I guess *Sully* as they called him—voices to the not-so-distant memory of my name being shuffled around the locker room an hour prior.

Once Sutton and I were in our apartment and she slammed the door, her hands fell to her hips. "Great, now my breakup is going to be the talk of campus. It's already floating around everywhere online that has any interest in the NHL."

"Don't worry, it'll blow over soon. No one will linger on your breakup for too long," I tried to reassure her, but we both knew it was a lie. College was one thing. The NHL was idolized. The players were a hot topic everywhere, and it just so happened that Sutton's ex, Crew Hart, was one of the best players the NHL acquired for the new season. "He's an asshole for letting you go. All hockey players are *assholes*, remember?"

She tried to laugh it off, but it wasn't very convincing. Her eyes glossed over, but she turned around and took in her new apartment.

"This is so much better than my old place." Her tiny nose wiggled. "Smells better too. Do you know what it's like to live in a house with sweaty athletes?"

"After being trapped in the locker room and smelling a bunch of hockey players after they discarded their pads, I think I can imagine."

Sutton took my response in stride and nodded. "*Pigs.*"

I laughed. "Total pigs."

"Just like Crew's *friends* who tried to keep me from

putting my shit in my car earlier. They begged me to stay. Lennox got on his knees and everything."

My jaw dropped. "You're kidding."

"Nope. They don't fool me, though. They've been trying to swoop in to mend my heart since Crew left, which just so happened to involve their penises."

I laughed out loud. "Definitely pigs."

After giving her the short, two-second tour of our apartment, we headed for the door to grab her things.

"There isn't much—" Sutton stopped mid-sentence. I bounced off her back when she stopped walking, and a huff of air left my chest. I peered around her while rubbing my forehead.

Ford, Efrain, Berkley, Graham, and—to my displeasure —*Aasher* were each stacking Sutton's boxes on top of one another in front of our door.

Ford smiled, showing off his perfect white teeth. "All done, babes."

Sutton recovered quickly after the initial surprise. She leaned forward and pecked Ford on the cheek. "You always were my favorite. Thanks, guys."

Once they disappeared in their apartment, Sutton glanced at me and shrugged. "Okay, maybe they aren't *all* assholes."

I scoffed, knowing better. "Don't worry. There's still plenty of time for them to show their true colors."

[5]

THE DISTRACTIONS WERE NONSTOP.

Gunfire, screeching tires, and explosions vibrated my bedroom door so hard that I had a hard time focusing on the warm mouth wrapped around my cock. Liv's silky hair weaved through my fingers, and she picked up the speed, trying to get me off faster so I could do the same for her.

I shut my eyes and focused. It was stereotypical for a jock to "*date*" around instead of settling down with someone in college. We were predictable, and it rang true for the majority of us. I was your average college hockey player, refusing to have anything serious with a girl, no matter how talented her mouth was. On occasion, there were some that I frequented more than once, and I say this with respect, but they were *easy*. As long as they knew it wasn't a secure relationship and that I didn't give two shits about how their best friend insulted them behind their back, then we were good. I didn't disrespect them. I just looked at it more as a working relationship rather than an intimate one.

"God." Liv choked me down and stood on wobbly legs. She wiped her mouth on the back of her hand, and I smirked. Her lips were swollen, and her cheeks were flushed. It was a hot look for her. "There toward the end I thought you might not get off. What's up? Are you distracted?"

You could say that.

Not to mention the fucking war zone occurring in the living room with Ford, Berkley, and Efrain screaming at the TV.

"Nope." I buttoned my pants and gripped her curvy waist, dismissing her questions. *That's not what we did.* I pulled her in close before shoving her on my bed. A quick, breathy laugh escaped her, and my fingers quickly got to work.

I pushed her short dress up. The cotton stayed bundled around her waist when I hooked my fingers into her panties and slowly pulled on them, revealing her well-groomed pussy. She was already anticipating my touch. I glanced at her face and saw that her eyes were closed with thick strands of dark hair fanned out behind her.

I bent down and began working my magic. I knew it wouldn't take long. Liv had frequented my apartment on a few different occasions, so I knew what she liked. Her smooth legs wrapped around my shoulders, and she dug her heels into my back. I sucked, licked, and flicked her tight clit, using my fingers and mouth for a quicker release.

After she came, she sat up quickly with her flushed face and smiled. I stood near my desk, chugged some water, and watched her put herself back together.

There was no time wasted between us, and the best part about it was that there were no feelings other than satisfaction. She grabbed her purse from the floor and furrowed her brow at the time. "I gotta go to work. Thanks for getting right down to business. That was fast and *intense*."

I noticed the pink on her cheeks, and my lip pulled into a grin. My arrogance was seeping all over the room. I was a man of many talents, and I knew it. "I'll see you later."

Liv opened the door at the exact time the video game cut off. I whipped my head toward the sound of a high-pitched voice echoing throughout the living room and down the hall to my room.

"We thought you guys were having a party."

"Why don't you beautiful girls join us, and it can be a party." It was obvious Ford had been drinking by the sound of his flirty, Southern drawl. *"Sutton can hold her own, but can you?"*

If Sutton was here, that meant the other voice belonged to my little subordinate. Riley had been easy to keep track of. She hadn't shown her innocent-looking face at any of our parties, and as far as I was aware, she stayed holed up in her apartment with her nose in a book.

Which was perfectly fine with me.

I followed Liv down the hallway, and my irritation kicked up a notch after seeing Coach's daughter in my living room. Riley commanded the room with her presence, and whether she was aware of it or not, her choice of clothing was like holding a neon sign that said *fuck me*. Was she baiting us—*them*? Her big, round, blue eyes were a slap to my face. The faint markings of freckles on the very tip of her small nose were the first things I saw when she swung her attention in my direction. Tendrils of dark hair framed her heart-shaped face, fallen from her high bun, and the little crop top she was wearing pissed me off because it did nothing but flaunt her medium-sized breasts and toned stomach. I hated that she was gorgeous. *Damn it.* Why couldn't Coach's daughter be ugly?

I briefly glanced at my roommates, and the loose hold of my composure quickly fell. *Who the hell invited Sully over?* I had the urge to stalk over and rip the video game controller out of his hand. He was already lusting over Riley. They all were. Sutton was nonexistent standing next to her roommate. The team had known her for years because she dated a former Bexley U hockey player. She was old news, and no one in the room had their eye set on her to win some stupid fucking bet.

"Where are your clothes?" My question was laced with disapproval, and everyone noticed. I ran my eyes down her body, cursing her smooth legs. I hadn't planned to be an asshole, but by the faint gasp that came from her mouth, I absolutely came across as one. *Oh well.* If I had to be the bad guy, then so be it.

Riley's soft, shy gaze hardened. Her nose wrinkled at my tone. I stood back against the bar and watched as she moved out of Liv's way so she could get through the door. *Shit, I forgot all about Liv.* Once the door latched, Riley crossed her arms over her *braless* chest and snapped back a response that I felt against my face. "You have the audacity to ask where my clothes are? Where were *her* clothes?"

"Probably still on his floor," Berkley said under his breath, snickering like the instigator he was. I shot him a glare because whose side was he on anyway?

Riley's smug grin was victorious. *I was totally going to hurt her feelings before the night was over.*

"What happened to you being the sweet, quiet Coach's daughter?" Efrain asked.

"I have never been described as sweet." Riley rolled her eyes at me before looking at Efrain. "Unless that's something you guys say about me the second you think you're alone in the locker room?"

"Who says we're talking about you in the locker room?" I pressed farther into the granite counter, forcing it to cut into my spine.

Sutton rolled her lips together before crossing her arms and glancing at her roommate. "They're *definitely* talking about you in the locker room."

I purposefully kept my attention on Riley instead of Sully because I knew my poker face wasn't up to par. I was certain he didn't know that I knew of the bet, and I had pretty good evidence that if he knew I disapproved, he'd try to score even harder.

A big part of me wanted to pull Riley aside and tell her what was going on, but there were obvious problems with that plan. Who knew how she would react? Would she run to her dad and throw the team under the bus and bring me down with them?

Sully's smug tone pulled me back to the present. "Why do you care what she's wearing, Aasher? Gonna send a picture to her dad or something?" I kept my face even, but he had no idea how tempting that idea was. *It would put her in her place real fast.* "She looks fine."

She looked more than fine, which was exactly what was bothering me.

Riley headed for the door. *Yes, good girl. Go home.* She called over her shoulder, "We just came to see if you guys could turn down the volume."

"*Or*...if we could join the party." Sutton's smile was flirty, but we knew her well. She wasn't the type of girl to find herself in another hockey player's bed after her breakup with Crew.

Ford popped up from the couch and began his usual

antics. "Sure, Riley. We will turn down the volume, but why don't you two stay and hang out with us?"

Riley choked out a laugh. She pulled the door open. "No thanks."

She and Sutton shared a sideways look. What was up with chicks having silent conversations that anyone with the XY chromosome couldn't decipher?

"You got other plans for the night?" Berkley asked.

"As a matter of fact, we do." Riley spun around, and I automatically stared at her ass. I cursed under my breath at the peach. Perfectly rounded cheeks were peeking out from below her soft, pink shorts, and if I thought she looked good, chances were my teammates did too.

"Do you now? Well, let's see what you two got going on for tonight." Sully wasted no time before standing up and moving through the apartment like the slithery snake he was, rounding Sutton like she wasn't even in the same room.

"Leave them alone," I said, crossing my arms over my chest. *And just like that, I showed my interest.*

Sully stopped mid-step. He squinted as he tried to read me. There was a spark there—a challenge brewing. And I was instantly fucked. *Great.*

Riley and Sutton were already halfway through the door when Sully began following them out. If Sutton wasn't with Riley, I would have followed after him.

"What's the deal?" Efrain's question was warranted, but that didn't mean I wanted to answer it. There was no sense in all of us heeding caution when it came to Riley and wondering which teammates were trying to score with her. I had everything under control.

"Nothing." My answer was sharp and a total lie. I kept

my attention on our closed door, wishing I could see through it. *Why did she have to wear those tiny shorts?*

"You still got beef with Sully?" Efrain probed. "I thought you two moved on from that after the first go around during preseason."

We had words. That was it.

Efrain sighed. "This won't be good for the team. You've gotta let that shit go."

Something snapped inside my body as muffled, girly laughter crept under our door from the hall. Oh, he was making her laugh now?

"You want to know what isn't good for the team?" I kept my tone level, but I was irritated. "The little competition going on between some of the players over who can be the first to fuck Riley."

"What?" Berkley's head snapped so loud I heard a crack.

"There's an ice bet going around, and guess who's at the center of it?"

"He didn't." Ford gasped dramatically.

Oh. He did.

"An ice bet? That's the oldest trick in the book and the stupidest idea anyone on this team has had, and that's saying something because Ford was looking into getting a real fucking wolf for our mascot." Efrain said.

"Blasphemy," Ford cursed under his breath, and we all gave him our attention—something he enjoyed. "Both the fact that it's illegal to own a wolf and the fact that half the team is trying to fuck Riley. What are they thinking?"

A rush of air flew from Berkley's mouth. "Coach will lose his shit if he finds out."

"And half the players will lose their spot on the team, meaning we can say goodbye to the Frozen Four." I sighed with agitation. The more I thought about it, the more anger that surfaced. "That's not all."

"There's more?" Efrain asked.

I rolled my lips. "Remember when Coach pulled me into his office the other day? He basically deemed me as Riley's babysitter. He wants me to watch out for her. Treat her like I would if she were my sister." *In other words, keep the team's hands off her.*

There was a beat of silence as each of my friends downloaded the information I had given them. Ford snapped his fingers at Efrain and Berkley. "It's time to intervene, boys."

"What does that mean?" Berkley was leery. We all were.

Efrain stole the glass of whiskey out of Ford's hand and handed it off to me so I could pour it down the sink.

"Whoa, whoa, whoa! Why did you do that?" Ford asked.

I raised an eyebrow. "We have conditioning at seven in the morning."

He pouted, but it didn't last long. "Let's go see what little Miss Riley's plans are for the night. I can assure you it won't be spending time with an asshole like Sully." Before we followed after him, he ruined his act of righteousness with a cocky remark. "Plus, if that girl is sleeping with anyone, it's going to be me."

My jaw flexed.

"I'm kidding. Chill, *dad.*"

[6]

"So how have you been, Ry?"

I knew one of them would follow, but to my surprise, it was Sully instead of Aasher.

What was I thinking? Stomping over there in my pajamas and yelling at them? I had tried to ignore them, but the louder they became, the more irritated I grew. I couldn't focus on the syllabus posted in my business ethics class, and one too many huffs later, Sutton was pulling me off the couch. "Come on, let's go see what all the ruckus is."

Then Aasher just *had* to make a comment about my attire. It fueled my irritation even further. What a jerk.

I slowly turned around with Sutton by my side and found Sully resting against the wall with his arms crossed over his chest. He waited patiently for my answer, and he could have fooled me, because instead of looking smug, like the rest of his teammates, he truly seemed curious.

Graham Sullivan was attractive and had no problems

getting girls. I highly doubted he was part of his team's locker room chat. Not to mention, I knew him from Rose-wood. If anything, he'd put a stop to the bet after watching my very public and humiliating breakup with his previous team captain.

"I've been good." I shifted and attempted to cover my boobs by crossing my arms. All I could hear was Aasher's patronizing voice in the back of my head, and I was slightly embarrassed. That wasn't to say there wasn't a burning desire to strip down even further, just to prove a point.

"You look like you've been better than just okay." Sully grinned, and his white teeth peeked from behind his lips. "Last time I saw you, things were a little intense."

I stilled. Intense was one way to describe my parting from Rosewood.

"I'm sorry," Sully blurted. "I didn't mean that in a bad way. You look good is all I'm trying to say."

"You're doing a shit job at it," Sutton said matter-of-factly. Her hip popped out, and she gave him a look that was nothing short of annoyance.

I forced out a quick laugh. "You're fine." Sully was stumbling over his words because the topic was touchy. *My breakup. The fall. Transferring schools.* "I fled Rosewood in a hurry, and the picture I left behind wasn't the prettiest."

Sutton studied me closely, aware that she didn't know the whole story.

"Have you been at Bexley U this whole time? I could totally use a tour guide. I'm still trying to get used to the campus. I see more of the rink than I do the courtyard."

The door across the hall opened at the same time Sutton shot Sully's implied invitation down. "A tour guide? Campus isn't *that* big."

Ford was the first to step into the hallway. "Sutton is right. Plus, we live in the twenty-first century. You have an iPhone with a map."

Sully smiled. "She's prettier than a map, though."

My cheeks grew warm. It was nice to hear after being reprimanded by Aasher for my lack of clothing, but there was skepticism that cooled my blushing almost immediately.

Sutton's hand found mine, and she turned her head in my direction. I could read her thoughts like they were my own. We'd both been burned by hockey players in the past, and neither of us fell for their compliments anymore, even if it was simply *just* a compliment.

"So, you said something about plans?" Ford interrupted the conversation by whisking across the hall. His steps were a little slower than usual. I pulled back out of his way, and he slipped past me and pushed on our apartment door to make himself at home.

"Hey!" I rushed toward Ford as he walked farther into our apartment. Sutton was hot on his heels.

I was stuck in time as Aasher waltzed through the door next and angled his chin in my direction. "I'll get him out in a second. He's tipsy and uncontrollable." *Yeah, just like my need to take my knee and ram it between your legs.*

Aasher's warm breath fanned over my face, and I blinked back the surprise of my inability to speak. I snapped out of it when his gaze slipped down to my lack of clothing again.

A bratty reply fled my mouth. "I don't need your help. I can handle a tipsy hockey player on my own." *I can handle an asshole hockey player too.*

His smooth skin gave way to zero imperfections, but just

below the faint scruff of his facial hair, his puffy lips—probably from kissing that puck bunny—curved into a cocky grin. "I didn't ask if you needed my help."

"And I didn't ask for you to comment on my clothing moments ago, either."

Aasher's eyebrow curved with the jerk of his head. A thick piece of brown hair flipped onto his forehead, and I wanted to reach out and pull it. "Oh, so you want him in here? Is that it?"

His accusation burned my cheeks. I didn't know how to read Aasher, and it drove me wild. Was he kidding? Or was he being serious? I'd already told him hockey players weren't my type, but his question made me trip over my thoughts. Was he manipulating me because *he* was the one behind the bet? I recognized the hint of disapproval in his tone. Maybe *he* was the one who said I wasn't his type because I was uptight and cold.

Aasher and I were at a stalemate. Instead of stumbling over my denial of wanting his roommates in my apartment, I turned around and left him to make his own assumption.

"Wow." Berkley's shoulder brushed mine. "This is a nice place. Way cooler than ours."

"Cleaner too," Sutton added.

Efrain came through the door after Aasher and flicked one of our twinkle lights hanging above the window. "Can I live with you instead of these two?"

Ford sighed. "If you do, can I have your room? I'm sick of the dorms, and your couch sucks."

I was coiled so tight from my little spar with Aasher that I couldn't keep the huff in my mouth when he ran his finger along the seam of our couch. *Don't touch our stuff.*

Sutton was standing beside me, and a quiet laugh tumbled from her. She was hardly even moved in yet, and here we were, surrounded by a bunch of irritating, pompous athletes.

"You can't just storm into our apartment," I said, letting my words trail off at the sight of Sully flopping onto the couch. He took up the entire length of it.

"She's right. Let's go." Aasher was standing near the door, appearing impatient with his flitting gaze and loud sighs. I almost said, '*Never mind, you guys can stay,*' just because he was agreeing with me, but the truth was, I didn't want them to stay, and I surely didn't want to catch his scathing gaze on my legs again.

"I thought you had plans tonight." Ford put his hand on his chin and looked around the apartment and our lack of plans. "What were you two ladies getting into?"

We didn't have plans.

Not a single thing was planned other than watching Netflix on the couch. Our course load was light right now because it was still the beginning of the semester.

"You know..." Sully got up from the couch. "I haven't seen you at any of the parties, Riley."

I shifted along the wood floor. There was a chill in the air, and I was certain it was because my warm and snug apartment felt cold and disturbed with unwelcome guests inside, but if Aasher said something about my outfit already, I wonder what he'd say if my nipples suddenly appeared through my shirt. I crossed my arms. "I'm not much of a party girl."

Sully tilted his head. "You used to be. You two should come to the next one."

Pass. "I was only invited to Rosewood parties because of Gray. You know how he was." He liked to flaunt me in front of his teammates.

Ford's eyebrows furrowed. "Well, I don't. Explain."

I immediately felt insecure. My chest tightened, and sweat beads formed on the back of my neck. Aasher had moved into my kitchen and leaned with his elbows propped on my counter, waiting for my explanation.

I had just enough confidence to muster up four little words. "Can you guys leave?"

Ford strode closer and looked me dead in the eye with pure sincerity. "Sore subject. I'm sorry, Duster."

"It's not a sore subject," I lied. It was obvious. Gray wasn't the love of my life, but our breakup was brutal, especially on top of everything else.

"He's a dick. I never liked him. The way he treated you..." Sully's sentence drifted, but he inched closer to stand shoulder-to-shoulder with Ford. They shared a questionable look when neither one of them moved.

"The way he treated her?" Ford's curious gaze stayed pinned to me. "Now I'm really interested."

Everyone was waiting for me to speak up. My mouth grew dry, and my palms were sweaty. I wished for a black hole to appear beneath my feet so I could vanish, but instead, Aasher appeared like some mystical, egotistical hero to save me. His hands fell to his teammates' shoulders, and he pulled them apart like the splitting of a tree. "That's enough. Out. All of you."

"Aw, come on." Ford suddenly sounded like he was from Texas with the hint of a Southern drawl. "We were just getting to the good stuff."

If it were anyone else who swooped in to ease me of the embarrassment of Gray's breakup, I would have been thankful. But there was something about Aasher that provoked me. I was willing to self-sabotage myself just to go against him.

"I'll tell you what happened." I changed my tune quickly, skimming right past Aasher's double take. My brain was yelling at me to retreat, but I didn't listen as I hauled myself up onto my kitchen counter, letting my legs dangle below. "My breakup isn't a secret."

Sutton snapped her head to me so quickly I felt the breeze of her hair. She was just as perplexed as I was at my behavior. "My boyfriend—"

"Gray Loretto." The name flew from Sully's mouth, and there was a wave of recognition that moved through the room. Everyone knew Gray Loretto. He was the best player Rosewood had. The humblest too.

Berkley mumbled, "Enough said."

I continued on with my explanation that Ford asked for. "We dated for about a year, but then he broke up with me at a party by pulling one of my best friends into his lap and making out with her in front of everyone."

"Wait, in front of you? He knew you were there?" Sutton's jaw dropped. She didn't know the whole story, but now she did.

Of course he knew I was there. He was the one to invite me. It was his way of proving that he would rather be with someone who shared his same goals. He wanted to be with someone who wouldn't choke under pressure like I did in the rink. Those were his exact words.

My confidence wobbled when silence filled my apartment. My poised explanation lacked the courage I had minutes before, so I looked over at Aasher, hoping his haughty gaze would have the same effect as earlier, but his green eyes were soft around the edges instead of firm with impatience. He stood back with his arms crossed over his chest, *watching* me.

"Oh, he knew," Sully answered for me. I released a shaky breath, pulling myself out of the strange sense of sadness I felt. He walked over to me and placed his hand on my knee, giving it a gentle squeeze.

I felt Aasher's scathing eye on us before his cool tone hit my ears.

"Did you know he was going to do it, Sully?"

Sully snapped his head over to Aasher, and tension rose. "Of course not. I would have told Riley." He squeezed my knee again, but I stared at Aasher as he zeroed in on Sully's palm on my leg. *What is his deal?*

Ford stole the attention of the room. "Well, that was a sad story, Duster. But don't you worry. We will demolish him on the ice. I'll even cross-check him for you." He winked, and a soft laugh left me. I smiled and decided that Ford was my favorite, even if my dad thought he was the most annoying on the team.

"Let's go." Aasher pushed himself off the far wall while his roommates groaned. He shook his head, clearly irritated with them. "Do you guys really want Riley to go off and tell her dad that we were all in her apartment? Especially after she asked us all to leave? Go. *Now*."

The fact that he was deeming me as a little tattletale had me sliding off the edge of the counter. My bare feet slapped against the hardwood floor, and my stomach hollowed. "Despite what you think," I snapped, choosing to ignore Berkley's hand around one of my trophies that he had pulled from the shoebox near the door, "I don't run and tattle to my dad every time something happens."

Berkley and Efrain made their way across the floor, and soon, all five guys were near the door, ready to escape to their apartment. I thought I was in the clear until one set of eyes shot down to my chest, eyeing my *very* pronounced nipples from the chill in the air. It probably had to do with Aasher. He was a cold, bossy asshole.

I refused to cover my chest. "Unlike *Aasher*."

"What? Unlike Aasher?" Sully repeated.

A deep crease appeared in between Aasher's eyebrows. There was an instant charge in the air that warmed the chill between us. The room crackled. His steely jaw flexed, and I smiled sweetly.

I knew, without a doubt, that Aasher would be the one on the team who would gladly rat me out. I wasn't sure if he was just an ass-kisser when it came to my dad, or if he was a leader by choice and took it upon himself to keep his team in check, but either way, his self-righteous personality prompted me to shove it right back in his face.

There was a flicker against his temples, but I stood my ground and stared at him from across my apartment. A small twitch of his lips was more condescending than amused, and it seemed like a warning of sorts. A smile tugged against his mouth as he turned around and shoved his teammates out the door.

Efrain slowly walked behind him and tipped his head at Sutton and me. "Good night, girls. Let us know if you need anything."

Ford shouted from across the hall, "Yeah, like strong arms to keep you warm at night."

I watched Aasher shove him through their door, and soon, their laughter faded, and Sutton and I were alone again.

"Those boys." She shook her hair out before pulling it up into a high pony. "They're gonna be trouble. But the best ones usually are."

They weren't *so* bad, except for Aasher and his assumptions. The fact that he thought I was going to go off and tell my dad that they came into my apartment uninvited was irking. It could have been worse, though. Living across the hall from the hockey team wasn't ideal with Aasher goading me every three seconds, but I could still be at Rosewood with a cheating boyfriend and the lingering taste of success on my tongue that only reminded me of my shortcomings.

[7]

AASHER

BEING on the ice was second nature, but it was like that for most of us. I slipped behind Theo, and eyed each Westin player slowly as a victorious, cheeky grin crept onto my face. *Fuckers.* Success coursed through my veins when we skated to center ice to celebrate.

It was a rough game, which was expected because it was our first. Practices had been top-notch with minimal mistakes, but when you put a real opponent on the ice for the first time, things were bound to shift. Our team was able to adapt and overcome, though, even with my irritation directed toward Sully. He was a good right wing. I knew when to admit someone's attributes and when to focus on their bad qualities all the same.

When we were on the ice together, our quiet rivalry was hidden, and that was exactly how it should be if either of us wanted to hit it big with the NHL.

I glanced up at the crowd, and the waving of the black-and-silver jerseys was more gratifying this season than last.

We were destined for the Frozen Four this year, and we had some of the strongest hockey players on our team.

After dropping my stick and watching the rest of the team climb over the wall to rush us on the ice, I shouted in our captain's ear over the roaring, "You're coming out with us tonight. Don't even say no, Theo."

"I always go to parties after games," he shouted through the back pats. "No need to beg me."

"No one is begging you," Emory joked. He inched his head toward the side of the rink, and we followed after him. He mumbled something about puck bunnies, which pulled at my stomach. I was a big fan of rewarding myself after playing a good game, and what better way to do that than with a girl who appreciated your hard work on the ice just as much as the team did.

I hadn't talked to Liv since the night Riley came stomping into our apartment with hardly any clothes on, and I was still kicking myself for bluntly calling her out, because without any context, like knowing that she was absentmindedly encouraging Sully to achieve the team bet, I acted like the world's biggest fuck boy. Now, she and I had this quiet cat-and-mouse game going on. She threw jabs at me—when she wasn't pretending I didn't exist—and I snapped right back at her. If I happened to pass her on the way to the elevator, or vice versa, I almost always skimmed my gaze down her body to see how revealing her clothes were.

They hadn't been revealing at all, but I still couldn't help but stare.

I was optimistic that the bet was a long-lost thought, though I knew it was highly unlikely. Coach's threat lingered in the back of my head like a grating reminder, and each time he pulled me into his office and asked about Riley

—like he couldn't just pick up the fucking phone—I was reminded of the position he had put me in.

I was a bit resentful.

Theo and Emory's conversation pulled me back to the present. They were talking about the party, and I was hoping that none of the Westin players decided to stick around and show their faces. They played dirty. Their shit-talking was up to par, and if Coach knew what they were saying, he would have been thrown out of the game.

I thought I had it under control until a familiar voice hit the back of my neck as I rounded the corner of the locker room.

"You may have won the game, but I'm going to be winning later."

Is this guy serious?

I was the first to admit that I had a bit of a temper when I was younger. I struggled with controlling the raging testosterone flowing throughout my teenage body, but after my high school coach showed me how to channel my anger on the ice, I knew how to cool my jets.

But I had my limits, and I was reaching the end of them.

I stopped walking, letting Emory and Theo get farther ahead before I spun around. "We're off the ice, man. You can stop with the mind games." *You lost. Time to go home.*

Just the sight of the Westin jersey made my fingers twitch. Each defenseman that I had the pleasure of going up against had been making remarks about which Bexley U girls they were going to fuck after they won.

It was a shame they didn't.

It was an even bigger shame that I was about to put him through a wall.

"I'm not playing any mind games." Sweat swiped down the side of his forehead, and I noticed that there wasn't a hint of humor on his red face. "I just wanted to know if you had Riley Lennon's number."

My jaw flexed. *Is this a joke?* I calmed my tone, but my arms were tingling. "What kind of player would I be if I gave you my coach's daughter's number after you and your teammates talked about running a train on our girls?"

I had a pretty big hunch that Riley wasn't the type of girl who would let one of these players take her behind the arena to fuck her brains out like they had been indicating. I would bet my life that she was just as uptight in the bedroom as she was out of it. Unfortunately for me, though, I instantly became engaged when her name was mentioned.

I could thank Coach for that.

"Is Riley your girl? You were awfully concerned on the ice after I said her name." He laughed, and my neck cracked. "Can I borrow her for the night?"

That isn't happening.

"If you lay a finger on her, I will break it off—*with* my coach's permission." He was right. I *was* concerned. I was riled up. *Too* riled up. "If you were talking about asking her out on a date like a real man, maybe I'd have no issue." Keyword being *maybe.* "But you and your teammates are a bunch of disrespectful dicks talking about her like that."

Number nine shook his head, and his grin boiled my blood. "Riley Lennon has been untouchable since being on the arm of Gray Loretto, but word has it that they've broken up, and with the way he talked about her during the preseason, I think everyone wants a piece of that pussy."

The hallway caved in. I pushed away the edging thought that maybe this whole thing with Riley was going to be harder than I thought. Assumptions had been made on my part, and admittedly, I didn't think she was going to cause me too much trouble. But here I was, standing inches away from a Westin player with my blood pressure flying through the roof.

"This is why you lost the game." I grinned, but it was a sick one. "You're focused on a girl, whereas I'm focused on winning." I stepped so close to him I could smell his sweat. "But now that we've won, I have no issues focusing on putting you through the fucking wall."

I watched the flare of anger burn in his eye, but before he could do anything, I wrapped my hand around his throat, relishing in the way his windpipe was being held hostage against my palm. For a split second in time, I was pulled back into the past, remembering the last time I had someone's throat in the palm of my hand. *It's always over a fucking girl.*

Things happened quickly. Theo's voice hit the side of my face, and Emory's hands dug into my jersey. He shoved me into the silent locker room where I came face to face with Coach.

Whoops.

"What the fuck was that? Can we get through one fucking game without there being some conflict? You're lucky we weren't on the ice when you pulled that shit." Theo turned to Coach and waited for his reprimand to follow.

His bellowing echoed throughout the locker room. "You better give me a good fucking reason, son. Or your ass is going to be running suicides at practice on Monday."

Anger rushed through me. *This is his fault.* "You sure you want to know?"

Murmurs traveled throughout the locker room, and I was damn lucky that someone spoke loud enough for Coach to hear, because if it were up to me, I would have told him, word for word, what the other players were saying about his daughter.

"For fuck's sake." Coach threw his hands up and stalked over to his office. "This is why I cursed the moment my wife told me I was going to have a baby girl."

His door slammed so loud the metal lockers rattled. My teammates wasted no time talking among themselves about how dirty the Westin players were on the ice.

I shut my locker and turned around half-dressed. "Those Westin players deserved to have their fucking faces bashed in."

I was hoping that some of my teammates had a guilty conscience and realized that it was just as bad to have a bet over who could fuck Riley as the shit-talking was from our opponents. If so, then maybe I wouldn't have to worry about their intentions with her.

After inhaling deeply, I pinched the bridge of my nose. I wasn't going to let the last few minutes ruin the rest of my night. We won our first game, and I was heading to the football house to celebrate, and the chances of Riley being there were slim to none.

━━

My mood lifted after Theo and I entered the party. I didn't envy the football players for having their own house, but I was thankful for the parties they threw. My shared apartment, even if Ford continued to couch surf and use up all my toothpaste, was perfect. Well, it was until a mouthy blue-eyed pain in my ass moved across the hall.

Nearly everyone was half-tanked when we arrived. Rush walked down the stairs with a girl following him that had clearly been fucked minutes before with the way her hair was tangled. He exchanged some words with Theo as I scanned the party for any Westin players. Admittedly, I was still tangled up over what had happened outside of the locker room.

"Beers on the house for you guys." Rush nudged my shoulder. "Oh, and I banned Westin players, bro. I heard about the fight. This is a chill environment. No fighting here. Our team can't afford it, and neither can yours."

"Solid." I nodded, throwing up a fist.

Bexley U's football team was number one in their division, like us. Although football at Bexley U had gained admirers for years, they still continued to pull in fans from all over the United States. Rush was a pretty decent guy too —especially for a quarterback.

"Problem solved," Theo muttered, giving me a side look as he caught a beer from Emory.

I was next, catching a cold can in my hand and popping the tab as I dragged my eyes through the crowd. I adjusted my backward hat and licked the foam spilling out from the top.

Theo hated the attention we were getting.

But I didn't mind it.

I grinned at a few puck bunnies as we continued walking through the party. Theo kept his gaze straight, not wanting to feed into the frenzy of hot admirers and back pats from some of the football players.

He leaned in, and I turned to listen. "You got a hard-on for Coach's daughter or something?"

I paused, feeling like I was just caught with my hand in the cookie jar. Anger quickly rushed to the surface and replaced the feeling of guilt. "What? No." It was true. I didn't have a hard-on for Riley. Finding her attractive wasn't a crime. In fact, I kind of detested her. Theo was unaware of

Coach's demand that I watch out for her, because knowing Theo, he'd swoop in and try to help, and he had enough going on with his new roommate situation. Not to mention, if he caught wind of the bet, he'd go ballistic. It would create a wedge between the captain and the entire team, and that was the last thing we needed.

"Good, because that would be a hard no."

Obviously.

The antagonizer in me wanted to poke at my best friend and ask if he had a hard-on for his new roommate, because I saw the way he looked at her the other day at The Bex, but I kept the remark to myself. Instead, I slugged back my beer and headed straight to the beer pong table because I had no desire to be questioned about Riley.

She wasn't at the party, so there was no need for her to take up any space in my head.

That was how the saying went—*out of sight, out of mind.*

[8]

RILEY

"You look nervous." Sutton blotted her lips on a napkin and threw it into the back seat.

I pulled at my dress and made sure there weren't any snags in my mesh tights. The last time I wore an outfit like this was when I was a student at Rosewood. I was a different person then, and I distinctly remember feeling confident, but right now, I was uncomfortable.

Sutton turned toward me. "Do you wanna go back to the apartment? Because I'm fine with dipping out."

"No." I was quick to answer, and she raised an eyebrow at me. The faint shimmer on her cheek sparkled against the lights on her dash. "I said I'd go."

"Okay, then." Her eyelashes curled to meet her eyebrows. "Plus, it's about time we both stopped being recluses. I'm posting a picture too, because what was it that Taylor said? Something about dressing for revenge?"

I snatched her phone and grinned wickedly. "That

needs to be the caption." I snapped a hot picture, and we laughed like teenage girls as she uploaded it online.

Before we made it all the way into the party, I pulled back on her arm and whispered, "Go find someone your ex would hate, and have some fun. You deserve it." I shrugged. "Maybe I'll take another picture, and we can post it too."

Sutton's lips split. "Mmm, the best kind of revenge." Then her smile fell, and she raised an eyebrow. "You should take your own advice. Gray Loretto needs to be put in his place."

I scoffed. "Maybe. But I'll never be caught dead with one of my dad's hockey players."

"Who said anything about hockey players?" Sutton was staring at a guy I didn't recognize. He was tall, dark, handsome and had the body of an athlete. When he caught her eye, he did a double take. It took no more than three seconds for him to stop mid-conversation and head directly for her.

"Want a drink?" His gaze drifted down her body before he realized what he was doing. He quickly zipped his eyes back to her face.

She sighed like she was already bored with him. "I don't need a guy to get me a drink."

"Well, what do you need a guy for?"

I saw the wheels turning in her head. "Do it," I whispered, urging her to take what she wanted. At least one of us could give a hockey player a run for his money, and I was *certain* this guy would do anything Sutton wanted, like purposefully touching her and letting her post the evidence online to irk her superstar NHL ex.

Good for her.

Bexley U parties were the same as they were at Rosewood. The only difference was the change of school colors hanging up in the windows and on the walls. Black and silver instead of red and white. I scanned the party, feeling more unlike myself the longer I stood alone. It was both exhilarating and daunting. At Rosewood, I was immediately greeted by everyone and offered a drink but only because of Gray. At least here I could be anyone I wanted without being in my hockey boyfriend's shadow and his disapproval of my future dangling in the outskirts of my reach.

As far as I knew, the only thing Bexley U students knew of me was that I was the daughter of their beloved hockey coach—unless there were any figure skaters loitering around. They'd recognize me right away. After all, they're anxiously waiting for me to join their team in a couple of months.

"You made it." Sully found me a few minutes after Sutton left, and it didn't take him long to give me a once-over with his glossed over gaze. "Now, *this* is the Riley I know." My black mesh tights suddenly felt a little suffocating, and my boots were heavy. Sully's warm hand found mine as he slowly spun me around. "You came to slay tonight, yeah? Too bad Gray isn't here to see what he's missing out on."

"I don't think he'd care." Gray wanted me for more than a short dress, despite what most thought. He wanted me for my name. He liked the attention I brought with my figure skating success because we were a *power couple*—his words, not mine. He always wanted the best, and when I was no longer the best, he no longer wanted me.

"Trust me. If he saw you, he'd care." I smiled at Sully's compliment. He took it and ran, pulling me farther into the party, like he wanted to show me off. "I wasn't sure you'd come tonight."

"I'm not going to stay long, but I told Sutton I'd come, so..."

Sully playfully nudged my shoulder with his. "Not one to back down on plans?"

Not unless it has to do with skating again. I may have been out of my element, but I'd done harder things. Making small talk at a college party was a breeze.

"Do you want a drink?"

"I can get it." I smiled at his attempt to be a gentleman, but I knew better. I made my way through the chaos of the party in hunt of a fruity seltzer or something I could sip on without feeling the pressure to down the entire thing. A hand landed on my hip, and alarm bells went off until I realized it was just Sully. His whisper coated the side of my neck. "I refuse to let you get your own drink. All it would take is one shady guy to see you in that dress and spike it. Stay put. I'll grab you one."

Since I knew Sully, I let him fulfill his need to be noble. I stayed put, like he wanted, and I opened my phone to text the only person I'd kept in touch with after leaving Rosewood.

> Me- I'm at a Bexley U party, and I have to admit, I miss my wing girl.

She texted back almost immediately with a picture. Underneath, it read, *I miss you more!* I felt a pinch of envy as I scanned the photo. It was a classic Mya selfie with her in the middle of a Rosewood party, wearing a tight dress, sans tights, ignoring that the New England states were heading directly for winter. A small wave of hurt replaced the envy as I zoomed in on the background and saw a hand that had touched every part of my body wrapped around one of my former teammate's tiny waist.

"See? He's a dick." Sully's smooth voice hit the side of my face, and I quickly shut my phone screen off. Heat slapped my cheeks. I wasn't embarrassed. Instead, I felt shame. I seemed desperate, and that was one thing I was not when it came to Gray. "I hope you like this flavor."

I grabbed the cup out of Sully's hand and let the liquid burn my throat as I took a much bigger swig than necessary. *Peach.* "I'm not picky. Thanks."

Sully stood beside me long enough for the silence we shared to become sticky. I shifted uncomfortably, regretting coming to the party, until he elbowed me gently in the ribs so I was forced to give him attention. I peered at him out of the corner of my eye and moved a piece of my hair that was in the way. "Yeah?"

He leaned his back against the wall. The party was loud and chaotic around us but his voice was as smooth as could be. "You're different."

I tipped my drink back and took another swig because I knew what he was reaching for. Gray's teammates were there the night I took a fall in front of the entire arena, and they were part of the gasps when I didn't get up. "How?" I asked cautiously.

"You don't smile anymore." He looked at my lips. "Did Gray break your heart that badly?"

I was slapped across the face with embarrassment that quickly turned into resentment. *Fucking Gray.* It always came back to him.

"He didn't break my heart, Graham. What is it with males and their cocky belief that they have such control over a female?"

Sully's eyebrow rose at my snarky response. I watched

the excitement take over his mouth as his lips moved into a smile. "*Ooh*, there she is."

I was beginning to hate that he knew me from Rosewood. But I knew him too, and I had never seen him talk to a female he wasn't interested in for more than three minutes. At nearly every Rosewood party, his face was buried in some girl's neck. "I'm going to find the restroom. I'll find you in a little bit."

I moved through the party in an attempt to escape him. Sutton paused her grinding—*or dancing*—and furrowed her brows at me. I mouthed, "Bathroom."

I didn't have to go to the bathroom, but I wasn't in the mood to talk about Gray, and I surely wasn't in the mood to obsess over the ice bet that Sully may have been a part of. The only thing that I *should've* been thinking about was how to get back to the girl Sully kept reminding me I was instead of worrying about the guys who frequented the ice more than I did.

Before running into what appeared like a brick wall, I paused my fast walking and glanced up to a guy with golden hair and a chiseled jawline. His eyes lit up like a Christmas tree. "I can't let you pass without you telling me your name."

I didn't recognize him. He was too clean-cut to be a hockey player, and none of them would be caught dead in a BU football shirt, so I assumed he was a football player. "Riley," my name barreled out of my mouth. *Now move.*

I eyed the stairs behind him and saw Aasher casually coming down with the same girl I saw at his apartment the other day. I hurriedly snapped back to attention and stared at the football player, hoping his large frame would hide me. I wasn't afraid of Aasher by any means, but who knew what insult would fly out of his mouth when he saw me.

Maybe I should ask him if he approved of my choice of clothing.

"Are you a freshman?"

"What? No." The football player was towering over me. "If you'll excuse me, I'm headed for the restroom."

Shit, then I have to walk past Aasher.

"Here, follow me." His hand fell to my wrist, and he began tugging me toward the stairs. "There's a long line. You can use the bathroom in my room."

And this was the part where the audience yelled at the naive girl as she followed the hot jock to his bedroom.

"Whoa, man. Where are you taking her?" Sully stepped in between us, and the football player freed my wrist. *Thank God.* I really didn't want to make a scene by stomping on this guy's foot.

"To the bathroom?" His answer was more of a question, and he quickly followed it with an apology. "My bad. Didn't know she was taken for the night."

I waited until we were alone again before giving Sully my best *what-the-fuck* look. "Trying to test the waters even though my dad threatened the entire hockey team and warned you all that I'm off-limits?"

Sully leaned against the banister and looked out into the party. "That depends. Am I going to sink or swim?"

I was surprised at his cool and collected answer. Graham Sullivan was totally relaxed. He turned toward me and raised an eyebrow, waiting for my answer. *He is serious.* I was beginning to wonder if the few sips of alcohol I'd had was clouding my judgment. Before I could regain my composure, a heavy presence filled the tiny air bubble that we shared. I didn't have to peek over my shoulder to see who it was because I knew right away.

"Lexy is asking for you." Aasher's smooth voice brushed

over my skin as he came around and leaned against the banister, blocking my view from Sully.

"I'm not interested."

"You were interested last night."

I stepped away from them and tried to sneak off, but when I glanced up to the top landing, I saw the football player watching me. *Great.* When I brought my gaze back down, Aasher was staring at me. He blinked once before turning back to Sully. "You were interested this morning, too."

Sully grumbled under his breath, but Aasher kept going.

"And after the game." He blew air out of his mouth. "Wow. Three times in twenty-four hours? She must be a special one."

Aasher spun around and blocked *me* from Sully instead of the other way around. It was obvious that he was trying to play *hero* again, but I played along. "Did you go to the game, Riley? I don't remember seeing you in the stands." He edged his chin and grinned at his teammate. "Better run. There's Lexy. She's coming over here."

Sully cursed under his breath before jogging up the stairs to hide.

"I saw your mom at the game but not you. Not a hockey fan?"

I took Sully's spot on the banister. "You saw my mom? Are you part of the family? Or just wanting to know my whereabouts so you can report back to my dad?"

Aasher snickered as he threw a fist up to someone walking past. They told him good game, and I silently agreed. Aasher didn't see me in the stands because I was in the box seat with Coach Lambert's family. I sort of acted as a nanny to the assistant coach's three daughters, but in between coloring and playing *Simon Says*, I caught snippets of black-and-silver jerseys rushing the ice and flinging the hockey puck at Westin's goalie. Theo Brooks was the driving force behind the win, but Aasher and a few other players definitely lessened the margin of being defeated. Number twelve, who just so happened to be Aasher, caught my eye numerous times as he rushed through the defense.

I hated to admit it, but he was *really* good.

Aasher adjusted his hat, probably covering his messy hair from the girl he was just with. "What are you doing here?" he asked, *clearly* annoyed.

I didn't answer. Instead, I pulled my cup to my mouth and slowly licked the top rim of it before tipping it backward. I had no idea what possessed me to do it other than to piss him off even more.

Aasher's eyes grew large, flaring with heat. His hand went around the rim of my cup, pulling it into his face. I huffed as he took a sip of it, and when his fingers flexed against mine, I pulled the drink away from his mouth.

"What the hell are you doing?" I asked.

I dropped my attention and watched as his tongue darted out to lick his bottom lip. *Ugh.*

"Who gave you the drink?" His tone gave way to his anger, and there was a little flex to his jaw.

I put my hand on my hip. "You do know that I'm twenty-one, right? I am *allowed* to drink. It's legal." *He's probably writing this down in his little tattletale book to give to my dad.*

"Who gave you the drink, though? Did you pour it yourself, or did Rogers get it for you so he could get you drunk and into his bed?"

I thought fast on my feet. "Who said I needed to be drunk to get into his bed?"

Aasher laughed, but it was as sharp as a knife. "Who gave you the fucking drink, Riley?"

I pictured myself splashing the drink in his face because his tone was full of conviction, and it made me feel like a child.

"You're worse than my dad," I mumbled.

Aasher tilted his head. "What was that?"

"I *said...*" I pushed my cup into his firm chest, and his heart beat wildly against the back of my hand. "That it's really none of your business." My fingers lifted, and the cup fell swiftly. If he wasn't so quick, it would have dropped to the ground and spilled all over his feet.

A grumble left his mouth, but I didn't stick around to hear what he had to say. I stopped by Sutton and whispered into her ear that I was going to head back to the apartment. She was kind enough to stop playing beer pong to say she was coming with me, but I told her I was totally fine on my own. Sutton was much more comfortable with the party crowd than I was. She was the center of the room with her pretty pink cheeks and a high-pitched laugh. Everyone gravitated toward her.

After making my way to the front door and successfully avoiding everyone, I sucked in the cool night air and let it blanket my hot cheeks. The brick porch was empty, which wasn't much of a surprise. It was a cold night, and I was in the minority with my love of winter, just like I was in the minority of wanting to get far away from all the jocks at this party.

"You shouldn't take drinks from guys you don't know."

I paused mid-step, pretending like I didn't hear Aasher. *You've got to be kidding me.* I stared at the houses lining the street, wondering if I could just slip into one of them to avoid him.

"You also shouldn't be walking by yourself at night."

"Excuse me?" I said, spinning around quickly. I spied his tall figure leaning against the pine tree outside of the football house with his arms and ankles crossed like he was waiting for me.

Aasher shrugged before pushing off from the bark. He looked like a black cat lurking in the dark with his piercing green eyes locked onto me. "I'm just saying, you shouldn't take drinks from guys you don't know. Haven't you seen any of the hundreds of documentaries out there?" He walked closer to me, despite the fact that I was making strides to get away from him. His hands casually dug into his pockets, and he seemed completely unbothered by my scowl, which only made me scowl deeper. "So many sweet, naive girls taking drinks from guys and ending up without clothes on the next day, unsure of what had happened to them." His lips flattened before opening his mouth to offend me. "Although, you're not really sweet, are you?"

"You truly do think I'm stupid, don't you?" It was a loaded question and one he probably didn't realize had a double meaning.

Aasher thought for a moment. "Well, I didn't until I saw you falling for Sully's bullshit."

The more I stood in front of Aasher, the angrier I grew. It was the way he was looking at me. As if *I* asked him to follow me out here. "What is your deal? Are you trying to impress my dad by coming to my rescue or something? Is there a camera out here somewhere?" I looked through the branches of the trees, even moving a low hanging one for dramatic effect. "Are you gonna record yourself walking me home like a gentleman? Or maybe tell him I took a drink from some guy and you swooped in and stopped me from getting roofied?"

His throaty laugh filled the quiet street, and my stomach clenched. "I have no need to impress him any more than I do now with my skill on the ice."

"I bet you impress him with how humble you are too." I rolled my eyes.

"There's nothing wrong with being confident. I'm good at hockey, and I know it. I'm proud of it too."

I understood where he was coming from, from an athletic perspective, but he annoyed me, so I called him out. "You're cocky, and it's unattractive."

Aasher threw his head back with laughter. He had a really good laugh, but I refused to let it show on my features. I kept my lips pinched tight. "You find cocky hockey players unattractive? Good. Then we will have no issues moving forward."

"Is that what this is about?" I asked, pondering his over-bearing attitude with me. It was all making sense. The disapproval of my lack of clothing, the comment about his teammates wanting me, being at this party, taking a drink from one of them. "Your teammates going against your coach's wishes and fucking me?" Aasher's eye twitched, and it was like pouring gasoline on a fire. I was starving, and his irritation fed me down to the very last crumb. "So what if they do? It's really none of your business."

I watched him very carefully, wondering which direction his concern leaned to. Did he want me for himself so he could win the bet, or was there another reason for his unprompted overprotectiveness?

"Actually, it *is* my business." Aasher took a step forward, and I met him halfway. My chest brushed his, and we both paused at the touch. I opened my mouth to say something, but he beat me to it. "Your dad would lose his mind if he found out that one of his players touched you...

let alone *fucked* you. The team isn't going to be jeopardized because of you."

The way that word rolled off his tongue should have been illegal. His green eyes flared, and his lips moved with ease. I was so riveted that I almost didn't notice his hands on my hips. He spun me around and pushed me in the opposite direction of the party. "Go home, Duster. I'll walk you."

I stumbled forward and whirled around in a wrath, more annoyed with myself than him. "*Stop* calling me that."

To most, I seemed uninterested in hockey, but growing up in the rink and having a father who coached, I knew what *Duster* meant. A duster was a benchwarmer. It was someone who was "collecting dust." I refused to give them the time of day—or anyone, for that matter—therefore I was collecting dust. But if Aasher kept it up, I was going to put an end to that nickname just to spite him.

"I'll stop calling you that." *Good.* "As long as you let me walk you home."

My shoulders fell. "I don't want you to walk me home. In fact, I think I'd like to go back to the party." I tried spinning around, but Aasher stepped in front of me, blocking me from the house.

"Are you kidding me?" I asked in a huff. "You're *that* afraid I'm going to sleep with one of your overly cocky teammates and ruin the team? You must think very highly of my pussy, Aasher."

His mouth opened, and a quick rush of hot air came with his surprise, but his comeback came even quicker. "Who's to say you won't? I mean, you came over to our apartment half naked the other day. For all I know, you're a wannabe puck bunny, or maybe you just wanna piss ol' daddy off."

My mouth flew open at his insult.

"Go home, Riley. You've already annoyed me by taking a drink from some random guy."

"Sully isn't some random guy. I've known him longer than I've known you." I turned and stomped away because I was arguing with an oversized toddler who was treating me like I was his favorite toy that he was unwilling to share. I picked up my speed at the sound of Aasher's thumping steps behind me.

"Stop walking so fast."

Naturally, I started to run.

His laugh followed me, echoing down the street. His long, easy strides caught up to mine quickly, so I stopped abruptly and swung around. "*Stop* following"—I tried to catch my breath—"me."

He wasn't out of breath in the slightest. "Sorry. Not only will your dad kill his players for touching you, but he'll torture us slowly with back-to-back drills during practice if he finds out that one of us let you walk home alone from a party dressed like that." I rolled my eyes. *I knew he'd mention my dress.* "You never know when Sully or Rogers is going to pop out from behind a bush and offer you a ride home in their sports car."

I scoffed and started to speed walk again. Aasher stayed a few steps behind me, and the only reason I didn't take off into a full sprint was because no matter how fast I ran, Aasher was going to end up at the same place as me since he was my neighbor.

He continued to half-chase me until I finally slowed my pace. The night grew cooler, and a chill shook me. The mesh tights did nothing to shield me from the wind.

"Here."

I peeked out of the corner of my eye and saw Aasher's hoodie dangling from his steady hand for the taking. I silently declined and kept walking, but *fine,* I'd admit it was a nice gesture.

Too bad he couldn't get me to surrender because of one nice act. I was fed up with his insults and constant watchful eye. I would never purposefully lure a hockey player into my bed simply to go against my father's wishes like he was suspecting. That wasn't to say that I wasn't going to flirt and tease every last one of them—except Aasher, because it was very clear that he detested me as much as I detested him—so they were tripping over their promises of being the first to have me.

"Just take my hoodie."

"No."

"So stubborn," he mumbled.

"Such a dick," I mumbled right back.

The moment the tall brick building appeared in front of us, I practically ran to the doors to get away. I reached for the door handle after swiping my card, but *of course,* Aasher was a step ahead, opening it for me. I raced up the stairs, refusing to get in an elevator with him. His patronizing laugh followed me until I was standing in front of my door, fumbling with my keys to get inside.

"Do you need help?" he asked, slinking up beside me.

I glared at him. "No. I'm just trying to get as far away from you as quickly as possible." I gritted my teeth and clumsily tried to work my keys into my door but couldn't because my stupid cold fingers were numb.

"Here." Aasher's steady hand fell to mine, and I quickly pulled away, frustrated at the warmth covering my skin. It was as if he'd burned me. My door was unlocked a breath later, and he stepped back into the hallway and ushered me through. "Now stay put."

A rush of rebellion zipped through me as I stood in my

apartment and stared at Aasher as he backed away toward his door. His jaw flexed, and he sighed. "I'm serious. Don't make my life harder than it already is."

"No one is asking you to be my shadow, Aasher. Mind your business, and stop assuming that I'm some little minx set out to ruin the hockey team." I rolled my eyes because did he truly think I was *that* pathetic? As if the only thing on my mind was how to get his teammates to sleep with me. "I'm the furthest thing from a puck bunny."

Aasher's lazy gaze slipped down my body, and I started to sweat. His eyes slowly brushed each of my curves before he snapped to attention and stared right at me. "Prove me wrong, then. Because so far, you seem to be nothing but a little tease."

I slammed the door to block out his cunning face. I tripped over my untouched skates and cursed under my breath.

I had nothing to prove to Aasher.

But with my eyes set on my skates, I knew I had something to prove to myself.

[9]

I TOSSED the souvenir hockey puck that I'd gotten when I was seven into the air. The apartment was loud, and my roommates were hyped on the promise of winning tomorrow's game.

It was poker night—something I didn't usually partake in because it was the one thing I wasn't good at. Plus, it was the night before a game. If Coach knew that half the team was over at the apartment, playing poker until well after midnight, he'd lose his shit, and I would not get stuck in the crossfire of that one.

"Ford!" I glanced at my bedroom door, recognizing the high-pitched voice right away. *Sutton.* I listened harder, wondering if she'd happened to bring over her roommate who wholeheartedly hated my guts. I had news for her, because I hated hers too.

She bled ignorance when she stomped her foot at me the other night and said that no one had asked me to be her shadow. That was exactly what was asked of me. Was she so dense that she thought I wanted to spend the entire season focused on anything other than hockey? Her bratty remarks drove me wild, and a few times on our "jog" home, I had the inclination to kiss her just to shut her up. That would have been impulsive and a grave mistake, but I bet it would have worked.

Admittedly, when Coach asked me to watch out for her, I thought it would be easy. Riley had never shown up at a party before—or at the rink, for that matter. But now, suddenly, she was showing up in places I never expected and ruining my mood with one short glance.

I tossed the hockey puck onto my bed and strode to the living room. I didn't expect Riley to be here, but I also didn't expect to see her at the party either, wearing that short dress and attracting stares from every male in a twenty-yard vicinity.

"Aw, look. The boss came out to play." Efrain slid his poker chips forward.

I took in the scene, and humor tugged at my lips. The only thing missing was a cloud of smoke and cigars hanging from my teammates' mouths. They were smart enough not to cloud their lungs the night before a game, though.

"If Theo gets wind of this, he's going to throw a fucking fit." I grabbed some water out of the fridge and rested my elbows over the counter, silently thanking God that Sutton was the only girl in the living room. She was concentrating on the cards in her hand with her tongue held hostage between her lips.

"Daddy Theo will be fine," Ford grinned. "Unless Daddy Number Two tells him."

I chugged my water before cocking an eyebrow.

"If you ever call me daddy again, I will slap the smug look right off your face."

Ford laughed. Sutton was still focusing on her cards, but she piped up beside him. "Aasher is too uptight for pet names in the bedroom."

"And you know how?" I leaned my hip against the counter and shot her a flirty grin. Without Riley here, sucking up all my energy, I was actually able to have a little fun.

"Riley told me."

I choked on my water and wheezed. Sutton failed at hiding her sneaky smile behind her cards. Each of my teammates' mouths hung open in confusion. I popped off the counter after catching my breath.

"Don't joke around about stuff like that. People will start rumors, and they'll think I've fucked her."

"You stare at her enough that people are probably already starting rumors."

I glared at her, wondering what her roommate had told her.

"You practically forced her to leave the party last week. I know that Riley despises hockey players, but no one else at Bexley U knows that. They probably think you took her home."

"I did." I rolled my eyes. "But that's all."

Sutton smashed her lips. "I'm just saying, it's pretty noticeable. If she's anywhere near you, your eyes are on her."

This is such bullshit.

My teammates kept their mouths shut because they knew why I was tied to Riley like her little ball and chain. I was about to march across the hall and admit that her father *did* ask me to be her shadow. I'd ruined one father/daughter relationship before. What was another?

"Where is she, anyway?" Ford questioned.

I was glad he asked, because God forbid I give Sutton any other ammunition to use against me.

"The rink."

My water bottle crinkled beneath my grip and caught the attention of everyone. "The rink? This late?"

I glanced at the clock and instantly became enraged.

"With who?"

Fuck, stop worrying. Knowing Riley, she probably felt more at home in the rink than anywhere else because of her icy personality.

Sutton shrugged innocently. She didn't pull her attention from the cards in her hand, and I couldn't decide if she was fucking with me or if she truly didn't know.

I snatched my keys off the table and headed for the door.

Efrain mumbled. "If we lose tomorrow because he plays like shit, it's your fault. He's usually asleep by now the night before a game."

"Maybe he should stop stalking my roommate, and he wouldn't be tired."

My jaw ached.

"Just play your hand, evil girl."

———

Well, Riley wasn't the brightest crayon in the box.

I slammed my door after pulling up next to her parked Honda. I knew it was hers because it was the only other car in the parking lot, which was a relief—except that didn't mean she was alone. The Honda wasn't a pile of shit, but it wasn't anything fancy either, which was surprising because, with how she acted most of the time, I assumed she was spoiled.

I put the code into the side door of the arena and tried to prepare myself for what I was about to walk in on.

I didn't know a lot about Riley, and I didn't care to get to know her either. She was already taking up too much of my time, and the last thing I needed was to befriend her. All I knew was that her father was awfully protective of her. She could be with anyone right now, and I wasn't sure I wanted to see who.

I edged my head toward the locker room, and part of me hoped that I'd catch her in there with one of the hockey players who was participating in the ice bet so I didn't have to worry about it anymore, but with that thought came a rush of something that I refused to acknowledge.

The door creaked, and I listened for the sounds that I'd heard many times before when some of my teammates thought everyone had left. It was a known thing on campus to christen the locker room at least once before you graduated and moved on to the pros.

It was dead silent.

I moved my way past the bench and sighed at the time. *I should be sleeping.* I was like Theo in a lot of ways. We both needed to be centered the night before a game and well rested, unlike my roommates, who played poker and used the distraction as a way to calm themselves before the storm.

Opening the door to the arena, I let my eyes adjust to the dark. I knew my way around the rink like the back of my hand, but the stands? I wasn't familiar with them. I was fifteen the last time I sat behind the glass and watched a college hockey game.

It was the last time my dad did too.

"*Just do it.*"

I almost tripped down the stairs.

Riley's voice was full of courage. *Do what?* I lifted up on the balls of my shoes and tried to make out where she was. There was a faint glow from her phone playing soft music. It illuminated her frame, and I ran my eyes down her curves as she stood and stared through the glass separating her from the ice.

She was alone and fully dressed.

There weren't any hockey players touching her in places they shouldn't have been.

But what the hell was she doing here by herself?

I could have been anyone, standing here in the shadows, watching her without her having any idea. Imagine if it were Sully—or worse, one of the many hockey players from Westin who openly fantasized about sleeping with her.

"Damn it." Riley reached up quickly and pulled on her hair tie, undoing her bun. Her dark hair tumbled down her back effortlessly, and I swore I smelled her shampoo all the way across the stands. Her little growl was angry sounding. I panicked when she reached down, grabbed her phone, and turned to leave.

Fuck.

I stepped into the aisleway and accepted my fate for what it was. I pulled out my imaginary weapon and prepared myself for another tiff with the coach's daughter.

"Rink is closed, Duster."

Her scream echoed throughout the vast space.

"Chill, it's just me."

Her huff made me smile.

"As if I should feel safe with you." She took her wrath of fury with her when she dipped down to swipe one of the ice skates that had fallen out of her arms. When she popped back up, I *definitely* smelled her shampoo. She smelled like a fucking winter fairy, and my dick twitched.

"Why wouldn't you feel safe with me?" I asked. "I

walked you home from a party last week for that very reason."

"You walked me home from a party to keep me safe?" She brushed past me, and if I didn't move out of her way, I likely would have been cut by the blade of her skate. "You mean to say that you *chased* me home so I wouldn't sleep with any of your teammates."

"You should put a cover on those." I pointed to her ice skates as she hurried past me to leave.

"Why are you here?" Riley stopped walking, and she placed a hand on her hip. Her blue eyes were wild with anger, and I kind of loved it. I couldn't help smiling at the way her little nose scrunched with irritation.

"Well, when I heard you were at the rink this late, I worried that one of my teammates might have talked you into a longtime tradition of theirs."

She had no idea what I was talking about.

I leaned back on the wall and put distance between us because I knew, without a doubt, I was about to piss her off.

"You know the tradition. Fucking a girl in the locker room the night before a game for good luck?" Riley's mouth dropped open at my bluntness, and I shrugged innocently. "Don't look at me. I'm not one to partake in such acts."

"Yet you think I am?"

Not necessarily, but I knew my teammates, and I knew they were manifesting that particular act with her. If she wasn't off-limits, I might have found myself doing the same.

"I don't know. I don't really know you."

I expected her to stomp away like the brat that she was, but she surprised me by sticking around. Her nose unwrinkled, and the angry lines on her forehead softened. There was a devilish glint in her eye that twinkled with mischief. I stood in shock as she absentmindedly gained the upper hand.

"Stop following me around, Aasher. Desperation isn't a good look on you."

I raised an eyebrow and couldn't help the curving of my lip. *Desperation?*

She walked over to me, and the toe of her skate dug into my chest. If I breathed too heavily, I was certain the sharp blade of steel would cut right through my shirt and slice my skin. "Was it your idea?"

I dropped my gaze to her mouth. She had whispered, and I was a fool because I was waiting eagerly to watch her soft lips move again. "Was what my idea?"

"I know about the ice bet."

Her confession was as sharp as the blade of her skate pressing into me. *Fucking stellar.*

"I'm beginning to think you're following me everywhere so you can be the one to get to me first."

I lowered my voice. "That is not true."

I grabbed on to her hips and flung her around so her back was resting against the wall. The pads of my thumbs had accidentally crept under her shirt and pressed against her warm skin. Her pupils dilated, and I refused to embrace it. I kept joking that she had an icy, cold heart, but she wasn't cold at all. She was warm, and soft, and...*shit.*

"You haven't told your dad," I said, not bothering to ask. We would know if she had. "Why?"

Riley's body brushed against mine as I crowded her space. I saw the lack of self-assurance as I stole her confidence. But she had it all wrong. I was the nervous one here because she had the power to ruin me.

"Maybe I will," she whispered.

Her sweet breath hit me square in the face, and I felt

drunk. I swallowed the words on my tongue and took a step back, releasing her. Her shoulders straightened, and her chin lifted with feigned confidence as she edged toward the door. Before she made her way through with her ice skates pressed firmly against her body, I followed after her and grabbed her by the arm.

My palm wrapped around the entire width of her bicep. The dark, shiny strands of her hair brushed over my skin like a feather. "Stay away from the team, Duster. They're planning to eat you alive." I tried to clean up their mess. "Don't tell your dad and ruin our chances at the Frozen Four because your feelings are hurt. Take it as a compliment. They think you're the whole package."

Take it as a compliment. Jesus.

The shovel was heavy as I continued to dig myself into a deeper hole.

Her clipped laugh distracted me enough for her to rip her arm out of my grasp. "They think I'm a toy they can play with once and then discard a moment later. That's not a compliment. That's an insult."

It was an insult. She wasn't the type of girl you fucked around with to win some stupid bet.

I stood back and watched Riley move across the parking lot like she was walking on water, and suddenly, I was feeling extremely thirsty.

[10]

RILEY

"ARE you ready for the game tomorrow night?" My dad's beer spilled onto the coaster as an older waitress placed it down on to the table.

"We're as ready as we can be," he said, glancing backward at the noisy booth in the corner of The Bex. It was the most popular restaurant at Bexley U, given the fact that it was *always* packed. This was a tradition. My parents started eating here the night before certain games for good luck, and sometimes, I tagged along. My father was extremely superstitious. I was pretty sure it was a requirement for all hockey players and their coaches. Gray was the same way. I couldn't even talk to him the night before a game because he liked to meditate.

Looking back, I wondered what kind of meditation he was actually doing.

I was surprised that Aasher followed me to the rink last week, because it was the night before a game. Maybe he was the exception—unless his pregame ritual was following college girls around only to offend them.

"Sutton." My mom took a sip of her Coke. "What is your major?"

I glanced over at my roommate, envious of how at ease she was in every situation. It didn't matter where we were or who we were with; she always seemed cool and collected.

I've gotten to know Sutton so much better since she moved in a few weeks ago, and I couldn't understand why her ex would ever let her go. She was kind, thoughtful, gorgeous, smart, and she knew how to have fun–even if we were just hanging out in the apartment, watching Netflix. She was much more outgoing than I was, and she was definitely more comfortable with the hockey team and parties on jock row, but she never made me feel bad for turning down an invite to go to the apartment across the hall. I'd rather poke my own eyeballs out than sit there and watch Aasher judge me.

"It's marketing, right?" I glanced at my dad after taking a bite of my burger.

"Um, yeah." Sutton laughed softly. "How did you know that?"

I was wondering the same thing.

"Crew mentioned it once or twice. How is my star player doing?"

Sutton's face fell.

"Dad." I silently tried to tell him to shut up, but he was completely oblivious.

I glanced at my mom who was eyeing Sutton. She turned to my dad and patted his hand. "Honey, they're not together anymore."

"What? Oh..." He cleared his throat. "Sorry."

Sutton put on a good front, smiling and brushing off his

mistake. I placed my hand on hers under the table and gave it a little squeeze, wanting to fix the situation because there was nothing worse than being in the spotlight when it was over something that made you uneasy.

"Your hockey players are acting like a bunch of children over there." I edged my head to the loud booth in the back that housed all four of my neighbors, plus some, and shifted the attention from Sutton. There were a few football players hanging around too, with an oversupply of puck bunnies and jersey chasers. I knew enough about jocks to know that they each had a certain nickname for girls who'd drop to their knees at a moment's notice for them.

My dad waved over his head, and before I knew it, Aasher and Theo were on their way to our table. His two superstars. I scowled at Aasher when my parents were distracted, already irritated with him.

I'd successfully evaded Aasher the several times he'd followed me or tried to ask anything that wasn't of his concern. Not only had he insulted me on numerous occasions, but I knew he'd bring up the bet. I was still reprimanding myself for telling him that I knew. It was all his fault. I grew unsteady around him. I fumbled over my thoughts whenever he smirked at me, let alone *touched* me. It was like climbing a never-ending rope. I kept trying to get the upper hand, but he beat me every single time.

"Hey, handsome boys!" My mom greeted Theo and Aasher like they were her sons.

I snickered, and Sutton quietly laughed under her breath. *At least someone appreciates my annoyance.* Aasher's mouth twitched, and it gave me more satisfaction than it should have.

"Are you two ready for tomorrow's game?" she asked.

Theo nodded. "Just about. Getting ready to head back to my room to start my pregame routine."

See, superstitious.

"And what about you?" I looked up at Aasher, unable to keep myself from poking him. "Do you have any pregame routines?" A sarcastic laugh left me. "I mean other than throwing poker parties the night before a game and keeping us up with the noise?"

My dad and Theo both whipped their heads to look at Aasher.

"Poker parties?" My dad was gone, and in his place was Coach Lennon.

I was amused. It wasn't my plan to provoke Aasher, but I was glad I did. He deserved it.

Sutton sucked her cheeks in, and I batted my eyelashes innocently at him. He played off his frustration well with a little smirk, but I could tell he was irked.

He put his hands in his pockets, seeming calm. "It's just a pregame thing with a few of the guys. I don't make the rules. I just win the games."

"We *all* win the games," Theo corrected.

The red blotches on my dad's neck told me he was irritated to find out that there were poker games going on the night before a game, but I didn't feel bad about throwing Aasher under the bus. Getting a reaction from him was refreshing, even if I knew I'd only have the upper hand for a second.

"It could always be worse, I guess," my dad finally said after seeming to think it over.

"It's better than what I used to do," Aasher replied.

Theo repeated him. "What you *used* to do?"

Aasher's crooked smile had me at the edge of my seat. I sensed the danger before he looked over at me. Our eyes snagged, and there was an immediate shift in the air. A silent threat. Or warning. I wasn't sure which.

"I used to sneak out of the dorms when I thought no one was awake, and I'd go to the rink after hours."

My cheeks blazed, and I gripped my glass of water tightly.

He was still following me.

I thought I was so slick, leaving the apartment well after I thought everyone was asleep. He followed me once. I should have known he'd do it again.

Instead of being embarrassed, I was *pissed*.

Did he really think he'd catch me in there with one of his teammates? Even after I confessed that I knew about the bet?

"To do what?" Theo asked.

I listened carefully, wondering if he was bluffing or not.

"I'd just stand there and stare at the ice through the glass."

My hand slipped against the condensation on my cup. Sutton grabbed it before it fell and soaked the table, because I made no attempt.

Aasher was standing near the foot of our table like a smug asshole, and I swore time had stopped. I blocked out the conversation and stared at him.

He wasn't fazed at all, but he knew he had hit the mark with me.

I was thankful when Ford walked over to the table and all the attention shifted to him, because I was sweating.

"My mama is comin' up to watch the game, Mrs. Lennon."

My mom bristled. "What did I say about calling me Mrs. Lennon?"

Ford grinned. "Sorry, sorry. My mom taught me

manners, though. Never go through a woman's purse, and always call her Mrs."

My dad looked over at my mom and rolled his eyes, but then he smiled a second later, which probably threw off the entire restaurant because not many people saw Coach Lennon smiling–unless they won a game. And even so, he usually kept his theatrics to a minimum.

"Anyway..." Ford took a seat beside me and wiggled his hips so Sutton and I would scoot over. My dad's eyebrows furrowed, but he didn't say anything. There was no point in commenting on Ford's behavior.

"My mom is bringing her famous country fried steak, *and* I told her to bring you the recipe." He wiggled his eyebrows.

"You remembered!" Ford's hand was taken in my mom's, and I quickly realized that it wasn't just my dad who had a relationship with the hockey team, but she did too. I would have realized that sooner if I hadn't stayed holed up in my childhood bedroom for the last year, hiding from the press and many articles floating around the internet, discussing my figure skating career and speculating about my fall.

"Are your parents coming?" My mom glanced at Aasher. I hadn't even noticed that Theo had left.

Aasher's entire demeanor changed. His relaxed shoulders tensed, and the muscles along his forearms flickered against his chest. The half-smile on his face fell. It was clear that he was uncomfortable.

"No. They usually just watch on TV. My dad can't take time off from work, and my mom isn't a fan of traveling by herself."

"If you give me her number, I will gladly record some of your ice time and send it over."

I couldn't pull myself away from Aasher's warm smile. One cheek tipped, and his green eyes were bright. "Sure, Mrs. Lennon. That would be great. She'd love it."

After he rattled off the number to my mom, my dad said they needed to get going. Ford slipped out of the booth allowing Sutton and I to follow. Aasher stood back with his hands in his pockets, watching me as I hugged both of my parents. Sutton did the same because once you were my friend, my mom treated you like you were her own.

"See you tomorrow, sweetie." My mom squeezed my hand and followed my dad over to the rest of the hockey team. He was scolding them for playing poker the night before a game. *Sorry, not sorry.*

Aasher leaned into my space. "That's on you, Duster." His whisper sent me into overdrive, but I recovered quickly after he pulled away.

"You're worried about him learning about your poker night?" I laughed. "Wait until I tell him ab—"

"*Don't,*" he interrupted.

Ford rubbed his hands together, unaware of our quiet conversation. "Do you girls want some milkshakes?"

Aasher scoffed. "Milkshakes? Bro, we have a game tomorrow. Stop putting shit in your body."

"It's part of my pregame ritual, though. I do this every night before a game. It's for good luck."

"I could go for one," Sutton said, following Ford. He draped his arm over her shoulders, and off they went, leaving Aasher and me alone.

A moment before, I was confident and masterful, throwing a jab at Aasher in front of my father. But now, I was the size of the french fry that had fallen on the sticky floor of The Bex.

"Really?" he asked, leaning back against the side of the booth with his arms crossed.

"What?" I pulled on my jacket and acted innocent. I leaned forward and grabbed my phone but snapped back up like a rubber band when I felt his warm whisper coat the side of my neck.

"You're a brat." He quickly stepped back, out of my space.

"And you're a stalker." I wanted my insult to come out harsher than what it did. Instead, I was breathy sounding and clearly affected by him. "How many times have you followed me to the rink?"

Aasher avoided answering. Instead, he reprimanded me. "You shouldn't be there alone at night. It's closed for a reason."

"You're treating me like I'm a child." *And for what reason?*

Aasher's smug look was a slap to my cheek. "Don't act like one, and I won't treat you like one."

I bit the inside of my cheek. My chest twisted, and anger ripped up my neck, and before I knew it, I was standing a mere inch from him. I tilted my chin and peered into his wildly inviting green eyes as he waited for my reaction. He loved sparring with me just as much as I loved sparring with him, but I was ready to knock him down a few notches. "Okay, Aasher. But just remember, you asked for it."

His head tilted.

"I'll see you tomorrow night." I made sure my voice was full of sugar.

He said nothing as I backed away and motioned for Sutton. She pecked Ford on the cheek and thanked him for the milkshake.

The bell on the door chimed over our heads. When I turned back to get one last look at Aasher, I watched him mouth the words, *"Tomorrow night?"*

I smiled deviously.

Before Sutton and I reached her car, I grabbed the milkshake out of her hand and gave it a quick sip before handing it back. "We need to talk."

"About you and Aasher? Because there is *definitely* something going on with you two."

There was, but it wasn't what she was assuming.

"I need to put him in his place."

If he wanted to follow me everywhere and watch my every move when his teammates were around, then I'd give him a show. Irritation was fueling my impulsivity, but that was what he wanted, right? To irritate me? The spark was long gone, but I still felt the after-effects of his warm breath on my neck with his belittling insults.

"Oh, I'm so in." Sutton did a little jump.

I thought for a second. "Actually, I need to put the whole hockey team in their place."

"The whole team? Why?"

As soon as we were both safely tucked away in her car, I stole another sip of the chocolate shake. "Remember when I was trapped in my dad's office?"

She nodded before putting her car in drive. She zoomed past Ford and Aasher so fast that gravel kicked up, and they were forced to take a step back.

"There's a bet."

Sutton glanced at me.

I sighed, looking out the window. "An ice bet."

She pressed harder on the accelerator.

"And I'm the prize."

[11]

I SHOOK WITH EXHAUSTION, but the exhilaration of winning backed my speed as I flew over the ice. Two Englanders' players shuffled as I dipped past with my hockey stick leading the way. Ford caught my eye, and he lifted the puck and sent it soaring in my direction. The contact traveled all the way to my bones, and there wasn't a single thought other than flinging the puck into the goal.

The buzzer sounded, and the crowd went wild.

Fuck yes.

The team flew over to me and tossed their helmets into the air, causing them to fall like rain droplets onto the ice. The fans screamed, and I smiled from the success.

"Fucking hell, that was a good game." Efrain patted me on the back, and I nodded, still out of breath.

"Aasher!" I caught my name through the crowd, and I found Coach's wife staring at me while she waved her arms frantically. I gave her a strange look when her blue eyes—the same color as her daughter's—widened. She turned her phone around, and I was surprised to see my mom's face on the other side of it, smiling proudly. She gave me a thumbs-up, and for a moment, I just stood there, wondering how different my parents' lives would be if I had never dated the mayor's daughter.

I smiled and put my glove up, signaling a wave. Then I turned around and skated toward center ice with the rest of my team to celebrate some more. Theo patted me on the back with his helmet in hand as sweat dripped down his face. "We're fucking unstoppable this year."

"We are." I grinned.

We both knew that having a winning season and progressing to the Frozen Four was vital if we wanted to start off in the NHL on steady feet, and so far, the chances of that were good.

It didn't take us long to get showered and cleaned up. The reporters kept their questions to a minimum, and Coach's departing words were short and to the point, like always.

I pulled my bag over my shoulder and almost made it out of the locker room before he shouted my name from his office. I stopped mid-step. *Fuck.*

I dipped my head through the crack in the door. "Yeah, Coach?"

"Get in here and shut the door."

My heart pounded harder when the door latched, shutting out the sounds of the locker room.

Coach sat on the edge of his desk with a loose tie and unbuttoned shirt. "How are things?"

I was sweating, and I really didn't have a reason to unless Riley had ratted out the team and told him about the bet.

"You mean with Riley?" I played dumb, like I had no idea what he was referring to. *Riley who?*

He gave me his *"obviously, you dumbass'"* look that he typically reserved for Ford.

"What else would I be talking about? I know how hockey is going." His expression had softened, and by that I meant he no longer looked like he wanted to smack me. "You did well."

I pulled my bag up higher on my shoulder and mumbled a thank you. It was hard to look him in the eye and not feel ashamed. I wondered if I should just tell him about the bet or mention that his daughter was a petty brat who was purposefully provoking me because she had caught my watchful eye, but I thought better of it. I'd push aside our little feud for now and let her have her fun as long as she didn't cross a line and take the team with her.

I cleared my throat. "Things are fine."

Coach eyed me suspiciously, so I gave a little depth.

"Well, actually, she did come to one of the parties."

He popped up from his desk. "She did?"

It was apparent he was surprised to hear that she went to a party, which only piqued my curiosity further. What happened to Riley at Rosewood that had made him so... *worried?*

As far as I was concerned, Riley Lennon could handle herself.

At least when it came to me, she could.

"She left shortly after she arrived," I added. "I made sure she got home safe."

It was on the tip of my tongue to tell him that she'd been coming to the rink late at night, but his abrupt laughter stopped me.

"And she was aware that you were making sure she got home safe?"

"Yeah." *And she was pissed.*

He laughed again. "And she was okay with that?"

I raised an eyebrow, and he nodded.

"I thought so. Now do you understand why she can't know you're watching her?" *Well, it was too late for that.* "If she knew I asked you to keep an eye out, she'd make it her mission to evade you every chance she gets."

My face stayed unmoving, but we were already there. Riley rolled her eyes if she caught me looking at her, and she bristled at our every interaction. It wasn't what I was used to when talking to a female, and as much as it annoyed me, I found myself thinking about her more often than not.

"Has the team been on their best behavior?"

Fuck no.

"If you're asking if any of them have touched her, the answer is no." It wasn't a lie.

He grunted. Red spread across his cheeks as he wound around his desk and sat down in his chair. "Good. Now get out of here."

I tipped my chin at him, but before I disappeared, he stopped me. *So close.*

"If she shows up to the party I know you all are going to—"

I didn't bother turning around. "I've got it under control. She'll get home safe."

My breathing didn't return to normal until I felt the cool night air fill my lungs. I caught up to Theo and walked in stride with him. "Are you going to Rush's tonight?"

"Yeah."

That was a surprise. I would have bet my left testicle that he was going to his dorm to lust over his roommate.

"I know damn well you are."

I scoffed. "You make me sound like a party animal—which I am not."

I'd never been a huge partier. The only time I got black-out drunk was one time in high school when Savannah and I pounded an entire bottle of vodka over the course of a few hours, skinny-dipped in our friend's pool until their parents came home, and then puked in the bushes outside her bedroom window until I hoisted her back through before the sun started to rise.

That was before everything hit the fucking fan.

The drive to Rush's took no more than ten minutes from the arena.

Their house was even closer to the football stadium.

Rush and many other seniors were destined for the NFL, just as most of the hockey team was destined for the NHL. Bexley U hadn't always been great at pulling elite athletes and furthering their careers to the pros, but over the last few years, the school had become one of the most sought-after colleges in the northeastern part of the United States. One good thing had come out of my hometown drama, I guess, because I wouldn't have attended Bexley U if it weren't for that.

"Party is in full swing," Theo mumbled, catching up to me. "As always."

I squeezed past a couple practically fucking on the porch, and though I couldn't see the guy's face, I had a feeling it was one of our players. It was too cold outside for it to be anyone else. Hockey players dug the cold.

When I was a kid, my mom used to have to dig through the snow to pull me back inside to rest for a while before I would put on my wet snow gear the second she turned her back and head right back out to practice slingshots on our icy driveway.

I'd pick winter over summer any day of the week.

I pulled on the collar of my hoodie when Theo and I moved through the party, because it was a fucking sauna inside. Berkley threw his fist in my direction, and we touched knuckles.

"What's up? Did you drive over?"

"Why?" He grinned. "Looking for a ride for when grandpa over here leaves immediately after getting his dick sucked so he can head to bed?"

Theo chuckled, and although we drove separately, he couldn't help but throw a dig. "Sorry. Some of us have to get their rest because they're too tired from carrying the team during that win."

We laughed because we all knew Theo was kidding. He was all for team morale, and we knew we were all working parts on the ice.

Theo slipped away and headed right toward Claire, his roommate. I scanned the party. I was on the lookout for a raven-haired, blue-eyed little devil that would likely show up just to piss me off.

I blew out a breath when I realized she wasn't here. I pulled out my phone. It was nearing eleven. I'd bet anything that she was waiting for the rink to clear so she could sneak in.

After our last quarrel, I cursed my need to irritate her, because I let it slip that I knew she was still going to the rink after hours. I understood that it made me look like a stalker, but in my defense, I saw her from my window while I was studying. She was walking down the street in the middle of the night. What was I supposed to do? Let her walk in the dark by herself? For the love of God, she didn't even carry mace with her. It was the least she could do, considering she was openly choosing to walk instead of drive.

Stupid.

Imagine if she were taken, or raped, or I don't know...fell into a sinkhole. Coach would throw *me* into a sinkhole.

I understood the loyalty the ice brought. The comfort. The solace. So I didn't judge her too harshly for going to the rink—just her way of getting there.

After everything happened with Savannah and my parents were named the town pariahs, along with receiving threats of me being hung like I was a piece of meat for something that I didn't have any control over, I used to go to the rink and hide out too. The only difference was that I actually got on the ice. Riley just stared at it.

I rolled out my sore shoulders and skimmed through my messages.

> Mom- That was a good game, honey! I'd love to send Karen something as a thank you for video-calling me. Dad and I are so proud. I wish we could be there in person to watch you.

But we can't afford it, was the last part of the text message that was left untyped. I knew why they couldn't make the trip up here to sit in the stands like most of the team's parents who were in the vicinity of Bexley U. My parents probably seemed unsupportive to most, never showing up to games and not making appearances. But that wasn't the case. I used to let the guilt eat me alive, but over the years, I'd come to the realization that it wasn't my fault.

"Hi." Liv slipped up beside me, and I instantly furrowed my brow at the sound of her shy voice.

I clicked my phone off and pushed it into my pocket at the sight of her small frown. *Here it comes.*

"Uh, hey." I looked at her empty hands. "You need a drink?"

I was a gentleman. Sort of.

She nibbled on her bottom lip. "Are you mad at me?"

Same 'ol shit, different girl. "Why would I be mad at you, Liv?"

She pushed a piece of hair behind her ear. "I don't know. I haven't heard from you."

That was because I was too busy following Riley around campus like an overprotective big brother—or stalker, according to her.

"I wasn't aware that there was a certain amount of time that I had to text you by."

"Is it because of that girl?"

Whoa. Hold up.

"What girl?"

"The one that you very obviously are into."

My pulse thrummed. "I have no idea who you're talking about." I knew damn well who she was referring to.

Liv smiled but squinted her eyes at me, like she was scrutinizing my actions. "You made a dig at a girl's lack of clothing when I left your apartment the other day." She patted my chest. "That's called being jealous. You didn't want your roommates looking at her."

She didn't seem bothered by this, just curious.

"You've never acted that way with me leaving your apartment with *just-fucked* hair and a missing bra." A soft laugh left her, and she shrugged, looking out into the party.

"It's fine if that's the case. I just need to know so I don't step on anyone's toes."

"I'm not into her." *And don't put that thought in my head.* "She's my coach's daughter. I said something about the way she was dressed because the last thing our team needs is an upset like one of them sleeping with her and pissing Coach Lennon off."

Liv's beer-scented breath fell graciously from her mouth. "Oh."

Silence passed between us, and I glanced out into the party, unsure of what to say to her. I'd love nothing more than to take her upstairs like usual, but things were beginning to feel sticky between us.

Too sticky.

"I'm sorry," she said, turning to me. "I hope you don't think I was jealous. I know that what you and I have is simple and there are absolutely zero strings."

That was what she had always alluded to.

I was busy with hockey, and she was busy trying to get into law school. Neither of us wanted anything more than a quick fuck, nor did we have the time for it.

"I just didn't want to be caught up in ex-girlfriend drama or whatever. I don't have time for that."

I took a sip of my beer, watching her relaxed movements. I wasn't sure if she was telling the truth, but I hoped she was. I didn't have time for drama either, and the sole reason for that was because I'd already been there and done that. I probably had the *most* ex-girlfriend drama out of everyone on this campus.

I chugged the rest of my beer and threw it in a nearby trash can before pulling Liv onto the dance floor. It was in the middle of the living room, but from the very first party I attended at Rush's, it had *always* been the place for people to dance and get a little touchy.

Liv put her back to my front, and her ass pushed up against my semi-hard dick. My hands flew to her waist, and she moved in front of me, rubbing herself against me so slowly that I only lasted a few minutes.

"Upstairs," I whispered into her ear, nibbling on the edge of it.

Liv and I were upstairs within ten seconds, and I had her up against the closed door with her pressed against my dick. Her head flew back, and she was looking for a quick fuck by the jerky movements of her pulling at my shirt.

I unbuttoned her jeans and shoved my hand down the front of her panties for a quick check. She was already wet and needy by the little moan that left her lips.

"You in a rush?" I moved my finger in and out of her slowly, feeling my dick harden.

"Kind of. I need to study for the LSATs. I'm taking them next week."

No-strings sex wasn't really emotionally fulfilling, but I didn't care.

I dropped her legs to the ground, and she undressed quickly. Her panties flew over my shoulder, and I chuckled.

"Spin."

Liv did as I said and placed her hands on the door.

After slipping a condom on, I crept up behind her and held her steady. "Spread."

She gasped when I pushed into her quickly.

"Ah," she whimpered.

I went to town as she moved up and down, chasing after her own high. I wrapped my arm around her hip and touched her clit, rubbing it out so she could get off faster. Her breathy moan was all the thanks I needed.

My phone vibrated from beneath my bundled jeans, but Liv was close. She started to milk me and it felt too damn good to stop.

The vibrating started up again, and I cursed the distraction.

Fuck. It was probably my mom again.

Ah, great. Now I was thinking about my mom.

Focus.

A text came next, and I pressed harder on Liv's clit.

What if it was Ford or Berkley texting me that Riley showed up?

I told them to let me know if she showed up to one of the parties and I wasn't around.

She better not be here.

I could see her now, smiling coyly while she flirted with the hockey team just to spite me while showing off too much of her creamy skin.

I rammed into Liv even harder. "Right there," she moaned, tightening around me.

My head was somewhere else as I tilted my hips and blew a load into the condom. I was breathing hard and dripping with sweat.

My jaw cracked when I pulled out of Liv.

I couldn't see straight. I couldn't even speak.

And I sure as hell would never admit that I got off while thinking of my coach's daughter.

Fuck.

Liv was fully content and had no idea what was going through my head as she got dressed.

After pulling on my jeans, I finally looked at my phone and was sucker punched.

Two missed calls.

One text message.

They were all from Ford.

There was commotion out in the hallway, and I knew it was him before his voice sounded on the other side of the door.

"Aasher, quit fucking a puck bunny and get out here."

Liv drew in a sharp breath. "I am not a puck bunny!"

I peeked over at her, and my lips flattened. *She kind of was.*

"Aasher! A puck bunny is when a girl is with multiple hockey players. Not just one!"

Ford opened the door and looked directly at Liv. "Look up the definition of a puck bunny, babe. You're one whether you want to admit it or not."

She angrily pulled her messy hair up in a bun. "Shut up, Ford. Bye, Aasher."

"Uh, later."

She stomped out of the bedroom, and I shot Ford a look. "Really?"

"Her feelings are the *least* of your worries right now." *Trust me, I fucking know.*

I bent down and snatched the condom wrapper and threw it in a small trash can near the dresser. "What is it?"

I didn't even need to ask. I already knew.

"Riley is here."

"Great." I sighed. "When did she show up?"

Ford walked beside me, nearly skipping. "When you were dick-deep in the puck bunny."

"Quit calling her that. It's degrading."

He shrugged. "It's the truth."

When we got to the top of the stairs, he put his hand on my chest, stopping me. "You're gonna need to prepare yourself."

My heart raced. "Why?"

"Because whoever just walked in with Sutton isn't the Riley Lennon that we all know as Duster."

The moment my feet hit the bottom of the stairs and I looked out onto the dance floor, I cursed. The last time I spoke to Riley, I told her she was acting like a child, and right now, she looked anything *but.*

[12]

RILEY

The lack of bra made my boobs itchy. But it was nothing a shot of Fireball couldn't lessen.

Sutton dressed me, and if my father saw my outfit, he'd have a heart attack.

I looked hot, even with my leather jacket on, and by the slacked jaws of some of the guys in the room, they thought so too.

Some of the rumors at Rosewood suggested that I had self-image issues because of how slender I became right before my last competition, but that wasn't technically the reason I had developed an eating disorder. It had nothing to do with how I looked and all to do with how I performed.

Still, it was nerve-racking to walk into a party dressed like *this*.

I lengthened my spine like I was full of confidence and followed Sutton through the maze of people. Aasher's insult was the real reason I had come tonight, but without his eyes on me, glaring with annoyance, I wasn't as eager to gain the stares of all his teammates.

"Get your game face on," Sutton mused from beside me.

She was the perfect wing-woman for this sort of thing. After I told her about the bet, she went into girl-power mode.

Sully walked toward us and grinned. "Wow." He completely ignored Sutton.

Red flag number one.

Sutton held my arm up and spun me around by my hand. "She looks hot, huh?"

"She sure does." Sully's voice had a little rasp to it, and I eyed him with wariness.

"Hands off, though," Sutton barked, edging in front of me.

I was surprised at her need to protect me since this wasn't really part of the plan we had concocted, but I couldn't blame her. She didn't know the old Riley. The one who would spend her entire day at the ice rink, working her body tirelessly, refusing to eat so she could be *lighter* on the ice while she strove to fulfill some crazy prophecy of perfection and then head to campus parties with her touchy boyfriend who didn't understand privacy.

I didn't need protection from any of these guys.

But of course, she didn't know that.

"Oh, come on." Ford slid up beside us and blocked Sully. "She can dance with me, though. Right?"

"I thought there was a hands-off rule when it came to the coach's daughter," I joked, snatching his drink and hurling it back in one gulp.

Sully hummed as he moved over to catch my eye. He peered at me from the top of his cup as he poured the rest of whatever alcohol inside his mouth.

"*Easy*, Duster," Ford warned, stealing the empty cup from my hand.

One eyebrow rose as he wrapped his palm around my waist. "Don't let your daddy know you're at a college party, slugging back beer like some wild party girl."

I let Ford lead me to the dance floor, relishing the burning alcohol in my belly. I could feel everyone watching me, and I wondered if Aasher was somewhere in the crowd since he was half the reason I'd decided to come tonight.

"It's a good thing I have Aasher here to babysit me, huh? He's gotta make sure I don't let you boys touch me too much and ruin the team."

Ford dipped me so far back that I almost touched the floor. "You are being awfully naughty, Riley." Air whizzed past my face when he pulled me back up. "What provoked this behavior?"

"You know as well as I do."

Ford laughed.

"You're driving him wild. It better not affect his time on the ice."

I searched for him, hoping to make my point very clear that his insults weren't going to stop me from doing what I wanted. I once let a guy take something from me. I wasn't going to let Aasher take something too, even if it was as trivial as showing up at the same party and shoving a bet down his teammates' throats.

"And what is he going to do? Put me over his shoulder and take me home like the good little boy that he is?"

"Damn." Ford's smile was full of mirth. "You're feisty tonight."

"Only when it comes to a certain meaty hockey player watching my every move so he can make sure I never get laid by a hockey player."

game. He got ice time, and that was kind of a big deal when you were a rookie.

He caught my eye, and it took less than two seconds for him to prowl over to me. He wore a hot smirk and was definitely attractive, but his arrogance was a little too potent. "Hey." His smirk only grew hotter.

"Let's dance. Or are you too afraid of the repercussions?" I teased.

"Repercussions?" he repeated, glancing around the party. Aasher was perched behind him, so he didn't notice the death glare he was sending our way. "I'll deal with them if it means I can dance with you."

As soon as we started to dance, I began rocking my hips slower. His hands cupped my waist as he pressed my ass to his front, and when his breathing sped up, I knew I was playing my cards right. These hockey boys were going to trip over me, and then I was going to clam up the moment they wanted something more. *Serves them right.*

A deep whisper came from behind, and I peeked over my shoulder. Ford was dancing with a pretty girl. "Tsk, tsk, Riley. You're being naughty."

"Who? Me?" I asked innocently.

Ford grinned, and I mimicked it.

"I'm just having a little fun." I paused. "In fact, I *bet* I can have more fun than you guys can tonight."

Ford's smile fell, but the girl he was dancing with pulled him away and told him to let me have my fun. I turned up the heat a little, swaying my hips even slower and rubbing against the hard bulge my partner in crime was sporting.

"Move."

Suddenly, I was jolted away from the rookie, and Sully was back, placing a drink in my hand.

"Oh, come on," the rookie whined. "That's not fair."

Sully's chest puffed. "Seniority. What I say goes."

I didn't remind Sully that he was just as much a rookie on Bexley U's hockey team as the underclassman was, but I wanted to.

I quickly snuck a glance at Aasher, and he was laser-focused on the rookie. He snapped his arm out so quickly I jumped. The rookie stopped walking, and whatever Aasher said to him had him nodding his head and sulking away.

I can't even dance with them?

I rolled my eyes, and Sully's face came back into view. "Did you hear me?"

"Huh?" I asked, feeling a sudden rush of warmth. The alcohol was catching up to me. "No, sorry. I...sorry. Let's take a break from dancing."

Sully led me by the hand to the opposite side of where Aasher was, and I knew he did that on purpose. "I was just telling you how good you look tonight."

I smiled and gripped the drink he'd given me without taking a sip. "Just tonight?"

He was quick to answer. "No, not just tonight."

Sully dropped his gaze to my mouth so I quickly changed the direction of the conversation. "You played well earlier."

"You watched? I didn't see you in the stands."

"Were you looking for me?" *So you could fulfill the bet?*

It was frustrating that I didn't know who was participating and who wasn't. It made my plan a little harder to achieve.

"If I was looking for you, I shouldn't say it out loud or else it'll get back to your dad, and I'm not necessarily in the clear with him just yet." He grabbed my hand and pulled me into a room that had a table in the middle with cups lining the edges. People were aggressively drinking and flipping them.

Flip cup.

I was the title holder at Rosewood, and I was pretty sure Sully knew that, even if he was finger-deep in a puck bunny most of the time.

"Wanna play, champ?" He gently elbowed me.

I laughed when everyone stopped playing and waited for my answer. There were multiple people lingering around—mostly guys, and they weren't all hockey players. I nibbled on the inside of my cheek, teetering between continuing to play my little game that no one was even aware of or to head home before I truly did cause trouble.

"No, she doesn't." Aasher's gruff voice came from behind, and just like that, my decision was made for me.

I turned around and looked him square in the eye, hating that although I wanted to punch him, I found him insanely attractive. His green eyes were bright with anger. The color was even more vibrant because his black hoodie made them pop. His square jaw flickered at the sides as he ran his gaze down my outfit.

I forced myself to stay still.

Aasher looking at me was ten times hotter than when anyone else did.

"Dude, chill," Sully said.

He looked at Aasher, and even though the room grew quiet, I heard the hidden words being spewed between them.

Sully stepped closer to me. "This isn't one of our stupid competitions. Riley is off-limits to the both of us."

Aasher moved closer. "*Exactly.* You're messing with something you shouldn't be."

"Am I a *something?*" I asked, becoming more irritated

the longer they talked about me like I wasn't standing right there.

Aasher snapped a glare over to me. "Dressed like that? Yeah, you are."

Asshole.

"She isn't off-limits to me. *Especially* dressed like that." A guy came and stood beside me. He was so tall I had to crane my neck to see his grin.

I stepped closer to him, and I thought Aasher was going to burst a blood vessel.

Sully's lips pursed as he pouted.

I slugged back the rest of my drink, holding back a choking cough, because apparently all the liquor had fallen to the bottom of the cup. I shoved it into Aasher's chest with as much force as I could. His hand covered mine, and the plastic cup crinkled. "It's been a long night," he sighed. "I'm not in the mood for this."

"No one is asking you to stay," I reminded him, peering up at his tightly drawn face and swollen lips, no doubt from some poor puck bunny. "What do you think is going to happen if I play a simple game of flip cup?"

"You *know* what I think is going to happen." The air crackled with us going toe to toe. "Let's go."

"What was that?" I shouted. "You want me to leave with you, Aasher?" I grew louder with each word and batted my eyes at him. "Are we heading back to your place or mine?"

Aasher's gaze dropped to my lips, then to my chest, and then down my legs. His nostrils flared. The cup I smashed into his chest dropped to the floor, and he tightly gripped my hand. "We need to talk."

Next thing I knew, I was being pulled through the party like a child. He shoved me through an open door, and I jumped when it slammed behind him. The light flipped on above our heads, and I realized we were in the pantry.

"What the hell are you doing, Duster?"

He was seething.

I ripped my wrist out of his grasp and backed up all the way to the shelf that was lined to the ceiling with protein bars. "I'm having fun," I snapped. "Why is that a problem for you?"

"Having *fun?* You're rubbing your tight ass all over Jones and Sullivan like you're asking to get fucked. Do I need to remind you that if you sleep with any of them, they are literally just doing it to win a *fucking* bet? If your dad finds out—"

"I'm not going to sleep with any of them." I rolled my eyes, interrupting Aasher's hissy fit. "I'm just trying to get back at them."

"You're just fucking with their heads." Aasher erased the space between us. "And mine. So stop it."

"You asked for it, and so did they. Stop treating me like I'm a child who needs a babysitter and let me put them in their place." I shrugged. "And then maybe I won't tell my dad how his team is a bunch of disgusting pigs."

Aasher grabbed the shelf right beside my head, and my heart raced. He mumbled something under his breath, and although I was a little tipsy, I heard him plain as day.

"So, it really is true."

For the first time, Aasher wasn't glaring at me. The divot between his eyebrows had disappeared. My heart raced faster, but my anger shifted to someone else.

"My dad seriously asked you to keep me from being with the hockey players?"

Aasher probably thinks I'm a slut. It's no wonder he was so worried. I assumed my dad had told the hockey players

Sj SYLVIS

that I was off-limits and gave them a little warning, but he *truly* asked Aasher to keep me away from them? It all made sense now.

"Is that what this is about? Keeping your word?" My jaw slacked. I didn't want to be angry at my dad, because I knew he was trying to protect me. Some guy hurt his daughter, and it caused a snowball effect, but his lack of trust was demoralizing.

"He asked me to keep an eye out for you." Aasher's tone was soft as he tried skirting around the truth. It amped up my anger. "He specifically told the team that you were off-limits."

"And he told you to intervene anytime I got close to someone?"

"Just knock it off and stop tempting them." The shelf creaked beneath his grip.

"Or what?" I spat.

I was beyond frustrated. My dad. Aasher. The bet. The quickly approaching date for tryouts. My stupid panic attacks anytime I got close to the ice. *Damn it.*

"*Riley.*"

I jutted my braless chest out and brushed against him. His head twitched.

"Are you going to bend me over and spank me, Aasher?" I laughed when his eyes widened. "Are you going to run off and tell my dad about the bet? I thought you were afraid that it would ruin the team? Isn't that what you're so concerned about? Your precious players getting kicked off the team and the Frozen Four slipping through your fingers?"

I was poking the bear, but it made me feel better, so whatever.

His smirk dug into me as sharp as the shelf behind my

back. "Nah. I'll just tell your dad that you've been trying to get the team to fuck you. I can assure you that every single hockey player will back me on that, because if they don't, they're going down too." Aasher's other hand came up to meet the shelf, and suddenly, I was trapped.

He wouldn't.

I stared up at him, and his perfect lips twitched. "Don't underestimate me."

"Fine." I sighed heavily. "I'll stay away from the team."

The look of surprise on his face almost made me laugh. *Don't underestimate him?* He shouldn't underestimate me.

His hands left the shelf, and he took a step back, freeing me. A shaky breath fell from my lips, and I hadn't realized how tense I was with him so close.

"Good, now let me take you home." I waited until he was almost to the door to take the reins back, because I wasn't leaving this party until we were even.

"No."

He spun around and scoffed. His brown hair flopped on his head, and his slacked jaw tightened again. "What?"

"I came here to have a good time, and I'm assuming my dad didn't tell the football team that I was off-limits, right?"

I'll admit, it wasn't *as* good as my original plan, but it would still drive the team crazy and knock them down a notch. They could all look, but no one was scoring points with me tonight.

I waited to see what Aasher would say, but instead of hearing anything, I felt a shift in the air. The room grew smaller, and it was hard to breathe. Aasher crept over to me slowly, and his features were drawn tight with impatience. His hands were right back to the shelf beside my head, and I was too shocked by the look in his eyes to slip out from underneath him. "Is that what you want, Duster? To have fun with some guy?"

Not really.

"Maybe." I shrugged.

His neck moved with a slow swallow. I gulped when his tongue darted out of his mouth to moisten his lips.

The words were effortless. "Fine. Tell me what you want, and I'll give it to you."

[13]

AASHER

I WANTED to kiss her just to get her to shut her bratty mouth.

Riley Lennon was a true player of the game, and up until now, I didn't even know we were playing one. There was a small crease in between her eyebrows that I wanted to smooth out with my finger, but I remained still. I crowded her space to intimidate her.

"Cat got your tongue?" I smirked. "What exactly is it that you want? Did you want one of them to kiss you? Wanted to prove that you weren't a duster after all?"

I was being such a dick, but that was what she deserved after pulling this stunt.

I studied the perfect curve of her lips. They were pouty and painted pink with shiny lip gloss. There was a quick lapse of time when I wondered what they tasted like. Being this close and having her at my mercy made me feel uncontrollable, and I suddenly understood the desire that the team felt. The temptation was strong, and my thoughts were spiraling.

"None of the other hockey players can have me, but you can?" Her breath was drunkenly sweet. "It sounds like you wanna win that silly little ice bet, after all."

If I were participating, I'd fucking win.

Riley shifted her chin and placed her hands on my chest to push me away. I let her, but only for a second. I wanted to blame it on my impatience with her and the provoking sound of her voice, but truth be told, she was irresistible.

The room caved in, and the only thing I could see was her. My hand snapped out, and I gripped her wrist just as she was storming out of the pantry to go flirt with some football player. I spun her, and her big blue eyes widened with confusion. I gripped her chin tightly, opened her mouth with my thumb, and pressed her lips to mine.

Fuck.

She tasted of something fruity, and I wanted to smother myself in it. I ran my tongue over hers, gulping up the remnants of the drink, and instead of pulling away like I should have, I found myself bringing her closer and going back for seconds. I swallowed her mouth not once but twice, moving my lips against hers so hard that our teeth clanked together. I'd never felt so possessive, and I'd never kissed someone as feverishly as I just did her.

A small whimper left her, and I snapped out of it, pulling back abruptly with my body on fire.

Shit. Shit. Shit.

Her mouth was still open, lips parted with shock. I put on a good front and lifted the back of my hand and wiped my mouth, removing the vanilla-scented lip gloss. "I'm not trying to win the bet, Ry. I just know kissing you won't fuck with my head like it will theirs. So if you want a hockey player, I'm the only one you can have."

It totally fucked with my head.

Riley cleared her throat before smoothing out her revealing shirt with her hands. I was crazed, wild with thoughts of touching her, so I stalked over to the door and opened it. "Let's go," I snapped, angry at myself for kissing her. "Your dad gave me strict orders to make sure you make it home from parties, so we're leaving."

Riley began to walk past me, but right before she made it through the threshold, she glanced over and smiled deviously.

Shit.

I had made a colossal mistake, because kissing her didn't affect her in the way that it affected me.

Her singsong voice rang throughout the crowded room. "Is it my turn?"

"Yes!" Taytum, our goalie's sister, grabbed Riley's hand and pulled her toward the end of the table.

"Sorry," I gritted between tight teeth. "Riley is leaving." I stole the cup that Taytum had placed in Riley's hand and put it down.

Sully snickered from the other side of the table, and I flicked my eyes at him.

"*Anddddd* Taytum is leaving too." Ford walked over to Taytum and tried to pull her away.

He failed.

Taytum and Riley shared a look, and I knew that I was in for a long night. I sighed angrily and stormed off, finding a perfect spot on the wall to keep an eye on her. I thought kissing her would put her in her place, but it did the opposite. She was laughing louder, smiling wider, and flirting so much I was about to take her back in that pantry and try again.

She wasn't just messing with the hockey team because of the bet. She was messing with me too, and she was *clearly* enjoying it.

"Hey! I recognize you." I eyed the girl who was staring at Riley. She was petite with hair so blonde it looked white. She blinked a million and one times before snapping her fingers. "Oh my god! You're Riley Lennon. The—"

Riley flipped the last cup and threw her hands up in victory. Then she looked over at the girl and said, "Yeah, the hockey coach's daughter. Don't remind me."

"No, you're more than just the hockey coach's daughter."

I agreed.

"I'm Gianna."

Riley froze. "Oh, Gianna..."

Gianna nodded. "Future teammate...I hope?"

Teammate?

I pushed off the wall. "Teammate for what?"

Riley completely ignored me by turning her back and shutting me out of the conversation.

One of Rush's running backs elbowed me. "Figure skating?"

What?

He must have sensed my confusion. "You didn't know about her figure skating career?" His beer-filled breath filled the space between us. "You're awfully protective over her for not knowing much about her."

I mused over his dig for the next two games of flip cup. *Figure skating?* I would have asked her about it, but she'd probably throw her drink in my face instead of answering, so I didn't ask.

Riley's eyes were becoming glossier by the second. Taytum had left after the second game, getting a phone call that pulled her away, but Riley was still going strong and talking some major shit to Sully, who I couldn't help but notice was encouraging her to keep going.

"I'm not stopping until I lose," Riley teased, pulling her long, dark hair up into a bun on top of her head. Her bare neck gave way to smooth skin and an even bigger window to her sexy top. I was almost positive she wasn't wearing a bra either.

After throwing back the last of my warm beer and watching every guy at the party fall under the spell that Riley had been putting on, I stepped up to the table and shoved Sully out of the way.

"My turn," I quipped, cracking my neck.

Sully opened his mouth, but I stopped him before he could even get started.

"You lost," I reminded him. "It's my turn."

Words died on the end of his lips when Riley beat him to the punch. "That's fine," she said. "But prepare to be put in your place, Aasher." She turned away and mumbled the word *again* under her breath.

I couldn't help but smirk at her dig.

She was sharp, and I was becoming duller by the second.

Sully rounded the table and stood beside her. *Why was he standing beside her?* His challenging gaze caught mine, and I couldn't stop the words from tumbling out of my mouth. "You know what, Duster?" I said, looking at her before snapping back to him. "Why don't we make a *bet?*"

I chuckled as surprise flickered over his face.

Riley's glossy eyes widened. There was a competitive

spark there because she knew the significance of the word. For a brief second, we were on the same team.

"Okay..." Riley's smile was lazy. *She was becoming drunker by the second.* "What's the bet?"

"If I win, you leave with me." I knew how it sounded, so I added, "And go back to your apartment." I let my words hang in the air for a moment before dipping down low for only her to hear. "*Alone.*"

She rolled her glassy blue eyes. "And if I win?"

"Then we stay until you're ready to go." I acted indifferent, but there wasn't a fucking chance I was letting her win.

"She doesn't need you to take her home. I can take her."

I completely ignored Sully and the rest of the guys at the party who were nodding. If I wasn't standing here, they'd all openly volunteer just so they could be alone with her.

Riley's gleaming white teeth sunk into her bottom lip. I zeroed in on her mouth and my stomach hollowed out. I was going to have to figure out how to deal with the repercussions of our kiss, because I was all sorts of fucked up.

"How about *you* leave and I'll stay until I'm ready to go?"

Not a chance.

I stuck my hand out over the table lined with cups. "Bet."

Her palm was soft and warm. I squeezed it tightly for a second before letting go.

Sully's hands landed on the top of Riley's shoulders, and he rubbed them a few times before whispering something in her ear that made her lips twitch. I held back a growl but was thankful for his encouragement, because seeing his hands on her pissed me off even more than her purposefully goading me.

"Ready, Duster?" I teased, seeing her little body sway to the right a little. It wasn't a question of whether she needed to go home or not.

"Ready when you are."

"Three, two...one. Go."

The thing about hockey players? We worked well under pressure.

Although, after watching her for the last hour, I could see that she worked well under pressure too.

We were neck and neck. Usually in flip cup, you had a partner and switched off like a relay, but it was her and me against each other. But we were used to that by now.

"Come on, Ry!" Sully was Riley's number one cheerleader, and in between flipping my cup and grabbing the next to down, I managed to sneak out an insult.

"Why the encouragement, Sully? Want her even drunker than she is?"

"I wish you would stop talking about me like I'm not here," she slurred.

Even if I didn't flip the last cup before her, I would have flung her over my shoulder and pulled her out of the party regardless, because I'd had enough.

"Time to go, Duster," I said, rounding the table and wiping the back of my hand against the leftover beer on my lips.

Her arms crossed. "No."

I bent my head low. "I didn't peg you to be a cheater, Duster."

"I am *not* a cheater, *Broom*."

"Broom?" I repeated. *Did she just call me a broom?*

She giggled, and it was sort of cute. "You call me a household tool; I call *you* a household tool."

I laughed out loud, and Riley's triumphant mood

quickly disappeared. Her shoulders dropped, and her arms hung down by her sides in defeat.

"You can call me whatever you want as long as you follow through on the bet. I won fair and square. Let's go."

"Make me."

"My pleasure," I said.

I quickly dropped down, wrapped my arms around the backs of her thighs, and flung her over my shoulder like a sack of potatoes.

"Aasher!" It was obvious that she was surprised, and part of me was worried someone would take a photo and share it with Coach, but I'd just have to rat her out and tell him that it was the only way she'd leave the party after getting smashed.

He said he trusted me, and I hoped he did.

I'm not sure he should after I threw her into the pantry and kissed her, but I'd make sure to leave that part of the night out.

"Put me down!"

I walked through the party with Riley's ass beside my head and her arms punching along my spine. It didn't hurt, so I let her work out her frustration. She didn't stop until we were outside and alone.

I turned back to the party and looked for Sully because it wouldn't be surprising if he tried to follow us. Anything to be Riley's knight covered in nothing but devious lies and fake chivalry, but no one was standing there except Sutton. She was drunk too, but I couldn't carry both of them home. Riley shouted for her to go back to the party. She made some dig about me stealing all her fun, but I ignored her and continued down the sidewalk, making sure my car was locked.

"Are you seriously going to carry me the whole way in

the freezing cold?" Riley hit me one last time before seemingly giving up.

"Well, if you would have left with me an hour ago, I could have driven us home, but instead, you forced me to play a game of flip cup, and now I'm half-buzzed, so thanks for that."

"I didn't force you."

"Do you really think I'd leave you at a house party while you are *this* drunk?"

Her chest rumbled against my body with a huff, and I stopped walking. "I can take care of myself."

"Can you?" I asked, noticing the way her voice dropped in between slurring.

She was quiet, and the only thing I could focus on was my overactive imagination as I continued on our trek. My arm was sore by the time we got to our apartment complex, but I kept her flung over my body until we made it to her door.

"Time to get down, Duster."

There was a slight whimper that left her lips.

"Riley?" I lifted my shoulder to shake her awake.

A warm sigh flitted from her mouth, and she readjusted herself on my shoulder, pressing her face into the crook of my neck. *Jesus.* She was warm, and the very tip of her nose brushed against my skin so lightly it sent a rush of heat down my arm.

My jaw flexed.

One inappropriate thought of Riley was dangerous, let alone the number I'd had tonight.

"Damn it," I mumbled. Despite her labeling me as a stalker, I wasn't a very good one because I didn't have a key to her apartment.

"Either wake up or you're staying in my room." I could

hear the rumors now. *The coach's daughter slept in Aasher Matthews's room after he dragged her from a party.* I'd be a dead man on skates.

Riley whimpered again, but this one was less breathy and resembled a whine. I fumbled with my key before rushing us into my apartment. No one was on the couch, but I knew I couldn't drop Riley there or else I'd be cleaning up vomit off the floor the next morning.

"Aasher," she panicked.

"I know," I said, attempting to soothe her. "Almost there, Duster."

My bathroom light brightened the room and gave way to Riley as she quickly slid herself down my body and ran over to the toilet. I turned my back, ready to shut the door and leave her, but I paused with my hands above my head, gripping the doorframe.

Seeing her like this brought back a feeling I didn't want to recognize.

I shut my eyes and listened to the sound of her retching. There wasn't much that could get me twisted inside, especially after molding a thick skin from what had happened with Savannah, but I'd admit, I was a little riled. I put on a decent front most of the time and acted nonchalant, but I was jaded.

"Hey," I said, softer than normal. "You okay?"

She had stopped puking, and though I didn't want to spin around, I did anyway. Riley's lifeless body was curled around the toilet with sweat trickling down the side of her cheek and one arm wrapped around her lower stomach. "Riley?" I repeated, taking a step toward her.

Her nose scrunched, and I breathed out a relieved sigh, reminding myself that she'd just had too much to drink. *She's fine.*

I walked over to the cabinet and grabbed a washcloth, wetting it with cold water. I bent down and pushed a strand of hair away from her tacky forehead. I had the uncontrollable urge to scoop her up, give her one of my shirts to wear, and put her in my bed for the rest of night so I could keep her close.

It was a fleeting feeling, but it was there.

"Here." I placed the rag against her sticky skin. She sighed but shook against the floor with a chill. "Are you okay? Do you think you're going to be sick again?"

"No."

"No you're not okay, or no you're not going to be sick again?"

Her eyes were shut, so I scanned her features and saw her bottom lip trembling. I almost ran out the door. *Fuck, is she crying?*

"I'm...you won't understand."

Sitting back on my butt, I rested my back against the tub and put my legs up so I could rest my forearms against my knees. "Try me." I swallowed. "Talk."

"Why?" she asked, gripping her stomach again. Her eyes were still shut, but maybe that was what she preferred. I didn't blame her.

"Because I just carried you for twenty minutes over my shoulder. You owe me."

"I don't owe you anything." She half-laughed, but it was weak, and her face was pale. There wasn't a lick of color on her cheeks, and I sighed, dropping my head.

"I'll be right back. I'm getting you a Gatorade."

She made a noise that sounded like she was on her deathbed, but before I walked out the door she whispered, "Blue."

"Huh?"

"I like blue."

"You get what you get, Duster," I said, but I knew very well that if we didn't have blue Gatorade in the fridge, I'd make sure to find one for her.

Thankfully, we had a blue one all the way in the back. I took my time getting back to my room, hopeful that my housemates wouldn't roam out of their rooms to see what was going on.

I trusted them because they were my teammates, but sometimes they had guests, and I didn't want it to get around campus that Riley was in my bedroom. I knew for a fact that if Ford was here, he'd make mention of it, because he didn't always think clearly with whiskey in his system.

I unscrewed the lid to the Gatorade, took a swig of it so it wasn't so full at the top, and opened the bedroom door. I stilled. The bottle of Gatorade nearly slipped out of my hand.

Riley was no longer in my bathroom, and her clothes were strewn all over the floor. The see-through top she teased everyone with was dropped inches from the bathroom door, and her jeans were bundled near the foot of my bed. I swallowed the Gatorade and ran my tongue over my bottom lip before cursing under my breath at her on my bed.

She was in nothing but her panties and one of my T-shirts. Thankfully, her cleavage was covered, but without her tight top on, I saw the true size of her breasts against the thin cotton, and they were a perfect, perky handful. The black lace of her panties peeked out from below as my T-shirt rode up over the curve of her hip, and I had a hard time pulling my eyes away. There was no fucking way I was sleeping in my bed with her looking like that.

Tear-streaked face or not, she was attractive.

And the kiss.

The fucking kiss.

She was dead asleep, chest rising slowly with her eyes shut. I reached over her and stole one of my pillows. I put it on the floor several feet away from her, because with my luck, she'd throw up on my face, and then I'd have to fling myself off a building.

I lay there for too long, listening to her soft breathing. I forced myself to keep my back to her in hopes that I would forget about her presence.

I should have been exhausted. I *was* exhausted, but instead of falling asleep on my makeshift bed on the floor, I opened my phone.

My fingers flew over the screen as I typed *Riley Lennon* into the search bar. The first thing that popped up was Coach and his stats and some other "suggested" searches on Riley that were nothing of interest to me.

Is Riley Lennon single?

How old is Riley Lennon?

How tall is Riley Lennon?

How much does Riley Lennon weigh?

But underneath those was a video with the title, *Riley Lennon's career-ending fall.* I was laser-focused on the video as it opened up on my screen, wondering what it was. When the ice rink came into view, I quickly silenced my phone and listened to make sure she was still sound asleep on my comfortable bed while I was down below on the hard floor.

I was pulled back to the video, mesmerized by the light-blue outfit she wore as she skated across the ice. She made it look effortless. Her hair was pulled into a tight bun, showing off her shimmering cheekbones, and there was a lightness to her that I had yet to see in person.

I felt an undeniable pull to continue watching her as she skated with vicious speed, and when she did a twirl in the air, my lips parted.

According to the captions on the bottom of my screen, it was a *triple-triple*. There was a brief clip of the crowd, and they were just as slack-jawed as I was. We were all in complete awe of Riley. My heart sped up when the camera pulled back to the ice, but it skipped a beat when Riley had landed her *triple-triple*. The pair of skates beneath her toned legs didn't look as steady as before, and she slowed her speed down tremendously, something that was noted from the captions. If I had to guess, Riley was dizzy or light-headed. Her head tipped to the side, and the blue of her tiny outfit swayed around her as she tilted one way and then the other.

My stomach was in my throat, and suddenly, I was watching a horror film instead of some figure skating competition. The battle was all over her face. She squinted and shook her head, but as soon as she took off to do another leap, she crumbled to the ice.

I'd fallen on ice before, and it hurt, even with pads.

Jesus.

Her head slammed against the ice, and my closed fist went up to my mouth in shock because she didn't get up.

There were other videos of her, and by the time I was finished watching her skate in numerous competitions, my eyes burned. I eventually turned on my back and glanced at her asleep on my bed. Her forehead was smooth, and her cheeks were relaxed without that adorable little scowl she always had when talking to me. The pout of her lips was soft with her quiet breathing.

That was the first night I went to bed thinking about something other than hockey, and I was pretty sure it wouldn't be the last.

[14]

I was sore. My eyes moved behind my closed eyelids, and I searched my memories in an attempt to figure out what I'd done to make my muscles ache.

As soon as I opened my eyes, the night came flying back, and I popped up. My tangled hair rushed past my face, and I reached for my head. I had a pounding headache, and my stomach was uneasy. The Bexley U logo on my shirt caught my eye, and I vaguely remembered scrounging through a dresser drawer for something to wear other than my uncomfortable outfit. I didn't have to look down onto the floor at the other human in the room to see where I was, because I knew if I had ended up with anyone, it would have been Aasher.

There was no way he was going to let me leave with anyone else.

My lips rolled as I stared down at his large frame lying perfectly still without any blankets covering his bare chest. The only thing he wore was a pair of comfy-looking lounge shorts with drawstrings outlining a very defined bulge against charcoal-colored fabric.

The night was a vague memory, and my eyes felt puffy against my shaky fingers. *Shit, I cried last night.* Mortification burned my cheeks, and I quickly crawled over his bed and scooped up my clothes, being as quiet as possible.

I was doing the ol' dash-and-pass that Mya and I used to do our freshman year before I'd started dating Gray. Except, this time, I was leaving with my dignity intact.

If anyone caught me leaving the hockey players' apartment looking like *this*, it would be bad. I was sneaking out of one of my father's player's rooms with his shirt on and my hair a mess. *God.*

I stole some toothpaste out of Aasher's bathroom and used my finger to brush my teeth. I used the leftover Gatorade to erase the gross taste out of my mouth, but I was still a wreck. I tiptoed out of the bathroom and grabbed the doorknob, thankful he hadn't woken up.

"Nope."

I jumped and flung around, slamming my back against Aasher's closed door. He jumped up from the floor, and it only took seconds until his weighty air surrounded me. "Do not go out there dressed like that."

His raspy growl pulled my mouth closed. I swallowed and pressed further onto the door, wishing I could somehow push myself through it.

Per usual, being this close to Aasher made me feel things I wasn't used to, so I tilted my chin and acted like I had the upper hand in the situation, even though we both knew I didn't. "Afraid it'll get back to your coach, and he'll think you did more than shove me into a pantry and kiss me?"

Aasher's entire face hardened, and I regretted bringing

up the kiss. *I should have pretended it didn't happen.* But it did, and I remembered very clearly how it felt to be kissed by him.

"Why did you transfer to Bexley U?"

I swallowed the taste of his minty toothpaste, and my cool breaths came out like crashing waves against a tide. One of Aasher's hands gripped my chin, and he forced me to look at him. I didn't like what I saw staring back at me. His mossy eyes caressed every curve of my face, as if he were trying to figure out an equation, and I prayed that he didn't figure me out.

"It's none of your business," I whispered, trying to turn away so he would stop looking at me.

He gripped my chin tighter and kept me in place. "If you're on the figure skating team, why haven't I seen you skate?"

The room cracked like we were in a glass house. *Of course he heard the conversation between Gianna and me.*

"Why do you just stand there late at night and stare at the rink instead of skating?"

My chin wobbled, but I tried to act angry. "I'm leaving."

I attempted to pull away, but he shook his head at me and kept a hold of my chin. "Not dressed like that." He dropped his hand from my face, but it fell to the hem of his T-shirt. He fingered the threads and tugged on it gently while raising his eyebrow.

"Fine," I said, pushing on his chest. I walked over to his bed and spun around in a fury of desperate anger, hating that he was trying to uncover shit that wasn't his concern. I wanted to get back at him, so I smirked before ripping his shirt off my body. His jaw slacked with surprise.

"God damn it, Riley!" he cursed. "You're such a brat."

He put his back to me quickly, and I peeled my eyes away from his flickering muscles. After I was fully dressed in my clothes from the night before, I dropped his T-shirt at his feet and waited for him to move out of my way.

I jumped when he snapped to attention. I braced myself for the battle we were about to find ourselves in, but I knew my armor wasn't nearly as tough as it should have been.

"Is it because you fell?"

My blood turned to ice, and the air through my nose was just as cold. I opened my mouth, but nothing came out. *How does he know about the fall?* I mean, the figure skating community knew about it, and students at Rosewood did too. But Aasher? The guy who thought of hockey and nothing else except for the occasional puck bunny?

"Is that why you're here?" He leaned his shoulder against the door and waited for me to answer.

I took a step back and shut my eyes, frustrated that they were growing blurry.

Keep it together.

I could count on one hand the number of times I'd cried since my fall, but leave it to Aasher Matthews to push me over the edge and make me bend with one little question.

"It's none—"

"Of my business. I know. But I'm still asking." His voice was softer than before. A shaky breath left me, and when I felt his touch on the side of my face, I nearly cracked.

I preferred his crass attitude toward me over this.

He pushed my hair behind my ear, and I hated how comforting the action was. Aasher was the last person I'd ever expect to make me feel comforted. Aasher Matthews was strength wrapped in a hockey jersey, and I was supposed to be repulsed by him and his annoying need to watch my every move. I was supposed to be repulsed by all hockey players, especially after knowing what they truly thought of me.

"It's only fair I know," he pressed.

I opened my eyes and was ready to argue, but his intense stare threw me off as he rattled off more questions.

"Why did you fall? Were you sick?"

It was in our human nature to assume things. To judge. And although Aasher was warm in all the right places, one wrong assumption and I'd freeze him out, and then we'd be right back to our exhausting sparring in the fickle war we kept clashing in.

"Were you hungover? That would explain why your dad told me to look out for you at parties. Were you a party girl?"

Anger skimmed the surface, and I wanted him to stop assuming things.

"Why do you care?" I asked, trying to get around him to leave his room.

He grabbed my hand as I tried to leave. "Who said I do?"

"Let me go." My voice quivered, and I wanted to rip my hair out.

Aasher's hand disappeared, and he took half a step back. I should have bolted for the door, but something stopped me. It wasn't that I wanted to tell him, but I wanted the assumptions to stop. I wanted everyone to stop asking me when I was getting back on the ice and what led to the potential end of my career before it even started.

"I can easily figure it out, Duster. But I'm asking you."

I snapped. Something hot bubbled in my chest, and my mouth was moving before I could stop it. "You know what, if everyone would just back the fuck off, maybe I wouldn't be so concerned about being a perfectionist and just get back on the ice!"

Aasher's eyes widened, but he recovered quickly, smoothing out his features and staying ramrod still against the door, blocking my escape.

"So, you're a perfectionist," he repeated, shrugging. "Me too."

I rolled my eyes. It went so much further than just being a perfectionist.

Aasher bit his lip as he studied me. When it popped out from being trapped beneath his teeth, he crossed his arms and poked me some more. "So you fell because you were a perfectionist? That doesn't make sense." He crept closer, but I didn't move. I wouldn't let him intimidate me into telling him all my secrets. "Did something happen to you? That made you fall? Was it your ex?"

Stop.

"Did something happen at a party? Sully obviously wanted you drunk, and I can only assume he had a reason. He's trying to win that bet after all."

My limbs shook. *Why does he keep pushing?*

Aasher pushed off the door and walked over to his dresser. "Did you and your boyfriend have a bad fight that day?" I refused to look him in the eye. Instead, I stared at the shirt in his hand and decided it was about to become a noose if he didn't stop assuming things that were outlandish.

I attempted to shift the conversation elsewhere because the more he poked, the tighter my chest became. "How do you know about my fall?"

"Did someone do something to you?"

"Stop it," I barked, stomping my foot. "Why do you even care?"

I wanted to leave his room, yet my feet remained unmoving.

Aasher rolled his eyes before pulling his shirt on. *Thank you.* I was getting pretty sick of his stupid abs moving right along with his annoying accusations.

"I don't care, but you were the one who was crying in my bathroom last night. You said you weren't okay, and I'm just trying to help."

"Or you're trying to weasel yourself into my pants by getting me to trust you," I mumbled, crossing my arms.

"What was that?" Aasher stopped mid-movement. He was stripping the sheets off his bed because God forbid my scent be on them.

"Nothing. I'm leaving," I said, sighing. He pissed me off, but he *did* take care of me last night, so I attempted to wave a white flag, too exhausted to keep arguing. "Thanks for..."

"Carrying you home, helping you while you threw up in my bathroom, letting you sleep on my bed, and not calling your dad the second you stripped off that leather jacket and showed your tits to a house full of horny jocks?" He scoffed. "No problem, Duster."

I gritted my teeth and turned around. I was fully prepared to put our sparring to rest, but then he flung another insult at me.

"Don't come to any more parties if you're just going to get wasted and make stupid choices. I'm not always going to be there to save you."

"Save me?" My heartbeats were like punches against my ribs. I breathed out like a dragon, and I wished fire came out of my mouth so I could burn Aasher in his spot. "I do *not* need saving."

He was winning our game, and I hated him for it. The next thing he said pushed me off the ledge. "Oh, and if I wanted to weasel myself into your pants, I could. You're just not my type."

I froze when the realization came to light. "It was you."

Unbelievable.

"You were the one who said cold and detached wasn't your type in the locker room that day while the rest of the team was scheming to get in my pants."

Why did it bother me knowing it was him?

Aasher's sighs were becoming as normal as blinking. He was so composed leaning against his dresser while I was sweating from anger.

"Fine," I snapped. "You want to know why my dad is so protective over me?"

"I actually want to know why someone as talented as you can't seem to take a blade to the ice even when she thinks no one is watching, but sure, I'll take that explanation too, considering I'm the one who has to deal with your behavior."

My anger was fiery, but instead of burning Aasher, I burned myself. "I wasn't some slutty party girl like you're assuming, and it has nothing to do with Gray. I didn't put *that* much stock in a stupid hockey player to give him the ammunition to turn me into this! It started years before I even met him!" I threw my hands up, and I knew I was acting crazy. My voice was shaky in all the wrong places, and by the look on Aasher's face, he thought I was acting crazy too.

"Turn you into what?" he finally asked.

"A failure."

I cracked. I was tight all over. My shoulders bunched, and my arms went around my unsettled stomach. "I can't even step foot on the ice without panicking."

The warmth of Aasher's body surrounded me, but I

wouldn't look at him because I was afraid to see what was on his face. I was afraid he'd assume something else, or worse, feel sorry for me. "You're not a failure because of one fall. Do you know how many times I've fallen on the ice? You just have to get back up."

He said it like it was easy, and his presumptions of the simplicity of my fall egged me on until I was stepping on his toes and peering up at his stern face. "You don't get it."

"Then explain it to me," he said matter-of-factly. His arms brushed mine as he crossed them over his chest, and when I looked away, I saw our reflection in the bathroom mirror. We were head-to-head. Toe-to-toe. He was towering over me with his dark features and arrogance, but he was about to rethink every thought he had ever had about me.

"It wasn't just a simple fall. I didn't trip or slip on the ice." I looked away, unable to fathom what his expression was going to show. "I fell because I hadn't eaten a full meal in weeks and was so malnourished that I fainted. Sleep was nonexistent, and I worked my body so hard that my muscles were too weak to hold me up."

Aasher's arms dropped abruptly, and he took a step away from me. It wasn't the reaction most people gave, but I kept going.

"I developed an eating disorder because I thought the thinner I was, the lighter I would be on the ice. I lost sleep because I spent so much time in the rink, perfecting my twists." My lip trembled, and my throat grew tight. "I was out of control, and it was all because I *needed* control. There was an incident with a guy, and it—"

I stopped talking the moment I realized what I was saying. This wasn't part of the careful explanation that I had planned over and over again in my head. I didn't tell people this part. In fact, I didn't tell most people *anything*.

"Don't stop now." His voice was nothing more than a whisper, and I knew if I backed down, he'd never leave it alone.

"A hockey player..." I glanced away, and I wasn't sure if I could keep up my façade, but suddenly, Aasher's finger was on my jaw, and he pushed my face back toward him. His eyes were soft around the edges, and they made me feel safe, despite the fact that I was jaded when it came to guys like him.

"Your ex?"

I shook my head. "It happened in high school. The hockey players and figure skaters shared a rink. They all used to watch me practice after theirs ended."

The hockey team always got first dibs when it came to their practice times. Hockey players took precedence over figure skaters, unfortunately.

"Let me guess. One of them didn't leave?"

For once, someone's assumption was correct.

"Yeah." I turned away, ready to run back to my apartment and away from Aasher because I felt naked in front of him, even though all my clothes were on. "I got over it. I *am* over it. But in the midst of trying to get over it, I formed an unhealthy obsession with being perfect. He took control from me that day, and in order to take it back, I controlled the only thing I could..."

"Being the best at skating."

I nodded.

"I controlled my eating habits—losing weight that I couldn't afford to lose. I stopped sleeping and stayed in the rink after hours to work on turns that Olympian skaters couldn't even hit. I developed terrible coping mechanisms. If I couldn't control what happened to me in that locker room, I *was* going to control what happened on the ice."

It took a long time to get to that conclusion. A year of therapy—a requirement of Dean Chiffon if I wanted to attend Bexley U and join their team, courtesy of my father pulling strings—and we'd finally connected the dots.

Aasher was quiet, and the more time that passed with an ugly truth in between us, the worse I felt. *I can't believe I just told him all of that.*

My face was on fire, and I wanted to run to my apartment and pull my blankets over my head. I rushed into the hallway, leaving Aasher in his room alone to digest everything. My psyche was shaking her head at me for spilling the truth.

My breaths were rapid bullets, and if any of the other guys were in my way, I was going to run right through them, but before I even had a chance to take in my surroundings, a tight grip pulled me backward. I was lifted off my feet and suddenly back in Aasher's bedroom.

"What the hel—"

Words slipped from my tongue when his hand cupped the side of my cheek, pressing it into his chest. Aasher's strong arms wrapped around my body like a blanket, and I felt the warmth all over. My chin trembled, and I squeezed my eyes shut, unsure of what to think. The beating of his heart matched mine. A painful thump every half second.

When his hand crept up my back and his fingers tangled in my hair, keeping my face pressed against his body, I felt something I never expected.

Safe.

And how ironic was it that I felt safe in the arms of a stupid, arrogant, overprotective hockey player that I refused to trust.

[15]

AASHER

"WHAT DID you do to her? Huh? Did you tell her she was fat? Tell her she needed to lose some weight? Is that what you wanted? For her to be skinnier?"

I stepped back toward Principal Larose's office door with my hands hung down by my sides. My coach, Principal Larose, and Savannah's parents were all staring at me like I was the cause of all this. I was in complete disbelief.

"I..." I opened my mouth, stuttering with confusion. "I didn't say any of that. I always told her the opposite."

"So you knew?" Savannah's mom's voice broke at the end, and tears rushed down her face. I can't remember the last time I cried, because, come on, teenage boys didn't cry, and if we did, we were told to lie about it. But shit, I felt a frog as big as a hockey puck in the back of my throat.

"No!" I managed to crack out. "I didn't know, Susan. If I knew, I would have said something."

"How didn't you know?!" Mike's face was red, and my coach stood up beside him because we all sensed the tension in the room. "Your fucking hands were always on her! You had to have felt how she was losing weight."

I'd never felt worse in my entire life than I did at that moment. Was it my fault? I didn't pay enough attention to her. I wasn't a good boyfriend. I knew it, but I never told her that she wasn't good enough or that she was too big. How was I getting blamed for this? And why did I feel guilty?

"You can kiss your scholarship goodbye."

I popped my head up and looked over at Coach who was just as panicked as I was.

"What?" I asked, dumbfounded.

"You think you get to have this successful future when my daughter's is destroyed? She's being shipped away to a facility halfway across the world as we speak."

"Now, come on, Michael. This isn't his fault."

I appreciated my coach's support, but I knew how this was going to go.

He'd be put back in his place within the blink of an eye by Savannah's father because Michael was at the top of the food chain in our small town. If Coach wanted to keep his job, he'd keep his mouth shut.

"I'm sorry," I said, backing farther out of the office. "If I knew how bad it was, I would have said something. I...I thought she had it under control. She told me she was fine."

I left school early that day, and things were never the same when I came back the following week. And technically, I was still paying the price of dating the mayor's daughter, because if I hadn't, I never would have been blamed for ruining her life; I never would have shown up at Bexley U, and I never would have met Riley. Now, my future was being fucked with again by another protective father.

Life was funny that way.

"Bro, focus." A hockey puck slapped against my practice jersey, and I slid around on the ice and glared at Theo.

"You're one to talk!" I shouted. I was frustrated because he was right. I wasn't focused.

Every time I left my apartment, I glanced across the hall. The prying need to knock on the door to see Riley was becoming a nuisance. It wasn't because I wanted to spend time with her or provoke her until she got those red cheeks and turned her pretty lips into a scowl, but more because I felt the need to rectify my own shit by helping her with hers.

It was a toxic thought process.

I knew that I couldn't erase the past and change things that were set in stone.

But there was a jaded part of me that wanted to swoop in and get closer to Riley to protect her or, at the very least, get her back on the ice.

Theo swept up the puck he flung at me. "I'm not unfocused. Did you see the stats of the last game?"

Ford skated over to Theo and me and popped his head in between us. "You're only unfocused when a certain roommate of yours is around."

Theo scoffed in the midst of skating away, flinging up ice in his wake. Ford laughed before we raced toward the glass and headed into the locker room to change. He sneakily looked over his shoulder after he whipped off his mask and leaned into my personal space.

"You're too close," I said, pulling away. "What do you want?"

"Did you and Riley hook up?"

The door almost hit me in the face as we piled through.

"Am I still alive?" *What a stupid question.*

Ford shrugged before pulling off his practice jersey. He scanned the chaos of the locker room before landing on Sully. He turned away at the last second and whispered under his breath. "I saw her leave your room last weekend. I was asleep on the couch. Well, I was until your little yelling match."

"You heard?" I asked.

I pulled on my gray BU long-sleeve shirt and twisted my hat around so it was facing backward. Truthfully, I just needed something to do with my hands because there was a nervous pit in my stomach at the thought of anyone thinking I had hooked up with Riley.

"Yeah, and then it was..."—his voice dropped even lower —"quiet after."

I rolled my eyes before shoving my shit into my bag. "It's not like that. Nothing happened."

"You sure about that? I wouldn't blame you if it did."

"I wouldn't cross that line." Because it would cost me everything.

Sully rushed past us and slipped out of the locker room like he was on a mission. After Riley told me about what had happened to her in high school, I was even more irate about the bet. I was glad she knew about it, and I kind of wanted her to put them in their place too.

"Ford," I said, flexing my fist.

His breath hit the side of my face. "Still right beside you, dude."

"If he touches her, you're gonna have to make sure I don't kill him."

Ford smirked. "But it would be so much fun to bury the body."

I shot him a glare and sighed. The only time Ford was serious was on the ice. Otherwise, the guy was all jokes and stupid grins. We walked out of the locker room together, leaving the rest of the team inside as they talked about tomorrow's night game. They were all about to head to The Bex to catch dinner before hitting the hay. Theo was long gone, and I knew it was because he wanted to get back to Claire.

"Sully isn't going to get far with her. If anyone's touching that girl, it's you."

"It's not funny to make jokes like that." I elbowed him in the ribs.

He gasped, dropping his bag on the ground. "Fuck, that hurt."

"About as much as it'll hurt if her dad finds out anyone touches her. So shut up."

"You're right," he said, pulling himself upright. He made a turn into the stands of the rink instead of heading toward the parking lot. He looked back at me and cracked the grin he used when girls were near so he could catch them in his *honey trap*—his words, not mine. "So you better get down there and intervene."

I skidded to a halt at the sight of Sully leaning against the glass window with his arms lazily crossed against his chest, smiling down at Riley, who was in her usual spot after our practices.

Second row back from the glass, third seat over.

She was a creature of habit.

But so was I, because I waited in the parking lot until she shuffled out of the double doors an hour after every practice with her head hung low and her untouched ice skates draped over her shoulder. I was just thankful she'd stopped walking to the rink alone late at night.

"Look at him trying to weasel himself in there." I seethed under my breath, prowling down the steps with my eyes pinned to him. "He's such an idiot that he can't see that she is playing him too."

"Persistent little thing, isn't he?"

"Hey, Sully," I shouted before erasing the distance between us.

Riley caught my eye but quickly looked away like she'd been doing for the last week. I'd passed her too many times in the hallway and even a few times on the way to class, and every single time, she avoided me. Not that it was unusual, but typically it was more of a sneer instead of an escape.

"Coach is lookin' for you."

"Yeah." Ford backed me up. "Said he needed to talk to you. Not gonna lie, he seemed a little pissy. What did you do?"

"What? Nothing?" Sully looked down at Riley, who was nibbling on her bottom lip. I really wished she'd stop. Didn't she know that was the ultimate *fuck-me* move? I thought for a second. She definitely knew. That was probably why she was doing it.

"I dunno, man." Ford began skipping up the stairs. "Maybe he got wind of some of that locker room talk you're always a part of."

I pressed my lips together to hide a smirk. Ford loved stirring the pot. Sully was in a full-on sweat but played it off well as he reached down and grabbed his bag. "See you later, Ry, and let me know about what we talked about. Yeah?"

"We'll see."

I stayed put, staring at the wisps of dark hair falling from her high bun. Her neck was bundled in a black scarf, but it still showed a sliver of her smooth skin. She purposefully kept her attention elsewhere as she spoke to me for the first time since last weekend. "Locker room talk. You know all about that, don't you?"

I sat down and stared at the ice with Riley, ignoring her insult. "Make any progress?" I asked, jumping in head first. She wasn't aware, but we were done skirting around what had happened in my room the other night, and to be honest, it was as innocent as it could possibly be. I hugged her. That was it. She was likely uncomfortable because of what she told me, but we all had a past. She didn't need to shy away from hers. Mine was just as messy.

She shifted in her seat, ignoring me, but I noticed the way she glanced down at her white skates resting on the floor in between us.

"Are you just gonna pretend like our last conversation didn't happen?"

"What conversation?"

I couldn't help it. I barked out a laugh.

"Has anyone ever told you that you're stubborn?"

Those icy eyes flung over to me, and I swore I felt ice prick my skin. "It's part of my DNA."

Her lip twitched, and I saw it as an opening that I absolutely knew I shouldn't have taken, but there was a loophole that I'd be happy to make a home in.

"I have a proposition for you."

Her eyebrow arched. "No."

There was a playfulness in her refusal, but recent revelations, it only made me try harder. I thought she was just a brat, hating on hockey players because of her loser ex, but it was much more than that.

I gulped as the rink seemed to grow quieter around us. I should have stood up the moment she said no, because *what the hell was I doing?* But instead, I continued balancing on the tightrope. "Let's make our own ice bet."

Riley's eyes narrowed, and she tilted her head. A coil of her wavy hair brushed against her high cheekbone, and I had the urge to move it so I could see her better.

"I bet I can get you back on the ice," I said.

A sarcastic laugh flew in between us, and I inhaled her mint-scented breath. "Is that so?" She rolled her eyes and looked back at the ice. She pulled her knees up to her chin and wrapped her arms around her legs. *She was so...cute.* "You may be the cockiest guy on my father's team."

I stretched my legs out in front of me. "Bullshit. Have you met Theo?"

She said nothing because we both knew Theo's ego was bigger than mine.

Barely. But it was.

A beat of silence later, she placed her feet on the floor and angled herself toward me. "Okay, fine. I'll bite. You want to bet you can get me back on the ice–"

I interrupted her and sat up taller to match her poised posture. "I want to get you back to the talented-as-hell figure skater that you are. Get you ready for...tryouts?"

"How do you know I'm talented?"

"Because I watched your competitions online."

Her mouth gaped. "You truly are a stalker, Aasher."

"I am not. Now continue." I wafted my hand out in between us, and for once, she did as I said.

"What's in it for you? What do *you* get if you somehow coax me back onto the ice?"

Coax? I liked the sound of that.

I cleared my throat and had to think quickly on my feet because this wasn't planned. Though, knowing Riley, she'd assumed this was all the start of some masterful plan to get her closer so I could watch her every move, but it wasn't. I couldn't explain my behavior even if I had a degree in psychology.

I hummed. "I want you to stop fucking with the team and trying to get back at them for their own little ice bet." Her mouth opened to argue, but I put my hand up and stopped her. "Before you say something bratty, I agree that they deserve it, okay?" Our eyes met, and it was as if her tiny hand was around my neck, choking me. "Do you know how many times I've wanted to tell your dad about their scheming?"

"Then why haven't you?"

I wanted to ask her the same thing.

"Because I don't want to be responsible for destroying the team by being a narc. Hockey means more to me than anything, and team dynamic is everything. You have to trust each other to work flawlessly on the ice together, and winning the championship will only increase my chances at joining a decent NHL team."

She sighed, and I felt her breath on my face as she turned away. "And if you don't succeed? If you can't get me back on the ice without having a massive panic attack? Then what?"

I shrugged. "Then you can tell your dad about the bet."

Her teeth sunk into her bottom lip, and I wanted to reach out and free it. Riley Lennon was a mystery, and the more time I spent with her, the more my assumptions about her were incorrect. Maybe she didn't know how hot she looked when she did that.

And would she tell her dad about the bet? Something told me that even though she claimed to hate all hockey players, she wouldn't throw the team under the bus like that. Maybe for her father's sake, but nonetheless.

"How about," she started, bending forward and grabbing her skates, "instead of me telling my dad, I'll make *you* tell him. Wait!" The spark in her blue eyes looked like she'd touched the fucking sun. "You can tell him you were the one to start it too."

Ouch.

I wanted to call her on her bluff, but I didn't, because at the end of the day, it didn't matter. She wouldn't win the bet, because I would.

I stood up beside her, and we were only a breath away. I towered over her with my six-foot-one frame and whispered, "Looks like we have ourselves an *ice bet*." I put my hand out to seal the deal, but the devious grin on her face had me lowering my hand.

"I have a better idea."

My pulse kicked up a notch, and I knowingly stood there and let her take all the control. She slowly pulled out her phone and opened up her camera. The bright light illuminated her deceitful features, showing off the gleam in her eye.

"Sit," she said, pushing me against my chest.

Why am I listening to her?

I sat down, and when she climbed on my lap and straddled me, I stopped breathing. I should have pushed her off or, at the very least, asked her what the hell she was doing, but I didn't. I let her do whatever she wanted.

"Now kiss me to seal our bet."

"Wh—" I stopped myself from asking because I was afraid she'd change her mind. I clamped my mouth shut and put my hands on her hips, holding her steady. She leaned down low, and our lips brushed. I attempted to control the situation when I gripped the back of her head. I thrust my hips up so fast it pulled a breath from her lungs, and I pushed her face to mine.

The kiss started off slow. A peck, really. When she pulled away—after taking a quick picture to use against me, I'm sure—I smirked and moved my hand to the front of her neck, just below her scarf. Her pulse was wild against my fingers. I gripped her a little harder than before, and even in the dark arena, I watched her pupils dilate.

I licked my bottom lip before whispering, "That one was just for the picture. Now this is the real seal to our ice bet...which I *will* win."

I gripped her chin with force and captured her mouth. My tongue slipped inside, and I ate up her sultry gasp, luring her into me. The hand wrapped around her waist moved to her leg, and I pushed it wider, opening her father. Our bodies were flush, and my lips moved against hers like I was starving and she was the only one to feed me. I licked every single part of her mouth until I was satisfied and felt the swell of her lips. Then I pulled back, but I refused to let her go. I took my thumb and swiped it over her bottom lip, wiping my taste away, and said, "Be here Monday evening. Seven sharp."

Riley climbed off my lap quickly and said nothing as I turned and began to climb the steps.

I knew her mouth was feeling ravished—branded, even.

Because so was mine.

[16]

RILEY

My mouth still felt different, even days later. Aasher continued to surprise me every step of the way with his behavior. Our own ice bet? Why did I agree to that? And why the *hell* did I slide onto his lap and make him kiss me to seal our deal?

Aasher was messing with my head, and I didn't think he even knew it. I'd been hyper-focused on tonight, wondering what it would feel like to have the ice beneath my skates again. During class, my leg bounced up and down a million miles a second as I counted the hours between then and now. Everyone stared at me like I was crazy, and a few younger hockey players smirked at me as they looked down to my thumping leg and back to my face.

I ignored them, though, because there was only one hockey player on my mind. He was so certain he'd get me back on the ice that he allowed me to take a picture of our kiss for blackmail.

It was all a ploy, though.

I'd never do something like that, unless severely provoked, but it felt good to have the upper hand for a second before he ambushed my mouth and tricked my body into thinking things that were downright forbidden.

"I see you are punctual." Aasher's voice came from behind me, but I didn't turn around.

I hadn't seen him since we made our bet, but when Sutton and I put their away game against Shadow Valley on the TV and watched them slay against an equally good team, I noticed how my eyes kept following him on the ice.

"And I see you are not," I countered, seeing his shadow move along the stairs before he made it to where I was sitting. He took a seat beside me, and I could tell he had showered after practice, because his clean, inviting scent was even stronger than before. *He smelled good.*

"I had to wait for everyone to leave before I could come back and lock myself in the rink with the coach's daughter."

There was an uptick in my pulse that I blamed on nerves instead of the thought of being locked away with him. *The kiss. It messed me up.*

"I didn't want anyone to get the wrong idea."

I chose to look over at him. I stopped breathing when our eyes clashed. He looked at my mouth before pulling away at the last second. Heat rushed to my cheeks.

"Sully and I have a bad reputation for competing against each other. If he thinks I'm trying to get to you before him, he'll *really* try to score with you."

I crossed my arms over my sweater and sunk back into my normal self, riding the wave of irritation at the mention of the other ice bet. "I can handle him."

Aasher reached over and tugged on a piece of my hair like an eight-year-old. I gasped and shot him a dirty look. His freshly shaven jaw was sharp with authority, and I shut my mouth the moment he opened his. "I know you can, but when I win this bet and get you back to doing triple-triples on the ice, you're not going to talk to a single hockey player again. Right?" His eyebrow crooked upward as he waited for my agreement. "That's part of the bet, Riley. Say it with me."

My scoff was as good as a refusal. His chuckle rubbed against me like ice on my skin. "You are such a brat."

I stood and peered down at his lazy posture on the seat. He was in the very first one, which probably wasn't a coincidence, because it was very clear that Aasher Matthews had a complex that bled confidence. He probably sat there because, in his head, he *was* number one.

"I'm waiting, Riley."

He was so irritating.

I sighed. "Fine."

His eyebrow rose. I rolled my eyes.

"I won't talk to a *Bexley U* hockey player if you win our bet."

Aasher chuckled. "You're too smart for your own good. Just had to add in that Bexley U part, yeah?"

"What's wrong with talking to other hockey players? That's not part of our little agreement."

He stood up and leaned down into my space. "Our ice bet, you mean."

I felt more amped up the longer I talked to him. Aasher had a way of making me feel everything deeper than usual. Irritation? I was ready to explode with insults. Desire? I had to force myself not to go in for another kiss after he let go the other day. "Whatever. Let's just get started."

"Follow me." Aasher slipped past me, but before he got too far, his fingers wrapped themselves beneath mine, separating them from my skates. "No skates."

"No skates?" I repeated, confused.

"No. Skates." He un-pried my fingers, one by one, and placed my skates on the ground.

Then he put his back to me and began walking down the aisle. I chased after him. "How am I ever going to get back to skating if I'm not even using my skates?"

Aasher didn't answer me, which was no surprise. He put his hands on the ledge of the side wall and flung himself over with ease, landing below with a precise thud. Hockey players were probably some of the most able-bodied athletes there were. Their precision on the ice carried over to the steady ground, and I was convinced they could do anything. Being on skates was a skill that had to be honed and most of the hockey players I knew had the dexterity of someone who lived and breathed athleticism and had room for nothing else.

"Come on," Aasher yelled from below, and I quickly rose to my tiptoes, placing my hands on the same wall he had hoisted himself over.

"I am not jumping."

"I'll catch you."

No. "Why can't I just go to the entrance like a normal person?"

He shook his head and adjusted his backward hat. It was really unfair how he looked so good in his black joggers, BU long-sleeve shirt, and hat. He was casual but still insanely attractive. "Because you aren't a normal person. You're Coach Lennon's daughter, and the last thing we need are rumors of how you and I were spotted alone in the rink together after hours."

He had a point.

I puffed up my cheeks and put my hands on the ledge, propping myself up. My muscles woke up, rushing with adrenaline from the thought of being on level ground with the ice. I gritted my teeth as I dragged a leg over the side and then the other. A rush of fear whipped through me as I dangled there with my fingers slipping against the tiny ledge.

"Jump, Duster," Aasher called out from below.

"I can't." The distant memory of my childhood coach flashed before my eyes, barking out an order to do three hundred pendulum exercises for saying the word *can't*.

"You're going to have to trust me if we want this to work. Now let go."

I didn't let go because of Aasher's demand. I let go because if I couldn't fathom a simple jump into his arms, I was never going to get back on the ice. A whoosh of breath left me as I landed in Aasher's arms, and I gripped his shoulders like they were my lifeline.

His hands fit around my hips like a perfect size of jeans —squeezing me in all the right places—and the only thing I thought of was the stupid kiss.

"Good girl," he whispered, breathing down into my space.

There was a flick of something in my lower stomach that was completely uncalled for with his praise. My cheeks were pink, and I wasn't close enough to the ice to blame it on the cool air.

The moment he put me down, I stepped farther away from the opening to the rink, for more reasons than one.

"That wasn't so hard now, was it?" He was smug while he grinned and put his hands in his pockets.

I tightened my scarf around my neck like it was going to hide my vulnerability. "What? Jumping over the ledge?"

He shook his head after adjusting his hat. "No. I was referring to you doing what I asked for once."

My mind went in a completely different direction than he was implying, and my cheeks fired up again. *What the hell is wrong with me?* I began analyzing my thoughts over the way I kept trying to escape the reality of what Aasher and I were doing alone in the ice rink.

I was well-versed in recognizing my defense mechanisms.

Avoidance was my best talent.

The door opened to the rink, and I stared at Aasher's back as he blocked the view. My breathing began to pick up, and I took a step back. He peered over his shoulder at me, showcasing his sturdy jaw and furrowed brow.

"Just opening the door bothers you?"

I made a face before turning away.

"Hey, put the claws away. I'm not poking fun at you. I'm just trying to understand so I can help you."

"What are you?" I snapped. "A therapist?"

I wasn't angry at him. I was angry at myself.

His lips twitched, and annoyance was ticking like a bomb in my chest. There was a self-proclaimed part of me that wanted to storm past him to get on the ice—just to prove a point. But I wouldn't.

"Have you always been this sassy? Or is it the fear making you that way?"

"It's you!"

There was a slip in my confidence around him. I was nervous, but it wasn't because I thought I wasn't safe around him. I wasn't sure if it was because he was one of the only hockey players that wasn't doing their best to manipulate me into their bed or if it was because, deep down, I knew he wasn't a bad guy.

"It's me?"

Aasher crept forward, but I refused to back away. My

heart thumped harder with each step he took, and when he was right in front of me, I held my breath. His hand slowly rose, and when it went around the base of my neck and slipped under my scarf, I finally inhaled our shared oxygen. I hated how shaky my breaths were.

"Fuck, Riley." Aasher's thumb brushed against the side of my neck, and chills raced to my flesh. "Your pulse is *this* fast because of me?"

"Don't flatter yourself," I said, panicking that he was right.

His hand stayed on my neck, and before I knew it, I was staring up into his green eyes, getting lost and forgetting where I was. His palm was a salve. I was calmer, but there was still chaos. It just wasn't the same chaos that I had felt moments ago. This was different.

The rink lights flicked off. I jumped and stepped closer to him. We were surrounded by the dark with nothing but the glow of the red exit sign in the distance. "Sorry," I murmured, trying to step away.

He tightened his fingers around my neck just enough to keep me in place. "That's what I was waiting for. Are you ready?"

"For what?" My lazy tone surprised me.

His white teeth looked brighter in the dark when he smiled. "For the first step in getting you ready for tryouts, baby."

My pulse fired up, and I refused to admit that it was partly because he called me baby. He rubbed the pad of his thumb against my skin, right over my pulse. "Relax." His warm breath smelled like mint mixed with ice, and I inhaled before letting out a shaky breath. "Now close your eyes and get ready."

[17]

AASHER

I WAS a confident guy with an ego bigger than the entire ice rink, but I was flying blind with Riley an inch away from me.

The ideas to make her comfortable on the ice were all off the table. If she were any other girl, I could distract her with one brush of my palm against her hip, but she was off-limits, *especially* after knowing how it felt to kiss her. So instead, I had to work in ways that were going to be infinitely harder.

I took a step back and rested my heels on the very edge of the opening, teetering back and forth over the ice. Riley stood unmoving in her tight black leggings and pink sweater. She had on fuzzy boots, and I thought about just picking her up and placing her on the ice, because how on earth would she even know the difference with those things on her feet? But I didn't want to push her too far. Her chest was heaving, and although mine was too—for different reasons—I decided to go easy on her.

"Walk to me." Riley opened her eyes, and the blue color

was deeper than before. Panic filled them, and instead of walking toward me, she stepped backward.

I laughed and threw my hands up. "You just did the complete opposite."

Her hands made a home on her hips. "You think that it's going to be *that* easy to get me back in the rink? By just demanding I get on there? Don't you think I've tried that before?" Her arms flung to her sides in defeat. "I start to... panic."

Typical of her to twist my words.

"I didn't ask you to get back in the rink. I asked you to walk to me."

Her hip jutted out with attitude. "You didn't ask me anything if we're being technical. You demanded."

I smirked, knowing this was never going to work if I continued to rile her up, but it was so fun to watch her cheeks fire with heat. "Oh, I'm sorry. I thought you enjoyed being the submissive one."

Riley's lips parted. She sucked in a breath, surprised by my words. I winked and shot her a playful smile before I walked a little closer to her, closing the gap. "Come on. Close your eyes and take a step."

Riley wanted to refuse. I could tell by the way she looked at me. But in the end, she did as I said and took one teeny-tiny step toward me.

"That was hardly a step, but progress is progress."

Her eyes remained shut, but there was a small smile on her lips. "You sound like my dad."

Good. The more she brought up her father during our time together, the more I could be reminded of who she was.

Silence passed between us, but I could feel the tension surrounding her. It was rare to see her relaxed, which was why it was bizarre to watch her sleep last weekend, but right now she looked as if she were ready for a fight.

Fuck, what can I do to distract her?

"Let's play a game." I rubbed my hands together and dove into the first thing that came to mind. "You tell me two truths and a lie, and if I get it right, you have to take another step toward me."

Riley opened her eyes. "Keep 'em closed, Duster."

"Or what?" she countered, laughing under her breath.

"I can always blindfold you."

She sucked her lips in. I wasn't sure if her head went where mine went, but there was a wicked visual of her on my bed, but instead of sleeping, she was blindfolded and in zero clothing. I got a very quick snippet of her bare chest when she decided to flash me last weekend to prove a point, but it was embedded into my brain. It *absolutely* proved a point.

Shit, stop it.

"Fine, but just a warning, I don't like to lose."

"Well, you won't really be losing if I get you closer to the ice without freaking out, right?"

She knew I was right, so she cleared her throat, leveled her shoulders, and started our little game. "My favorite color is blue. My favorite drink is pumpkin spice. My favorite season is summer."

I laughed. "Too easy, ice princess. Your favorite season is winter. Take a step forward, baby."

I looked behind my shoulder, knowing no one was there, but I still checked to see if anyone just heard me call her baby. *That's a no-go.* It was a habit, but I could only imagine what her dad would say if he heard me call her *baby*—not once, but twice.

She grumbled something under her breath before peeking one eye open and taking the *smallest* step forward.

I put my hands in my pockets to keep me from picking her up around her waist and walking her onto the ice myself. "You peeked."

"I didn't want to trip over something."

I smiled at her lie. "You're impossible."

"I agree. This *is* impossible." Riley turned around and stomped toward the doors. As much as I enjoyed her backside, I flexed my jaw and jogged after her. I gripped her waist and pulled her into my front.

A fleeting breath escaped her lungs when I said, "I wasn't aware that your father bred a quitter."

"I'm not a quitter." The heel of her fuzzy boot landed on my foot, and I grunted, dropping my hands and letting her slip through my fingers.

If only she'd use her anger at me to get back on the ice, then we'd make some *real* progress.

Wait, that's it.

The idea was as bright as her smile the other night when she was busy secretly seducing every hockey player on the team to piss me off.

"Then prove it," I whispered in her ear, grabbing her hips. I inhaled the scent of her shampoo and loathed how much it turned me on. Her fiery attitude toward me was fucking with my head, and everything about her seemed more desirable simply because I knew I couldn't have her.

Riley's back arched, and her ass rubbed against my front. I panicked and dropped my hands like she was a smoking ember. She rounded me, and her eyes burned with so much determination they looked like a blue flame.

I recovered quickly, flicking an eyebrow while lifting my lip. "I'm waiting."

"So this is your plan?" she asked, reaching up and ripping the hair tie out of her hair. Long locks of dark, wavy hair fell around her shoulders, cupping her heart-shaped face. "Bully me onto the ice? You're not going to win this bet after all."

My confidence never wavered, and I didn't feel bad for pushing her to her limits, because I knew, deep down, she was as tough as nails—especially when it came to me. There wasn't a single person I'd ever heard her talk to the way she talked to me. Not even Sully, who she knew was playing her like the strings of a guitar.

I stepped toward her, and Riley stepped backward. We did this all the way until her heels were at the very brim of the opening for the rink. She was so focused on sending me a scathing look that I didn't think she noticed when I dropped my eyes down her legs and eyed the ice behind her.

The rink was blanketed in darkness. The bright lights that were usually caught between the sheen of ice were nonexistent, and if I could just keep up our spar and get her to step backward, the hardest part would be over.

It was the first step that was always the hardest.

The first step.

The first look.

The first touch.

The first kiss...

I continued walking toward her, pretending I wasn't just thinking about the kiss we shared. "I'm not bullying you," I reassured her. "I'm only stating the facts."

"The facts?" Riley was offended. "I am *not* a quitter."

"Says the girl who is one of the best figure skaters of today's time but can't even fathom stepping on the ice."

I insulted her, but it was for the greater good.

Just how angry are you, Riley?

My fingers twitched inside my pockets. I wanted to grab her hand and pull her onto the ice with me and whisper into her ear that she was safe. There was no sense in panicking. She was born for the ice. I knew that without even truly knowing her.

The ice wasn't her problem.

It was everything else.

"You're an asshole," she spat, pushing on my chest and stepping backward.

Riley was trying to escape me so quickly that she didn't realize she was actually in the rink. Hardly, but if she were to look down, she'd see ice.

"You don't really believe that, do you? I'm here helping you get ready for tryouts. I'm the one who has been trying to get you away from the team because I know they don't have your best interest in mind."

"Don't act righteous," she countered, crossing her arms over her pink sweater. "You're doing it for your own selfish needs, and you know it."

I shrugged, acting nonchalant and stepping right up to her. Our chests were touching, but the closer I got to her, the more she'd be distracted. "Maybe. I'm not a bully, though. It may seem like I'm bullying you, but this is the only plan that I won't be killed for."

"What does that mean?" she asked, scrunching her cute nose.

I leaned down to her level and tilted her chin with my finger. "If you were any other girl, I'd do more than creep into your space and offend you. I'd touch every part of you until you were so sweaty you *had* to get on the ice."

Her tongue slipped out of her pouty mouth and misbehaved. It swiped over her plump bottom lip.

I was the one sweating.

Fuck.

"Look down."

"Huh?"

I pulled her face down with my thumb on her chin.

Her gasp was as loud as the snapping of her back. When she stepped away, fully flustered, she slipped. I caught her around the waist before she face-planted, and when her nails dug into the skin of my arm and we both went flying backward, I decided that the risk was totally worth the fall, because she was in my lap, and I enjoyed it.

18

RILEY

Falling was the least of my concerns.

My chest squeezed, and my vision grew blurry. Everything was dark, and I knew that Aasher's hands were around my waist, but with my throat closing, it felt like they were around my neck.

I was desperate for the chilly air to cool my lungs. My hands shook as I tried pushing off Aasher's hard chest to get away, but he pulled me in closer. His fingers got lost in my hair and my face fell into the warm crook of his neck. His scent attempted to calm me as it canceled out the icy-scented mist flying up all around us.

"Breathe," he demanded, pulling on the strands of my hair.

I gasped for air. I was straddling him, but all I could think about was the hard ground against my knees. My thin leggings did nothing to block out the ice through the cotton. From the outside, our position probably looked like something more than it was.

"Riley, you're safe." Aasher's warm breath wafted in between us, and he pulled me in closer. Our bodies were mended together. I made no attempt to move, because truth be told, I did feel safe with him. Much safer in his arms than I did standing on my own a moment ago.

I squeezed my thighs around him when I felt him stand. His fingers dug into the backs of my thighs, skimming the curve of my butt. "Keep your eyes closed, okay?"

The only response he got from me was a gulp, but I made sure to do as he said, comforted by the darkness behind my eyelids. His breathing was steady, and the more I focused on it, the more mine became steady too. "That's it," he reassured. "You're doing great, Ry. Just remember that I'm the only one here with you. No one else is watching you or waiting for some miraculous jump on the ice. All you have to do is breathe. You're safe. You won't fall, and if you do, I'll catch us both."

His words are comforting.

I wanted him to keep going. I *needed* him to keep going. I was beyond frustrated that panicking was the result I got when I tried to skate now. But PTSD had a strange way of tricking your mind into thinking the worst, and there were snippets of falling in front of what felt like a million pairs of eyes, and the trembling in my limbs was something that both Aasher and I noticed.

"Keep going." My voice was a rasp. I blew out a breath of air into the safe part of his neck. The fighting between us was a long-lost thought, and the only thing I was focused on now was how to make the intrusive thoughts disappear. News article headlines were stomping all over the place in my mind, and Gray's breakup reasoning crept in, reminding me that he was the one who broke the last stable part of me. My parents' worried faces after I woke up in the hospital. It was coming at me full swing.

"What do you need me to do? Tell me." Aasher's voice cut through the noise. My heart pounded so hard it hurt. I pulled back and stared at the worry lines on his forehead below his backward hat. It had been so long since I breathed in the fresh air of the rink, and I wanted it to relax me like before instead of spin me into a spiral.

"Get me to relax."

"Tell me how, and I'll do it." His eyes bounced back and forth between mine, and though he usually used his brash, arrogant tone with me full of nothing but snippy remarks and insults, right now he was soft and sincere.

"Treat me like any other girl." I surprised us both.

My body grew tense after I said it, knowing very well that I was crossing a line.

"Wh—what?" Aasher's heavy browline deepened, and his eyes grew hooded when he realized what I meant. "Riley..."

"I can't think of any other way to get through this." I was reaching. "Holding me in your arms and telling me to breathe isn't enough, so just do what you said you'd do if I wasn't your coach's daughter." I was pleading, begging, and it went against every single thing I stood for, but I'd deal with the repercussions of that later.

I needed a solution, and the longer I was surrounded by the cold and my eyes adjusted, the choppier my breaths became.

Aasher eventually sighed. My hands rested against his shoulders as my hair came down like a curtain around us. "Are you sure?" he asked with a tone that stained my cheeks pink.

Gray's face faded from my head when I stared into

Aasher's eyes. I nodded curtly, adjusting myself in his arms. I glanced at the ice and sucked in a breath, closing my eyes.

It was unfair to feel this unsettled.

The rink used to be my happy place, my home. Now, it brought back nothing but an ugliness that I couldn't hide from. I was afraid to fall into the same mindset as before and dip into those coping mechanisms that put me here in the first place.

I held on tight as Aasher walked with me pressed against him. When I felt the glass wall against my back, I slowly pried my eyes open and found him staring at me. "This means nothing," he whispered, taking his hand and dragging it up my leg to rest against my groin. He pushed my leg open farther and crept closer. "You got it? And you tell *no one*."

I nodded. My heart was racing even faster than before, but the more I focused on Aasher's mouth moving, the more I thought about the devilish things it could do instead of the bite of his insult.

Of course it means nothing to him. I'm not his type.

It meant nothing to me either, except for a brief act of saving.

"Wait."

Aasher's lips rolled together as he raised an eyebrow, waiting for me to continue. I couldn't tell if the look in his eye was relief or disappointment. "Second thoughts?"

I shook my head. "I want you to have all the control."

His eyes widened but only for a second. "I don't think you know what you're asking for, Duster."

This entire problem started with me needing to have control. I knew *exactly* what I was asking for. I never let Gray have control in the bedroom, and after a while, he grew sick of being the submissive one. I was too far along to realize why I was so afraid to let someone else have the power. But I understood it now.

"Please, Aasher," I begged. "I know what I need."

He paused before licking his lips. He looked down at the ice before staring right at my mouth. "Fuck it."

One of his hands disappeared, and he held me up with the other one like I was as light as a feather. The brush of my scarf being unraveled from my neck sent chills flying down my arms. I blushed at how needy I felt with Aasher in charge. Instead of fighting to take back control, I was falling into a trap of submission and anticipating what he was going to do next.

"Put your hands in front of you."

I did as he said, putting my hands together. My back pressed harder into the glass behind me, and I was thankful that Aasher kept my legs pinned behind his back as he wrapped the scarf around my wrists, tying them together. "Is this okay?"

I nodded, appreciative that although I was handing the reins over to him, he was still being respectful and going slow. I knew it was because of what I'd told him happened to me, but it was much more than I could say for any other guy that I'd been with.

"Good." His voice dropped low as he moved his hands back to my butt. The warm whisper in my ear was like stepping close to the sun. Sweat threatened to prickle my temples as I inhaled his scent, falling for his words harder than I expected. "Now spread."

I swallowed my tongue as I followed every one of his commands. A breath hitched in my chest as he lazily dragged his finger over my hip and down the crease of my groin, rubbing his knuckle over the seam of my leggings.

How does that feel so good with a layer of clothing in the way?

"You're already wet." His teeth grazed my jaw before he nipped at my earlobe.

Oh my god.

"And it's a fucking turn-on, Riley."

It is?

"It's even hotter because I'm not supposed to be touching you. Who knew that I turned you on this much?"

Aasher's breathing picked up in pace, right along with mine. His hand slowly crept up past my hip and dipped underneath my sweater. He kept his eyes on mine, and I couldn't decide if he was trying to see if I was going to panic or trying to see if I enjoyed it.

I wasn't panicking, because I was too busy anticipating his next move.

I didn't really care if he was a narcissistic hockey player with an ego bigger than the universe, nor did I care that this didn't mean anything serious, because his touches were way too inviting to want to stop.

"It's been a long time," I murmured, trying to blame my arousal on the fact that I hadn't been with anyone since Gray.

I was hyper-focused on his finger trailing up my ribcage and underneath my bra. His palm cupped me, and I arched my back, thrusting my hips into him. He grunted before I felt his hand disappear from under my shirt. His fingers dug into my waist, and he shoved us apart.

My mouth formed a pout—something I could feel before he commented on it.

"Stop pouting. I'm in control, remember? Keep still so I can remember every part of this." His mouth brushed over mine with his reminder. "Because this is the *only* time I will touch you."

Got it.

I nodded, sucking in a shaky breath. I forced myself to stay still against his lips, refusing to kiss him. With every word that left his mouth, I felt the faint sweep of his lips against mine. A quiet whimper crawled out of the depths of my body, and I knew he heard it.

"Breathe in the scent of the rink," he whispered, dragging his finger along the crook of my neck and all the way to the outskirts of my leggings. "Can you smell the ice? Does it feel like home to you too?"

I didn't answer him as I inhaled. Sorrow was distant through the chaos I felt from his teasing touches, but I still recognized it. The rink didn't feel like home to me anymore, and that made me panic.

I stopped breathing when I noticed that Aasher's finger didn't move. He was right at the brink of sinking into my pants, but he leaned back and raised an eyebrow. "Answer me, or I'll stop."

I zeroed in on the faint smirk ghosting his lips when he saw my eyes widen. I rushed out the truth and wiggled in his arms. "It makes me feel homesick. Like I'm home, but not really."

Aasher resumed his exploration and swiped the very top of my panties with his long finger. My stomach was in hot knots, burning hotter and hotter as he touched and whispered things about the ice that I longed for.

The smell.

The temperature.

The feeling of it beneath his feet.

"Do you miss it?" he asked, pausing over my clit. *Is he trying to kill me? Provoke me? Make me beg for it?*

"No," I lied, growing impatient.

His teasing was painful, and I wasn't focused on my nerves, or the ice, or figure skating in general anymore. I was centered on his mouth and how his hand hovered over the spot that throbbed for him.

"Wrong answer." He pulled his hand out of my panties, and I tried to stop him, but my hands were tied.

He smirked. "I'm in control, remember?" His loud swallow echoed around us. "Answer correctly, and maybe I'll reward you. Do you miss the ice?"

"Yes." My answer erupted around us. I stared at his mouth and prayed that he'd put me out of my misery. "I don't feel like myself without skating."

I glanced away, uncomfortable for admitting the truth, but Aasher didn't allow me to succumb. Instead, he pulled all of my negative thoughts into one single focus, and that focus was him. He pushed his finger into me and teased me with long, tediously slow pumps.

I was panting.

My hips moved to meet his hand. I was chasing the rush that he was giving me and forgetting about everything else. There was a ring of fire surrounding us, melting the rink from my sight. His kissable lips were opened slightly as he stared down at me with a lustful gaze that I couldn't bring myself to look away from.

Aasher tore his hand away, and I whimpered at the loss of pleasure. He licked his bottom lip before kissing me. His tongue swept inside as he pulled me closer, kissing me to the point that I was withering in his grasp. The kiss was deep and sensual, and my mind was a mess. I took my tied wrists and pulled them up over his head to trap his face to mine.

I'd never felt so desirable from a single kiss. The way he

lapped at my tongue messed with my emotions to the point that I didn't know who we were.

He moved backward, breaking our kiss. "You're driving me wild." His fingers dug into my sides as he shoved me away. He was hard through his sweats, and it threw me off. "This was such a bad idea."

A gasp escaped my chest when he pushed our bodies together again. His mouth was everywhere. He pressed quick kisses against my jawline, sucking and nibbling until he landed on my earlobe. "Do you want me to keep going? Is it working?"

Oh, right. I'd forgotten how we got here and why he was kissing me.

"Yes." I rasped out a breath. "Don't stop."

Aasher shut his eyes and tilted his head away. It gave me the perfect view of his chiseled jaw. I leaned in and placed a sweet kiss against his thrumming pulse, feeling satisfied for a split second at the feel of his skin against my mouth.

The desire went both ways.

I was totally and irrevocably his at this moment.

When he pulled his attention back to me, something had changed. "It's getting hot in here."

Sweat trickled down the side of his flushed face at the same time it crept against my neck. He followed the little bead with his eye before whisking me away from the glass and placing me down on the ice.

I tensed as he hovered over me. He quickly untangled himself from my arms that were trapping him and pulled at the end of the scarf. It fell swiftly, and Aasher intertwined one of his hands with mine and slowly pushed it over my head and onto the ice.

"Eyes on me."

He knew I was back. He knew I was remembering where we were and why he was touching me.

I nodded shakily.

"Open your legs." Our eyes met, and my stomach hollowed.

Aasher pushed the inner part of my knee, releasing himself from the vise grip I had on him.

"Good girl," he whispered. "Now I'm going to need you to come for me."

His dirty words swept me away. I relished in the burn of the frosted floor as he pulled my leggings down in one quick motion. His rough palm rubbed against my clit as he cupped his fingers inside of me, pushing farther and farther until he hit a spot that my body liked.

Oh my god.

"You like that?" he asked, staring down at me like he wanted to devour me. "That's it," he coaxed, rubbing faster. I moaned, and he cursed under his breath.

"Come for me, baby, and make it good, because I'm the *only* hockey player that gets to see this."

My body betrayed me, and I completely shattered around him, arching my back against the hard, frosted rink. He squeezed my hand tightly, keeping it pinned to the ice. He pumped his finger in and out as I squeezed and whimpered, shutting my eyes to enjoy the way my body came alive.

Aasher pulled his hand away. But instead of releasing me altogether, he cupped my waist and rested his sweaty forehead on my lower belly, inhaling deeply. "I need to burn this from my fucking head."

His tone was a bite to the air, and chills flew to my skin with his hot breath. With the ice beneath my back and his warmth on my front, I felt unraveled. We stayed like that for so long my back started to grow numb, and a chill cracked down my spine.

But it worked.

I was on the ice.

Aasher eventually pulled me to my feet and made sure my leggings were back in place. I looked down and knew that standing on the ice was nothing compared to putting skates on my feet and landing a triple again, but it was a step in the right direction.

It was too bad he couldn't touch me like this all the time.

We stayed silent as he pulled me off the ice. We walked slowly, and my chest grew tight as I slid beside him. When the door shut, he pulled me into his chest. His thumb gently tugged at my chin, and his finger swept across my lips.

"Not a word, Duster. If you tell anyone..." He looked away, full of guilt. "Be here tomorrow night, seven sharp." He put distance between us and walked away. With his back to me, I still heard the sharp warning. "*And wear a fucking chastity belt.*"

19

AASHER

> Dad: Keep your head in the game this
> weekend. I know it'll be tough because of
> who they are, but we've raised you right.

I leaned against the glass and typed several different varia-
tions of messages to my father but ended up clicking my
phone off instead. I'd already managed to text Savannah
back, and that was enough to get my blood flowing with
dread.

Hockey was comforting to me, but when you were
forced to play against your ex-girlfriend's brother who chose
to believe a lie instead of the truth, it didn't feel so
comforting after all.

"Sorry I'm late." Riley clambered down the dark hall
toward the ice. Her dark hair was down, and I thought of
nothing but wrapping my fingers in it again and swallowing
her sweet little gasps.

I was ruined.

We needed to have a five-foot perimeter around us at all times after last night.

I cleared my throat and pushed off the wall to the rink. I gripped my bag and slung it over my shoulder. The lights were still gleaming above the glistening ice, and after we crossed the line last night, I wasn't tempting fate again.

The lights were staying on, and a barrier as strong as the Great Wall of China was going to be built between us. *How dare she ask me to treat her like any other girl when we both knew she wasn't, and fuck me for agreeing.*

"Did you bring them?"

Riley's baby blues popped up, so innocent looking, but after knowing what her pussy could do, I knew she wasn't as innocent as everyone assumed. "Yeah." She held up her bag. "That's why I'm late. I had to run back home to grab them." She looked at the books in my hands. "Why do I need my schoolwork?"

"Well..." I turned around and put my back to her. The door to the rink opened up, and her tiny gulp had me turning and looking at her over my shoulder. "We're going to get you comfortable on the ice."

"More comfortable than last night?" She giggled.

My blood sang at the same time my shoulders tensed. I was on edge, and it truly had nothing to do with her and everything to do with the upcoming game on Friday. "You're breaking the promise you made me."

"What promise?"

My tone sliced through the chilly air. "You promised not to speak of last night—*ever*." I slipped my attention to her legs. She wore jeans. *Good.* "And where is your chastity belt?"

Riley snorted, and her smile was infectious. *She was so damn pretty when she smiled.* She hid it from me nine out of ten times. If I was lucky, I could catch a smile when she was with Sutton or whenever she was fucking with the team to get back at them, but right now, she was smiling at me.

I hated myself for liking it.

Her hand crept to the bottom of her black sweater, and she pulled it up.

I couldn't hold back my laughter. *She thinks she's hilarious.*

"Is this good enough for you, Dad?"

Dad. That's right, her dad was my coach.

"You think you're funny, huh?" I shook my head, trying to hide my own smile. Her tight jeans fit around her waist to perfection, showing off her long legs, but hanging from the thin black belt was a padlock.

"I *am* funny."

I was fully amused but pretended I wasn't. "Get on the ice."

She stepped backward, and it took everything in me not to storm her, put her over my shoulder and onto the ice. I knew she'd follow, though, because she wasn't a quitter.

"Get on the ice and bring your backpack."

The rink still felt chilly to me, despite being used to the freezing temperature. It was different without my pads and practice jersey on. The long-sleeve shirt I had on didn't quite cut it, but I pulled my beanie down a little farther over my ears and sat on the ice, waiting for my ass to grow numb through my jeans.

"I don't have all night," I shouted, pulling open my backpack.

I was taking easy college courses, but I would still graduate with a degree in management—something my parents thought would be good if playing pro didn't work out or if I got a career-ending injury. At least I would still have one foot in the hockey world and use my degree to manage a team or even the NCAA.

That was what Tom Gardini did, and he was practically a legend—especially to Theo, who was stopping at nothing to get in his good graces.

"Fi–fine."

I smirked. Riley's shoe popped into my peripheral vision, and her tiny steps into the rink were that of a toddler beginning to walk for the first time.

"My eleven-month-old cousin takes bigger steps than that, Riley. Get on the ice."

"You're such a dick," she muttered, picking up the pace and heading to where I was sitting.

I mumbled, "Not what you were saying last night."

Her gasp was as loud as my chuckle, but when she slipped beside me, I quit laughing altogether. I used my honed reflexes and caught her before she fell. I cursed when her ass landed right on my dick. My book flew to the ice, as if it were making room for her on my lap instead of it.

"Good thing you're wearing that padlock," I whispered, trying to make a joke. But it wasn't funny. All it took was one touch, and I was a goner. I wanted to kiss her again.

Shit.

I shoved her gently and ended up sliding her several feet away on her butt.

She swallowed slowly and breathed out of her nose. "What are we even doing?"

"Taking another baby step." I pulled out two more books from my backpack and rested them in between us, horizontally. Riley furrowed her brow before pushing her dark hair behind her ear. I caught the shine of the little hoops she wore and wondered why the change in earrings. *Trying to look nice?*

"And the books between us...?"

I flipped open my notebook and pulled off the cap of my highlighter with my teeth. I kept it there, paying her no attention as I mumbled, "A barrier."

Her lively laugh echoed around the rink. "Are you kidding me?"

Our eyes met, and her gaping mouth was more of a smile. "When was the last time you laughed while in the rink?"

The apples of her cheeks turned pink. *I thought so.*

I raised an eyebrow. "You have a paper due in your marketing management class, so get to writing. We know how you like to formulate plans. Come up with one to keep your chosen marketing campaign on track."

"How the hell do you kno—"

I held up the book closest to her.

An idea sparked when it blocked her face for a second.

I started to stack my books on top of each other. "Your class is right before mine. I see you walking with Sutton every Wednesday. I also saw Sully and Jasper walking with you two. What did they want? To get you drunk at the next frat party to help their chances at winning their bet?"

I continued to stack my books, blocking her altogether.

"You are such a stalker."

"And you're a tease."

The books between us came clambering down to the ice. One slid to my foot, and the other slid to hers. I reached forward to grab it at the same time she did and grabbed her hand instead.

Tingles raced up my arm at the touch, just like they did last night with my hand between her legs.

"Yep." I pulled the book out of her grasp and began

stacking them again. "A total, fucking tease. Ask anyone on the team. They'll agree."

"I'm *purposefully* teasing them, though. Of course they'd agree."

"After I put those skates on your feet and get your ass back on track for tryouts, you won't be teasing anyone."

I heard her bratty tone through our wall of books but ignored whatever she had to say.

"For the next several days, we're going to do our homework on the ice, eat dinner on the ice, and hell, maybe even sleep on the ice. You're going to get comfortable with it again before we put our skates on. Got it?"

"Yes, *Dad.* I've got it."

"And one more thing." I leaned back and caught her soft gaze. "Stop fucking calling me dad."

Riley rolled her pretty eyes and sucked in her lips to avoid smiling. She put her hand to her forehead and saluted me before going back to her paper.

I did the same.

———

My phone vibrated, and I knew it was my mom this time instead of my dad. If I ignored a text from him, he always made sure my mom sent me one too.

Mom: Your father said he texted you and that you didn't text back. We're here if you need us. Good luck tomorrow night. Wish we could be there.

. . .

I typed a quick response because I knew they'd keep it up if I didn't acknowledge the elephant in the room. I was doing my best to ignore the worry over the game, but I knew that Coach had noticed my distracted mood in practice earlier. He pulled me aside, and for a second, I thought he was going to ask about Riley, but he didn't. He drilled into me and told me to get my shit together. Theo was right behind him to do the same.

They weren't wrong.

I was playing like shit.

Even knowing that Savannah wasn't coming to the game, I was still dreading playing against her brother. He wasn't a better player than me, but his vendetta was just as large as his father's.

"No book wall tonight?"

I sat up a little taller and watched Riley skim over the ice with more confidence than I'd ever seen from her—well, except for when she was knee-deep in booze, winning flip cup against the entire hockey team at the last party.

A thought came to mind, and it was perfect timing. I was too on edge to sit here in the rink with her soft breaths in my ear, looking all pretty and tempting while scribbling in her notebook as I sat a yard away, forcing myself to stop thinking about the face she made when I gave her an orgasm.

"Why are you looking at me like that?" She hesitated, taking a step back. Her brows furrowed, and the slight shimmer on her high cheekbones caught the lights from above.

I pulled out my phone and sent a group text to my roommates, plus Ford because I'd never hear the end of it.

"Follow me, Duster. We're doing something new tonight."

[20]

THE LOCKER ROOM WAS EMPTY, but the lingering scent of athletes and their body wash remained. I glanced at my father's office and saw the light off with the door shut.

"What are we doing in here?" I asked.

Aasher opened his locker and pulled out his practice jersey, along with a face mask and pads. His smirk was a permanent fixture on his face as he walked over to me with confidence. He dropped the gear at my feet.

"We're gonna skate tonight, baby." He winked, and the amount of nerves that filled my stomach was enough to make the blood drain from my face.

I opened my mouth to protest, but Aasher dropped the shoulder pads onto my tiny frame and I stumbled backward. The door opened, and another pair of hands flew to my waist.

"Good thing I was here to catch ya." I turned around to see Berkley holding me steady. "You ready to play?"

"Play?" I spun around and glared at Aasher, but his eyes

were on Berkley's hands around my hips instead of the confusion that was absolutely evident on my face.

Berkley backed away and disappeared when Ford came through the locker room door next, slurping on his milkshake from The Bex. Sutton pushed him out of the way a half-second later, stealing the milkshake from his hand and sucking the last few remnants down. "I hear we're playing hockey."

"No, we're not," I corrected, glaring at Aasher. I knew I looked ridiculous because I was standing there in my skinny jeans with oversized pads draped on my shoulders.

"Wasn't aware you were a quitter." Aasher was in front of me, and the ghost of a knowing smile was the only thing I focused on. I almost stepped on his foot because I was pissed that he was putting me in this position, but I was sort of appreciative too. Aasher knew that the last thing I wanted was to become a spectacle again and to lose my shit on the ice in front of anyone else.

He knew I was nervous, and he was aware that he was pushing me out of my comfort zone. I could tell by the way his hands brushed my hair away from my face gently before pulling the face mask down. Sutton was pulling on the same gear from Ford. She fake-bit his finger when he tried to help her.

"Relax," Aasher whispered, pretending to mess with my mask. His bright-green eyes shifted between mine. "It's just another baby step. No one is asking you to do a quadruple axel out there. This is for fun."

"It's not fun for me."

He tightened my helmet. "Exactly. That's our goal for tonight."

"And how do you even know what a quadruple axel is?"

I tried adjusting the pads on my shoulders after Aasher pulled his practice jersey over my head.

His attention shifted, and I was half tempted to place my hand on his jaw and turn his face to mine like he always did to me, but there were too many eyes.

"Did you...research figure skating terms?"

"So what if I did?"

A tiny smile fell to my mouth.

Aasher rolled his eyes before stalking over to another locker and grabbing some more gear.

I continued to grin all the way to the rink, because it was kind of cute how dedicated he was, but as soon as the skates were dangling in my peripheral, my lips fell, and if there wasn't a mammoth-sized hockey player blocking the exit, I may have turned around and pretended to be sick to get out of this.

"I hear someone needs a goalie."

Emory, the best goalie in the NCAA—something my father bragged about—was standing behind me, blocking my only plan of escape. A petite girl popped out from behind him and began pulling her blonde hair up into a pony. I vaguely remembered her from the party.

"And an extra player for the girls team!"

Emory rolled his shoulders and glared at her. "She wouldn't stay put."

She walked toward me while talking to him. "It was the perfect excuse to leave dinner with our parents."

"Hey! We haven't officially met. I'm Taytum." She smiled at me. "Are you ready to put these guys in their place?"

Her arm wrapped around mine, and she pulled me on light feet. Sutton dipped her head in between Taytum and me and whispered, "I'm not good on the ice. Just a fair warning."

I snorted because, truthfully, I wasn't sure I was either. Not anymore.

"Look at them, already planning and scheming together." Ford scoffed.

All four guys stood there, and their smiles danced with mirth. They each had on their knee pads and skates and were holding out a pair for us to take. Sutton took her pair from Emory because Taytum walked right past her brother as if he didn't exist. Taytum took hers from Ford, and I had no choice but to take mine from Aasher because he pushed me to sit and began lacing them up for me.

"I kind of hate you right now," I said between tight teeth, hoping he could see the irritation through the overly big mask on my face. "I'm not ready."

He didn't even look up. "You are ready, and you don't hate me." My ankle jerked when he tied my skates even tighter. "You know this will be good for you."

I sighed, and he glanced up, showing off his smooth features and sincerity. "I'm gonna win our bet, and I'm gonna cheer you on from the stands when you're back in action." He winked, and my stomach flipped.

"Listen up." Ford was on the ice, skating circles swiftly and without any difficulty. "This is totally going against our pregame rituals."

"Here we go," Taytum mumbled, stepping onto the ice. It took her a few seconds, but she was skating around just as swiftly as Ford. "Your *stupid* pregame rituals."

Berkley climbed on next, right after Sutton. "It's in our DNA. We're hockey players."

Emory shook his head like he didn't agree. He had on more gear than the rest of us, but that made sense because pucks were usually flying at his face. Being a goalie was tough, but it suited him. He was the rugged one of the team, and I knew for a fact that he had a temper, because my dad had to clean up several of his "messes."

"Here's what I propose." Ford said.

"A bet?" I snarked, unable to help myself. "Should I call the rest of the team? We all know how they like to make silly ice bets." I smirked as I threw the dig out into the open space, and truthfully, I had no idea who was aware of the bet and who wasn't, but if they were, they now had an inkling that I knew.

Aasher growled from behind me and put his hands on my hips, shoving me onto the ice. "Knock it off."

"Wait, what? An ice bet?" Taytum asked, halting her skating.

Her voice faded when I felt the ice under my skates. A taste of familiarity stained the back of my tongue, and I felt the cold seep into my blood. "Breathe, Riley." Aasher's voice came from close by, and his skates appeared in my vision. I waited for him to put his hand on my chin and tip my face to his like usual, but he didn't touch me.

"Eyes on me."

I fell for it. I looked right at him, and his lips twitched.

"I knew that would work. Does this part of the rink look familiar to you?"

A rush of adrenaline forced a breath from my tight lungs, and suddenly, I was thinking about what we did several nights ago, because this was the *exact* spot where he made my back arch with his fingers deep inside of me.

"It does to me." He winked, skating past to meet Ford at center ice. "In fact, it's all I can think about."

I was left standing near the opening with a flushed neck and face. He was so good at pushing my buttons.

"Poker? That's what you guys do the night before a game?" Taytum tightened her ponytail before taking a stick from Berkley. He held one out for me, and I took it hesitantly before catching up with their conversation.

"Yeah," I answered for them, holding on tightly to my stick to ground me. I skated—just a little—toward her, pushing back on the anxiety squeezing every muscle in my body. "They're loud and rambunctious too, playing until well after midnight."

"If we win tomorrow night, you girls have to come over and play poker with us instead of going to Rush's for the party. To make up for tonight." Ford wiggled his eyebrows.

Berkley skated to center ice and pointed his stick at us. "And this will become the new pregame ritual?"

"Yes!" Ford snapped his fingers.

"Deal," Taytum said. "Now let's play."

Aasher skated forward as Ford twirled the puck in his hand with a shit-eating grin on his face. "We play half-court. Emory is the goalie." His eyes snapped to me, and I gulped. "Riley and I will do the face-off."

I shook my head, but there was no point. Aasher would get me over there one way or another, and with Sutton and Taytum cheering me on, as if we were truly on our own hockey team, I pushed past anxiety and thought of what he'd said to me.

No one is making you do a quadruple axel.

I had been skating since I was old enough to walk.

The skill didn't just disappear.

It was all a mind game.

I put one skate in front of the other, and although everyone was in their own conversations, shit-talking each other, I knew that Aasher's eyes were stuck to me like glue. I slowly skated over to him, and the slight splitting of his lips was all the encouragement I needed. When we both placed our sticks on the ground, waiting for Ford to drop the puck, he said something that took me by surprise.

"I'm proud of you."

"Wha—"

"And I expect you in the stands tomorrow night. I want you as close to the ice as possible."

[21]

AASHER

I was nervous, and it was obvious.

I stayed quiet through warm-ups and didn't even crack a smile at Ford's jokes. My team was ready to demolish Green University, but they had no idea that one of them had a *big* fucking problem with me.

It was evident the moment Van slid onto the ice.

Savannah's brother's head swiveled until he found me. His arrogance was far heavier than most. He wasn't your typical rival.

"You look worried." Sully skated toward me and started looking into the stands. "What's wrong? Afraid my stats will be better? They were pretty close last game."

Like I cared about his stats during a time like this.

Okay, fine. I did a little bit.

"We're on the same team." My snippy response bit through the air like a snapping turtle, and I was so on edge that I almost bit him while I was at it. "As long as we both do well, there isn't an issue."

Sully hummed. "Something really must be off with you. Are you sleepy from your *game* last night?"

My blood ran cold.

"Excuse me?"

"I heard you were up late...playing with the coach's daughter."

I pulled my glove off, canceling out the sound of the roaring crowd. The lights changed from multicolored to bright, telling us that the game was about to start. "Careful what you say, Graham." I grimaced and tried to reel in my temper. *I needed to be careful too.* "I could get you kicked off this team if I wanted, but I care more about our chances at winning the cup than I do about your infatuation with me. You're a good player, but remember, skill won't keep you afloat forever. We work better together, so get your fucking head in the game."

I was one to talk. If I wasn't thinking about Riley and her sweet laughter last night after she got over the initial shock of being on the ice, then I was thinking about Savannah's little brother and how he had been waiting for this day for a long fucking time.

Sully scoffed. "You could get me kicked off the team? That's unlikely." He pulled his mask down as we headed onto the ice. "And no offense, but *you* need to get your fucking head in the game. What the hell was up with that warm-up?"

He looked past my shoulder. I didn't question the flicker of realization because I didn't have to. The wind of someone skating too closely behind me told me who it was. "Remember me?"

I squeezed my stick and stared into the stands, trying my best to avoid anyone wearing green and black.

"I know who you are," Sully said.

He directed his next sentence to me. "And now, I suddenly know why you're distracted."

He skated away, and it was just Van and me.

"Too much of a pussy to turn around and face me like a man?"

"Not a pussy at all," I said, skating around quickly and flinging ice up in my wake. *Don't let this fuck with you, Aasher.* "It's called being civil. We have a hockey game to play, and I plan to win, despite your obvious attempt to bring personal shit onto the ice."

I learned a long time ago that when players chose to taunt you on the ice, it was because they were fearful about losing. They wanted to get in your head. Sully had done it every single time we played against one another, and it was because he didn't have the confidence he has now on our team. But Van had a different reason for badgering me, and knowing his father, it was probably premeditated.

"I'll never be civil with you."

I laughed sarcastically, keeping my eye on the referee in the middle of the ice, holding the puck steadily in his hands. "Savannah warned me that you'd be like this, and I know she told you to drop it, because the truth is, her issues had nothing to do with me."

"Don't you dare say her name."

I sighed, knowing this game was going to be tougher mentally than it would be physically. I pushed away and got into my position on the ice. I shut my eyes and waited for the horn to blow, trying to calm down. At the last second, I looked up in the stands and saw Riley sitting with Sutton, Taytum, and Theo's roommate. Riley's smile was like the sun—so warm it melted the chill I felt from Van.

At least I had one good thing going for me tonight. I knew the moment I was cross-checked by a player in a green-and-black jersey, I was either going to end up severely injured or in the sin bin for the majority of the game.

I wasn't sure which option was better.

———

"What the fuck is going on?" Coach grabbed me by the mask, pulling me in so closely I could smell the blue Gatorade on his tongue. *Like father, like daughter.* "Tell me right now what you did to them."

"I did nothing." Everything was tight. Even my words.

"Then whose sister did you fuck, Matthews? Because they are all targeting you."

I ignored the question.

"And why the hell are you taking it?" That came from Berkley. He skidded next to me and glanced at Coach. "Can I fuck them up? They're literally targeting him."

They were. I had fallen more in this game than I did collectively last season. Green University players were more like hound dogs at this point. It was so bad that the audience grew quiet after every fall. Whether they felt bad or were waiting for me to explode didn't matter. I was getting eaten alive, and the refs weren't calling them out either.

"No! We play clean. It's part of our reputation. But I need to know what the hell is going on. Right now."

The intermission was almost over, and I could hardly focus. I scanned past Coach's reddening face and stared right at Savannah's father. His arms were crossed over his freshly pressed dress shirt, and the smug smile on his face was a change from the last time I saw him. He was happy I was getting mauled, and the longer I looked at him, the shorter my fuse burned.

Savannah and I were never at odds with one another. It was always her family against me, forcing guilt down my throat until I choked on it. And that was what I was doing right now. *Choking.*

"It's his ex's brother that's causing trouble. He's their captain."

Coach eyed Sully with skepticism.

Theo skated forward. "Explain." The attention was pulled from Sully, and the entire team was waiting. *Fuck me.*

"Number three. Van Klein. He has it out for me. His sister had some issues, and they blame me."

"What kind of issues?"

"None of your fucking business," I spat, glaring at my teammates. "It's personal."

The last thing I wanted Coach to know was that Savannah's parents blamed me for their daughter having an eating disorder. It was too similar to Riley's past, and that was just a little too sticky for me.

"The only thing you guys need to know is that it wasn't my fault. Her parents just wanted someone to blame, and that someone was me."

I wouldn't let Van make me feel guilty for something that wasn't my fault. However, I wasn't going to stoop to his level and ruin *my* future, because that was exactly what he and his father wanted. Michael Klein, mayor of my hometown, crippled my ambitions once. He wouldn't do it again.

"That's why you lost your scholarship to Rosewood, huh?" Coach's usual temper-filled tone came down a notch. *He knew?*

"Sure is," Sully snipped.

Theo glared at the uptick in his voice, but I didn't bother to say anything. I was too concerned with keeping myself steady on the ice and not ending up in the sin bin. Anger was bursting at the seams, but thankfully I had honed the skill to place my anger on the game instead of the players.

Off the ice was a different story.

But on the ice, I knew what to do. That was, if I could stay off my back from the constant cross-checks and shoves.

Coach wrapped his hand around the back of my neck and pulled me down to his level. "Keep your head in the game, Aasher. I trust you, and I know that you can handle their shit. If you're going to retaliate, do it subtly. I don't want you suspended, or I'll be ten times tougher on you than they are right now."

I nodded and rushed onto the ice beside my teammates. I let the cool ice flow into my blood and feed me from the inside out. I thought of everything possible to calm myself down and fought like hell to regain stability, but the truth was, I was spiraling. More cross-checks came my way, and with every elbow thrown, I was spent.

We had four minutes left in the third period. Theo and I were on the line together, and he nodded to Ford, silently working with him to pass the puck. Dax came in from the left, and I skated forward, blocking out the sounds around me, but the moment I made contact with the puck, I flew forward and collided with the ice. The air was knocked out of me, and I clutched my chest.

Words were too hard to fathom or else I would have cursed.

Fuck, that hurt.

"Need a hand?"

It was a voice I didn't recognize, so I didn't take the bait. *Don't do it. Don't do it.* If I retaliated, especially on Van, I could see his father going above and beyond and getting me thrown out of Bexley U. I wouldn't jeopardize my future. I wouldn't fall for it this time. I was older and wiser. That was what happened when someone broke you and you had to build yourself up again.

Coach was on the ice, yelling at the referee. A collective *"Boo!"* from the crowd came roaring in like wildfire, and when I tried to get up on my own, ignoring the green jersey to my left, I was shoved back down to the ice. Another strained puff of air left me, and the Green U player was hauled back and thrown up against the glass. Ford, who *rarely* showed his temper, was foaming at the mouth. There was chaos everywhere, and it made me think of Riley. *Is this what she felt while on the ice?* Out of control of her emotions?

Coach yelled louder. "The entire fucking team needs to be put in the sin bin! Number three needs to be thrown out! At the very least, it's unsportsmanlike conduct! Are your eyes even open? I don't give a shit that we're winning by two! This goes far beyond winning, ref!"

Fuck me.

Everyone was wondering what was going on.

The news would soon start circling, and people would dig into my past.

All it would take is one overzealous news reporter to pull up my hometown paper and see the drama that unfolded after Savannah left school that year. My poor parents were about to be the center of the town gossip again.

I turned to my side as my teammates worked together to pull Ford away from the opposing player. "Ford, don't," I croaked.

"*Aasher!*"

Her sweet, melodic voice cut through the roaring crowd.

Coach was still shouting at the ref, and Green U's coach was attempting to calm his players, but all I heard was her. I was on my knees, forcing breath through my rigid lungs, when I saw her wide eyes from the stands.

"Get up," she demanded.

The two tiny words were magic. I climbed to level skates and gasped for air, ignoring pain I felt from forcing air into my lungs. Everything moved in slow motion as I kept a hold of her stare through the glass. *Look down.*

What?

I looked down at the ice. The blue line was visible, but only because her body wasn't writhing over it like the other night when I had her at my mercy. I slowly brought my attention back to her, and she winked.

Thank you, Duster.

I nodded and shook out my shoulders before skating over to Ford. Half the team was holding him back, one of them being Sully. *Oh look, he's finally showing up for our team.*

"Hey, chill." I rested my gloved hand on the back of his head. "Let's score on them again, and maybe next time, they will worry about winning the game instead of fucking us up on the ice."

"Fucking *you* up," Sully corrected.

We all skated to center ice, waiting for Coach to stop shouting at the ref. The game was almost over, but there was plenty of time to score again.

"What the hell did you do to your ex?"

I glared at Sully, and I couldn't help but swing my eyes to Riley one more time. She was no longer looking at me. Instead, she was staring at her dad with a frown.

The whistle blew, and the moment I looked back at Sully, I knew I was going to regret whatever decided to come out of my mouth. I'd blame it on Savannah for being on my mind and the insults from Van, but later, when I was alone, I would admit that it was because I cared about Riley.

"No more than you and some of our teammates have planned for Riley."

Sully did a double take, but we quickly got back in the game, and this time, not a single Green U player touched me. I didn't let them. Instead, when Theo passed me the puck, I took it straight to their goalie, and if he were to step a hair to the left, it would have cut him with the speed.

[22]

RILEY

"WHAT A FREAKING GAME."

I followed Sutton, Taytum, and Taytum's friend, Claire, down the hallway bustling with every other person in the stands. I typically stayed in the box with Coach's Davis' daughters, coloring in a Barbie coloring book, until the stands cleared, but with Aasher putting me on the spot in front of everyone last night, I opted to sit in the stands—just like he demanded.

To make it clear, though, I didn't do it for him.

I did it for me.

"They were totally targeting Aasher." We followed Sutton into the bathroom.

"They definitely were." I fixed my Bexley U shirt and adjusted it over my torso, staying off to the side while Sutton and Taytum used the bathroom. Claire was staring at her phone screen, grinning. I watched a few girls fix their hair in the mirror, but it did nothing to distract the irrational anger I had behind my nonchalant attitude.

I wanted to rush onto the ice and grab those players and bust their heads in for purposefully attacking Aasher. Questions circulated around the stands as everyone sat back and watched him take every insult, jab, and cross-check. It got to the point that I almost marched down to where my father was to tell him to do something.

I didn't, of course, because what would everyone think if I did that?

"Is Aasher the one that kept getting taken down?"

My lip popped out from behind my teeth, and I stared at the girl reapplying her pink lipstick in the mirror. She puckered her lips, and I held back an eye roll when I read the back of her shirt. It said *Puck Bunny* over the number three.

"Obviously." Sutton didn't even look at her as she washed her hands.

I, however, couldn't seem to look away. She threw her lipstick back into her purse and leaned against the sink, seemingly not caring that other people needed to use it. "Do you girls know him? You go to BU, right?"

"Yes, why?" My response was snippy, and everyone noticed.

"Can you introduce me to him?" *Um, no.*

Taytum snickered, and Claire pulled on her arm, hauling her away. I stayed put against the wall, waiting for Sutton to finish washing her hands.

"No offense"—Sutton turned the water off—"but I highly doubt that he will want anything to do with you if you're wearing the number of the guy who continued to blast him all over the ice."

My jaw hurt from clenching my teeth together. *Who does she think she is? And why am I so irked?*

"Trade me?"

I was struck speechless when she whipped her shirt off. Her boobs spilled out of a black bra.

"Are you that desperate?" I asked. I purposfully ignored looking at myself in the mirror because I knew my cheeks were red, and it had nothing to do with a pair of boobs in my face. "As if we would let him climb into bed with you!"

Sutton laughed loudly. Her hand flew to her mouth, and when I turned back to the girl, she was slowly putting her shirt back on. "Who said anything about a bed?"

I stepped forward, but Sutton's hand fell to my arm. "Well, good luck with that!" she called over her shoulder before dragging us through the bathroom door.

Taytum and Claire popped up from the wall they were resting on.

"What's so funny?" Taytum asked.

Sutton looked back and forth between us and shook her head after letting her laughter die down. "Nothing. Just some crazed puck bunny in there."

What the hell was that? I didn't even act like that with Gray, and there were *tons* of puck bunnies that tried to get his attention—and apparently had succeeded.

"Let's go! We have a poker game to gear up for."

"Poker?" Claire asked, slipping her phone into her pocket.

"Yes, *Little-Miss-Workaholic.* When you were rehearsing in the studio last night after your shift, we were busy playing a little game of hockey with the guys." Taytum paused. "Except for Theo. He wasn't there. I wonder where he was?"

We stepped outside, and Claire was quick to turn away from Taytum. She shrugged. "Beats me."

"Liar," Taytum whispered. "I'll see you tomorrow. Love you!"

Claire didn't deny lying, but she quickly said bye to us, and we watched as she crossed the street and climbed into her car.

Headlights crept around the swarm of fans as I nibbled on my lip. Every green shirt caught my eye, and I kept watching for the player that was harassing Aasher, though I knew that they wouldn't go through the front doors like the fans—unless they had a large ego and liked the attention.

Which most of them did.

Sutton, Taytum, and I lingered over the curb of the sidewalk when people started to rush past us to get back inside.

"What's going on?" Sutton asked.

"Hey." Taytum grabbed on to a girl rushing past us. "Where are you going?"

Her response cut through the pounding of footsteps against pavement. "Aasher Matthews is about to get in a fight."

I turned and put my endurance to the test. I may not have been actively skating, but I still stretched every single night, and it paid off. I was muscular from years in the rink, so I easily pushed through groups of college girls milling around and slipped underneath a few outstretched arms.

My heart sank.

Aasher, with messy damp hair and a flexing jaw, stood in the middle of a crowded hallway with too many sets of eyes pinned to him. There was an older man talking to him, but with the way Aasher's fists were flexing at his sides, it was clear to everyone that he didn't want to be standing there.

The crowd gasped when the man grabbed on to Aasher's T-shirt, bundling the fabric between his fingers. I looked around, bypassing Taytum and Sutton's gaped mouths. *Where is my dad?*

"Where is security?" Sutton asked.

She and Taytum took off, and I assumed it was to find security, but I knew that it would be a long shot. After watching the game unfold and seeing the referees do nothing to rectify the beating that Aasher was getting, I knew that strings had been pulled. I had been in the hockey world for almost as long as I had been in the figure skating world—it was how these things worked.

I slipped between a few guys and went down the opposite hall that I knew wound back to the locker rooms.

An *ooh* from the crowd followed me like a shadow, and when I skidded to a halt in front of the locker room door, Theo walked out with this bag slung over his shoulder. "Lookin' for your dad? He's in his office."

Theo's head whipped in the direction of the rising noise and snapped his attention back to me. "Aasher's in trouble."

He took off in one direction, and I took off in the other.

"Dad!" I shouted, ignoring the starstuck, half-naked hockey players.

"Riley? What the hell are you doing in here with my team undressing?"

His eyes flew to his players, one of them in nothing but a towel, and I definitely got a glimpse of a bare ass.

"Aasher is in trouble. There's an older man, and he's—"

"Shit!"

My dad was hot on my heels, and we both jogged down the hall like the good ol' days when we'd race around the bend in our neighborhood.

"What the hell is going—" Theo's words were cut short.

There was an audible gasp that traveled through the growing crowd like a wave, and I clutched my stomach when I saw Aasher's head snap to the right from the hit.

To everyone's surprise, Aasher righted his footing and

rubbed the blood away from his lip without raising a fist. Aasher either thought he deserved the punch, or he knew that the man was baiting him. I watched everything unfold in complete and utter horror. My father stepped forward, and I went with him, knowing he had a temper when it came to his players.

He was tough on them.

But he had a soft spot for them too. No one messed with his own and got away with it.

"If you ever touch one of my players again, I will get the board involved, and you'll be banned from ever stepping foot in an arena again."

"Dad!" A pretty girl rushed through the crowd, completely out of breath. Her gasps cut through the silence like a knife, and everyone turned to look at her. "What are you doing?!" She slipped right in front of Aasher and pushed her dad away. "You can't just accept it, can you?"

"Savannah, not here." His jaw twitched, and he glared at Aasher over her high ponytail.

"Not here?" she screeched. "You just punched him in front of everyone and don't even get me started on that game! I cannot believe you."

She turned around with owl-like eyes that brimmed with moisture. "I am *so* sorry, Aash. I..." Her mouth was hidden behind her palm. Her watery gaze swung around the crowd and she shook her head.

"It's fine."

I stared at Aasher, and my throat narrowed. I'd never seen someone look so defeated, and it should have surprised me that it bothered me so much, but it didn't.

"It is *not* fine," Savannah snapped, turning to look at Theo and the rest of the team who were shooing away the bystanders. "I knew this would happen. The second I got a text about Van's behavior, I rushed over here."

"They want someone to blame. It's fine."

"It isn't fine." She spun around and headed to follow after her dad.

I pulled back when Aasher reached out and grabbed her hand. I was baffled at the jealousy I felt. *Why is this bothering me?* I wanted to turn away, give him the privacy he deserved.

But I couldn't look away.

"It is. I can be the bad guy."

Savannah looked down at Aasher's hand. I wanted to hate her, but I knew nothing about her. If Aasher didn't hate her, even after her dad attacked him, how could I? "But you're *not* a bad guy."

Aasher let go of her hand. She turned around, and that was when I pulled my eyes away from her. I stood quietly as everyone continued to push the crowd away. His long arms were down by his sides, and his cheeks were flushed with anger or embarrassment, maybe even both.

I stepped up to him, zeroing in on his busted lip. "Are you okay?"

He sighed, turning the rest of the way around, and began heading toward the way I came. "I'm fine." His answer was a brush of cool air in my direction. He wouldn't meet my eye, and though I knew I shouldn't have followed after him, I did anyway.

The locker room was empty when I entered, except for Aasher. He was tucked behind the second row of lockers with his forehead pressed against the silver metal, and his hands flattened on both sides. The gray BU shirt he wore was stretched tightly against his back with little specks of sweat dotting his spine.

"What are you doing here?"

I jumped at the brash tone he used.

When he turned to me, I stared directly at the blood still trickling from his bottom lip. I went into the showers that lingered with steam and grabbed a rag off the shelf, wetting it. When I returned, Aasher was sitting on the bench with his head hung low and his hands resting on the tops of his knees.

"Look up," I whispered, stepping into him. He spread his legs, and his head slowly rose. His high cheekbones were stamped red, and there was an ache in my chest.

My breath quickened when his hands splayed against the backs of my thighs, and he pulled me in closer, angling his head so I could press the rag against his mouth. I wanted to ask what just happened, and I wanted to know who Savannah was. It was only fair after all, since he knew so much about me. But instead of asking, I wiped at his busted mouth and relaxed in the silence that surrounded us. It was just as calming being in a silent locker room with him as it was when we were on the ice, working on college papers with nothing but the buzzing lights above our heads, which was surprising because the last time I was alone with a guy in a locker room, I was left tainted.

Aasher knew my secrets, and he had seen my fears first-hand. Knowing someone's secrets and keeping them close was how you built trust. The fact that I was standing in a deserted locker room with Aasher told me all I needed to know.

I trusted him more than I thought.

"Your lip is split," I whispered, dabbing at his mouth again.

"I don't care."

"Be honest. Are you okay?" My hand shook when he peered up at me.

"I'm fine." He tightened his grip on the backs of my legs, a tell to his lie. Denim separated the pads of his fingers along my skin, but warmth still rushed to the spot he was touching. "It's nothing you need to be concerned about."

"But I am concerned," I whispered, wiping at his mouth once more. The blood seemed to stop.

"Why?" he asked, keeping his face tilted toward me. His green eyes stood out against the flushed color of his skin and richness of his still-damp hair.

I really shouldn't be concerned.

Up until this moment, I swore to never be vulnerable when it came to another hockey player, no matter how genuine they may seem. I swore I'd never fall for another hockey player, either—or trust one. Yet here I was.

It was the way he looked at me with pride when I got onto the ice.

It was the sincere tone he used when he told me he was proud of me.

The warmth that pooled in my lower belly with his approval was something I hadn't felt in years.

Asher pushed away the rag that I tried to use on his lip again. It fell to the bench beside him with a smack. "I could have sworn that you told me you hated me last night. So why are you in here wiping the blood off my face and asking if I'm okay?"

"Because." I looked away, but he pulled me in even closer. A ragged breath squeezed out of my tight chest.

"Eyes on me, Duster."

Heat flooded in between my legs, and I knew he could sense it. My brows folded together, but his words worked into my skin like a scar.

"You don't hate me after all, do you?"

"Maybe I'm just taking care of you because I owe you one. You took care of me after the party, so I'm just repaying you," I lied right through my teeth.

His lip tipped. "You are such a liar. I think you're finally realizing that not all hockey players are assholes."

"Don't get ahead of yourself," I warned, reaching down and grabbing the damp rag again. I used a little more force when I pressed it against his lip this time. "You just got sucker punched by someone's father."

His body stiffened.

"You're right," he whispered, reaching up and putting his hand on top of mine to take the rag. I should have pulled back and let him take control, but I didn't want to. I liked being close to him.

Temptation tugged at my belly, and his stare was unwavering. "You should step away or else I'm going to be punched by two fathers tonight, and I'll actually deserve the one from your dad."

"Why would you deserve it? You've been watching out for me since he asked you to, have attempted to keep the hockey team from making me another notch on their bedpost, and I skated last night. You've found a way to get me to trust you." *That is no small feat.*

Goose bumps covered my arms when Aasher's hand crept from the back of my thigh to the front of my hip. His fingers pressed into me when he stood and the rag dropped to the ground. "Because I touched you, and I shouldn't have."

Snippets of him above me with hooded eyes flashed in my mind. "But that was different. I asked you to and—"

"Don't ask me again."

I swallowed my pride and tried to step away. First, I was

jealous, and now I was wounded because he obviously regretted the other night. But why wouldn't he? It wasn't like he sought me out because he wanted me. He was forced to step into my life because of my dad and now because of his team. Why did I all of a sudden *want* him to want me?

"Stop it."

His hands slipped down to my waist to keep me steady.

"Stop what?"

"Stop looking disappointed at the thought of me not touching you again."

I blinked to hide the truth on my face.

"If I agreed to touch you without knowing how you looked while being pleasured, what makes you think I wouldn't say yes now after watching you come apart from my touch?"

My cheeks burned. The cold metal locker behind my back didn't come close to touching the heat rushing against my skin. I looked at Aasher's mouth, busted lip and all, and wanted him to kiss me in the most desperate way.

"Tell me to let go of you, Riley."

I sucked in a breath, prepared to do just that. But I surprised us both when I said, "No."

[23]

SHE IS SO GODDAMN ALLURING.

Her shiny dark hair that made her blue eyes stand out even more than before, and the light-pink sheen of arousal painted against her cheeks went straight to my dick and jumbled all my thoughts. I was mentally spent, and every muscle in my body ached, but standing in front of Riley, holding her hostage with her gaze set directly on my mouth, like she was begging me to kiss her, threw every thought out the locker room door.

"Riley," I warned.

Walk away. Walk away. Walk away.

I knew I was about to make a mistake, but having her in my hands felt so right, even if we both knew it was wrong. *Especially* me. I never said I was a saint, and after getting manhandled by Savannah's father and having used all my self-control, I had none left to spare for her.

"*Christ,*" I cursed, keeping her steady.

The entire locker room disappeared when my mouth

captured hers. My lip stung, but her sweet, needy mouth was what I desperately craved. The pain disappeared when a sexy little moan vibrated against my mouth. Her hands flew to my wrists, digging her nails into my skin, and I pressed into her further, wanting so much more than she was probably willing to give.

I wanted to claim her.

I wanted to claim her in front of my entire team and tell them I'd break their necks if they continued with their little games.

She jumped up when I cupped her ass. She pressed herself against me, and I held back a groan. I mauled her face, sucking, licking, and nipping her sweet taste. My hands were everywhere, and my kissing was urgent. I knew this couldn't go any further, and I knew I'd regret it the second I was alone again, but for now, I was acting like she was mine.

I dragged my lips against her jawline as she fiddled with the waistband of my sweats. Her shaky hand dipped inside, and I saw red. I flexed my hips, anticipating her warm palm squeezing the life out of me.

"This is so fucking wrong, but I have zero self-control right now." I took hold of her teasing hand and shoved it down farther until she gripped me. I forced out a breath. Riley's devilish tongue slipped out of her mouth, and I went in for the kill until we both froze at the ringing sound of her father's voice shrieking with anger outside the locker room.

"*Shit.*"

Riley slipped down the front of me, and her panic matched mine. Her wide eyes, full of unwavering fear and surprise, told me this wasn't just some sick game that she was playing—because, trust me, the thought did cross my mind once or twice.

"Stay quiet," I demanded, hating that I was shoving a girl like her into a locker.

What the fuck am I doing?

The locker slammed, and her father appeared two seconds later with Ford, Theo, and Emory standing behind him.

Theo was frustrated.

Ford's eyebrow was slanted to his sweaty hairline, and when his eyes moved to the locker, I knew that he knew.

I didn't have a chance to look at Emory, because Coach stepped forward, and I prepared myself for another sucker punch.

It would be so fucking worth it, though.

"I need you to tell me what the hell just happened, son."

Son.

He would not be calling me son if he knew his daughter's warm palm was just wrapped around my dick.

"Aasher." His tone was low, but there wasn't an ounce of anger lingering.

He'd never used that tone with me.

To Riley? Yes.

To his wife? Yes.

To the team? Never.

Especially not if he had any indication that I was lusting over Riley to the point that I was *still* hard, even with an audience.

Clearing my throat, I turned around and leaned against the locker Riley was in. Warm breaths coated the back of my neck, and a shiver worked down my body. "What do you want to know?" I asked, knowing I had to explain everything, even with Riley listening from inside a locker.

"For starters, I want to know how you were able to keep your temper intact. Weeks ago, you nearly put someone through a wall because they talked about my daughter. Today, someone punched you, and you stood there and took it."

Please, God, don't let him look too much into that. I've sinned, and though I'm not sorry, I'm not ready to die.

Emory, with his grumbly, gritty voice, cut through my desperate prayer. "Took a page out of my handbook, huh? Throwing people through walls." He laughed but shut up as soon as Coach glared.

"Why did you let him hit you?"

"Because he thought he deserved it." Theo crossed his arms and leaned back beside me. *Fuck.* Our eyes met, and when he shifted his attention to the locker behind our backs, his eyes widened.

"Deserved it how, exactly?" Coach asked.

The nerves pushed me to spill, because the sooner I answered his question, the sooner he'd leave.

"My high school girlfriend was sent away our senior year because she had a severe eating disorder. I didn't know about it until it was too late, but her parents blamed me. They assumed that I had told her she was fat or not good enough because, truthfully, I was a shitty boyfriend. I didn't treat her with respect, and I blew her off a lot. But I never said anything negative about her appearance. Ever."

I cleared my throat. I *hated* talking about it, and it was even more demeaning to have to explain it to several people —one of them being Riley.

"Her dad lost his shit. Pulled strings and called the dean at Rosewood, which is—"

"How you ended up at Bexley U instead." Coach added.

I nodded. "Savannah's dad is the mayor of my home-town. He's made my parents pariahs, and they were forced to help me pay for Bexley U because my scholarship magically disappeared."

"Wow." Both of Ford's eyebrows rose. Either he forgot that Riley was locked in the locker behind me, or he was baffled at my story.

"That's why they never come to the games. They can't really afford to make the drive."

"What a fucking asshole," Emory mumbled. "And the girl?"

"Savannah?"

He nodded.

"She's fine. She got treatment, and after she was released, she apologized to me and told me she reassured her parents that I had nothing to do with it." I shrugged. "They still want someone to blame. I knew it was going to be a tough game. I knew her brother was coming for me."

Coach stood, and angry lines carved into his reddening face. "That's complete bullshit. There are plenty of fucked-up little shits doing far worse to young girls in high school *and* college for him to come at you and openly assault a player of my team for doing nothing wrong."

I tensed because I knew exactly why he was so fired up.

I tried to lighten the mood. "It's alright, Coach. I probably deserved a punch. He'd been saving that hit for, like, three years."

Coach put his hands on his hips. He looked at me for so long I started to think he knew that Riley was behind me. I watched Ford and Emory out of the corner of my eye, as they threw up hand movements behind his back to move the meeting along. It was apparent to all of my teammates that we weren't alone.

"You didn't deserve to be punched." He shook his head. "I know you are a good guy, Aasher."

My fate is sealed.

If he ever found out that I made his daughter come all over my fingers in the rink, he would retract that statement in a heartbeat, and I would be dead. It would be even worse if he opened the locker behind me and his daughter stepped out with my blood on her mouth because we'd been kissing moments before—and *kissing* was putting it mildly.

"Be ready for practice on Monday," Coach threw over his shoulder. "If we're lucky, we'll make it to the cup and have another chance to pay back Green University for everything they did tonight."

I stayed pressed against the locker even after we all heard the locker room door shut. Theo slowly turned to me, and he would probably kill me if he knew that Riley was a breath away from us, hidden away with swollen lips that I caused. If there was anyone on the team that had more riding on a good season and impressing scouts, it was him. He wouldn't be happy if he knew I was playing with fire and potentially messing everything up.

"Finish fucking your puck bunny and go get some sleep." His hand landed on my shoulder, and he gave it a squeeze. "You deserve it."

I shrugged his hand away. "Uh, thanks. Did you wanna suck my dick too, or...?"

Theo rolled his eyes and stalked off, hauling his bag higher on his shoulder. Emory and Ford turned to me when silence filled the locker room. Ford's shoe squeaked over the floor, and I tried to block him, but he was too fast. His hand sprung forward, and he undid the latch and out barreled Riley, red-faced and sweaty.

"Aw, fuck," Emory mumbled, moving his way around the bench and disappearing. "I saw nothing."

Ford caught Riley by the waist and hoisted her up

before she fell to the floor. "And what exactly were you two doing before we came in here?"

He knew exactly what we were doing, but Riley attempted to lie anyway.

"I was just making sure he was okay."

"With what? Your mouth?" he asked, taking her by the shoulders and directing her to the mirrors. My blood was on her lip, and she hurriedly wiped it off.

What was I thinking?

It was very clear that I couldn't be trusted.

Not tonight, anyway.

"I need to go." I grabbed my bag and rushed through the door.

That night in the living room, her sweet laugh was the only thing I could hear over the shuffling of cards and clanking of poker chips. I wanted to be the one making her laugh.

I was in timeout, though.

I stayed locked in my room because now that I knew Riley was just as tempted as I was, we both needed some space.

[24]

THE RINK WAS EMPTY. Just like it had been for several nights. I had been doing *just* fine with the sting of disappointment from Aasher not showing up. Maybe it was all part of his plan—forcing me onto the ice without his help. Or maybe he didn't trust himself around me anymore.

I could say the same.

I should have listened to him when he told me to back away. But I didn't, and now I was forced to live with the consequences. I secretly hoped that I'd catch him in the hallway or run into him on campus after my marketing class, but he was nowhere to be found. I even stooped so low to act interested in Sully's attempt to squeeze his way into my pants by acting righteous, but it didn't bait Aasher like I thought it would. Instead, it just made me feel desperate and stupid.

I replayed the conversation that I was forced to listen to while stuffed in a locker. It only proved what I already knew about him. Taking a hit from his ex-girlfriend's father, years after their breakup, because he thought he deserved it for being a shitty boyfriend was a pretty honorable thing to do.

But it was painfully obvious that there were some similarities between his ex and myself. I couldn't help but wonder if Aasher was trying to make up for his past by helping me, and I understood why he was so adamant that I stay away from the team. His future had been messed with before, and his goals—along with his parents' bank account —were the casualties. It was something he was *still* paying for, whether he deserved it or not.

He had a second chance at securing his future. No hockey player was picked in the first draft after having a shitty season, and especially not if he seemed disloyal to his teammates. Word of mouth was everything. He couldn't tell my father about the bet, even if he wanted to, because the team would suffer, and then his future wouldn't be set in stone.

Who was I to think that Aasher would screw up his future and his relationship with his coach for me?

I was angry that I thought his kisses were something more than attraction. It was hard to fault his need to put necessary distance between us so he didn't screw everything up.

His future meant everything to him.

My future meant everything to me.

We were alike in that aspect.

"Have you thought any more about what I said?"

I jumped at the sound of Sully's voice echoing down the arena. It bounced off the glass, and I spun around, putting my hand on my chest. "Jeez. Make a noise next time!"

I wasn't afraid of Sully. He was a dick, but he didn't scare me.

"I did. By talking." He chuckled and hopped down the steps on light feet.

I saw the jersey in his hand and pushed Aasher out of my head, because even if he was avoiding me, he wouldn't be happy with this.

It had nothing to do with Aasher, though, and it wasn't like I was spreading my legs for Sully. I wasn't doing it for him to gain points for their ridiculous point system either—something I would make sure to let him know because I didn't have time for their games. Making them pay didn't seem as appealing anymore.

I stretched out my hand to grip the Rosewood jersey Sully was handing to me. "You know Gray is going to lose it, right?"

Sully didn't let go when I grabbed on to the fabric. Instead, he crept his hand closer to mine and brushed my fingers with his.

He waited for a reaction, but there was none.

His touch did nothing but annoy me.

"Are you trying to score some points?" I asked, arching my eyebrow.

"What?" His grin wavered. "With you? Always."

I snatched the jersey and shoved it into my bag. "I hope this isn't your attempt at a bargain, Graham." I used his first name to really gain his attention. "Wearing your jersey to the Rosewood game doesn't mean I'll sleep with you."

His jaw slacked. I crossed my arms and popped out my hip. I knew he was going to lie, so I made sure to beat him to the punch. "I know about the bet. I've known the whole time."

I put my back to him and sat down to lace up my skates.

Maybe tonight will be the night I climb onto the ice by myself.

He remained quiet, and when I finally glanced at him, he looked caught.

"Are you going to tell your dad?"

I shrugged. "Should I?"

He moved to rest against the glass and pulled his hood up. His sweet-and-innocent act was gone. Instead, it was the Sully I briefly got glimpses of while attending Rosewood. He was that same smug college guy that started a bet with his teammates over who could sleep with me first.

"Aasher told you, didn't he?"

I played stupid. "Aasher? He wasn't in on the ice bet that you started."

Sully looked like he was thinking over something, but I didn't pay him too much mind as I finished lacing my skates. I wiggled my toes, happy with how tight they were. He finally broke the silence.

"You've been playing us this entire time, haven't you? That night at the party? When Aasher made you leave? You both have known this whole fucking time." He scoffed with humor, but I sensed the discomfort.

I stood and grinned. "You shouldn't underestimate me, Graham."

"You really shouldn't."

I snapped my head to the right, and my lungs deflated. Aasher stood at the top of the stairs, wearing the same hoodie that Sully had on, except Aasher looked ten times more dangerous and a million times hotter.

Sully pushed off the glass and stared at Aasher as he walked down each step slowly. His stride was confident, and I smelled his arrogance like a shark sniffing out blood.

"Everything suddenly makes sense now," Sully said, shaking his head.

I sensed the tension well before Aasher reached us. It

was hard to look at him. My cheeks burned, and I quickly put my back to both of them and walked down the aisle. When I made it to the hall leading to the ice, I paused to listen to their arguing.

"You've been keeping your own score, haven't you?" I recognized Sully's sarcastic laugh, and the thought of Aasher participating in their bet was the push I needed to scramble onto the ice. *Alone.*

Aasher didn't answer him. Instead, he said, "Can you make yourself disappear please?"

I smiled at the smooth way he'd said it.

Sully was unsettled. It was clear in his desperate attempt to goad Aasher, but Aasher seemed as cool as a cucumber. I looked through the glass and met his eye. He was sitting in the seat that I sat in, leaning back with his arms crossed over his chest, with a smooth face, free of any emotions.

"You're off the hook, Sully. No one is going to run to Coach and tell him what a disrespectful ass you are unless I find out that you or anyone else on this team has touched her. Then all bets are off." Aasher dropped his eyes to mine. *"All of them."*

I gulped before spinning on the ice and blocking him out. There was something so incredibly hot about his threat. I also realized that there was something seriously wrong with me, because up until now, I had been trying to soothe the sting of him avoiding me.

I pushed off the wall and slid forward, picking up speed the more I tried to push Aasher out of my head. Instead of thinking about his mouth moving against mine and how it felt like the start of something dangerous, I thought of how he told me that it meant nothing. Instead of finding a serenity in his calm breathing while we studied on the ice, I remembered how he made sure there were several feet in between us at all times. Instead of brimming with heat when he hoisted me up and pressed me against his locker to swallow my kiss, I recalled how it felt to be shoved aside like it was a mistake.

Damn it.

It bothered me.

I hated that it bothered me.

All of a sudden, I was flying in the air, spinning and in the midst of a triple lutz—my go-to move. When Aasher's arm wrapped around my waist to steady me as I landed, I gasped with surprise. He tightened his grip before I fell forward from the momentum, and I froze. My lungs screamed, and my muscles tightened. *Holy shit.* I whipped my head up to him, wide-eyed and confused.

Aasher smiled, showing me his perfect white teeth. "Good girl," he said, dropping his hands and stepping away. "Now go do it again."

"I..." Confusion left me speechless.

I looked back at the marks my skates left over the ice and then down to my feet. My eyes blurred, and I blinked back the moisture. "But—"

"No buts. Do it again."

I spun with my chest still heaving. We were alone. Sully was no longer standing behind the glass, and I had been too busy skating, lost in my own world that seemed to revolve around Aasher, to know if he'd left on his own or if Aasher had said something else to make him leave.

"Go, Riley," Aasher urged.

"Or what?" I asked, hearing a bite in my tone.

I was feeling more confident than ever, standing here on the ice, looking at him like I actually had the upper hand.

I did it. I felt so much satisfaction that I wanted to cry.

My eyes welled, but I pulled it together.

Aasher's Adam's apple bobbed up and down before he shook his head. "Don't tempt me, Riley." He turned and walked off the ice.

The disappointment was enough to push me further. I skated away quickly and couldn't believe my ability to glide over the ice without my chest constricting.

I blew out a shaky breath and shoved him out of my head. I spun when I heard the clink of a blade against the ice. Aasher skated over to me, and the arching of his eyebrow was a challenge like no other. "Show me what you've got."

"I thought you left." I looked at his black skates and pretended I wasn't pleased that he'd stuck around.

"Nope." He skated to center ice. "I was just putting these on in case you kept tempting me."

"I'm not tempting you to do anything. No one invited you here tonight."

"You tempt me by breathing," he said. "Now do it again before I throw you in the sin bin."

I sucked in a smile. "You'd have to catch me first."

"Better run, then."

[25]

AASHER

I THOUGHT I stayed away long enough to get her out of my system.

Unfortunately, I was wrong.

The moment I saw her alone with Sully, I had only an ounce of control. That control kept me from punching his lights out and then *zip*. I was spent.

There were 800 reasons why I should have continued on my way after removing my hands from her waist. She did it. She skated. She did a triple lutz—something I knew because I studied a diagram of figure skating lingo. The only reason I scrambled onto the ice after I watched Sully leave was because I could tell she was unfocused, and being unfocused on the ice usually resulted in injuries.

But then she smiled at me, and I was too foolish to stay away. I'd been in timeout like a toddler since Friday. I fell asleep that night, listening to her sweet, singsong laugh while she sat in my living room with my friends, playing poker. And every night since, I refused to make myself known while she stood on the ice and contemplated skating. I watched from afar, like a stalker. I knew she would do it eventually. I just didn't know that all it would take was for me to reveal a possessive side to myself that I *rarely* ever showed.

I might have scared her or, at the very least, confused her.

But regardless, she flew over the ice gracefully, like an angel, and I'd regret it for the rest of my life if I turned around and went home.

"Aasher!" The echo of her shout made me smile. "You're a lot faster on the ice without all your gear."

I leaned to the right as I turned and reached out to grab her. She yelped, and I chuckled. I scooped her up and placed her over my shoulder, just like the time I carried her home from the frat party. Only this time, I couldn't fester in my irritation with her to keep my hands to myself.

The shelf of her ass rested against my arm, and I looked down, wanting to take a bite out of it. *Shit. I needed another timeout.*

"Put me down!"

Ignoring my conscience, I threw her words back at her. *"Or what?"*

She wiggled against me, and I finally let go of her. I smirked before skating away and falling to center ice. My arms rested against my knees, and before I knew it, she was only a foot away, sinking down to her butt and then eventually lying on her back. I only let myself look at her for a few seconds, but it was plenty of time to feel the punch in my gut. Her ribcage extended with heavy breaths, all the way to the knot tied below her belly button from when she shrugged off her thin hoodie and tied it around her waist. The light-pink long-sleeve shirt she had underneath was more of a second skin, and the tiny pebbles of her nipples were hard enough to see through her bra.

I couldn't get her out of my head. I couldn't stop craving her sweet breath, and I couldn't stop silently rooting for her to get on the ice and prove to everyone that she was the best, because I had truly never met a more determined person.

It was inspiring, honestly.

If getting on the ice made me panic to the point that I couldn't breathe, I would have given up a long time ago.

Not Riley, though. She was stubborn, fierce, and determined. It was beyond attractive.

"Can I ask you something?" she asked.

I stared at the penalty box, wanting to put her in there for all the trouble she was causing me. I had a feeling her question was only going to add to that trouble.

"Sure," I replied.

"Have you only been helping me because of Savannah?"

I stifled a groan. I knew she'd ask eventually. After all, she was forced to hear my side of the story on Friday, just like I was forced to shove her in a locker to save my ass. The scruff of my facial hair against my palm was the only sound between us. I could feel her eyes lingering on me.

She huffed. "You told me I could ask you something."

"I didn't say I would answer."

A pouty noise left her, and my mouth twitched. I glanced down, and her blue eyes trapped me. If anyone else would ask me about my ex, I'd blow them off and move on. But Riley was different. I'd never felt so comfortable around another person. She wasn't asking to be nosey, and I knew, after everything, I could trust her to keep anything I said to herself. Somehow, after being forced together the last several weeks, I'd built a relationship with her that was full of trust. She trusted me with her fears and failures, and who was I to deny her mine?

"No," I finally answered her, but I turned away when I did. I flicked the tongue of my skate to give my fingers something to do besides twitch with the need to pull her in. "I mean, not specifically. After everything with Savannah happened, I...changed."

"How?"

I shrugged. "Well, after I got over the guilt of fucking up my future—"

"It was unfair, though. You shouldn't have guilt over something you had no control over."

I looked at her. "I could say the same to you."

Riley's cheeks reddened, and she pulled her eyes away and stared at the ceiling. I traced the outline of her delicate jawline, wondering how a guy like Gray Loretto could *ever* let her slip through his fingers. *What an idiot.*

"I deserve to have some guilt," she whispered. "I allowed some guy to mess with my head and turn me into something that—"

"You never want to be again."

She clasped her hands on her belly after I finished the sentence for her. "Yeah."

"After everything calmed down and I realized I could attend Bexley U, with the help of my parents, my priorities shifted. I grew. I matured...*some.*" She giggled, and I grinned before continuing. "Things that I didn't realize were important became important."

Like when your coach asks you to watch out for his daughter or your future will be fucked, it's a no-brainer. Only I was having a *really* hard time staying on task. The thought of having her and securing my spot in the NHL with a team that would value me and secure a career that I had dreamed about from a very young age was becoming harder and harder to ignore.

There was no use in pretending that what I felt for her was only attraction. We weren't even touching and my heart was skipping beats. I had avoided her for five whole days, and the only thing it did was make me irritable. It was so bad at practice that Theo pulled me aside and asked if I was still bothered by the whole Savannah thing.

I wasn't.

I didn't give a shit about her dad sucker punching me.

The only thing I thought about from that night was the hidden moment between Riley and me in the locker room.

"Can I ask you something?" I went back to flicking the tongue of my skate so I could distract myself from the insanity of my thoughts. *Why can't I stop myself from wanting her?*

"It's only fair," she answered.

"Why do you skate?"

I heard her head roll over on the ice, but I couldn't look at her. "What do you mean?"

I shrugged. "I mean, before everything happened with the guy I'm going to hunt down and murder one day…"

I chose then to look at her, and I raised my eyebrow. She rolled her eyes.

"Why did you skate before all of that happened?"

"That's easy. Skating felt right."

"Right for who?"

She was quiet for a second. "Me…I guess. Why? What are you getting at?"

I leaned back and rested my hands against the floor before the icy bite worked itself down to my bones. "And who did you skate for after?"

"After…?"

"Yes, *after*."

She knew what I was implying, and if she made me say it out loud, she'd see just how much it bothered me knowing that someone touched her without permission. I was well aware that it happened in the past, but to my benefit, I only found out about it recently. I wasn't over it.

Riley's neck moved with her swallow, and her eyes bounced all around the rink as she thought about her answer. She slowly turned, and her eyes were glassy. She blinked once and then twice before opening her mouth and whispering, "I see your point."

"Skate for *you*," I said. "Don't try to prove something to him or try to fix what happened in the past. Don't skate to prove something to Gray, because if he broke it off with you over the fact that you stopped skating in the first place, then he's the biggest fucking idiot in the hockey league."

She smiled, but it didn't reach her eyes.

"Don't skate for your parents to make them proud, because as much as your dad loves you, he's already proud. And don't skate for the figure skating team, because none of those people matter when it comes to what you want. You were afraid you'd get lost in the demands of figure skating again to prove something to everyone else, but if you just skate for yourself, that won't happen. The only approval you need is yours."

I reached over the ice with my thumb and pulled her bottom lip out from her teeth. Then I ran my finger over the little indents and said, "Skate for you, and you'll do fine."

The only indication that she heard what I said was a slight nod after I dropped my hand. We sat in silence for so long that it made me feel things that I had no business feeling when it came to her. I rested my palms against the ice again, but this time it was to ground me because the hold on my control was slipping the longer I listened to her soft breathing.

Fuck. Do something.

"Can I ask you one more thing?"

She slowly sat up and met my eye. "Yes."

It was a poor attempt to irritate her, because maybe if I did, she'd get up and leave, and I wouldn't have to fight with myself about whether I should grab on to her hand and drag her closer. "Does it make you mad that I won our bet? We both know how you hate to lose."

A laugh abruptly flew from her mouth, and I smiled.

She stood up on her skates and skated a circle around me with her arms crossed. She was adorably annoyed with her nose scrunched and her cheeks flushed.

"You're annoying when you win."

"And you're cute when you lose."

The next thing I knew, I was being pegged in the head with a hair tie. I snatched it up before standing and towering over her. I held the thin elastic in between my fingers and dangled it above her face. "Was that supposed to hurt?"

Her lips smashed together to smother a laugh. She failed, and her giggle made my heart skip. "It was either that or take my skate off to throw instead."

I lifted my hand higher so she couldn't reach the hair tie when she tried to snatch it. "Wow, an entire skate?"

She shrugged. "I decided to use my hair tie because if I hurt you with my skate and you couldn't play on Friday, my dad would lose it. Beating Rosewood was his New Year's resolution this year."

"Ah, Rosewood." I clicked my tongue. Her old stomping grounds. "Are you coming to the game?"

"I come to all the games." Riley tried to grab the hair tie

again, but I smirked and pulled it away at the last second. This was what we called flirting, and I shouldn't have been participating.

"You gonna sit in the first row again?"

"I guess you'll just have to see." She reached up one more time and failed.

Her hand landed on my chest as she steadied herself. My palm splayed on the small of her back when she peered at me.

A hot swallow worked itself down my throat. I briefly glanced around the rink when the temptation grew stronger. *We are alone. No one would ever know…*

I ground my jaw and chucked the hair tie halfway across the rink. "First one there wins."

She gasped in surprise when I took off skating, listening as she created tracks across the ice just as quickly as I was. I swooped down, snatched the hair tie, and put it on my wrist. I smirked and did a half-turn, only to be knocked backward by her speed.

My head nearly cracked on the ice, but I tightened my abs and gripped on to her torso, keeping her pinned to my front as I broke our fall. Her laughter vibrated against my chest, and I rested my head back, laughing too. "Fuck, you're fast as shit, Riley."

"You cheated. I want a redo."

"Sorry. You lost." I lifted my head and found myself an inch away from her face. My laughter faded, and my pulse flew. *Shit.* Her pretty lips fell open, and the very second she moved her playful eyes to my mouth, it was game over.

Riley didn't lose.

I did.

[26]

RILEY

Kiss me.

Don't kiss me.

Wait, kiss me.

I couldn't breathe, and it had nothing to do with being on the ice and everything to do with being on top of Aasher. His amused green eyes were all I could see, and when they darkened, I did what any sane girl would do.

I leaned forward and kissed him.

We'd been skirting around each other the entire night, and I could see that he was teetering between right and wrong. But how could something that feels this good be considered wrong? *So what, there was some silly ban on the coach's daughter?* It was a tale as old as time. And to hell with hating hockey players and never trusting one again, because I wasn't sure there was anyone that I trusted more than Aasher Matthews. He'd proven himself worthy on so many occasions that I couldn't use that as a barrier any longer.

"Riley." Aasher cupped the sides of my face, and he pushed me back. His throat bobbed. "I shouldn't."

I stayed quiet, trying to figure out what to say. I didn't want to seem desperate, but I also didn't want to accept his attempt at doing what he thought was right. I wiggled against him, hearing my skates scrape against the ice. My voice cracked through the tension. "If you don't want me like that, fine. But if you do, and you're only pushing me away because you think it's the right thing to do, then you're wrong."

"You're tempting me again," he whispered.

His hand trailed down my jawline, and the pad of his finger traced all around my lips before a gruff growl vibrated out of his throat. Suddenly, I was in his arms, and he was skating us over to the penalty box. The door flung open and bounced off the wall.

I trembled against him when he sat down on the bench, wrapping my legs around his back. He leaned up to kiss me, and I felt him everywhere. The knot around my waist loosened, and he pulled my hoodie off my hips, dropping it to the floor with a *whoosh*.

I moved against him, eager to feel what I was doing to him between my legs.

I wanted him, and he knew it.

He wanted me too.

I sucked in the air of the tiny penalty box when he dragged his hand over the curve of my hip and down to the laces of my skates. "On your back," he said, flipping me around and laying me flat against the bench. I withered as he worked his deft fingers through the laces of my skates, pulling them off one by one and setting them on the ground.

"I'm proud of you for getting on the ice tonight." His words were sincere, but his eyes were hooded, simmering with much more than satisfaction. A shaky exhale escaped my mouth at the faint touch of his nose skimming up my leg.

"Spread."

The playful Aasher that made me chase him on the ice had turned into someone I'd only imagined on my loneliest nights. He was bossy and commanding and took full authority over my body, and I was at his mercy.

My muscles ached from skating for hours, practicing my triple lutz and doing whatever Aasher asked me to show him, but I had no problem spreading my legs and feeling the stretch in my groin.

"I want you so fucking much that I can't find it in me to stop." Aasher buried his face between my legs and inhaled. Heat wrapped around my neck and crept up to my cheeks. The brush of his fingers gripping the waistband of my leggings gave me butterflies. "I couldn't live with myself if you thought that I didn't want you like this."

The slow tug of the fabric slipping past my curves made me pant. I leaned up on my forearms and watched as his tongue slipped out of his mouth to wet his lips. A fire burned in my lower belly, and when he flicked his attention to my face, my heart stopped. "I've imagined you like this for the past five days."

"You avoided me. I thought you regretted what happened."

goose bumps followed his calloused hands as they scuffed my legs. His fingers dug into my thighs, spreading me wider. "Don't you get it? I can't control myself around you."

His warm breath drifted over me, and I said nothing because it was too much. He cursed before sucking me into his mouth, and I was completely lost in pleasure.

Holy shit.

My pulse pounded, and I moaned softly, digging my fingers through his thick hair. We had so much pent-up tension and angst that it made this a million times better.

"Fuck, baby. This is better than I imagined."

He pulled his mouth away, and I panicked.

I popped up, and Aasher's eyes were like bullets, headed straight for me. "Hold on tight. I'm about to devour you."

I arched my back when his fingers dug into my thighs, dragging me closer to his face. He propped my legs up on his shoulders and went back in for more. I gasped for air. I was drowning. My orgasm built quickly, and when he sucked on my clit, the entire penalty box went black.

"God damn," he whispered against my neck, inhaling deeply. "That was well worth it."

I finally opened my eyes, and he was staring down at me with swollen lips, still glistening from my pleasure.

"You think that was worth it?" I asked through ragged breaths.

He thinks we're done?

Aasher ran a hand through his unkempt hair and shook his head. "Don't look at me like that. I've already crossed too many lines tonight."

He backed up against the glass and flexed his jaw as I moved toward him, righting my leggings and ignoring the wet spot between my legs. I cupped him with my palm and relished in the carelessness I was feeling. The entire hockey team could be in the rink and I'd still drop to my knees, because as much as he wanted to taste me, I wanted to taste him too.

"Riley," he warned, peering down at me with wild eyes.

"Yes?" I asked sweetly, sinking my teeth into my bottom lip. He looked straight ahead and shut his mouth. *My turn.*

"Fuck," he whisper-cursed. "I'm going straight to hell."

I smiled when his pants slipped down to his skates. There was something *so* enticing about driving Aasher even crazier than he was moments ago while he touched me and had me succumbing to him.

His length sprung out of his boxers, and I paused to relish how hard he was. My legs clenched when he took his hand and ran it over himself, milking his cock like he was beating off alone instead of me falling to my knees to take him in my mouth.

It took one hot glance in my direction for his hand to press on the back of my head as I sucked him long and hard.

"There goes my ability to say no to you," he grunted, thrusting his hips to meet my face.

I ran my tongue along his base before taking him into my throat. I sucked, and he pulled my hair.

"I knew you'd be good at this by the way you sassed me." His breathing picked up, and I sucked harder. "Fuck, Riley. Stop or I'll come straight down your throat."

"Do it," I mumbled with him still in my mouth. *Break for me like I broke for you.*

He hissed and gripped the back of my head before pulling himself out. His hand fell to my chin, and he gripped it tightly, staring down at me with a carnal look. I licked his finger, tasting myself on his skin.

"*Fuck.*"

He pressed himself to my mouth and watched in awe, but before I could take him all the way, he dropped to meet me on the floor and pulled me on top of him. "Someone's here."

"What?" I was startled. "Who?"

He exhaled in my face, and for some reason, instead of being afraid that we were about to get caught, I was excited.

What is wrong with me?

"I think it's Bob."

The sound of the Zamboni machine echoed through the penalty box, and I looked past Aasher's head and saw that the door was still halfway open. Aasher must have had the same thought, because his arm reached up, his long finger crept beneath the lower edge, and he slowly closed it.

"There," he whispered. "We can wait until he heads to the opposite side and then sneak out."

I nodded and wiggled down some more to hunker against his body. I was certain that Bob didn't see us. He was as old as a bat and had fallen asleep on the Zamboni before...while it was on. But he knew my father well, and he would have no issues telling him that I was sucking one of his players off in the penalty box when the rink was supposed to be closed.

Aasher was right. Even if my dad was okay with me dating one of his players, he would kill him for this.

"Quit moving." Aasher gripped the back of my neck and shoved my face into the crook of his neck. His pulse hammered against my cheek.

"Why?" I asked, tilting my hips a little. I was surprised to find him still hard. I guess the fear of being caught wasn't enough to send his arousal packing.

"Because your mouth on my cock drove me fucking crazy to the point that I'm about to fuck you right here," he seethed under his breath. "And don't you dare tell me to, because I have no self-control when it comes to you."

The Zamboni machine whirled louder as it got closer to us. I shifted against Aasher again, rubbing my damp leggings against him. He bit onto my earlobe. "You are trouble. Stop teasing me."

"I'll stop if you stop," I whispered against his pulse.

He continued to nibble my skin, tracing a path of soft kisses against my jaw, all the way to my mouth. I turned, and his tongue slipped in between my lips, coaxing a silent whimper from me. I moved against him, feeling his hard length rub against my clit. He pushed up, pressing harder, and neither one of us could stop.

We were in sync. Pushing and pulling. Rubbing and moaning. The sound of the Zamboni started to fade, but neither one of us halted our movements.

Aasher bit my lip as I moved to straddle him. I stayed down low, but with the new angle, even with our clothes on, I felt a pinch of an orgasm peaking.

"Fuck," I whispered against his mouth.

Aasher pressed harder, touching every part of my body, and then we both jolted. Another hot orgasm took me by surprise, and when I peeked at him, he mouthed, "Holy shit."

"Are you fucking kidding me?" he whispered, keeping his hands on my hips.

"What?" I asked against his neck.

"You got me off and both of our clothes are still on."

I looked down and blushed at the wet spot on his pants. Some of it was from me, and some of it was from him.

Aasher shut his eyes and angled his head backward. "What the hell am I going to do with you?"

It was a rhetorical question, so I didn't answer. Instead, we stayed still against the dirty floor of the penalty box until the Zamboni was farther away. He tapped me twice on the butt, and I slid off him slowly and gripped my skates by the laces.

Aasher glanced up over the ledge before ushering for me to go.

I jumped over the side and landed on quiet feet before

snatching my bag and racing up the steps. I darted into the hallway with Aasher hot on my heels. We didn't say a word as we walked through the dark, and when we found ourselves in the lobby, he looked down at his pants and shook his head.

I sucked in my amusement and opened the doors, feeling pretty damn proud.

"Not a word, Duster."

I pretended to zip my lips and began heading for my car with him following me. He opened the door for me and leaned over the edge when I sat down. "I'll wait until you head home before going back inside."

"Why are you going back in?"

He stepped back from my car door and looked down at his pants. "Because I have cum all over my pants. Imagine my roommates when I show up looking like this with you following me looking like that."

Aasher crowded my space and ran his thumb over my swollen lips before reaching over to buckle my seat belt.

"Get home and stay there."

I was tempted to say, *or what?*

But I chose not to.

Lines had already been blurred, and the more time I spent with Aasher, the more I was going to be confused when morning came.

27

RILEY

"ARE you *sure* you don't want to sit with us?" Sutton pulled on her Bexley U Wolves shirt and worked a little knot in the front to show off some of her stomach.

I scrolled over the messages on my phone, and the slimy feeling of dread weighed me down.

> Mya – We can't wait to see you!
>
> Me- Same!
>
> Mya – Has Gray messaged you?
>
> Me – Yeah, he wants to see me.
>
> Mya – That ought to be fun.

The last thing I wanted to do was sit in the Rosewood section with a group of girls who weren't half the friend that Sutton was. Or even Taytum and Claire, which was kind of pathetic because we'd only hung out a handful of times. But if I went back on my word and didn't sit with them, that'd only give them ammunition to start more rumors, and those rumors would follow me to the rink when we competed against one another down the road.

Sometimes being civil meant breaking your own boundaries, and not to mention, I wasn't going to back down from Gray. He was probably knee-deep in the cologne I'd once told him I enjoyed, because he thought he was going to find me after the game.

Yeah, not happening.

He was going to learn that I wasn't that same girl who fell into a trap of self-deprecation and allowed him to embarrass me in front of the entire Rosewood campus. I was all for putting hockey players in their place, and tonight, I'd put him in his place like I should have the night he cheated to put *me* in my place.

"Riley?" Sutton elbowed me, and I tried to click my phone off, but she snatched it at the last second. "If I look at this, what am I going to see?"

She was asking for my permission to snoop, and I didn't stop her.

"Look for yourself," I said, draping Sully's old jersey from Rosewood on my shoulders. The number thirty made me think of all thirty reasons why I shouldn't be wearing it, but Sully was on par with his cruel joke. It was the perfect revenge bomb to drop on Gray.

Sutton's mouth hung open. "Gray has some fucking nerve, doesn't he? Does he truly think you'd want him after everything he did to you?" She paused with my phone in her hand after seeing what I had on. "What are you wearing?"

"What?" I asked, turning around and eyeing the name Sullivan in the mirror. "Does this make me look as devious as I feel?"

Her nose scrunched. "Sully? Really? He's so...ugh."

She was right. "It'll put Gray in his place."

"Mm. You're right," she agreed, standing back with her hands on her hips. "I've gotta give you credit. You're brave."

I put my phone in my back pocket and followed her out the door. I knew the guys were already at the rink, warming up, so I wasn't worried I'd run into Aasher, and even if we happened to cross each other's paths in the hallway, I was pretty certain he'd keep his reservations to himself.

Before we crossed a million lines the other night, I didn't think twice about his reaction to me wearing this to their game, but then I wondered if it was a good idea.

That thought vanished when I showed up to play hockey for our night-before-a-game tradition, and he was nowhere to be found. I stayed and participated with Taytum and Sutton because I enjoyed their company, and the more I was on the ice, the better, but there was no sign of a tall, dark-haired hockey player who'd had his mouth between my legs the night before.

He went right back to avoiding me.

It did nothing but leave the taste of confusion behind. He was playing mind games, whether he meant to or not, and I was pretty certain I was losing.

"Why am I brave?"

Sutton and I climbed into Taytum's car, and she answered for her.

"Um. That's why." Taytum pointed to the Rosewood jersey. "The guys will never stand for this."

Claire laughed. "That's something I would do to make Theo mad."

Taytum pulled away from the curb. "Honestly, it's a good idea. I might steal it."

"To make who mad? Ford?"

Taytum grinned, but all attention was on me again.

"I'm not trying to make any of the guys mad. I'm doing it to irritate my ex." I leaned back and stared at the red color on my chest. "They won't even know. I'll be sitting on the opposing side."

Even though it felt all wrong.

Sutton squinted at me.

After Taytum parked the car, she turned around in her seat. "They'll know exactly where you are, Riley."

"Well, then, they'll just have to deal. This isn't about them. It's about me."

It was Aasher who told me I needed to do things for myself and no one else.

Watching Gray's face twist with confusion was one minor tweak I needed to make to show everyone at Rosewood that I was back. Their rumors would die on the end of their lips, and the pity would turn to envy real quick.

Just wait until they find out I'm skating again.

There was a dimple digging into Sutton's cheek. "I like this new attitude. I'm all for it, and I am totally on your side. Fuck hockey players." She grabbed my hand and pulled it to the center console. Taytum put her hand on top of Sutton's, and Claire put hers on top of Taytum's.

"Solidarity, besties," Taytum mused.

We all laughed and piled out of Taytum's car. We linked arms, and although I was wearing a Rosewood jersey and looked out of place, I felt right at home.

Sutton leaned in. "Don't worry. We will save you a seat

just in case you want to ditch those loser Rosewood friends and root for the team that I *know* you want to win."

My confidence didn't shake, but I placed my head on her shoulder as we disappeared into the crowd, because no matter what happened in the future, I was beginning to think that everything happened for a reason. I was right where I needed to be at Bexley U.

———

Mya's slender arms wrapped around my neck, and her familiar rose-smelling perfume engulfed me. "I've missed you so much!" Her hands fell to my sore shoulders—thanks to the quick pregame hockey sesh last night. "You look good, Ry."

I knew that would be the consensus tonight. My weight loss and lack of sleep wasn't noticeable to everyone while I attended Rosewood, but Mya had paid attention. She was the only one who announced her concern, and I blew her off.

Something I still felt guilty over.

"Thanks," I said, smiling. "I feel good. Balanced."

She leaned in close to my ear and whispered, "Um, what are you doing wearing Graham Sullivan's old jersey?"

My teeth sunk into my bottom lip before answering. "Just putting Gray in his place."

Mya burst into laughter. "This is going to get interesting, isn't it?"

I shrugged. "That depends on his reaction. But according to his texts, he thinks he's able to get back in my good graces after what he did to me, and I'm hoping this will show him that he can't."

"He was an asshole. I tell him that every time I see him."

He is an asshole. Not was.

"Let's go. The rest of the girls want to see you."

That was funny because not a single one of them asked how I was after I left.

After multiple awkward, stiff hugs and forced smiles, I slid down into my seat beside Mya and dropped my attention to the ice. "We Will Rock You" by Queen was playing overhead, and the dark-blue lights flashed to the beat. Instead of looking for Gray to flip him the finger and hopefully send him the right message with his old teammate's jersey, I immediately looked to the opposite side of the rink and found the black-and-white uniforms moving up and down with their warm-up stretches.

My belly dipped when I stared at the number twelve below the name *Matthews*. His head was tilted to the stands, but his legs were resting on the rink floor. I bit the inside of my cheek when he stretched forward, tilting his hips to move against the ice like he did to me a few nights prior. The arena was chilly, like always, but I gripped the collar of the jersey I wore and blew a shaky breath out.

He had been invading my head from the very first encounter we had. Only now, my thoughts were filled with dangerous temptations instead of annoyance and anger. I stopped myself from looking at him when he skated over to the glass to talk to someone, because I knew that my grip on our *situation* was full of slack, and I didn't want to let him mess with my head again.

"Riley." I looked down, knowing it was Gray who had said my name. *Here we go.*

Mya scooted closer to me, and a hush raced down the aisle. *Oh, goody. An audience.*

"Gray," I replied.

His face was as handsome as ever, sporting his angular jawline and cleft chin.

Too bad he was a total power-hungry dick.

He kept a hold of my eye. "It's good to see you. How have you been?"

I smiled, pretending that nothing was unusual. "I've been great."

"You look good." He showed off his coy grin, and I hated that I used to fall for it. He ran his eyes down my body, and I watched with amusement when his confidence veered. A sick smile curved onto my mouth. If I could have curled up in the divot between his eyebrows, I would have.

"Wait. What are you wearing?"

"Is there a problem?" I asked, tugging on his attention. His expression was no longer welcoming but, instead, fueled with hatred. If there was one thing I learned about my ex-boyfriend, it was that he didn't like to be second-best. It was the entire reason he broke up with me. I was no longer the unstoppable figure skater with stats that ruled the entire figure skating division, so he dropped me faster than my fall on the ice.

"You're wearing the wrong number."

His nostrils flared.

I looked down at my jersey innocently. "Mmm, no. This is right." I turned around and showed him the back, glancing at him over my shoulder. "It says Sullivan, right?"

"*Sullivan*? Really? Are you with him now?" Something flickered over his face. "I always knew you liked to be second-best, so that makes sense."

That was his anger talking, and I knew that I was truly over him, because it didn't hurt like he wanted it to.

"Isn't that what you'll be tonight when Bexley U beats you? Second-best?"

"Oh. She came back swinging, bro." I waved at Elliot, who had joined his teammate on the ice. He gave me a thumbs-up behind Gray's back, and I held back a smile.

Every hockey team had a douche, and now that Sully was gone, Gray was Rosewood's biggest one.

Gray glared, and I silently laughed at his fleeting looks to the people listening to our conversation. It was probably more than we both thought. People had a way of pretending they were distracted when they were actually paying close attention. "Ry, baby."

"Don't you dare," I snapped. I burned with anger. "You don't get to call me that anymore."

He was shocked.

"Don't tell me. You heard I was skating again, didn't you? Do you want me back now?"

Someone whispered from beside Mya, "*She's skating again?*"

I heard my name from across the ice, but I didn't look at who was calling it. I wasn't shying away from Gray. The last time he saw me, I was messy.

I was well put together this time around, and I was pretty sure he was regretting how he treated me.

"Take it off," he demanded, apparently thinking he still had a chance.

I crossed my arms and smiled at him. "I don't think I will."

28

AASHER

THE SONG *"WE WILL ROCK YOU"* by Queen didn't clear my mind like it usually did before a game. This was our typical warm-up song, but my focus was thrown when I saw Sutton, Taytum, and Claire sitting in the stands with an empty seat to their left.

I did a double take.

Then a triple take.

Then I found myself loitering below them with a startling rapid heartbeat.

"Where is Riley?"

Silence buried their laughter, and I waited for them to answer me. They shared a look, and I instantly beat myself up for avoiding Riley again.

I pussed out, and I knew it.

I was too wrapped up in my thoughts, trying to right a wrong that I couldn't even convince myself was wrong. The number of times I got up in the middle of the night, walked over to her apartment door, and then back to mine was pathetic.

"What's going on?" Ford asked, skating up beside me.

I turned toward him. "Where is Riley?"

"Not sure," he answered. He leaned in close, and I backed away, but not before I caught his snarky remark. "But just to let you know, she didn't ask where you were last night."

My brows fell.

He waited to add, "But she wanted to."

A few other players skated up beside us, Theo being one of them. He only had eyes for Claire, though, oblivious to anything else going on.

I turned at the sound of Sully's smug tone. "She's sitting with a few of her old friends."

My skates dragged over the ice, and I found her immediately.

Ford threw his hands up. "How dare she?!"

What the—

My blinks were slow, and I wanted to reach my hand out and strangle Sully. She had Graham Sullivan written all over her, *literally*, and it confirmed my suspicion that he had a part in this.

I could see her sneaky little grin all the way across the rink as she smiled down at Gray Loretto. I made sure to find him the moment Rosewood slid onto the ice.

"You're unbelievable," I seethed, skating past Sully and heading for Coach. Ford had his hands on his hips and was pointing over to Riley. Berkley and Efrain were backing Ford's attempt at making Coach feel bad for his own daughter rooting for our opponent.

Coach's face was growing redder the more he stared at Riley talking to the guy who broke the camel's back. I did another take and thought I was going to shake right out of my skates.

I knew of Gray Loretto well before I met Riley. He was the top player at Rosewood, and if the articles online had any accuracy, he was an even worse boyfriend to Riley than I was to Savannah. The only difference between us was that he didn't feel bad about what he did to her.

The internet was a dangerous place to be. Actions didn't disappear when they were caught on camera, and the look on Riley's face when he pulled one of her friends in close and swallowed her face to *break up* with his long*time* figure skating girlfriend was a permanent fixture in my head.

"Will you idiots focus?! She's just sitting with her old friends. My daughter isn't your concern," Coach's voice echoed, and I watched as his blood pressure rose each second that the guys were giving him shit about Riley wearing the wrong colors. "Sully!" he roared. "Get over here!"

Sully skated over, and I rolled my eyes at his fake heavy breathing. He wanted to act like he was busy warming up when I knew he was skating as slow as a toddler so he could have a listen. "Yeah, Coach?

"Why the hell is my daughter wearing your old jersey?"

He put on his good-boy act, pretending he was innocent. Ford and I shared a look, and I clenched my jaw. "I don't know. She asked me if she could wear it, and I said sure. I didn't ask questions."

Fucking liar.

Coach's patience was running thin, and so was mine. Did she wear it to make Gray mad? Or was she punishing me? Either way, I was growing tired of the push-and-pull game I was playing with her. I brimmed with possessiveness. The name Sullivan on her back fucked with my head, and I wanted to rip Gray Loretto to pieces for even looking at her.

Let alone talking to her.

He was mine tonight.

And Sully had better be thanking his goddamn stars that he was wearing a BU jersey instead of a Rosewood jersey. He may have been untouchable, but this would be the last time that he ever persuaded my girl to do something.

My girl?

"Coach." I skated forward and pulled his glare away from Riley and Gray. "Let me go get my practice jersey. She can wear it instead."

The entire team paused and waited for Coach's reaction. I cleared my throat and pleaded with him silently. "The team is distracted, and they're obviously not focused. It's messing with their heads." I was lying through my teeth. They were fine. It was messing with *my* head.

His bushy eyebrows folded. "She told you what he did, didn't she? That he broke up with her in front of everyone when she was at her lowest?"

"Riley!" Ford yelled, skating to center ice with his hands thrown up into the air. She didn't hear him. She was staring down at Gray, and he was peering up at her. When I turned back and looked at Coach, he was giving Gray the same look I was certain he'd give me if he knew what I'd done behind his back.

"Go," he bit out, sparing me one last look. Before I rushed to the locker room, he grabbed me by the arm and gripped my jersey in his tight fingers. "You all better make him pay on the ice tonight."

I smirked. "We already planned on it."

▭

"Take it off."

My blood ran cold when I heard the way he spoke to her.

I dropped my eyes to her ass when she stuck her hip out. "No. I don't think I will."

"I agree," I hummed, startling her.

Riley jumped and spun around with her blue eyes round like saucers. I thrust my white practice jersey into her chest while wrapping my hand around her lower back to keep her steady. I breathed down into her space and watched her lips part. "Take it off."

"Wh—"

My lips skimmed her ear when I pulled her in close. I stared down at Gray angrily looking up at us from the ice. "Are you forgetting the stipulations to our bet, baby?"

She gulped and hated that I couldn't watch her neck move up and down with her nerves. "You're back on the ice, which means I won. You're not supposed to mess with the team's head anymore, remember?"

"I'm not messing with anyone's head but Gray's," she said quietly, glancing at everyone staring at us.

I gave her some space but shoved my jersey into her chest again. "You're messing with *mine*."

Her mouth opened, but I peered around her and stared at her ex. "I'll see you on the ice." I winked and then grabbed her hand and forcefully pulled her behind me. Once we were in the hallway between the two locker rooms, I gently shoved her against the wall, hoping that none of her Rosewood friends would follow after her.

"I'm messing with your head?" she asked, clearly pissed that I'd been avoiding her again. She blew a strand of her dark hair away from her face. "You're messing with mine! Where were you last night? Too busy with regret?"

"Take it off," I demanded. I stepped back and waited for her to strip right there.

Her bottom lip popped out with a pout. I saw her refusal without hearing a word she said. I silenced her by gripping the hem of the Rosewood jersey tightly. I shoved it up so forcefully that more strands of her dark hair fell from her ponytail. She stood in nothing but a scandalous black bra that made my mouth water.

Fuck.

"The *only* name I want to see on your back is mine."

"But—"

"You're mine, and I'm done pretending that you're not."

After dropping Sully's jersey to the ground and kicking it several feet away, I pulled my jersey over her head and shoved it down past her face. My hand slid around her delicate waist, and I pulled her flush to my body. Even with all my gear on and layers of clothing separating us, I felt the heat simmering. "And if you wanted to pay Gray back, all you had to do was ask me."

"What do you mean?"

"It means I'll be in the sin bin tonight, baby." I landed a quick kiss on her lips, just to make her want more. "And so will you for wearing that jersey."

[29]

RILEY

It may not have been noticeable to the entire crowd that Bexley U had it out for Gray Loretto, but it was absolutely obvious to me. The black-and-white jerseys were scheming with quick looks and flicks of their steely chins. The vicious skating toward Rosewood's best center was subtle, but if Gray tried to pass the puck to someone and make a goal, a Wolf was right there to swoop in and steal it while making sure to shoulder-check him on their way past.

The first cross-check that Aasher landed on Gray sent him to the sin bin. Gray shook his head but kept his cool and didn't react, which was very unlike him. The second cross-check made him irate, though, because the ref let it go. Aasher grinned like a kid in a candy shop, and I stood silently beside Sutton and bit my fingernails.

"He has it out for Gray," Sutton said, clearly pleased by the way her dimple stuck out.

"They all do." Taytum laughed. "What did that boy do to you?"

I nibbled on my bottom lip. The heat from Aasher draping his jersey on my body had long died out as I stood completely still and watched him provoke my ex like it was more important to him than winning the game.

I shifted my attention to my dad, and surprisingly, he wasn't losing his shit. His face wasn't red, and the tiny vein on his temple wasn't protruding like it usually was during games. In fact, he looked *pleased?* Smug, even. He'd definitely get shit from my mom later—I was positive of that.

"Aasher!" I shouted, knowing he'd hear me from above. "Get your head in the game!"

I had already put Gray in his place. Aasher was wanting to right a wrong for me, but he didn't need to ruin his reputation to do so.

However, it was a little bit of a turn-on.

"My head is in the game," he shouted back, keeping his glare on my ex.

Aasher's stick slapped against the ice. He said something to Gray before flicking his lively green eyes to mine. I choked at the sight of his hot smirk, but when Gray threw his stick to the ground, my hand flew to my mouth.

"Oh shit." Taytum looked at me, but I didn't have the ability to look back at her because I was too busy silently losing it over the fact that Gray's helmet was off, showing his sweaty head full of blond hair.

Don't do it, Aasher.

My dad was going to kill him. He hadn't mentioned a single thing to me about Aasher, but after this, he'd know that our *friendship* went far beyond the normal scopes.

Aasher's mouth moved, and time stopped. "*She's mine, Gray.*"

His back was to my dad, which meant I could read his lips perfectly.

Gray leaped forward like a lion, and the next thing I saw was Aasher's bloody smile as they hauled Gray to the sin bin.

"Well, that was interesting," Sutton whispered from beside me. "I think you have some explaining to do."

I shushed her and spent the next half of the game sweating in the stands, praying that my dad didn't kill Aasher.

My hands were shaky as I stacked my poker chips together, waiting for Aasher to walk through his apartment door. The girls and I left the game the moment the buzzer sounded in an attempt to avoid Rosewood's student section. Mya had texted me a few times, but I didn't respond because I wasn't sure how to answer her questions about Aasher.

We weren't together.

But we weren't apart either.

And what if Gray stuck around to confront Aasher? I wouldn't be surprised. Gray didn't like to be embarrassed, and not only did Bexley U win the game, but Gray lost his cool on the ice.

"What's got you so quiet, Duster?" Ford pretended to act concerned, but I think everyone at the table was dying for information. "Worried about Aasher?"

I shifted in my seat.

"Why would I be worried?" I asked, knowing that it was complete and utter bullshit. *I was wearing his freaking jersey*.

Emory snorted under his breath, but no one answered. Instead, Ford hummed the *Jeopardy* song.

"Where is he?" I finally asked, slamming my poker chips onto the table.

Berkley sat down beside Sutton and put his arm around the back of her chair. "Coach called him into the office as we were leavin'. Said he'd be home in a few."

Oh god.

"I wonder what they could be talking about?" Ford asked in a singsong voice before kicking me under the table. I kicked him back, but he didn't even flinch.

Taytum, who refused to follow her brother's commands of her not coming over to play poker, mumbled, "He's probably wondering why he was in the sin bin so many times."

I started to sweat the more they talked. Words were ping-ponging across the kitchen table, but the only thing I thought about was what the hell my dad was talking to Aasher about and why it was taking him so long to show up.

What if he went back to avoiding me?

"I've gotta pee," I announced, standing up abruptly and leaving the conversation. I needed to get my thoughts straight and simmer my nerves. I sucked in a deep breath and pulled out my phone, wondering if I should have texted Aasher. There were multiple texts from Mya and one from my mom, gently probing on the drama that occurred with me sitting with my old *friends*. I quickly texted her back and told her I'd chat with her tomorrow over lunch.

I clicked my phone off and stared at myself in the mirror.

My blue eyes were bright with life when I thought about Aasher's hand splayed on my back as he pulled me in close and told me I was his, but they dulled a second later with questions that were unanswered. Our interactions were fickle at best. There was undeniable chemistry between us, but my guard was up. Rightfully so. I pushed loose strands of hair away from my cheeks and breathed in and out, fogging up the glass.

It was dangerous to be trapped in my head with thoughts of Aasher. Before our bet, I was ready to take him down, along with the team. I wanted to bring them all to their knees, Gray included. But now, I was afraid that he was tied up to the bench in the locker room with my dad breathing down his neck because he found out that one of his most trusted hockey players was finger-fucking his daughter instead of keeping her away from the hockey team.

Shit.

I cared about Aasher.

I cared about his future.

And surprisingly, I cared about the hockey team's season, and it wasn't only because my dad was the head coach.

My fingers dug into the sides of the sink as I dropped my head. The poker game was about to start. The dealing of cards was beginning, and I knew I needed to get back out there. As soon as I spun around, I flung backward with a gasp. The porcelain cut into my lower back, and my hand flew to my chest.

"Hiding?" Aasher shut the door with his foot and dropped his bag down to the floor before advancing in my direction.

"Wh–what if I was actually using the restroom?" I stuttered, pressing myself farther onto the sink.

He smirked, flipping his hat backward. *Does he know how hot he is when he does that?* "I knew you weren't."

"I'm surprised you showed up," I said, shifting my attention away from his dangerous smile. I traced the letters of the words Bexley University in the center of his shirt to distract myself.

He took another step toward me, but it was more like a prowl. Dark lashes outlined his glittering eyes, and instead of seeing the familiar battle between right and wrong that always followed his slip in restraint, I saw something that made my stomach knot. "I live here. Of course I'd show up."

"Why are you late?" I teetered around my real question: *What the hell did my dad say?*

"Your dad pulled me into his office."

I waited for him to tell me more. Aasher's hands found my waist, and he dropped his eyes to my mouth, which did nothing but tighten the knot in my belly.

"Not going to ask why?"

"I'm afraid to know the answer," I whispered, tilting my head back to get a better look at his face. Damp ringlets of his hair stuck out beneath his hat, and the smell of his shampoo made me feel tipsy.

"Are you?" he prodded.

"Well," my voice croaked, but it wasn't out of fear. I was feeling something much more potent than fear. "I guess not anymore since you're standing here with your hands around my waist with that look in your eye."

"What look is that?" Our mouths were getting closer and closer, and this time, instead of Aasher acting like he was out of control and unable to stop himself from touching me, he acted like he was in charge. This moment seemed premeditated.

"Like you've been thinking about what you want to do to me since leaving me in the hallway after stripping another guy's jersey from my body."

Aasher dragged his hand up my side, brushing over the

curve of my heavy breast before cupping the side of my face. "You know me better than I thought."

My mouth opened willingly when his lips fell to mine. Chills blanketed every inch of my skin at the slip of his tongue, and suddenly, I forgot all about his aggression on the ice when it came to Gray. I didn't really care to know what my dad said to him either.

When he pulled away, I blinked several times, trying to right the room. I was left breathless.

"I meant what I said earlier, Riley. You're mine, and I'm going to prove it to you."

My voice was hardly above a whisper. "And here I thought you were proving it to me by putting Gray in his place."

He smirked. "That was just an added bonus."

"But—" I swallowed his minty taste. "What about my dad? What did he say to you? Does he...know?"

Aasher threw his head back and barked out a laugh. I peeled my fingers away from the sink and crossed my arms at his laughter. I wasn't sure what was so funny.

"Does he know that I couldn't stop thinking about his daughter wearing nothing but my jersey as I made her scream my name during that entire game? No. Otherwise I'd be thrown off the team and likely be in a six-foot-deep hole."

I rolled my eyes. "That is not true." *Is it?* I'd been burned by two hockey players, and any normal father would be leery of their daughter dating another. Roy Lennon took "normal" to an entirely different level. His protectiveness was downright lethal at this point.

"Wanna bet?" he asked, peeling my crossed arms away from my chest and wrapping them around his torso. "You're O and 1."

My lips twitched. "Okay, I'll tell him. It'll soften the blow."

Aasher's head snapped so quickly I heard the crack in his neck. "And what will you tell him? That in the midst of me keeping you away from the rest of the team, I decided to just keep you for myself? That I decided to spread you wide on the ice and watch you come all over my fingers? Or maybe we should start with what we did in the sin bin?"

I went to move my arms, but his hands landed on my forearms, and he kept me there.

"Fine," I snapped. "Then what? You're going to go back to avoiding me after you've gotten your fill?"

Aasher's eyes hardened. "I'll never get my fill of you, Riley."

That shut me up.

He cupped my face, and I was flush against his body. "We have to be smart about this."

"*This?*"

A hot gasp rushed from my tight lungs when Aasher spun me around and pressed himself against my backside. I caught his stare in the mirror and gulped. "Yes, *this.*"

His hand curved around my neck and traveled down to his last name settled between my shoulder blades. I shook with every faint touch of his finger tracing the letters. "We will keep it under wraps until the end of the season. I broke a promise to your dad, and he won't take that lightly. Trust me." Aasher lowered his voice. "I have to think about my future, and whether you want to admit this or not, your dad can crumble it with his fingers if he wanted to."

He wouldn't do that.

"And then what?" I let my head fall back. Aasher's lips brushed the side of my neck.

Why am I so needy when it comes to him?

My blood sang when he touched me.

Just like when I stepped foot on the ice—something that he helped me find again.

"Well, when he isn't my coach anymore, he has nothing to hold over me. As soon as the season is over and I sign with the Boston Hops, I'll make sure everyone knows you're mine. I respect your dad but not enough to keep me from having you."

I felt faint from his words, and there wasn't a single guy I'd ever been okay giving full control to, but with Aasher, I *craved* it. So I egged him on by biting down on my lip and staring at him through the mirror. "Do I get any say in this?" *I don't want any say.* "What if I don't want to be yours?"

Aasher's teeth sunk into my neck, and I dragged in a breath. He slipped his hand into the front of my jeans, and everything burned bright. He blew cool air against the mark he left behind, and I stopped breathing when he slipped his finger inside of me. "You do."

I whimpered with desperation when he pulled his finger out and stepped away from me. I was dizzy from how fast I spun around to glare at him. The smile on his face only distracted me for a second.

"See?" He held his wet finger up in between us and stuck it into his mouth, licking my arousal off his skin. I swallowed and gripped the sink again, hoping it would hold me up. He was so goddamn hot, and I truly didn't care that he wanted to keep me a secret. I understood it in a way that not many would. The NHL to him was what figure skating was to me. He wasn't one without the other, and I wouldn't stand in his way of getting that. Just like I wouldn't allow my dad to either. Now that I knew what happened to him before attending Bexley U, I understood why he was hesitant. His future was taken from him before, and what was to say that it wouldn't be again? I could look him in the eye and say it until I was blue in the face, but at the end of the day, I wasn't my father, and I didn't have any power over his decisions.

The knock on the bathroom door startled me. I knocked the soap off the sink at the sound of Sutton's voice. "Riley? Are you okay? You've been in there for a long time."

Aasher put his finger up to his mouth and shook his head. "Yeah, I'm fine. I'm coming."

I went to walk past Aasher, and he grabbed me by the arm. "You most definitely will be coming later."

I half-smiled with a roll of my eyes.

"Wait for my text. When it's safe, I expect you to sneak your pretty little self back into my room."

"I thought you said I was going to the sin bin," I joked, remembering his threat from earlier.

Before I walked through the door, he whispered something that made me pause. "Oh, baby. You *are* in the sin bin."

[30]

AASHER

Two hours.

That was how long I'd had to sit here beside her and act completely composed about it.

Every time I shifted in my seat, I made sure my knee brushed the side of her thigh. Every time we laid our cards down, my finger touched hers, and it lingered for a second longer than it needed to. We were down to Ford, Taytum, Sutton, Riley, and me. This never-ending game of poker was just the tip of the karma iceberg that I'd continue being served until I told Coach the truth.

I lied right to his face tonight, and I was too infatuated with his daughter to care. The more time I spent with her, the more I fell for her. And the more time I spent away from her, the more desperate I became. I practically had to chain myself to my bed last night to stay away from the rink, knowing she was there with my friends, gliding over the ice with her pretty smile chinking away at everyone's need to keep her at an arm's length, per her father's request.

The few slips in time and my lack of self-discipline wasn't nearly enough to quench my thirst. She was all I thought about. I wondered what she was doing even when I was supposed to be avoiding her. I wondered if she had tightened up her Biellmann spin in preparation for her upcoming tryouts. I wanted to know if she told her parents that she was skating, because I knew it was something she was looking forward to doing. I wanted to see the glow of elation on her face after sticking a jump on the ice and watch her cheeks turn pink after telling her that I was proud of her.

It was the first time, since Savannah, that I'd ever let myself think of a girl as more than just a means to an end, and no one was more surprised than me. I had loathed Riley the moment her dad named me her babysitter, but now I was here, sneaking behind his back, counting down the seconds until this game was over so I could show her just how much she meant to me.

I couldn't say it out loud, but even as I sat there and lied to Coach, convincing him that Riley and I were nothing but *friends*, I was pretty certain that if I had to, I would choose her.

"I'm folding." Taytum slapped the cards down to the table. "I've gotta go anyway. I'm supposed to be up early."

"For what?" Ford shifted his attention to her, and I took the opportunity to move closer to Riley. I cleared my throat before putting my hand on her thigh under the table. Two hours was long enough. This game needed to end.

"The bigs are waking up early and making shirts for the game with the littles."

"Cheering for the football players now, are we? *Interesting.*" Ford was poking her, but Taytum didn't fall for it. She ignored him and looked over at Riley and Sutton. "If you girls want to come to the game tomorrow, text me. You can sit with us. Claire is coming too."

Emory grunted from the couch at his sister's statement. "Theo ain't letting that happen."

"As if Claire is going to *let* Theo tell her what to do."

"You sure about that?" Ford asked.

Everyone on campus knew that our team captain was totally obsessed with his roommate/fake girlfriend. His actions spoke louder than words, and the fact that he almost showed up late for one of our games because he was with her proved that they had a secret of their own.

"I'm sorry, are you talking to me?" Taytum asked, batting her eyelashes at Ford.

Sutton snorted at their bickering.

I stared at Ford's lip twitching as I dragged my finger up Riley's thigh. Her quick glance in my direction was like the sting of a bee, but I pretended to be as interested in Ford and Taytum's arguing as Sutton was.

Ford threw his cards down, and he lifted an eyebrow in Taytum's direction. "You know what, I'm folding too. In fact, I might just head to Rush's. I bet the party is still going on."

Emory popped up from the couch. "I'll go with you. After that game, I could use a reward, if you know what I mean."

Taytum gagged.

Riley squeezed her legs together when I gripped the inside of her thigh. My pinkie brushed against the zipper of her jeans, and my dick twitched at the sound of her shallow breathing.

Ford snapped his fingers. "You know what, you're right, Em." He popped up and looked at Taytum but directed his statement at Emory. "Let's go find a few rewards, shall we?"

I pulled my hand away at the last second, and I swore I heard Riley's pout.

"Besties..." Taytum mused, slowly rising from her seat. "Are you up for a party?"

Ford's growl caught my ear, and I chuckled.

Emory crossed his arms over his puffed chest. "You're not coming."

"You're not her boss," Sutton said, linking arms with Taytum. "Or mine."

Emory glared at Sutton. "I don't care if you go, but Taytum doesn't need to go."

"I agree." Ford pushed off from the table and walked to the bar to grab his keys. "Let's go, Em."

"We're coming." Taytum stomped after her brother and stole the keys out of Ford's hand. "And I'm driving."

Emory didn't catch his cheeky smile, but I did.

Ford wanted her to go all along.

"Are you coming, Ry?"

"She absolutely isn't," I answered for her. "Word has it that Gray Loretto is there."

Riley was perturbed by this. "He's still on campus?"

Emory leaned down in between us and looked me right in the eye. "Then you're staying put."

Fine by me.

"Is that what Coach wanted to talk to you about? Staying home tonight because of Gray?" Ford asked.

Riley stood up. She was annoyed along with being all hot and bothered by my constant teasing. *The perfect combo.*

I shrugged. "He may have mentioned it."

"Did my dad tell you to make sure I stayed put?"

He may have mentioned that as well.

I didn't answer. I leaned back in my chair and stared up at her. She clicked her tongue and turned around, leaving me at the table alone. Where the hell did she think she was going?

"Are you coming?" Sutton asked, moving her gaze back and forth between me and Riley.

I squinted one eye from across the room and thought, *Don't you dare.*

A ghost of a smile raced across her mouth. "I'll think about it." Then she walked out the door, knowing I wouldn't chase after her in front of everyone.

Ford gripped my sore trap and bent down beside my ear before following after everyone. "Careful."

He was one to talk. I saw the way he looked at Emory's little sister. He wasn't fooling me.

When I was alone, I quickly stood up and snatched my phone. I rarely texted her because I wasn't stupid enough to leave proof behind, but I pulled open my texts and typed the name Duster.

Me: You better be in your apartment, Riley.

The temperature of the fridge did nothing to cool me down. I popped open the top of a beer and swallowed a bitter mouthful when my phone pinged.

Duster: Or what?

The things that went through my head were sinful. My heart was pounding, and the beer can crumpled in my grasp. Did she think I was playing with her?

Me: Come over here and see.

My beer was empty faster than I meant for it to be. Sweat prickled at the back of my neck. I ripped off my hoodie and threw it onto the couch.

Duster: Sorry, I was told to stay put.

I dropped my head and laughed. She was so stubborn.

Me: Get over here right now, and I swear to God, if you say, "Or what?" I will break down your door.

My phone rang three seconds after I hit send. I made her wait until the last second, and then I finally answered. Her pretty face appeared, and I made sure to look at her surroundings before saying anything.

"You're lucky I can tell you're home."

Her eyebrows raised. "I'm lucky?" The gloss of her lips caught my eye as she smiled. "I'm not afraid of you."

I hummed, dropping my gaze down and seeing that she

was still wearing my jersey. "You should be if you continue acting like that with my jersey on."

"I can always take it off," she replied.

I followed her movements like a lovesick puppy as she walked through her apartment, finally stopping as she made herself comfortable on the couch.

"I don't know why you're sitting down."

She acted confused by batting her eyelashes. I knew she was fucking with my head. She was so good at it, and she knew it.

"Why wouldn't I? I'm just getting comfy." She placed the phone in front of her, and I assumed by the clanking of it that she rested it on the coffee table.

"You're still in jeans," I noted, starting to walk to my room before glancing at the front door to make sure it was unlocked. She'd be coming over sooner or later, but I'd let her have her fun first.

"You're right. I guess I'll take them off." I stopped in the middle of the hallway when she popped up from the couch and stood in front of the phone. Her fingers fiddled with the button of her jeans, and I stopped breathing when she pulled the zipper down, revealing black, lacy panties that I *knew* were soaked from all the teasing I had done during the poker game.

I licked my lips at the slow pace of the denim slipping over her curvy hips, revealing toned legs the color of sand. *Fuck me.* I stared at her covered pussy and remembered how good she tasted. I wasn't sure I *could* let her have her fun.

"That's better." She sighed, sitting back down. The cushions swallowed her whole, and I'd never been jealous of a fucking couch before, but I wanted to rip it to shreds. *This is ridiculous.*

"You're really good at getting under my skin," I admitted, in hopes that my defeat would make her come over.

She laughed, and the sound raised my dick to the standing position. I looked down at it before she stole my attention again. "You think you can tease me for the last two hours, tell me what to do, and expect me not to retaliate? It's like you don't know me at all."

"I know you're soaked right now." My voice was as strained as my dick inside my boxers.

"Am I?"

"Why don't you show me?" I teased.

Riley giggled like a little devil, and I couldn't believe that the team nicknamed her Duster. We were all fooled by her sweet-and-innocent act.

I rested my back against the wall and gripped my phone so tightly I thought it may snap. A plea for her to stop fucking around was at the tip of my tongue, but when she slipped her fingers beneath the black silk, I died a slow death.

By the sound of my voice, it sounded like I'd swallowed a handful of rocks. "What are you doing?"

"I thought you wanted to see?"

"Then spread your legs and let me look." I was desperate. I pressed my heels into the floor and shoved a breath down my throat.

Fuck, fuck, fuck. She was driving me absolutely wild. I almost began pacing.

My mouth watered, and I wanted her taste to replace the beer I'd chugged moments ago. Her soft movements and dragging of silk down her legs were enough to bring me to my knees.

Once her panties were off and I looked at her perfect pussy, she threw the black scrap of fabric at the phone and covered almost all of the camera. I felt the arrow go straight into my chest.

"Two can play that game."

"Hmm?" It sounded like a moan.

I strode to my bedroom and flipped the light switch.

"Can you see okay?" I asked, locking onto the tiniest fucking sliver of her through the stupid black silk. "I wouldn't want you to miss the show."

I tore my T-shirt off, but I didn't throw it over the camera. I wanted her to see exactly what she did to me. My abs flickered with every deliberate movement, and when I pulled my sweats down and revealed my throbbing dick, I smiled at her sharp intake of breath.

"What was that?" I asked.

"Huh?"

"I thought I heard you say something."

My blood pressure shot to the roof when I caught a quick glimpse of her hand moving over her legs. "Don't. You. Dare," I snapped, gripping my cock. I sighed with plea-sure. It wasn't as good as it would be if she were here doing this, but it sufficed.

"Are you telling me I can't touch myself?" she asked in a breathy voice.

I groaned at my tight grip. "That's exactly what I'm saying, Riley. If anyone is touching that pussy tonight, it's me."

Fuck. She better get over here.

I pumped myself up and down, all while staring at her unmoving hand. *Good girl.* I clenched my teeth and looked away because no matter how good it felt to beat myself off, I wanted nothing more than for her to get her ass over here so I could show her everything I'd been holding back since the very first kiss.

"Riley," I groaned. "Better throw in the white flag, or I'm going to finish, and then there will be nothing left for you."

Lies. I was certain I could get off and then be hard minutes later for her. Every interaction I'd had with Riley from the very beginning was foreplay, and the fact that I knew what laid on the inside too made me want her that much more.

I picked up my pace, moving my hand faster and faster.

Come on, baby.

"Ugh!" she finally said, springing up from the couch. She grabbed the phone and pulled her panties away. I stared at her red cheeks. "Fine! You win."

I removed my hand slowly. "Door's unlocked."

The phone call ended, and I waited for her to walk into my room so I could show her what she did to me.

[31]

RILEY

THERE WAS no point in putting on my underwear, but I did anyway because knowing Aasher, he'd be pissed that I walked across the hall nearly naked.

I stumbled through the front door and went directly to his room, refusing to waste any more time.When he saw me, he gripped my wrist so hard I fell into him. His fingers dug into my butt when he picked me up and put me on top of his dresser. I inched closer, dragging myself over the wood in a rush and looked at his flushed face.

"You're beautiful," he whispered, angling my head back and slipping a kiss onto my neck. A chill racked through me. My ankles locked themselves around his waist, and I whimpered at the feel of his hard length pressing into the wet spot on my panties. "Even more so when you want to get fucked."

A tease halted at the edge of my lips because denying it would be absurd. He knew my body well enough by now to know just how much I wanted him.

His calloused hands crept up my stomach and landed at the bottom of my lacy bra. The tickle of his hot breath caressed my ear, and I inhaled deeply. "I've thought of nothing but stripping this bra off your body since ripping Sully's jersey off you."

I arched my back with the slip of his hand winding around and unlatching it. My hands were uncontrollable as I quickly pulled the straps down my arms and threw it to the floor. When I went to pull his jersey off, he bit my earlobe. "Leave it."

"What?" I asked breathlessly.

Aasher pulled back, and his green eyes were nothing short of carnal. He looked drunk on lust. "You in nothing but my jersey? A fucking dream, Riley."

His mouth swallowed anything I was prepared to say, and he licked up any doubt that I had. I lifted my butt when his fingers raced down my sides and crept underneath the black silk. A rush of surprise left me even more breathless when I heard the tear of fabric and then the silky shred of my panties dropping to the floor. A sexy smile covered his face, and the room spun.

He is perfect.

We could keep us a secret for the rest of my life, and I might just be okay with it if he kept looking at me like that.

I licked my lips when he pulled open a drawer to slip on his condom. My teeth sunk into my bottom lip, and he quickly reached up and freed it. "Are you okay with this?"

There was no hesitation.

"I've never been more okay."

I sighed wistfully at the heat between us. The edge of the dresser dug into the very tops of my thighs as he pulled me closer. "Wait," I said, digging my nails into his shoulders. He paused. There was a slight flicker in his jaw that I noticed right away. "Are *you* okay with this? You're not going to regret this after, right?"

"I'll regret lying to your dad." He positioned himself between my legs. "But I'll never regret touching you."

I spread wide, and the anticipation was enough for me to hold my breath.

"Fuck," he hissed, pushing himself into me and pausing. "You *do* want this."

I pulled back, and we both looked down. Every line drawn between us was obliterated.

My stomach dipped at the sight of him inside me. Since the very first time I gave myself away to someone—willingly —I never once had the inkling to let them have *all* of me.

Up until now, I didn't realize that I had never allowed myself to be this vulnerable. There was always some sense of control that I had to hold on to. But with Aasher, I was his for the taking.

Butterflies swarmed me when his finger tilted my chin up to meet his face. His eyes bounced back and forth between mine, and a timid smile moved against my lips. I moved my hips, and he shut his eyes at the pleasure. "What have you done to me?" he asked, gripping me by my rib cage and slamming into me.

"The same thing you've done to me," I replied, holding on to his shoulders and letting him take me any way he wanted. "I've—" I lost my train of thought. It was a type of pleasure that I'd never felt before. "I've never been like this."

"This wet?" Aasher's talented finger dipped down, and he rubbed his thumb over my clit, stealing my thoughts for a second.

"No, this willing to let someone have me any way they want."

Aasher slammed into me harder, holding me steady so he could fill me up completely. My throat grew tight, and the ripples of pleasure were everywhere. "Don't say things like that to me when I have you like this."

Our mouths sealed, and our kiss was urgent, like something was about to pull us apart. I whimpered when he quickened his pace. He rubbed against my clit, and I cried out. "Aasher." I tore my mouth from his before he growled and pulled my mouth back. He kissed me so hard my thoughts jumbled, and my body went into a frenzy.

"Let go for me," he said before slowing his pace. My eyes shut and a blinding wind started in my lower belly.

"God...*damn*." His words were strained.

I opened my eyes when he slid me off the dresser and spun me around. I slapped my hands onto the wood, and his palm moved up to my throat, holding me up by the chin. "Actually, let go for *us*."

I locked onto his feral gaze in the mirror. My body went stiff, and Aasher turned my face to swallow my name on his lips. He thrust into me one more time, and I didn't even notice the grip he had on my hip until his fingers peeled themselves away and he lifted his jersey.

"Fuck, I left marks on you," he pulled himself out.

I spun around and drunkenly said, "You left your mark on me way before this moment, Aasher."

His eyebrows dipped before he wove his hand through my hair and kissed me. It was a softer kiss this time, but it still had the same effect.

I was his.

My eyes fluttered with sleep, and I snuggled back into the soft pillow. I inhaled and shifted, trying to get closer to the warmth along my back.

"Better quit."

My eyes sprung open at the sound of Aasher's voice, but the surprise only lasted for a second as the night came flooding back in. I looked at the dresser through blurry eyes, and my cheeks flared with heat. *Last night.*

Aasher's breath tickled the back of my neck, and goose bumps appeared on my skin.

"Are you cold?" he asked, draping his heavy arm over the dip of my hip. He pulled me in closer, and I laughed quietly.

"What's so funny?"

"I'm not cold."

Air whooshed from my lungs when he spun me and forced me to lie on my back. His messy dark hair was adorably sexy, and his sleepy eyes blinked several times before he looked at my mouth. "Tell me why you have goose bumps, then."

I sucked my lips in, refusing to answer. *Why am I so... turned on?*

"You look embarrassed."

My cheeks heated even more—something that he noticed if his classic half-grin said anything about it.

"Answer me." His fingers moved over the part of my belly that was showing. I was still wearing his jersey—something he forbade me to take off last night after he carried me over to his bed.

The sun was barely peeking through the clouds, but I saw the eagerness in his gaze.

"I remembered last night."

One eyebrow rose. "And that gave you goose bumps?"

My lips rolled together, and his amused smile was annoying. "Don't be embarrassed," he whispered, climbing on top of me. My legs spread, and I gasped because I forgot I didn't have any underwear on. His hard-on rubbed against me. "I'm not."

I swallowed as I let my hips fall open even wider. His head went into the crook of my neck. "I can't believe I've waited this long to have you in my bed."

I trembled with need, and he noticed.

"Do you like knowing how much I want you?"

I kept my mouth shut but nodded. *I do. It's addicting.*

"I want you so much that I want you to scream my name so loud that everyone in this apartment complex knows you're mine."

"But my dad—"

Aasher sucked the words off my tongue, keeping our mouths sealed as he moved to lie beside me. A shaky sigh fell from my mouth when his finger skimmed over me, lightly brushing my swollen clit. It tingled, and he smiled, moving his mouth to mine.

Against my lips, he said, "Addicting." Then he slipped a finger inside before slowly pulling it out and moving back to my clit. He rubbed me over and over again, playing with me, before I was withering beside him with need. His finger disappeared inside, and I tilted my hips to meet his palm as it rubbed against me. "I want you in my bed every night, you got that?"

A sharp knock sounded on his door, and both our heads turned at the noise. "Aasher!"

Berkley huffed loud enough for us both to hear it through the door, but Aasher didn't move his hand.

"You're running out of time," Aasher whispered, pulling in and out a little faster. My hand fisted the sheets, and he gripped my other one and placed it over my clit. "We work well together."

I throbbed in all the right places, ignoring the constant knocks on the door.

"Yeah?" Aasher shouted, staring at my hand rubbing myself. His tongue darted out to lick his bottom lip, and I threw my head back at the way I tightened. Aasher put his palm over my mouth, and I bit down, pulling in my moan.

Holy shit.

"If Riley is in there, you better hide her."

Aasher pulled his hand away quickly, and we both sprung up.

"What?"

"Someone beat up Gray Loretto last night, and Coach is on his way over here to ask if it was you."

I said nothing as I pulled on random sweats—sans panties, thanks to Aasher. I kicked my bra underneath my bed, and he flung open the door while pulling his shirt down.

Berkley found me immediately.

He shook his head at my appearance and erased the distance between us. He ran his fingers down my tangled hair, clearly on a mission. "This won't do. You look..." His words trailed off as he grabbed my wrist and pulled me down the hallway, disappearing into his room. Aasher followed closely behind. His jeans weren't even on yet when there was a knock on the door.

We shared a panicked look, and Ford popped up from the couch. "Who the fuck is at the door this early?" His hair was just as messy as Aasher's, but they had a way of shaking their heads once and looking just as put together as they usually did.

"Uh-oh," Ford said, looking at me while Aasher buttoned his pants.

Berkley came back and handed me a small Bexley U shirt.

"Strip."

"Whose is this?" I pulled Aasher's practice jersey up.

"Close your eyes," he barked at his teammates. Berkley rolled his before turning for a quick second.

"Wolves!" My dad was about to wake up the entire complex.

"Is that—"

"Yes," Aasher and I answered at the same time.

Berkley threw Aasher's practice jersey into his room, and my stomach filled with nerves.

"Not a word," Asher warned everyone, walking over to the door.

"What is your plan?" Ford whispered, stumbling over his shoes that were in the middle of the floor.

I didn't have one, but by the look of pure fear on Aasher's face, I hoped someone else did, because his confidence from last night was clearly wobbly with my dad's booming voice on the other side of the door. It hurt to see the shame on his face, and I definitely didn't like knowing that I was part of the reason it was there.

"Take whatever you're thinking and throw it right out of your head," Aasher said to me. "I don't regret it."

"You will if he finds out," Berkley stated, edging his head to the door.

"Jesus. Follow my lead, you lovesick puppies. I've got this." Ford smoothed out his wrinkled shirt as he walked over to the door. He lowered his voice. "Riley, go make us breakfast."

My jaw slacked. "Excuse me?"

"It's part of the plan!" he urged. "I'll take you for pancakes later to make up for bossing you around."

I eyed him but did as he said. Aasher sat across from me, slightly amused at my obedience.

The door opened, and my dad walked in with his eyes pinned right on Aasher. "You better have a good fucking alibi."

Oh, he does.

Too bad we can't tell him the truth.

AASHER

My life flashed before my eyes. What a shame it would have been if I only got one night with her before her dad killed me.

"Riley?" Coach stopped mid-step, freezing at the sight of his daughter in the kitchen with a puff of flour surrounding her.

"Hey, Dad." She was as poised as ever, but I knew it was fake, because her sweats were definitely damp from the orgasm I just gave her.

"What are you doing over here in my players' apartment?" Berkley, Ford, and I stood casually, pretending like nothing was unusual.

Nothing to see here.

"Riley is making us breakfast." Ford yawned.

"She's making you breakfast?" he repeated. Then he turned and looked at her. "You're making them breakfast?" Question marks were carved into the wrinkles along his forehead. "Why?"

"Uh..." Riley grabbed the eggs out of the fridge. *Thank God Efrain went grocery shopping.*

"*Becauseeeee,*" Ford sang. "She lost a bet."

I coughed. My glare was a permanent fixture on my face. Riley dropped an entire egg in the pancake batter and sucked in her cheeks.

Nice, Ford. Nice.

"A bet?" Coach pondered, clearly becoming distracted.

"If we beat her loser ex's team last night, she had to make us breakfast this morning."

Coach thought it over and glared at his daughter, seemingly forgetting why he was at our apartment. "Is that why you were wearing a Rosewood jersey? Because of a silly bet between you and my players? Or were you trying to get that asshat's attention?"

He had no idea the irony in that statement. *A bet.* My heart beat harder and harder.

"I wasn't trying to get Gray's attention."

Oh, she absolutely was, but she got mine instead.

"And you?" Coach's tone changed *real* fast when he directed his question to me. "Were you provoking him on the ice so he'd come after you later?"

"I provoked him beca—"

Ford stepped forward, interrupting me. "*We.*"

I sighed. "*We* provoked him on the ice because he did your daughter dirty." *For once, I didn't have to lie to his face.*

Not to mention, he was totally on board with it during the game.

Riley slammed down the skillet a little too forcefully. "I didn't ask you guys to do that. I had it handled."

Coach ignored her and kept his unwavering glare on me. "And who handled it last night at Chi Alpha Sigma?"

He stepped forward, and he eyed me closely. "I told you not to go. I told you—"

"You told him to keep me from going," Riley said under her breath, knowing we all heard her.

Coach opened his mouth to rebut her assumption. "*Riley.*"

"Don't," she said, putting her hand up.

Silence filled our apartment, except for the sound of oil in the pan. Coach placed his hands on his hips while he watched his daughter move around comfortably in our kitchen, making herself right at home.

"I can't believe you're making them breakfast."

If I was reading him correctly, he was a little jealous.

"You haven't made me breakfast since you were seven."

She grinned while pouring pancake batter into the pan. I was completely captivated by her movements, and I hoped that her dad didn't notice the way my eyes followed her.

"Well, I'm not doing this willingly."

"I hope you aren't poisoning us." Ford took a seat beside me at the bar.

"Where were you guys last night?" Coach asked, ping-ponging his attention between me, Ford, and Berkley.

"I was at the party for a little while, but I...left." Berkley looked away.

"You left?" Coach asked. "And came home?"

"Not at first."

"Where did you—" He shook his head before briefly looking at Riley. "Never mind. Ford?"

Ford's smug smirk told me all I needed to know. "I went with Emory, but I didn't stay long."

"Let me guess, you also went somewhere other than here? I hope you two have someone to back that statement up."

He smiled while wiggling his eyebrows. "Oh, we definitely do."

"Not in front of my daughter!" Coach scolded Ford.

I refused to look at Riley, because if he knew that his daughter was here getting rammed by me the night before...

"Sorry, sorry!" Ford mumbled.

Coach turned to me as the scent of pancakes filled the apartment. "And where were you?" He dropped his eyes to my knuckles. There wasn't a nick on them. The only thing that was on them was his daughter's dried cum.

I'm dead.

"Uh..." I kept my face as smooth as possible, even if I was picturing Riley spread open in my bed.

"He was with me."

My heart stopped.

"What did you just say?" Coach's face was green, and I couldn't tell if I was relieved or ill.

"We were at the rink." Riley placed the spatula down slowly, and she seemed completely at ease. Meanwhile, I was sweating through my shirt. "He's been helping me get ready for tryouts."

The shock was enough to pull her dad's murderous thoughts away from me. The lines around his eyes softened, and the vein above his left eyebrow magically disappeared. "So Bob was right?"

Riley's eyes found mine, and my entire spine stiffened.

Fuck us.

"Bob?" I asked, taking some of the weight off her shoulders.

Coach nodded. "He said he thought he saw you two sneaking out of the rink the other night, and I chalked it up to his old age and poor vision."

"We've been going almost every night for weeks."

Riley's voice was timid and sweet—something that worked over her dad like magic.

"Really?" He walked over and leaned against the bar beside me. I pictured him taking his hand and slamming my face onto the granite if he were to find out the truth, but thankfully, he seemed blinded by surprise that she was back on the ice.

"And how is it going?"

Riley's smile was real. It was bright, beautiful, and a complete sucker punch right to my chest. "Good. Really, *really* good."

"There it is," he whispered, tapping his knuckles against the counter. "That's what your mom and I have been missing."

"What?" Her cheeks ripened with embarrassment. She turned around and flipped a pancake.

"Your smile," I said in a low voice. *Fuck, did I say that out loud?*

All eyes were on me. I waited patiently for Coach Lennon's hand to make contact with the back of my skull. *This is gonna hurt.*

Ford swooped in and saved the day. "It's the only time you smile, Ry-Ry. But we all get it. We like the ice too."

Ry-Ry?

I cleared my throat and walked around the edge of the counter to inhale oxygen that wasn't stained with guilt. The plates clinked together as I gripped them with force and placed them beside the stove. I went to take a pancake, and Riley slapped the top of my hand with the hot spatula.

"Ow, fuck!" I said, snatching my hand away from the stack. A red welt was forming.

The guys snickered, and the tension lessened. Coach chuckled under his breath.

"I have nothing to worry about with you anymore, do I?" he asked, looking right at Riley. I walked around the bar and sat down, waiting for Riley's permission to get a pancake, because apparently, I wasn't allowed to.

"No." She peeked over her shoulder, showing off those baby blues. "You don't."

Coach waited for a beat before pushing off the counter. He looked at us. "If I find out any of you are lying and you are responsible for knocking Gray Loretto's lights out..." His threat faded as we waited for him to finish. But he never did. "Well, okay, then."

My lip twitched.

I looked away as he hugged Riley. They had a quiet conversation, and I was sure he was probing her confession of skating again, so we gave them the privacy they deserved. When he left, after telling us to gear up for tomorrow's practice, Riley blew out a breath so hard it moved her hair out of her face. She turned the stove off, and we all reached for a pancake, but she pulled the plate back.

"These are for me. Make your own!"

"What?!" Ford shouted. "I just saved your ass!"

"Technically, you saved Aasher's ass. Maybe he'll make you pancakes." Her coy smile had me by the balls. I moved closer to her and slipped the spatula out of her hand.

"Nice save," I whispered.

Then I got to work making pancakes.

———

"Do a triple." I skated backward as I challenged Riley. Loose hair framed her face, and I forced myself to put space between us because I knew that the arena wasn't officially empty yet. Not to mention, her dad knew that she'd been here daily after our practices. We had to be careful in case he came and watched from afar.

It didn't matter, though. Not being allowed to touch her only ramped up my touches for later when she crept into my room. Every night since Friday, she was in my bed. Sometimes we watched Netflix, and other times, we studied. It always ended the same, though. Her on her back, and me unable to keep my hands to myself.

The obsession was growing unhealthier every day.

She was mine behind closed doors, but I wanted her to be mine all the time.

"Are you gonna catch me if I fall?" The graceful way she spun on the ice grabbed me by the throat. I followed every sway of her hips and longed to run my hands down the curves of her legs.

"You won't fall." I dropped my voice. "Remember who you're skating for, baby. If you dig down deep, you'll find that skill still nestled inside. You don't need me or anyone else."

I wanted her to need me.

But she didn't.

Her soft breath hit me square in the face, and my nostrils flared. She knew the effect she had on me, and her knowing little smile was the last thing I saw before she backed up and shook out her hands.

I stayed put.

My skates itched to slide me forward, but I didn't.

Riley was skilled beyond belief on the ice. She was better than me. More poised, more in control, and more at ease. The ice became compliant to her, not the other way around.

When I played hockey, it was loud and always a rush. For Riley, it was serene and calm. She was captivating. Her

fluid movements sucked me in, and when her leg straightened out with a soft turn, I found my lips parting and my
jaw slacking. She was right at home. I was pretty sure she
forgot I was in the rink with her, but I could never forget
where she was. My thoughts were wrapped around her like
a blanket, and my future was looking a lot like pretty blue
eyes in the morning instead of stark-white ice beneath my
skates.

Riley skated backward, and her fluid movements
became sharper. I straightened my back and prepared
myself for the triple I knew she was trying to perfect. A
breath was lodged in my throat, and I couldn't help myself. I
skated over to her mid-spin, and when she landed and
leaned forward, I wrapped my hands around her lithe waist
and hoisted her up to my chest.

"You're leaning forward too far."

The fast pace of her ribcage in my hands did nothing to
distract me from glancing at her pouty mouth. "I am not."

"You are. Do it again." I wanted to kiss her so fucking
badly. I peeked up in the stands and saw nothing but empty
seats. Her shaky fingers gripped my biceps.

"Is there anyone behind me?" I asked against her ear.
My stomach filled with loose knots that I was pretty sure
were a direct cause of having her in my grip.

Instead of enjoying the last few games of the season
before the cup games, I wanted to get through them so I
could make her mine.

"No one is behind you."

I cupped the side of her face, and I kissed her so deeply
a strangled noise left her throat. A gasp floated out of her
mouth when I let her lips go, and her eyes glossed over with
need. "Do it again."

I dropped my hands and skated away. Her arms fell

beside her thighs, and she moved her neck to the left and then to the right before evening her breathing and doing it again.

I caught her by the waist. But this time, she tightened her stomach and pulled up quicker than before.

"*Again*," I said, letting her go.

Three more times, and every time she got better.

"Don't wear yourself out, Ry."

I almost slipped at the sound of her dad's voice. There was a pain behind my ribs, and it very well could have been the sign of a heart attack.

Riley's shocked gape found me, and I shook my head, silently telling her to calm down.

"Skate for you," I mouthed.

She nodded before looking over my shoulder.

"I've almost got it," she shouted to her dad. "This is the last time."

I skated away, giving her space. He walked farther down the stairs and met me near the penalty box. *That damn penalty box*. I refused to look at the bench where I had tasted Riley for the first time, because this was *not* the place.

"I can't believe she's on the ice." Coach used a tone that I was certain he only reserved for her. I understood it, though. Riley had a way of bringing out a softer side.

"You sound proud."

I kept my gaze on her.

"I am."

I couldn't help myself from stating the obvious. "You know she wants to be the best to make you proud, right?"

Coach's hands dropped to the edge of the sin bin, and his white knuckles caught my eye. "That's what got her into this mess in the first place. Her desire to be perfect. The *best*."

I nodded, understanding her more and more as time went on. "She let the control take over." And it all started with that little shit who took advantage of her.

"Too busy trying to prove something to everyone else."

"Except herself."

We both followed her spin, and I stood straighter, knowing she was gearing up for the triple.

I sighed before shouting across the rink. "Do it for you, Riley."

Her father said nothing.

We stood in silence with too many unsaid words shared between us.

I held my breath, and my knuckles grew white with tension, just like his.

The jump was breathtaking. Her dark hair was a halo around her head with the angelic spin. The arch of her back and gentle landing had me drowning in satisfaction.

"Yes!" I shouted, elbowing her dad, forgetting that he was my coach. "Did you see that?"

He was smiling, and I was thankful he was too blinded by Riley landing her turn to notice how proud I was. *I couldn't hide it even if I wanted to.*

"I did," he finally answered, shaking his head with astonishment. He turned around after giving Riley a thumbs-up. Before he left, he looked over his shoulder at me and said, "Thank you for keeping her away from Gray the other night."

I nodded.

"Who knew that having you keep an eye out for her would lead her back to herself?"

That's not all that I've led her to.

Coach disappeared, and Riley's skates against the ice caught my attention. I turned around, and her smile made me unsteady. "I did it."

The guilt lessened the more I stared at the bright light in her eyes. *Shit, I am wrapped around her finger.* I wanted to spend the rest of my life putting that pretty glow on her cheeks. My heart sped up the more I stared at her gleaming smile.

"Come on." I pulled on her hand, and she skated into my chest. A strangled noise left her, and I picked her up around the waist and carried us to the locker room.

"What are you doing?!" The blades of her skates dug into my lower back. "My dad probably isn't even in his car yet."

Fuck it.

The locker room was empty. I knew Coach was the last to leave. He was finalizing game plans for tomorrow. Typically, I was excited for away games. It was always a breath of fresh air to play in a different rink, and the guys were usually pumped up to defeat someone in their home rink, but I was frustrated that Riley wouldn't be in the stands.

"I don't care," I said, pushing her up against his office door.

"Aasher," she warned.

Her eyes moved all around the locker room.

"We won't be alone for long. We have a hockey game to play, remember?"

Oh, right. And yet...

"I don't care," I repeated, shoving my hand into her pants. Her chest jutted forward, and my smile felt dangerous.

"If my dad forgets something..."

She was acting like she didn't want me to touch her in

fear of someone walking in, but her hips tilted, and she gave me more access.

"I'm doing what I want." I kissed her long and hard, stroking my tongue against hers. Our little makeout session went straight to my dick, and I wasn't sure if it was because we were in a rush, or if it was because I was so proud of her, but either way, I was uncontrollable. "It's what you want too," I said between a groan, pulling my fingers out of her. She was wet as hell, needy for my touch.

I bit down on her earlobe and fingered her again. Her hips moved against my hand, rubbing her clit on the heel of my palm. "Do you know how torturous it is to watch you move on the ice and not be able to touch you? I can't go back into the rink without witnessing this."

I loved watching her command the ice, but I loved watching her orgasm more.

"Watch what?" She dragged in a heavy breath, shutting her eyes as she tightened around my fingers.

"You riding my hand against your dad's office door, knowing that someone could walk in at any moment." I was acting absolutely feral, but I couldn't help it.

She moaned, and I smiled. "You like the idea of getting caught, don't you?"

I curled my finger against her, and mid-orgasm, I pulled my hand away and placed her back on the ground. I flipped her around and shoved my pants down. *Fuck this.* No one was stopping me from having her.

We both groaned when I entered her. I bit down on her sweaty neck. She tasted like salt and winter, and I wouldn't have it any other way.

She threw her head back. "Harder."

My eyes rolled into the back of my head when I rammed inside of her, catching my name on her mouth with her quick orgasm. I pumped my strained cock in and out of her a few more times, frantically racing toward my own release. I pulled out quickly and shot my cum on her dad's office door, dropping my head to her shoulder.

"Jesus Christ," I muttered, completely shocked at my behavior. I knew how to fuck, but that was *intense*.

We were both out of breath. I tucked myself away and pulled up her pants, knowing that her own pleasure was still dripping down her legs. Her sweaty and freshly fucked face was trapped in between my hands, and I kissed her slower this time, edging back and looking down at my cum sliding against the office door. "You make me do wild things."

"I promised myself I'd never be with another hockey player, and yet, I just let you fuck me against my dad's office door. So, yeah. I guess I could say the same."

I chuckled, and her soft laughter filled the locker room.

The door opened, and I thanked my lucky stars that it was the crew, ready to play our ceremonial hockey game the night before our own. "Let's gooooo! I have a milkshake to get!" Ford walked farther inside with Berkley and Emory following closely behind. They started grabbing their pads, but I watched silently as Ford jerked his head over his shoulder and looked at the wet spot beside Riley.

"Is that—"

Emory sniffed the air. "It smells like sex in here."

Ford bent over and howled with laughter. Riley's teeth sunk into her bottom lip, and she glared at me, but nothing could hide the afterglow of an orgasm. I flashed her my teeth, and she sighed wistfully, walking out of the locker room, knowing we'd all follow her onto the ice.

Ford threw a towel at me, hitting me in the face. "You are so fucking screwed, Aasher. It's too bad you aren't a part of that little ice bet Sully arranged, because you'd definitely win after *that*."

I cleaned up my cum, ready to have a little *chat* with the rest of the team about Riley.

Team bond be damned. Not a single one of them was allowed to have an impure thought about my girl, or I'd cross-check them and not even think twice about it.

[33]

AASHER

I shrugged out of my suit jacket and loosened my tie. Crown Point's locker room was nice and roomy, which worked in my favor because I had my eye on a few select Wolves that required my assistance.

Required my assistance, threat, whatever.

I put my phone into my pocket after texting Riley and letting her know we made it. She was staying home tonight. She and Sutton were going to watch the game on TV with pizza and beer after she did some stretches. I'd asked if she'd show me some stretches next time we were alone, and she sent me a naughty emoji and said she would.

My dick twitched, even hundreds of miles away.

"You ready to make these guys our bitch?" Theo asked, slapping me on the shoulder. He had been in a good mood lately because he and his little fake girlfriend were no longer *fake*. His future was shaping up with a good girl by his side and a confirmation from his dream team—something I was still waiting for.

It wasn't too late to receive an offer or talk with a scout. And if I played my cards right, Coach wouldn't get in the way of me signing with the Hops.

Theo just so happened to secure his before anyone else in the league.

"I'm ready," I answered, throwing my fist up. Theo went around and gave a few more fist bumps, even stopping by Sully and allowing him to touch knuckles with our captain.

I paused, breaking my neck to look at Sully's hand after the blackened color caught my eye.

Wait a fucking second.

"Why are your knuckles busted, Graham?" I couldn't help but mention it.

Theo glanced down at his hand.

"That's why you've been ready to go for practice this week, huh? Fully dressed and on the ice before anyone else. You've been hiding those healing cuts beneath your gloves."

Theo shook his head. "Fighting. Really? Save that shit for the ice and be smart about it."

"Meaning, don't get thrown into the sin bin like our boy over here?"

Efrain snickered at Sullivan's attempt at being in good standing with Theo.

Our boy. I knew he wasn't talking about me.

Theo launched into a team "talk," reprimanding the guys and warning them about keeping their head in the game and making good choices. It was our last game in the regular season, and we'd had nearly a perfect season, setting us up well for our conference tourney.

I tuned out the chatter after Theo was done playing *Dad* and changed into my warm-up gear. I kept my eye on Sully, knowing we had a shit-ton of beef that we needed to work through before our attempt at securing a spot in the Frozen Four. *Stay calm.*

I shuffled in a quick, calming breath before spinning to pin him with a look. The locker room was dwindling, and the chatter had died down. "Your plan failed."

He flicked an eyebrow, arrogance falling on his face like a mask. "What plan? Scoring with the coach's daughter?"

Just the thought of her in his mind caused havoc in my body. "Beating the shit out of Gray and wanting me to take the blame for it."

There was a quick movement of something on his face. He pulled his helmet down in an attempt to cover it. "Not sure what you're talkin' about."

My voice strained with a gritty noise. "You think I don't know that you were the one to spread the rumor that I beat up Gray at the party? He told the press that he had been jumped. All fingers pointed to me. Except, I wasn't there that night. You were."

Naturally, after Coach showed up at my apartment that morning, I dug into the accusations that flooded around campus. There was zero proof that I had touched Gray, and with Riley's admittance that I was with her that night, Coach made sure to send the right message to every news article that inquired a response.

It had Graham Sullivan all over it.

He was throwing a hissy fit because Riley and I had played him at his own game.

Our feud ran deep, but he needed to drop it before I ruined his career.

"So where were you that night? Tryin' to win your own bet?" he asked, knowing very well where I was. He was an asshole, but he wasn't dense.

"You think I won't throw you under the bus? Because I

can march right into Coach's office and tell him that you made a bet with the underclassmen on this team to see who could fuck his daughter first."

He threw his head back and laughed, slipping on his gloves to hide the marks from his tiff with Gray. "And how ironic is it that you're the one fucking her? I can throw you under the bus too, Aasher."

"Does our rival run *that* fucking deep that you'd ruin this team's chances at winning, Sully? Just let it go and tell your little fuckheads to let it go too, or I'll take them down with you." I'd tried being patient, but my patience was running very fucking thin.

He smiled, and I pictured ramming my fist into his face and knocking his teeth out all over this goddamn floor.

"I don't know, Matthews. You tell me. I called dibs on her first, and you just had to swoop in and beat me. Like usual."

There was a big difference between us.

I didn't give a shit about our feud.

And my interests in Riley had nothing to do with him.

It had everything to do with her.

"See you on the ice. Make sure to steal the puck from me too. God forbid you let me score for once." Sully stomped away.

Emory popped around the edge of the lockers and stood beside me to watch him leave. My blood rushed with so much anger I shook. A few seconds passed before he leaned in. "Take that shit out on the ice. Pretend the puck is his face. Do whatever you have to do, but don't stoop to his level and fuck us all."

My teeth ground against one another with frustration, but I planned to do exactly what Emory said.

After all, Sully could threaten me all he wanted.

He couldn't take me down without going down too.

———

The Hawks were lethal, and their student section was even rowdier than ours. Their goalie gave Emory a run for his money—both of them blocking pucks left, right, up, down, and every other direction you could think of.

I hadn't forgotten about the conversation with Sully, but I did let it fuel me with swift speed on the ice. Coach pulled me aside at one point and asked if I needed to sit, but I brushed him off, slipping past Sully while managing to keep my stick to myself.

There were only two minutes left to go, and we were tied.

One to one.

Theo zoomed past me, ice slicing up in his wake. "I don't know what has gotten into you, but keep it up and pay attention. Coach wants us to do the *whip*."

Sully tapped his stick against the ice before taking off after Theo. We'd practiced this drill so many times, but I had a feeling that Sully was about to fuck it up because of me. I wanted to believe that he wouldn't stoop so low because his future rode on this team's back too, but I also didn't know him as well as I thought. We had unresolved issues, but I thought we were both man enough to keep it off the ice until now.

"Fuck," I mumbled, skating toward center ice. Riley crossed my mind for a brief second, and I could see her now, pacing back and forth in front of the TV as she watched us strive for our last win of the season.

"*Whip!*" Coach yelled from the side.

I followed his cue and nodded to Theo.

Time moved in slow motion. Sully slipped to the right when he was supposed to go to the left. Ford zipped past, and there was a hint of confusion there as we caught eyes. *Fuck.*

"If you fuck this up, you're dead. Don't make me clean up another one of your messes," I seethed under my breath.

Sully's lips flattened, and my stomach turned.

One of the Crown Point players saw the diversion in our team, and they knew it was a gap they could weasel themselves into.

"Crow!" I yelled to Theo.

His rebuttal of me changing the play lasted only a second before he looked over to Sully, seeing that he wasn't in line with the rest of us.

The problem with adding a new player to a team full of seniors was that the new player was never quite in sync, especially if they were as slithery as Sully. It was a good thing Theo could adapt, though, because when he flew forward, shifting back and forth over the ice, we all followed suit.

The puck zipped over to Ford and then to me, missing the edge of a Crown Point's stick by a hair. I channeled my anger and focused on what I needed to do for the team, and the puck zipped underneath Whiteshaw's padded knee, and the buzzer sounded.

Relief sunk onto my shoulders, and I took my first full deep breath since my chat with Sully in the locker room.

I threw my stick to the ground and ripped my helmet off. My team rushed over and crowded me as our fans raved in the background. Theo's bare hand slapped my shoulder as he brought me in for a hug.

"What the fuck was that?" he asked under his breath.

"That was me getting us a win," I answered. "I'll explain later."

His jaw flickered, but he was happy with the win, just like the rest of the team. No one truly cared how we won, just that we did.

Unless you were Sully.

He acted with fake glee, skating around the rink with his hands raised above his head, egging the crowd on. I scanned the stands, watching them lose it over his encouragement and froze at a distant sight that hit me square in the chest.

"What—"

My parents.

They were beaming with pride. My mom had her cowbell, still painted blue and white—my high school's colors. Her graying brown hair was pulled into a low bun, but she must have shaken the bell so hard that some thin strands had fallen out.

"Thataboy, Matthews!" my dad's shout was raspy.

How are they here?

I wasn't an emotional person by any means. But my vision grew blurry.

"Is that your mom?" Ford asked, wrapping his arm around my shoulder.

I nodded, pulling my attention away from their overjoyed faces. I didn't understand how or why they were here, but what I did know was that my pride swelled.

"Your mom is hot in person."

I snapped my neck over so fast that it popped. Ford ducked as I wound my arm back and tried to punch him. His laughter echoed through the hall as we made our way back to the locker room where Coach was elated.

The team was celebrating our last win of the season, even as we descended to the bus. I spotted Coach talking to his wife, and I stopped mid-step.

My parents were huddled close. My dad's hand was intertwined in my mom's as she laughed at something Coach's wife said. I shuffled over the pavement, glancing at the starry sky behind them in the distance.

"Hun." My mom pulled away from my dad and wrapped me in a hug.

She was small. I towered over her, and my arms could have wrapped around her slender body twice.

"What are you doing here?" I asked. They couldn't afford it, and we all knew it.

"Don't you worry about that," Riley's mom—*er, Coach's wife*—patted my arm.

Did they do this?

"That was a good game, son. I didn't realize how much I missed watching you play in person."

I grinned at my dad after pulling away from my mom's warm grasp. There was a tight feeling in my gut, reminding me how much I owed my parents for sticking by me, even when I thought my world was falling apart.

After everything happened with Savannah, my dad asked me what happened. He wanted to know if I did something to cause her spiral. There was no anger, just curiosity. I told him the truth. I told him how guilty I felt for not speaking up and for not being there for her like I should have been.

He stayed quiet, patted my back, and told me that we learned from our mistakes. And then he and my mom found a way to get me to Bexley U. He worked double shifts during my freshman year to cover my books because the loans weren't as hefty as we would have liked. Savannah's dad fucked us, but my parents held their chins high and got me to where I was now.

"I'm glad you came," I managed to choke out.

The bus lights flickered, and Coach shook my dad's hand, knowing we needed to get going. We talked for a few more minutes before Coach and his wife walked over to the bus, giving me a private moment with my parents.

"You look so handsome."

"Mom." I grinned as she tried to fix my tie. "The game is over. We're going back to the hotel, and I'm crashing until morning. My tie is fine."

She brushed me off. "Just let me take care of you."

I laughed. "Fine."

My dad shook his head and grabbed my mom's waist, pulling her into him. "You better go." He inched his head toward the bus.

Shrugging, I hoisted my bag up higher on my shoulder. "Not until you two tell me how you got here."

I did the math in my head. It was a six-hour drive from my hometown to Crown Point. My dad's 2007 Ford F150 was a gas guzzler—and front row tickets?

"Did you get a bonus that I'm not aware of?"

Highly unlikely.

My sigh matched his. The Bexley U logo on his shirt stretched when his chest puffed out. Both of my parents were hesitant to tell me. Their eyes were shifty and they shuffled on their feet.

"Coach?" I probed. "His wife?"

I paused as a flicker of realization nestled into my chest. *Riley.*

"You know what." I pulled my mom into another hug. "It doesn't matter. I'm just glad you two made it."

They'd be at every game if they could.

I knew it.

They didn't have to tell me.

"We love you," my dad said, shaking my hand before pulling me in for a hug.

"I know." I nodded. "I love you too."

"Aasher! Let's go." Ford stuck his head out the door. "Hello, Mr. and Mrs. Matthews!"

My mom waved to Ford, already knowing exactly who he was because he had FaceTimed her several times from my phone. He had a way of slipping into everyone's lives.

"Text me when you get back to school tomorrow so I know you've made it."

"I will," I said, knowing I'd hear from my dad if I didn't.

Once I climbed on the bus and pulled my phone out, I opened my texts and tapped on her name.

Duster: Impressive, Matthews. Very impressive.

I pressed myself back into my seat, and heat coated my chest.

Me: It was you, wasn't it?

It was late. She may have been sleeping.

I clicked my phone off, but it buzzed a second later. Swiping up, I turned the brightness down and blocked out the continuous celebration from my team. They were rowdy, some planning on sneaking away to hit the bars before needing to get on the bus at eight a.m. sharp. I had no desire to go out. In fact, I wished we could drive through the night so I'd be back to Bexley U faster.

Duster: What are you talking about?

I smiled. Who did she think I was?

Me: Don't play coy with me, Duster. You had something to do with my parents coming to my game.

Duster: Don't be mad, please.

How could I ever be angry with her for doing something like that?

> Me: I know you're used to an asshole like Gray, but I'm not him. You somehow managed to get my parents to one of my games—something that I know they will be forever grateful for. That is probably the nicest thing anyone has ever done for me, Duster.

She was out of her mind if she thought I was angry. If anything, it made me fall for her even harder. Not only was she on board with me keeping us a secret until the end of the season—even without knowing that her dad threatened my chances at the NHL—but now she was making moves like this? Riley Lennon had nestled herself right next to my heart.

You couldn't live without a beating heart, and I was pretty certain I couldn't live without her either.

> Duster: So, you're not mad?

> Me: I'm the furthest thing from mad. I want to do nothing but kiss you right now, so get ready for tomorrow night, baby, because I'm going to prove to you that I'm nothing like Gray, and I fully plan on appreciating you the way you deserve.

Only, she deserved to be flaunted around.
    Not shoved behind a closed door.

[34]

RILEY

THE HOUSES along Bexley U's party street were quiet—all except the one that was holding the end-of-season hockey celebration. It was the biggest fraternity at Bexley U, therefore they had the biggest house, and leave it to Taytum and her flirty smile to get them to agree to host the party.

Everyone was wearing black—*a black-out party*. The only thing in the midst of the dark color were the shiny silver streamers hanging over every archway. The bowl of black punch—something that screamed bad decisions—smelled of liquor and blackberries. I opted for a beer instead, but mostly everyone had a cup with the liquid sloshing out the top.

There were so many bodies packed in the living room that I was forced to stay in the kitchen with Sutton sipping on her drink. Butterflies filled my belly at the thought of seeing Aasher. I wanted nothing more than to stay in my apartment and wait for their bus to weave through the winding roads toward the hockey rink, but Sutton got word that Crew was making an appearance to congratulate his alma mater on their season, and I knew she'd need all the support she could get.

"It's only *this* packed because of Crew coming." Her eye roll told me she was less than pleased about his appearance.

"Do you wanna leave?" I asked.

Sutton and I had both been burned by hockey players, but her heart was still broken.

Mine wasn't.

Her blonde hair whizzed past her face when she looked over at me. "No. I don't want him to have that power over me."

I completely understood. My beer bottle clanked with her cup, and we tipped our drinks back and took a gulp. My phone buzzed, and I knew it was Aasher. I'd missed nearly all his texts from this afternoon because I was in the rink, practicing.

My tryout for the figure skating team was a formality, according to Coach Chen-Wong, but the entire board would be there. First impressions meant everything, and I wanted to be ready.

Aasher: If you aren't at this party, you're in trouble.

A wicked grin curved onto my face as I typed back.

. . .

Me: What are you going to do if I'm not?

Aasher and I were on a whole new level. Instead of our usual antics of denying our attraction and hiding our desires, we were embracing them in the only way we could without messing everything up.

I liked knowing he wanted to see me.

I had butterflies every time I thought about him, and just a simple glance from him made me pause.

The anticipation of him walking through the front door had me on the edge of my seat. I nibbled on my bottom lip and watched as several hockey players walked through with their confidence as haughty as ever.

Where is he?

"What am I going to do, hmm?"

I shrieked, making Sutton jump beside me. I spun and gripped my beer bottle by the neck.

Aasher was standing against the kitchen bar with his arms crossed over his gray Henley. *How long has he been there?* The first two buttons were undone, and I gulped at the sexy smirk he was wearing.

"Jesus," Sutton said, placing her cup on the bar top. "You scared me."

Aasher's gaze didn't leave mine. "Sorry."

He wasn't sorry.

Sutton grabbed her drink again and put her back to Aasher and me. Ford and Emory slipped in past us, and after they said hi to me, they ushered Sutton farther into the party. The guys knew that Crew was showing up. It was all over campus. They would take care of Sutton. She had nothing to worry about.

"You're lucky," Aasher said, staring directly at my lips.

"Am I?" I asked, popping my hip out. I leaned against the edge of the counter beside him. I stared at his strong profile, watching his dark lashes move up and down with his slow blinks.

"I'd find you one way or another." He grinned, and to anyone else, it would look like he was talking to the person in front of him instead of talking to me.

"And what would you do to me if you found me?" I baited, feeling edgier than usual. Just talking to Aasher made the few gulps of beer in my belly bubble.

The muscle lining his jaw flickered, and when he turned toward me, my knees buckled. "Want to find out?"

I tipped my beer back and chugged the rest of it. Aasher's jaw clenched, but he said nothing. I pushed the bottle into his chest, feeling his ramming heart thump against the back of my hand. "Yes," I whispered. "You've gotta find me first, though."

His lips parted at the temptation.

I giggled and turned on my heel and weaved through the party, knowing he'd come find me. I stopped and talked to a few people—Taytum, some of her sorority sisters, and even one of the freshman figure skaters who stumbled over every word when she recognized me. Some of Aasher's teammates followed my every step, probably still attempting to secure that bet they had, but I slipped right past them and darted up the stairs.

I felt Aasher's eyes on me, even if I didn't have the notion to look back. Most of the doors were locked, so I slinked down the dark hallway and slipped into a closet.

A laugh brewed.

Why is this so fun?

I was giddy with nerves at the thought of Aasher

opening the door and finding me.

My phone buzzed, and I pulled it out of my back pocket.

Aasher: You're going to be sorry.

Me: I highly doubt that.

I jumped when the door unlatched. I pressed myself farther into the shelves. The door creaked slowly as he pushed it open. It revealed nothing but his shadowy figure in the hall. My breath quickened.

"A duster in the cleaning closet? How ironic."

I rolled my eyes at his joke.

"You aren't very good at hiding, Riley." The door slammed behind him. "Some would think you wanted to be found."

"I did," I said, surprised at how sultry my voice was.

My breasts pushed forward when his hands fell to my hips, slipping underneath my black long-sleeve shirt. It was mesh, so I paired it with a lace bralette, knowing I'd catch more attention than usual. "I like your outfit," he whispered over my ear. "But I'm about to rip it to shreds."

"That's what I hoped for when I put it on."

I weaved my hands up his chest and wrapped them around his neck. My fingers teased his unruly strands of hair, and when his teeth grazed the sensitive part along my neck, I pulled on the ends.

"You smell so good." He pulled back and pressed himself into me. He was already hard, and suddenly, our touches grew more frantic. I tore my top off at the same time as he undid my pants and shoved them down my legs. The button hit the door behind him when he threw them, cutting through the booming music from downstairs.

One second, I was on flat feet. The next, I was slammed onto the shelf behind me. My legs spread when he crowded my space, and the moment our mouths touched, his fingers dove through the front of my panties, and his palm scratched against my throbbing clit.

"*God*," I whimpered.

"It's only been a couple of days, Riley. Yet look at how wet your pussy is for me."

His words made something curl inside of me, and I moved myself against his hand, chasing the high only he could give me.

"Oh, she likes it when I talk dirty to her?"

I whimpered, grabbing on to his hand to keep it steady as I rocked my hips back and forth.

"Sinful," he moaned.

I felt drunk, but it had nothing to do with the beer I had.

His other hand that was keeping me steady crept underneath the lace of my bralette, and he squeezed, sending tingles down past my waist.

"Fuck," he said. "I feel how close you are."

"I am," I gasped when his mouth fell to my nipple. He licked and sucked. My head hit the back of the wall when I came against his fingers, but the pain only lasted a second when he pulled my panties down my legs and entered me a second later.

"I can't wait any more."

My body shook as my heels dug into his lower back, keeping him as close to me as possible. He moved fast and took what he wanted, and I let him.

I moaned his name. His teeth sunk into my lips, and my back arched. There were voices outside the door. People were walking down the hall.

"Aasher." I dug my nails into his shoulders, but he wasn't stopping. "Did you lock the door?"

"No," he groaned, tilting his hips to hit a spot that took my breath away.

"But—" I moved against him, unable to stop. "Someone could walk in and see us."

His mouth fell to mine, and he swallowed my worries. Our tongues tangled, and we were both sweaty. I pulled on his hair again and matched his pace. I was close to orgasming again, and he knew it.

"Let them. I want everyone to know you're mine."

"But—"

Aasher's thumb brushed over my clit before he pressed hard and rubbed me.

"*But* nothing."

He sent me over the edge. His hot, needy mouth ate away at my moans, and he pumped in one more time before pulling out and shooting his cum out beside me.

We were both out of breath and stayed put for so long that the sweat dried on our skin. I was surprised when his hands found my hips again, pulling my naked body to meet him. We made out again, except this time, it wasn't rushed. It was slow, sensual, and he cursed before pulling away.

"I could fuck you again."

He bent down and pulled my panties up my legs, righting them on my hips before placing me on the ground. Once I was fully dressed and I ran my fingers through my hair, Aasher grabbed me by the hand and kissed my knuckles.

The door opened, and a blast of cool air floated around

us. He turned and peered down at me with his slightly red cheeks and swollen lips. "I need a beer after that."

I laughed. "Same."

35

AASHER

"Wait." Riley let go of my hand, and I stopped walking to look down at her. *She is breathtaking.* In fact, she did a lot more than take my breath away. When I had her in my hands, I thought of nothing but her.

"Yeah?" I scanned her body, making sure I had put her back together correctly after acting like a wild animal in the stupid fucking broom closet.

"Um, you go first."

"What?"

It only took a second to remember that although I considered her mine, she wasn't really. Not in front of the entire campus where it could get back to her dad. I was on his good side right now, but I wouldn't be after he found out I had been lying to him and fucking his daughter behind his back.

"Oh, right." Our hands dropped to our sides. "You go first."

322 / SJ SYLVIS

She gave me the side-eye and her lip tilted. "Why? You want to watch me from behind?"

I grinned and nodded, but it was a complete lie. I wanted to add more names to my shit list, because every guy who followed my girl's swaying hips was officially an enemy to me.

I leaned against the banister as Riley descended the steps. She was only a few ahead of me when I started after her, not wanting to be too far. The party was packed—too packed for my liking.

Too many eyes.

Too many poor decisions.

Too much alcohol.

"That wasn't obvious at all," Ford said under his breath, pretending to cough. He pressed a beer into my chest, and I willingly took it, peeling my gaze from Riley for only a second. "Maybe you should just tell Coach. What's the worst that could happen? You already have the girl."

"Trust me," I said, forcing another sip down my throat, "I've thought about it."

"But?"

I searched the sea of black for Riley, spotting her with Taytum and Sutton. Taytum put her beer up in the air, and the girls cheered with her. My nostrils flared at the cup in Riley's hand instead of a beer bottle. *What is she drinking?*

I sighed and turned toward Ford. "Coach didn't just ask me to watch out for her. He told me to treat her like a sister. To make sure none of the guys fucked with her. He specifically told me not to break his trust."

"Well, you don't fuck your sister, so there went that."

I ignored his attempt to make a joke.

"You don't get it. He...threatened me." That sounded way worse than it actually was, so I backtracked. "Kind of.

He insinuated that he could fuck up my future if I betrayed his trust."

Ford seemed to have an ah-ha moment. His head tilted before he turned away and nodded. "Now we're getting somewhere. Does she know?"

I shook my head.

We both leaned against the railing of the stairs.

"Does Sully?"

I laughed sarcastically. "Fuck no. I don't think I have to worry about him, though. If he tries to take me down, he'll go down too. Plus"—I shrugged—"during the game, I think I showed him that I have more pull with this team than he does."

I pulled my attention away from Riley and looked for him.

He would be here. I was certain of it.

"Sully already left." Efrain slipped up beside us, knowing who I was looking for.

"He did?"

His mouth twitched. "He left with that girl you always fucked."

I paused, thinking over his words. It was like now that I had Riley, I forgot there was anyone before her. "You mean Liv?"

I'd been avoiding her.

She was smart enough to know why.

Efrain snapped his fingers. "Yep, probably his attempt at messing with your head."

He was sorely mistaken if he thought sleeping with a previous puck bunny was going to mess with my head. I should warn Liv about him, though. I made a mental note to do that next time I saw her. Graham Sullivan had poor morals. That much was obvious.

We stood back against the stairs and watched the girls take off to the living room. It was hard to keep track of them between all the dancing and before I knew it, one song turned into three, and my beer was empty.

Grabbing Ford's and Efrain's bottles, I headed to the kitchen to replace them, but they followed me. "I think I can handle grabbing some beers," I joked.

Efrain tugged on my arm. "Wait, stop. What's going on over there?"

I followed his line of sight. Sutton and Taytum were slack-jawed, and their eyes were beady. Riley's face was hidden behind Sutton's head, but I knew with the way they were looking at me, it had to do with her.

Taytum rushed over to us, and we met her halfway.

"Tay, what's wrong?" Ford grabbed her by the arm, and instead of her usual annoyance with him, she looked scared and maybe a little pissed.

"Riley said she feels off. She's a little wobbly. Like she's drunk, but she only had a few sips."

No way.

The room slowed as I pushed forward and found Riley leaning against the wall. Her breathing was shallow, and her blue eyes were unfocused. Her dainty fingers dug into Sutton's arm.

I zipped around and found the cup I knew she'd put up to her lips when we first came downstairs. It was sitting on top of the mantel above her head. It was half-empty.

"Who gave her that drink?" I asked, unlatching Riley's fingers from Sutton's arm. There were crescent-like marks left behind.

"I don't know," Sutton replied. "I asked her the same thing."

I held on to her tightly and noticed how quiet she was.

My gaze swung around the party, and everyone else seemed fine. Sure, there were hazy looks and drunken laughter, but no one was stumbling around or causing a scene.

I met the eyes of Ford and Efrain. They were already rounding the troops.

"No one else looks drugged." I said.

Riley wasn't completely knocked out, but it was clear she wasn't herself.

"Drugged?" Sutton's mouth fell open, and she quickly put her cup on the mantel beside Riley's empty drink. Taytum took off, whispering in every female's ear. They all dropped their cups a moment later.

"Shut this fucking shit down," I growled.

I was so angry I couldn't even see straight. My teammates got to work. They grabbed Rush, who gathered his football players and then snagged a couple more of our own.

Sutton trailed me out of the party and propped the back door open. She stopped for a brief second when she heard her ex from behind.

"Sutton, are you okay?" he asked.

I didn't plan to stick around to hear her reply, but Sutton's and Crew's footsteps followed closely behind as she filled him in. The lights to his brand-new car flashed, and he opened the door. "Get in," he ushered. "Are we taking her to Coach Lennon?"

"No!" Riley's head leaned on my shoulder. I hoisted her up in my arms and climbed in the back seat of Crew's car. Sutton took the front.

"He's going to lose his shit." Crew said when his car revved. My heart was beating faster than it ever had, but Coach's reaction to Riley getting drugged—because it was clear that someone slipped something in her drink, even if she didn't guzzle it down—was the last thing on my mind.

"Sutton, please tell me you didn't drink that fucking punch."

"Don't act like you care!" Sutton snapped, shutting her ex down. She peered back at me. "Do you want to take her to our apartment?"

"Do not tell my parents." Riley slurred.

Fuck.

"Shouldn't we at least take her to the hospital?" Crew asked.

"No," Riley repeated slowly. "Guys... I'm fine. I'm..." Her lip wobbled. "I didn't drink that much of it. It probably won't even show up on a drug test."

Sutton looked at me. I contemplated calling Riley's parents, but she tugged on my shirt, and even though her eyes were droopy and glossed over, she silently pleaded with me.

"Please," she whispered.

"Just take us home." I sighed, giving in to what Riley wanted.

I'd wait until she was in her right state of mind before running to her father, but one way or another, he was going to know what had happened. I would get to the bottom of who spiked her drink, but my first priority was taking care of her.

Once Crew parked the car and we piled into the elevator, I was shaking with adrenaline. Riley tried to climb out of my arms at one point, telling me she was fine, but I held her tighter. A girl like Riley didn't want help, and she sure as hell didn't like to be taken advantage of—not that anyone did. But given her past, this was hitting her in a way that it didn't hit most.

It was the reason she didn't want her parents to know.

Things had *just* become normal for her. *For them.*

"She's staying with me," I said, bypassing Sutton's lead to their apartment.

"Don't tell me..." Crew put his hands on his hips while looking at his previous coach's daughter in my arms.

I rolled my eyes at his attempt to act authoritative. Sutton made sure to put him in his place, but I was too busy staring down at Riley's smooth face as she drifted in and out of sleep to care what Sutton had told him.

"Aasher." Riley clutched my shirt when we got into my room.

"I'm here. You're okay. I've got you."

I kept my door open, knowing that my roommates would be home as soon as they deescalated the party. They would want to check on her.

There was no way I could keep this from Coach. It would be all over campus soon.

How could I let this happen?

After placing her down on my bed, I stripped her out of her clothes and draped one of my T-shirts over her slender shoulders before pulling her into my arms.

"What are we doing?"

"We're sleeping, baby." I kissed her on the temple.

She snuggled into my chest and draped a leg over me before sighing wistfully. I could smell the berry punch on her breath. My stomach was in knots, and my phone was vibrating nonstop in my pocket. I couldn't fathom looking at what was on the screen, in fear that Coach had already found out and was sending me my own obituary.

There was only one person at the top of my list that would have done something like this.

The only problem was that Sully wasn't even at the party, so who the hell drugged my girl, and how could I get away with murder?

36

RILEY

Hushed voices pulled me from sleep. I cringed at the rising nausea and clutched my belly. *God, why do I feel so sick?*

My eyes moved back and forth behind my eyelids. The movement was making me more nauseated, and before I knew it, I was falling onto the floor and trying to make it to the bathroom.

Strong arms embraced me, and the toilet appeared a moment later. My back ached as I emptied my stomach and sweat trickled down my cheek. Once the room stopped spinning, I took a deep breath and realized that I was in Aasher's bathroom.

"Here, baby." A blue Gatorade was placed in front of my face, and I took it with a shaky hand. I felt dizzy and confused.

After taking a small sip, Aasher took the drink back and put the cap on. My head fell against the wall, and I stared up at the ceiling, breathing in and out of my nose.

"Are you okay?" he asked gingerly, sinking down beside me so our arms brushed.

"I just puked in front of you. *Again.*" A short laugh left me. "I've been better."

Aasher didn't laugh. His chest didn't tumble with a chuckle. Nothing. Curiosity pulled my attention to him, and his lips were pulled into a frown. "Aasher?"

My cheek pressed into his warm hand when he cupped my face. His finger brushed against my skin gently, and warmth flew through me. "Do you remember anything from last night?"

I thought long and hard—so hard it made my head pound.

Shit, that's a killer headache.

My first worry was if I was going to be ready for tryouts tomorrow, and then I quickly moved past that thought and worried over Aasher's tightly drawn face and worried gaze. "Um..." I shrugged, hugging my stomach tighter. "I remember going up the stairs and..." My cheeks instantly felt hot.

He cleared his throat. "After that."

"Dancing." I tried to piece together the rest of the night. My chest grew tight, and my stomach rolled. "Wait." My heart raced when things started to come back to me. The broken thoughts were sharp enough to cut me.

"Hey." Aasher's fingers softly brushed my cheek again. "Take a breath. You're okay."

"Why can't I remember everything, though?" My bottom lip trembled. I frantically scratched at my throat because it felt tight. For someone that likes to be in control, I felt completely unstable and *out of control*.

"Baby, calm down." Aasher pulled me into his lap, and he pressed my head into his neck. I inhaled his scent and focused on the way he was rubbing my lower back. "Please." A few long seconds passed, and I breathed in and out of my nose, focusing on his warm skin against my cheek. "There you go."

I was teary-eyed, and I knew, with the little memory I had, what had happened.

"How could I be so irresponsible?"

"No." Aasher pulled my face up and wiped my tears with his thumbs. His green eyes hardened to stone. "This is *not* your fault. Don't you dare."

I couldn't fathom it. I couldn't wrap my head around the fact that someone else, someone I couldn't even put a face to, took my control away. *Again.* I was upset, but I leaned more toward anger than anything.

"Did anything happen?"

It was a girl's worst nightmare.

"Nothing." Aasher's fingers dug into my hair. "I had my eye on you the entire time. We're still not even sure who could have slipped something into your drink."

"Sully?"

"He left before we came downstairs."

I was confused, and my head hurt. I vaguely remembered coming home—if I thought really hard—but the more I tried to unblur my memory, the more my head pounded. "Was Gray there?" I asked, trying to think of anyone who would want to get back at me for something.

"No." He was just as confused as I was.

"One of the guys who was involved in the bet?" That made the most sense, but would they seriously stoop *that* low?

"That's what we've been trying to figure out." We turned toward Ford lingering in the doorway of Aasher's bathroom. Berkley and Efrain weren't too far behind him, listening. "Do you remember who gave you the drink?"

The drink.

What drink?

Aasher unscrewed the Gatorade for me again as I sat and thought. I sipped on it before handing it back. "I only remember getting some of the punch because someone in the kitchen said they were out of beer."

It was rule number one in the college girl handbook: *Don't drink anything you didn't pour yourself.*

"I'm sorry," I blabbed. "I'm so stupid."

I let my guard down, and although Aasher was there, and I knew that nothing more had happened, it could have been so much worse.

"You have nothing to be sorry for," Ford snapped before storming away.

Efrain and Berkley followed after him, and I was alone with Aasher again.

His long legs were out in front of him, and that was when I realized he was in the same dark jeans and Henley from last night. "Did you sleep at all?"

I looked at the dark bags beneath his eyes, and he shrugged. "I was afraid you'd need me."

"I do need you," I whispered, grabbing his hand.

I shut my eyes when they blurred. My thoughts were messy, and my emotions were all over the place, but the one thing I was certain of was my need to keep someone like Aasher in my life—*no matter what.*

"Ry." He swallowed so loud I glanced over at him. "We have to tell your dad."

I sprung up quickly, knocking the Gatorade bottle halfway across the tiled floor. "No."

Aasher was behind me faster than I wanted. He caught me around the waist and spun me around, pressing our bodies together. My ear pressed against his chest, and his ramming heart stopped me from wiggling free. "Riley. Someone fucking drugged you, and even though Sully wasn't there, I am almost positive he had something to do with it."

"Why would he do that?"

I leaned back and peered into his eyes.

"Sully and I have had it out for each other since high school. When I found out about the bet, I made sure to play my cards right. I didn't want him to know that I was aware because I *knew* it would egg him on, and now he knows that you and I are..."

"Did you tell him about us? How could you do that? He is gonna be the first to run to my dad, and who knows what he'll tell him. My dad is going to kill yo—" Aasher's finger fell to my mouth, silencing me.

"I don't give a damn if your dad finds out about us. You were drugged, Riley. I refuse to let that go, so please don't ask me to."

This was a mess.

"Is that why you have been hiding me? Not because you think my dad will disapprove but because of Sully?" *That is ridiculous.*

Aasher darted his attention to the left.

"You're lying about something."

"I'm not lying about anything."

I pulled myself away and sat on his bed. I wasn't going to let the spinning room stop this conversation from happening. "Then answer my question."

Aasher pulled on the ends of his hair in frustration. "Riley."

"I will walk out of this room right now."

He snapped to attention, dropping his arms by his sides. He didn't bat an eyelash when the truth fell from his mouth. "Your dad said he'd ruin my chances at the NHL if I broke his trust. It was after he had asked me to watch out for you, to make sure you stayed safe."

My mouth parted.

"I'd already broken his trust by not telling him about the bet. I thought I could handle things on my own and keep you away from the team, but with doing that, I fell for you. I've broken his trust a million times over again, and I wanted to wait until I signed with the Hops before doing anything rash, but I won't play on a team with someone who is capable of this. You're not a toy, Riley. I won't stand for it." Aasher pushed off the edge of his dresser and flung his bedroom door open.

"Where are you going?!" I asked, jumping up from the bed before wobbling and nearly falling. Aasher was right there to catch me, pushing me down to sit.

"Sit." He turned to walk away. "I'm going to go fix this."

"Don't tell him, Aasher."

"I'm done hiding you, and I'd rather die by the hands of your father than let Graham Sullivan or his little following have even one tiny goddamn impure thought about you. They made a mistake with that bet, and it's time they knew it."

"Wait!" I shouted. "Just wait."

He paused before shaking his head. "Riley, I'm not playing on a team with someone like him."

"I don't expect you to. I'm just as angry, Aasher."

"But?" he asked, waiting for me to continue.

I dropped my hand. "Just get the facts straight first. Don't tear apart the team because you *think* he had something to do with this. It means too much to you and my dad to throw it all away because of me."

Aasher laughed, but it was edged with sarcasm. He dropped to a knee in front of me. "Riley, don't you get it? Nothing means more to me than you."

I was speechless after he walked away and left his apartment.

My hand flew to my mouth and then to my chest as I rubbed the spot my heart was slamming against. His confession was full of truth, but I hated knowing that he was about to throw a wedge into everything he'd worked for.

Because of me.

I stayed on the end of his bed and realized that the apartment was empty. In the midst of trying to figure out a way to find out who was responsible for last night, my phone vibrated. I grabbed it, hoping it was Aasher to let me know he'd changed his mind, but when I saw who it was, my heart sank. Three missed calls and a text from Assistant Coach Davis.

She was informing me that tryouts had been rescheduled.

For today.

I popped up, ignoring the roll of my stomach, and rushed across the hall to my apartment.

Sutton was sipping on a cup of coffee with her phone in her hand when I flew through the door. "I was just about to text you." She placed the mug down and followed me into the bathroom as I quickly turned the sink on to wash my face. "Are you okay? How are you feeling?"

I turned to her with wide eyes. "Nervous."

I couldn't even think about what had happened last night or how I wanted to rush after Aasher and plead my case again. "My tryouts got rescheduled."

Her brows fell. "For when?"

"Right now."

37

AASHER

"What the fuck were you thinking?"

Theo wasn't nearly as angry as I imagined he'd be, but he still slapped the top of my dashboard.

I glared at him from the driver's seat.

"Riley? *Really?* I thought you said nothing was going on between you?"

I leaned back, eyeing the parking lot for Coach's shiny black Dodge Ram with the BUWolves license plate. "Just like you said nothing was going on between you and your fake girlfriend?"

Theo thought twice and sighed, ripping off his BU beanie and throwing it in my back seat. "So what's your plan? You just gonna walk into Coach's office and say, '*Hey, I'm fuckin' your daughter, but don't throw me off the team. Banish Graham Sullivan instead because he started a bet to see who could fuck her first. Oh, and I think he may have tried to date-rape her while I was supposed to be watching her. Sorry.'*"

My jaw flexed.

"Fuck, Aasher. Think with your head, not your dick."

"My dick? Really?" I seethed. "I'm pretty sure you of all people know that I'm not thinking with my dick."

Theo blew out a breath, and I did the same. *Relax.* There was no way I would make it out alive if I walked into Coach's office to tell the truth with anger riding my nerves.

"Fine. Sorry," he said, flying back into the seat once more. "I'm just...we're *this* close to the conference tourney, and now the entire team is going to be on edge."

I know. I fucking know. "But," he started, placing his hand on the door handle, "I would rip someone to fucking shreds if they pulled that shit with Claire."

We made eye contact and silently agreed on a plan. Theo and I would do whatever it took to keep the team together while informing Coach about what happened. I knew Theo would back me because he understood where I was coming from. At the beginning of the season...maybe not. But now he and I both knew there could be something more to the future than *just* hockey.

My phone rang just as the crisp winter air swooped into my car. We paused when Ford's voice came through the speaker.

"Get to the arena."

"I'm already here."

Theo added, "With me."

I heard Berkley say, *"Good. He's gonna need you."*

"What's going on?" I asked, pretending I didn't hear Coach's shovel digging my grave in the background.

"Sully just slipped out of Coach's office, looking more smug than ever."

Efrain's voice came through the speaker next. "He was practically walking on sunshine."

Theo and I were out of my car before I could even manage to hang up.

I may have been walking right into my own death, but at least I'd die an honest man.

—————

"Out." Theo snapped his fingers once, and the entire locker room emptied. It was time for conditioning anyway, so not many players were lingering around, most of them already hitting the weights.

"Shit." I forced a breath to leave my mouth. "I'm fucking nervous."

"You should be."

I rapped my knuckles against the door before Theo and I walked through the threshold. I took one look at Coach and knew that he had been told a lie. Beads of sweat rested below his hairline, and the vein above his left eyebrow was loud and proud.

Theo was the first to say something. "Coach, before you throw him off the team, I need you to hear him out."

Theo was a good man, a phenomenal hockey player, and an even better friend. I'd owe him forever after sticking his neck out on the line for me—not that he had much riding on this conversation. He had already signed an exclusive contract and was headed to the NHL regardless.

"Let's hear it, then." Coach threw his pen across the room, missing my head by no more than a centimeter. "Please inform me how one of the best players on this team has been lying to my face the entire season and shoving my daughter into closets at college parties, doing God knows what with her!"

R.I.P. Aasher Matthews.

"I didn't shove her into a closet." It was a poor opening line. I recognized that immediately after Theo elbowed me so hard in the ribs that I grunted. Coach's knuckles were begging to touch my nose. I could tell by the shuddering white color as he squeezed them together.

Standing up, I rounded the back of the chair I was sitting in and gripped the top. "You told me not to break your trust, and I did. I'm sorry for that." I made sure to look him in the eye, even if it was like looking down the barrel of a gun. "But I'm not sorry for falling for your daughter."

"You are not making a good case for yourself." Coach leaned back in his chair and leveled me with a glare.

"There was a bet."

His eyes flared with anger.

I threw my hands up. "I didn't start it, nor did I participate. But I knew about it. Riley did too."

Coach's glare hardened further, but he remained quiet.

"I thought I could do as you asked and keep her away from the guys, but..." I wanted to smile at the boldness that Riley possessed, wanting to make the team her bitch, but I made sure to keep my facial expressions to a minimum. "Riley overheard the guys making the bet. She was angry and had plans to put them in their place. You told me to keep her away from them, so Riley and I made our own bet. If I helped get her back on the ice in time for her tryouts, then she'd stop that unnecessary flirting and quit screwing with their heads." I rolled my eyes. "I knew it would only egg them on further anyway."

"And what makes you think I believe you?" Coach remained in his seat, which was surprising. I thought by now he'd have me by the throat. "I had someone come into my office mere minutes before you to tell me that *you* were the one to start the bet."

"I would never do that." *How could he think I'd do that?*

"I also have pictures of you pulling my daughter out of a closet at last night's party—where she just so happened to get fucking roofied!" His hand slapped on the table, and the photos flew down onto the floor, just like my confidence. I picked them up slowly, zeroing in on Riley's flushed face and timid smile as she followed me out of the closet.

Fuck.

I slapped the photo down on the table. "You think that smile is one of someone who was roofied and taken advantage of?" I shoved the flimsy photo off Coach's desk.

Theo gripped my shoulder and pushed me back down to my chair. I was too angry at the accusation to take a breath, so I continued to shout.

"Kick me off the team, screw my chances at signing with the Hops, get the dean involved and expel me from Bexley U, but don't you *dare* accuse me of treating your daughter like she's something you can play with and then throw away a moment later! I *love* her."

Shit, do I?

I threw my hands up and walked over to the door. I flung it open before pulling back and looking him right in the face. "And what the hell did you expect?" My question was full of mockery. "You know how perfect she is. You forced me to make friends with her but expected me *not* to fall for her at the same time?" I shook my head. "And you know what makes her so perfect?"

The room was silent.

"Her imperfections."

goose bumps rushed as I dug down deep and pulled out a truth that I hadn't known was there.

"She was trying so hard to be perfect at everything

because of that one fucking incident in high school, and it wrecked her."

I pointed at my chest. "I was the one who put her back together and helped her find herself again. I was the one who told her to skate for herself and no one else."

"Aasher—" Coach started to say something, but I cut him off.

"Make your decision. I'll be in the rink."

Before I made it through the locker room with my skates in tow, Coach shouted at me from his desk. "Rink is closed."

"You're already banning me from the rink?"

For fuck's sake.

"No. Figure skating tryouts are today."

"No," I corrected him. "They're tomorrow."

"No, they rescheduled. They're *today*."

I dropped my shit on the floor and ran right to the stands because knowing Riley, she would be here.

[38]

RILEY

"Are you sure you're okay to do this?" Sutton followed me around our apartment as I left various colors of leotards behind in my wake. I turned around, sucked in a slow breath at the lingering nausea from last night, and nodded at my choice of ballet-pink.

Aasher's T-shirt was in a pile at my feet. After slicking my hair into a tight, ballerina-like bun, I changed into my skin-colored tights and slipped into my leo that felt more like a second skin than anything.

"I don't have a choice. I *just* got the text that they are happening in twenty minutes." I argued, taking my blush brush and applying some highlighter to my cheek bones and the very tip of my nose. The dark bags under my eyes weren't going to go away, no matter what I did, so they had to stay.

I turned and looked at Sutton leaning against the doorjamb.

"I do have a choice," I corrected, knowing that I didn't

have to do this. It was up to me to decide my future, and it was up to me to decide if I wanted to continue with figure skating. Aasher was the one who opened my eyes to that.

"You're right." Sutton nodded. "And let me guess...you *want* to do this."

"For me," I whispered, running my hands down my velvet leo. "Someone once took the choice from me, and I refuse to let them do it again. Before leaving Rosewood, I only skated to prove something to someone. I didn't think I had a choice. It was either I *was perfect, made no mistakes,* or *nothing.* This isn't about that anymore."

I snagged my keys and rushed to the door, knowing I would be late if I didn't leave now. "No one is going to take my choice away. Someone roofied me last night, and if I let that stop me from doing something *I* want, then I'm no different than who I was at Rosewood."

Sutton opened the door for me and grabbed my hand. "You're such a badass."

I couldn't help but laugh.

Then she slapped me on the butt. "Go kill it, Ry. We are all rooting for you."

First, tryouts.

Second, find Aasher and we go talk to my dad together.

━━━

I smelled the cool ice of the rink the moment I stepped into the arena. The hockey team was there, their cars all parked in a single row toward the side entrance. I didn't let it distract me, though.

"There she is!" I was hurriedly pulled down the stairs by a senior skater, who I recognized from prior competitions. My skates bounced over my shoulder, and every step was like a pulley tugging on my sensitive belly.

"I'm not late," I announced, eyeing my future coach. The figure skating committee sat in a single row with their clipboards hugged tightly to their chests and glasses perched on the edges of their noses.

"Is that Riley Lennon?"

"I think so."

"Well, fuck us. We're out."

I leaned down to the young girls that were likely hoping for a full ride to Bexley U—or maybe just a spot on the team in general.

"There's room for us all," I whispered, winking at them. I'd already made the decision to treat this team differently than my last. I would be a senior, and there was no way I was going to run a team like the seniors did at Rosewood.

Lead by example, not by fear of competition.

"You smell like alcohol," Gianna whispered. Worry worked over her features, and her eyes widened. "Oh my god, tell me it wasn't you."

Shit. It was already around campus.

I gulped and sat down to tie my skates. "I'm fine."

Her hand landed on my arm. "Are you? I'm certain the committee would understand. You're Riley Lennon. You are already number one on this team."

"I don't want special treatment. Plus, I have to stop the curious looks and worries."

Gianna lifted her hands. "Alright, well...good luck. We could really benefit from having you on the team."

The way figure skating worked was we were all scored individually, but every point added up to one overall score. You skated for yourself, but you skated for the team too.

"Thanks." I smiled and headed toward the ice to meet

with the coach. We'd only had a handful of conversations over the last year, but she was well aware of who I was, and she already had my song choice lined up. It was the one that Aasher chose for me one night while I was training as his eyes followed my every move.

"Good luck, Riley."

I froze, turned, and then glared. My lungs were on fire, and my fingers twitched to slap him.

"How dare you show your face here."

Graham Sullivan looked guiltier than ever. His temples flicked back and forth as he rested along one of the seats within a row lined with his younger followers. "All of you," I said, looking at them.

Most of them swung their eyes in different directions, but Sully kept his eye on me. "What?"

"You think just because you weren't there last night that I don't know you were behind it?"

Sully's throat moved. I wanted to wrap my small hands around his neck to choke him. "Behind what? The bet?" He sighed and looked remorseful, his mouth drooping at the sides. "Riley, it was Aasher's idea. He's been fooling you from the beginning."

"Unbelievable," I whispered.

His hands went into his pockets as he stood and headed toward me. I stayed unmoving. "I know. I'm sorry. I should have told you."

I laughed. It sounded manic. "No. I mean it's unbelievable that you can stand there and lie *so* well. It's kind of scary."

He opened his mouth, and I knew that anyone within earshot was listening. My nerves were lessening the longer I talked to him, because it felt good to steal the power back from someone who took it.

"It wasn't Aasher's idea," I said, bending down slowly to make sure my skates were tied tightly. "It was yours." I popped up and smiled boldly. "I was in the locker room that day, listening to everything you said. The point system, *everything*."

Sully knew he'd been caught.

His eyebrows dipped just enough for me to keep going.

"And how fucking *dare* you slip something in my drink."

"You put something in her drink? Dude, what?"

I leaned around and eyed one of the younger hockey players. "Well, he didn't. But he had someone else do it because he can't even do his own dirty work."

"Nothing happened." Sully rolled his eyes. "It's not like you were touched. Jesus."

"Taking away someone's control, even for a few hours, isn't *nothing*." My knee met his groin, and he bent over at the waist, gasping for air. "Don't you *ever* do something like that again, or I swear to God, Graham, you'll regret it."

After I backed away, I turned around and shook out my arms. I slid onto the ice with a winning smile on my face. I'd never felt more like myself with the ice beneath my feet and fully capable of making my own decisions without trying to prove something to someone.

Skate for you, Riley.

I moved backward, creating little divots in the ice as my pink wispy tutu flew up beside my hips. After taking center ice and shoving away the jumbling in my belly, I inhaled and dug down to the part of myself that I was happy to show off.

"Let's go, Riley!"

I glanced up to the top of the arena and smiled. Ford, Berkley, Efrain, and even broody Emory were standing with their shirts pulled up, showing off their muscular bodies that were painted with the letters R-I-L-EY.

They were one person short.

Where is Aasher?

Ford pointed, and I scanned the arena before landing on him. He was still wearing the same clothes from last night but somehow still looked put together. My dad walked up behind him, and I froze. I put one skate forward, but Aasher raised an eyebrow and shook his head. *"Skate for you,"* he mouthed, keeping me level.

I exhaled and took my position.

I would skate for myself, but afterward, I would fight for him.

AASHER

MY HEART GALLOPED LIKE A HORSE.

I put my knuckle up to my teeth and bit down when the familiar song played. Riley looked more beautiful than ever as she commanded the ice. The arena was silent. I wasn't breathing, and although I knew her dad wanted to lay me flat on my ass, he stood beside me, unblinking as his daughter swayed with the music and made leaps and bounds against the frosty floor. Riley's mom had snuck in the moment the song started and sat with the guys in the top seats, probably wanting to stay out of Riley's sight so she didn't make her nervous.

"*Amazing*," I whispered, watching her back arch with a spin that would make anyone double over and throw up— especially someone who had been roofied the night prior. It didn't matter if she only had a couple of sips, I knew she wasn't one hundred percent.

But still, she was unstoppable.

"She is," Coach agreed from beside me, gripping the

same edge of the wall that I was. Our hands were nearly touching, both of us white-knuckling it. "I've never seen her so at ease."

I nodded.

"This is the routine she did when she fell."

I turned toward him. "What?"

He nodded. She'd been perfecting her spins and leaps for the last couple of weeks, but never once did she tell me that they were a part of the routine that she *thought* had ended her career.

Riley's pink skirt brushed against her hips as her skating slowed. She swayed back and forth, making her rounds against the ice before meeting at center ice again. My pulse was hammering behind my neck, and I sucked in a deep breath.

Skate for you, baby.

"She's got this," I whispered, hearing the creaking in my voice.

Coach briefly looked over at me before we both stood paralyzed as she did one turn, then another, and then the one that was easily the most difficult. When she landed and pulled her shoulders straight, showing off her relaxed and smooth expression, I slapped my hands together and had forgotten all about her dad standing a foot away from me.

"You do love her, don't you?" he finally said.

His voice was overcome by emotion.

I nodded. "I meant what I said. Kick me off the team, rip away my future. It wouldn't be the first time someone did that to me." The music began to reach its end, so I turned toward my coach and told him the truth, right to his face. "I'd work a nine-to-five every day for the rest of my life and be fine as long as she was mine. Do what you want,

Coach Lennon. But my future is with her even if you kick me out of this school."

Coach smiled.

Then he laughed.

I heard applauding for Riley, so I brought my hands together and clapped, but I didn't look away. Why was he laughing? Did he think I was kidding?

"If you would have waited three more seconds before ripping open my office door, you could have saved yourself some turmoil."

"What?" I snapped, becoming impatient. "Listen, if you want to punch my lights out, can you hurry and do it so I can regain consciousness before she gets over here?"

"The only person's lights who are getting punched out are Graham Sullivan's."

I stopped breathing.

"You think I didn't know that you were in love with my daughter until today?"

"Wait." I took a step back. "You knew?"

He sighed. "I knew."

I shook my head in disbelief.

"And the only reason I'm allowing you to continue on with my daughter is because you were just willing to give up everything for her. You should have told me about the bet. I know why you didn't, thanks to Theo explaining your thought process behind that." I watched his expression change. "But listen…if you ever shove Riley into a closet again, I'll kill you."

I put my hands up. "I didn't shove her into a closet."

I did, however, shove her into a locker.

He glared at me, but we both turned at the sound of Riley skating up to the side. "Dad. Please, listen. Aasher did nothing wrong. He—"

"Loves you," I finished for her.

I leaned forward and put my hands around her waist, hauling her up and over the side wall.

Surprise took away whatever else she was going to say.

"And we're so proud of you," I whispered, staring down into her baby blues.

Is she really mine?

Riley slowly glanced up at her dad. She didn't move away from me, though. Instead, she moved closer. Coach Lennon didn't make a move to pull her away. He put his hands in his pockets, and his eyes glossed over. "All I've ever wanted was for you to be happy, sweetheart."

Riley blinked a few times as she bounced her attention back and forth between us. She was just as stunned as I was.

Relieved too.

"Coach," I said, seeing something out of the corner of my eye. "Can I do the honor?"

"If you're already asking for her hand in marriage, I *will* kick you off the team."

"I'll save that for later." I winked at my girl and then dropped the good-guy act real fast to ask his permission to lay Graham Sullivan out.

"Will you kick me off the team if you find out I've punched one of my teammates?"

Coach pulled Riley into his side and placed a kiss on her temple. "Graham is no longer on our team."

A devious smile curved onto my mouth, and when Sully saw me coming, he panicked. "Coach!"

"I'm not your coach!" he shouted. Then he took his daughter, and they disappeared, leaving me alone with my fist and Sully's face.

EPILOGUE

AASHER

Ten Years Later

My mom and Karen went completely over the top. They were two of the most spirited older women when it came to hockey—something every sports news station had mentioned time and time again over the years—and it was no different for youth hockey.

Mila took after me when it came to the ice. Instead of having grace and fluidity like her mother, she got my precise velocity. Although she was tiny, she was mighty. She was an angry little thing. We channeled it into a contact sport: *hockey*. I liked to tease Riley and say that Mila chose hockey over figure skating because my genes were stronger, but the truth was, hockey was in both of our genes.

Her grandpa retired as one of the best college hockey coaches the Eastern Conference had ever seen, and her dad was an NHL sensation.

"Mom." I leaned back. "Enough with the cowbell." It was the same ol' cowbell that she had used when I played hockey that was now painted green and white—the colors of Mila's hockey team. "The game is over."

Riley's mom laughed from beside mine and shook her own bell. *Yep, that's right. They both have their own bells.*

"We need to work on her focus," Roy mentioned, rubbing a hand over his five o'clock shadow. He may have been retired, but his coaching days were never too far gone.

"Now you know what Riley would say if she just heard you say that," I said, silently agreeing.

My dad stretched his legs out in front of him and mimicked Riley. "*Let your granddaughter have fun.*"

We all laughed, but Riley was in the right spot at the right time, because she peered up from below, on the ice, holding an abundance of little snack packs that she made for Mila's team. "Shush," she said, rolling her pretty blue eyes in our direction.

I chuckled after winking at her.

She scoffed with pretend annoyance, but I lived to see her pretty mouth twitch with amusement.

The moment the team saw my wife holding the snacks, they rushed over the ice to grab one along with a juice box. I was pretty certain that most of them *only* came for the snack, but not Mila. She was one of the last to head in our direction. The one thing she did get from her mother was the *perfection* gene. That girl was determined to win every game, even if she was the underdog.

She was one of the only girls who played at this age.

Most little girls moved on to Barbies and makeup.

Not Mila.

I kept my eyes on my daughter as she slowly skated toward her mom. One of the boys—who was much taller than her—whizzed past and knocked her down, causing her stick to go flying and her unstrapped helmet to tumble off her head. I stared lasers in the boy's direction, catching his number and adding it to my shit list.

When I looked back at Mila, she popped up quickly and had the same look on her face that Riley used to send to me before I made her mine.

"Down, boy," my dad said from behind.

I ignored him along with the chattering of my mother-in-law and my own mother from behind.

That little fucker, I thought.

Riley glanced up at me and raised an eyebrow, silently warning me.

Mila brushed herself off and grabbed her stick with anger. She was still glaring at the boy who knocked her down, likely sick of them always acting like they were better than her—even if she *was* my daughter. I watched another boy skate toward her. He bent down with precision and grabbed her helmet. Mila glanced at him, and I watched the anger disappear from her face as she gingerly grabbed the helmet from his hand.

What the fuck is that look?

My eyebrows crowded as they skated off together, acting *friendly.*

I looked over at my father-in-law and said, "I get it now."

"Get what?" he asked.

"I get why you wanted to kill me back then."

He smiled before patting me on the back. "Oh, you just wait, son. This is just the beginning..."

The End

AFTERWORD

Stay tuned for more Bexley U books by SJ Sylvis! Head to **sjsylvis.com** for information on upcoming releases!

ALSO BY SJ SYLVIS

Bexley U Series

Weak Side

Ice Bet

Untitled - coming 2024

Shadow Valley Series

Sticks and Stones

English Prep Series

All the Little Lies

All the Little Secrets

All the Little Truths

St. Mary's Series

Good Girls Never Rise

Bad Boys Never Fall

Dead Girls Never Talk

Heartless Boys Never Kiss

Pretty Girls Never Lie

Standalones

Three Summers

Yours Truly, Cammie

Chasing Ivy

Falling for Fallon

Truth

ABOUT THE AUTHOR

S.J. Sylvis is an Amazon top 50 and USA Today bestselling author who is best known for her angsty new adult romances. She currently resides in Arizona with her husband, two small kiddos, and dog. She is obsessed with coffee, becomes easily attached to fictional characters, and spends most of her evenings buried in a book!

sjsylvis.com

ACKNOWLEDGMENTS

First and foremost, I have to thank my family and friends for being *so* incredibly supportive of my career. There have been many long nights and weekends spent in my office and I am beyond thankful to have such a supportive husband to pick up the slack when I'm running behind on a deadline (as always). Thank you to my pink ladies (you know who you are <3) for being my village and doing whatever you can to help when my load is too heavy.

Thank you to my editors, proofers, publicist, PA, alpha reader(s), and beta reader(s) - Ice Bet wouldn't be as polished if it weren't for you and I wouldn't be as organized either (LOL). Your help and advice is *always* appreciated.

To my author and reader besties - we are in this together and I am so happy to have you by my side whether it's a shared post, a vent session through facetime, or a mile long text history. I love you lots!

My readers—how I love you all so much! Thank you for your patience when it takes me a little longer than most to release a book (#momlife) and for your continuous excitement. I hope to continue writing *all* the perfect book boyfriends for you to swoon over!

xo

SJ

Milton Keynes UK
Ingram Content Group UK Ltd.
UKHW041102030624
443552UK00004B/169

9 798985 802092